W9-CGQ-348

Captain Barney

Captain Barney

A NOVEL BY
Jan Westcott

CROWN PUBLISHERS, INC.
New York

Copyright, 1951, by Jan Westcott
Library of Congress Catalog Card Number 51–12010

Printed in the United States of America

For Jerrell and Mike

CAPTAIN BARNEY is fiction.

But the daring and vigor of Captain Joshua Barney, American privateer and United States Naval officer, have come down through the years so generously to quicken my invention and to augment the action of this novel that I must acknowledge my great debt to him. He lived his life in the finest tradition of the romantic hero.

PART ONE

1

AT TEN O'CLOCK ON THE NIGHT OF AUGUST 24, 1780, THE COMMANDANT of Mill Prison scribbled his initials on the last paper on his desk. They were all routine matters. The prison was overcrowded and understaffed, and there was hardly hope for a betterment of conditions while the war went on.

The commandant looked down at the top paper—tomorrow's guard duty. Idly, sleepily, his eyes wandered up the list. When they reached Thomas Browne, south gate, he wondered why the devil he was reading the list. He picked up the papers and handed them to his weary adjutant.

"Goodnight," he said.

Outside the summer moon rose. The night was still. The town of Plymouth and its harbor and inlets were bathed in moonlight. It was not till five in the morning that the fog began to roll in.

In the solitary cell, Benjamin Barney slept, sprawled out on his narrow cot, one hand dangling over the side; he slept the light sleep of a very hungry man. He was dreaming of food, then abruptly the dream changed and he was lying flat in the water drain, his big hands fastened in the grating, trying to shake it loose with the remainder of his strength. It wouldn't come loose, and he swore slowly and with deep venom; he muttered aloud in his sleep and this wakened him. He opened his eyes.

It was still dark. For a moment the blackness made him think he was still imprisoned in the black hole of a dungeon; they had kept him down there for forty days after they had caught him trying to escape through the dank water tunnel. But his hands were not manacled and now he was fully awake, and he knew where he was. He stood slowly. He went to the window.

[7]

He could smell the fog. It came off the sea and smelled of salt. It was like a breath of freedom and the image it conjured of the rolling vastness that lay murmuring so near these stone walls was a sudden sharp thrust of pain. But it was cold and damp too, so he took his blue service greatcoat off the nail and lay down again, spreading it over his long length carefully, so as not to muss it. He lay looking up at the blackness, rubbing his wrists, for they still ached, even though the wounds had healed and only the telltale scars of the manacles remained. Lying there, sleepless now, he went over again in his mind the details of his new plan of escape. He knew very well the consequences if he were caught; he did not permit himself to dwell on them, but only on the essentials of the scheme. Last time he had attempted to take six other men with him through the tunnel. This time he must try alone.

An hour passed. The fog was still thick. Gradually the walls of the cell took shape; he could see the crutches leaning against the stone walls, the barred door. With the passing minutes his hunger grew, the familiar gnawing pain; this was a kind of clock, always worst in the hour preceding the scanty meal. He reckoned it was almost six and—proving him right—the sound of the first bell came within seconds. He rose, hung up the greatcoat and opened his sea chest.

He began to strop his razor in long even strokes. By the time he had finished, he heard the guard's footsteps. His morning meal was bread and water; there was water for washing. The guard said, "Morning, Captain," and the door swung shut again. Barney couldn't resist wolfing the bread. With the basin of water still in one hand, he tore off a big hunk of the bread with his teeth and swallowed it too fast. He should eat slowly; all the men had told him that. He sat down on the edge of his cot and began to chew methodically, restraining his eagerness to swallow, and taking frequent sips of water.

He was finished too soon. He drank most of the water. Then he fished his tiny piece of soap out of its oilskin and began to soap his face. When he had finished shaving, the post-breakfast lassitude had settled over the prison again though he could hear the voices of the men in the big barracks down the hall. Roll call would begin soon. Impatience gripped him; he longed for the moment when roll call would be completed and his door would be unlocked and he would be allowed out into the courtyard for the rest of the morning. As was

[8]

his frequent practice, he began to pace the small cell, back and forth, back and forth, trying to ease the terrible restlessness that drove him. Perhaps today—

He answered as his name was called, his voice clipped and almost contemptuous. Then he stood at his barred door, towering there behind the iron, his dark face taut with unleashed anger. This morning the guards did not speak. After they had had a look at his face, they went on by.

Now he would be left alone for about thirty minutes. No one would pass his door. So he set himself his usual morning task. Methodically he began to remove the faded uniform of the Continental Navy of the United States of America; the gold braid was tarnished. He stripped it off and laid it carefully under his mattress, at the same time taking from the mattress another uniform, with the blue undress coat of the Royal Navy, smuggled to him by a guard named Thomas Browne, who had served in America. He had not even demanded a high price for this precious uniform, bought from a pawnshop where a lieutenant of the Royal Navy had left it and never returned to redeem it. Probably by now he never would.

Barney dressed. He drew his sock up over the heavy bandages on his left ankle; he adjusted his greatcoat so that it swung closed in front and did not reveal any of him save his shoes. Then he eased the crutches in place, closed the sea chest, looked around the cell.

Everything was in order. No one could perceive that he wore a British uniform under his coat. He always went hatless; fortunately so did many officers, even the British, and often, too, they had their hair clipped short. Men of the sea were starting a fashion which others would follow. He waited by his door.

In five minutes he heard the tread of his fellow prisoners as they marched two by two. When the group from the first barrack room had passed, his own door opened again, and he fell into step with Colonel Silas Talbot. They nodded their good mornings, and it was not until they were out in the courtyard that they finally spoke.

The yard in which they stood was made up of two courts at right angles to each other as they extended around two sides of the prison. The stone walls were ten feet high, pierced by four gates. Past those walls was another ten-foot wall, but these outer gates stood open, and were manned by two sentries. The inner gates were also manned, each by a pair of sentries, but these gates were always locked. With Talbot trailing behind, Barney hobbled along on his crutches as fast as possible, around the corner, looking toward the south gate. He stopped suddenly. Thomas Browne was one of the sentries on the south gate.

Talbot almost bumped into Barney. His eyes took in the figure of the sentry, he heard around him the noise of the men released from bondage. He was standing near the wall; he leaned back against it negligently and managed to convey a warning to Barney as he said:

"I saw by the paper last night that Charles Fox had been set upon by a highwayman, and succeeded in turning the tables and capturing him. Watch your coat."

"Yes," said Barney. "That was the *Morning Post* of three days ago." The south gate was the only gate that was not directly opposite the gate of the outer wall; further, it was set at right angles to the main yard.

"I take it you are not an admirer of Charles Fox," Talbot continued his conversation.

"I find the arrogance of the English Whigs almost as stinking as the Tories," Barney said truthfully.

Talbot smiled. "The *Post* suggested it was a pity Fox couldn't be hanged instead of the highwayman. Barney, are you sure you want to go through with this?" He looked sideways and up at the face of his fellow prisoner, at the thick, rough dark hair, and he met the gaze of the dark eyes as Barney turned toward him.

"Yes," Barney said. A boy was coming toward the two men. Barney's face softened and he smiled. "Good morning, lad," he said.

At ten o'clock the fog had lifted a little and was swirling over the lawns of the country residence of Lord Edgecomb, five miles from Plymouth on the river. The head gardener touched his cap as he saw a lady come down the wide stone steps toward the waiting carriage.

"Good morning, Lady Douglass."

"Good morning, Matthew," Douglass said, as the footman aided her into the open coach. She settled her skirts, raised a hand to touch her high-piled thick hair. Her grey eyes were wideset and fringed with heavy black lashes. Her red mouth was full; her chin dimpled. She yawned a little, and leaned back, while Lady Edgecomb gave her a brief envious glance. The carriage swung smartly out of the long drive.

"Have you ever seen the prison, Douglass?" Lady Edgecomb asked.

"No," said Douglass.

"It's not far. We do this quite often," she said, "because conditions at the prison are so bad; Bertram has spoken in Parliament about it. We take food and clothes." She had been speaking absently. With more wonder she asked, "Douglass, what are you going to do? Will you really meet your brother-in-law and let him make your decision?"

In answer Douglass Harris opened her gold-topped reticule, extracted a letter and held it out. "Read it," she suggested. Her delicate brows were drawn a little as she watched Clara run her eyes over the very brief message.

Clara Edgecomb read it twice, folded it and handed it back. "The Belgian packet to Brussels in three days, then," she said. "It's like a man, though. Will you go?"

Douglass replaced the letter. She shrugged. The shrug was belied by a gleam in her eyes. "I must. Sounds like a cold-blooded flounder, doesn't he? 'Considering that it is quite impossible for me to come to England, if you wish to confer with me, I suggest you take, etc.' " She stopped. "As yet he—this Joshua—has not paid me a cent from James's estate, and two years have passed." Her red mouth set and the dimple in her chin became more pronounced. "I must go to 'confer' with him. I—" She broke off again, deciding not to tell Clara she had already asked Lord Edgecomb for a loan for her passage. Clara might not approve. "Is that Mill Prison?"

Ahead was the massive stone outline of the prison.

The coachman was slowing his horses, he turned their heads toward the wide open gate; the sentries saluted. The coach came to a halt outside the south gate.

Within, Thomas Browne took the heavy keys from the ring attached to his belt and unlocked the iron gates. They swung inward, and the coach entered the yard while the other sentry walked forward and motioned the men back toward the center of the court. There were very few men here anyway, in this part. The footman jumped down and began unloading boxes. Douglass sat straight and looked into the yard.

The ground was bare, gritty. There was shouting and laughter from the men around the corner who were playing games. And just ahead of her, standing rather awkwardly, was a man on crutches.

Douglass' grey eyes fastened on him; she was sure it was he. She leaned over the side of the carriage to speak to the guard.

"Is that—could that be—Barney?" she asked, her eyes wide.

Browne nodded importantly. "Yes, ma'am."

She could not take her eyes from him. She had seen him pictured many times; he was one of those rarities of war—an admired enemy. She recalled one picture vividly, the pistols at his waist, the smoke curling around the dark head, and the legend written underneath: "Captain Barney, *le terreur des Anglais*." This had been reproduced in the English newspapers, and many English women were half in love with this raider.

She leaned forward a little. The sun had come out again and made her blond head gleam. He was coming toward her now, awkwardly, on the crutches, staring at her, as though there were no one else in this prison yard with its high stone walls. A bit of dust blew. Douglass' heart beat fast. Then a voice cut through.

"That's far enough, Barney!"

A man had swung around the corner, coming from the small guard house in the center of the middle court. He gave a few brief orders to the guards, but Douglass didn't hear what he said. Barney stood only ten feet away.

His handsome face was thin; the great wide shoulders looked thin, too, even under the big coat, but the superb and arrogant assurance was undimmed. She saw that quickly as he bowed very briefly, as if they had just met, according to their own code of introducing each other. His dark eyes went over her.

Douglass leaned over the side of the carriage toward him. For her he had a magnetic quality.

Blandly he appraised her. How bold an eye! Her sensation raised a telltale flush in her cheeks. The coachman cracked the whip. Douglass sighed, leaned back again in the seat. The carriage turned.

It moved slowly out of the gate. She heard, above the horse's hoofs, the sound of the gate's closing with finality.

At one precisely, the prison bells rang. Barney said, "Run along, lad." He gave no reason. And the boy obeyed him immediately. Barney watched the two sentries at the south gate.

Thomas Browne was unhooking the heavy bunch of keys from his belt. He was handing them, as was the custom, to the other guard. The other guard swung them in his hand as he walked by Barney.

At this time, when the prison guards ate their dinner, only one sentry was left at the gate. But he had no keys. The key-carrier passed around the corner.

On the lookout for this move, Talbot lounged around the same corner toward Barney. There was no one else in this portion of the court. Together, without a word, they moved toward the south gate. When they reached Browne, he whispered:

"Quick, then!" Browne's face was pale.

Barney dropped the crutches. Talbot braced himself against the wall. Barney stepped into his cupped hands; Talbot gave a heave; Barney's hands found a hold on top the wall. In a second he was perched on top. Talbot handed his crutches up to him. "Goodbye. Good luck!" The New Englander repeated that injunction. "Good luck!"

Barney nodded acknowledgment. He dropped from sight. Talbot brushed from his hands the mud from Barney's shoes that had clung to them. He said in his dry voice, "It is to be hoped they don't discover this for a while, Browne." Upon this understatement he walked away.

On the other side of the wall, Barney laid down his crutches, flat against the wall. The authorities would wonder about those crutches. He let the greatcoat swing open. With no sign of a limp, he strode easily toward the outer gate twenty feet around the corner. One sentry was standing there. He saw the undress uniform of the Royal Navy. He saluted.

Barney returned the salute with a brief wintry smile. He walked out of the gates. He turned right. Soon he was out of the sentry's sight down the dusty road on the way to Plymouth.

At five in the afternoon, Admiral Rodney was interrupted aboard his flagship "Sandwich." He had been writing a letter to his wife. The "Sandwich" was riding at anchor in the Hamoaze harbor, and the fog had settled down again over Plymouth. It was so thick it was difficult to see through it to the other warships of the fleet anchored near, in this harbor especially dedicated to the use of His Majesty's Navy.

Admiral Rodney looked up from his writing at one of his lieutenants. "Send the man in," he snapped.

He had never heard of Captain Underwood, of the privateer "Alice." He frowned a little as Underwood entered the paneled cabin, bowed, and wordlessly and diffidently laid a sealed letter before England's most famous admiral. Underwood said constrainedly:

"I was especially instructed to give this to you, and you only, sir."

Rodney looked puzzled. So did Underwood. The two men regarded each other for a moment, and then Rodney ripped the seal and opened the single sheet of paper. He read the one line of heavy writing. He read it again; he saw the signature. He set his mouth, and his eyes lifted to Underwood with blazing anger in them. He rose to his feet.

Under the piercing look of his icy blue eyes, Underwood retreated a few steps. "I—sir." He stopped.

Rodney was keeping silence till he trusted his tongue. Once more he glanced down at the message. It was simple and short. It read only, "The compliments of the Navy of the United States." And it was signed with a single name. "Barney." Rodney pounded his fist gently on the letter. He spaced each word.

"Where did you get this?"

Underwood stared back at the implacable face opposite him. "From a lieutenant of the Royal Navy, sir."

This further effrontery of the American Barney drew a blasting oath. "You fool, he tricked you!" growled Rodney. Then he said, "Tell me the circumstances. Well! Tell me them!"

Underwood wet his lips. "Sir, two hours ago I was coming into Plymouth." He searched for quick lucid words. "There was a fishing smack. I hailed her. Only one man was aboard." How could he comprise all that had happened into a few words?

"Go on," Rodney said.

"The man aboard told me he was sailing for France. I asked him what business he could have on the enemy coast. He said, 'Naval business,' and he threw open his coat, which was tied with rope, and showed me the uniform of a lieutenant of the Navy, sir. I said it was a strange business, whereupon he stared me down, sir, as you're doing now, and said it was confidential business, and that I was a damned fool to stop the Navy, sir. But—but, sir, I stuck to the point. I told him he'd have to prove it with his papers, sir, and he had none. He said if I took him aboard and brought him back here, I'd have to bring you a message from him. I did, sir."

The impudence of it left Rodney speechless. He went to the cabin door and flung it open. "Mr. Craig!"

Mr. Craig responded on the run. Rodney, his grey wig slipping in his perturbation, snapped out, "Send a messenger to Mill Prison to ascertain the whereabouts of Benjamin Barney!" Yet no one but Barney would have played this brazen trick. "No, inform them that Barney has escaped!" He stamped over to his table, wishing he could give more orders. But he could think of none. He himself had handed Barney over to the commandant of Mill Prison; he himself had brought him to England from New York. But the job of tracking him down now lay in other hands. Underwood cried:

"I left him aboard the 'Alice,' sir!"

Rodney swung around. "And you dream he'll still be there?" Then a thought struck him. "Had you the good sense to clap him in irons?"

Underwood looked amazed. "No, sir."

"No doubt you allowed him the freedom of the ship?" Rodney's voice showed his hopelessness.

"Yes, sir. But I left him under guard!"

"Thank you for being so kind as to bring me a letter from him," Rodney said. "Mr. Craig! Send a detail of men with Captain Underwood."

Underwood swallowed hard. He went to the cabin door. "Good day, sir," he said, and almost ran out on deck. Then he remembered it was the Yankee Barney who had caused this trouble. Underwood cursed Barney and all Yankees. There'd been nothing but trouble since they'd made a tea caddy of Boston Harbor.

2

AT ALMOST THE SAME MINUTE THAT UNDERWOOD'S OATHS WERE crackling the air around him, Barney walked the quarterdeck of the "Alice." Across two hundred yards of water lay a white beach, a straggling row of cottages; an inn sign swung back and forth in the light wind. Steps approached him from the rear.

"Lieutenant," said a dubious voice.

Barney swung around, keeping his grim expression. "Yes?" he snapped.

"Would you care for supper, sir? The other officers and I—"

Barney cut in. "No, thank you."

"I see, sir." The officer backed away. The ship was very silent; most of the men had been given shore leave so that if the Royal Navy sent men back with Captain Underwood, there would be no crew to impress. That happened too often. The officer disappeared.

Barney smelled the food. His stomach turned over. He started to pace back and forth like a caged animal; if he could not escape now, Rodney would have him back behind the walls of Mill Prison in an hour or so. Underwood must be aboard the "Sandwich" by now. But it had been the only way he could get a little time; otherwise Underwood would have carted him right to the Port Officer.

The "Alice" shifted on her ropes. The sound of the officers, voices in the aftercabin came plain. There was no one on deck. This was the time.

A boat was hitched way below him. He did not dare pull it toward him, and use the ladder. Instead he swung over the side like a cat and slid down the slender rope, almost hurtling. He struck his leg sharply on the edge of the boat, and fell into it. In a moment he had loosed the painter, and was pulling for shore.

His wits were working fast and coldly. He had only a little time. It was providence that the tide had swung the "Alice" about so that her bow was presented to the beach; the officers eating in the after-cabin could not see the shore from the portholes. On the beach were a few loungers.

The bow of the boat touched the sand. Barney stepped out, motioning to the men. "Help me with this," he commanded.

The men obeyed automatically. They eyed him and the uniform he wore with respect. They dragged the boat up onto the sand, well away from the tide. One of the men said:

"I'm the customs man, sir." He smiled.

Barney nodded alertly. "I'm the prize officer," he responded.

The customs man indicated the fishing smack riding close to the "Alice." "Is that a prize?"

"Yes," said Barney, starting to move away.

The other said then, "You've hurt your leg, sir!"

Barney looked down. Blood was trickling down his leg where he had hit the boat as he had jumped for it. "Yes. I'd best get something on it." Then he thought of something else. "Where are my men?"

The customs man said, "At the Red Lion, sir. Right down—the last house in the village."

"Thank you," said Barney. He would have to pass right by it. He would have to take a chance that if they saw him, they would not know that he was not the officer he appeared to be. Boldly he started down the road past the cottages. His nearest refuge was the maze of Plymouth's waterfront. Plymouth would have to do, for the anonymity of London was too far away. Yet he did not dare cross by way of the public ferry. Undoubtedly, by the time he would reach it, it would be policed, and they would be looking for him.

The Red Lion's windows were open, and he could hear a song sung by the men inside. He quickened his pace. He had almost passed by when he heard a voice say from the doorway:

"Lieutenant!"

Barney stiffened. He brought his head up, and made his voice curt. "Yes?"

The man who had spoken ambled toward him. He came to stand right in front of Barney, who could see more men clustered in the doorway. How much did they suspect?

"Speak up," Barney snapped.

"Are you all squared away with Captain Underwood?"

Barney perceived his hesitancy.

"Damn your impudence," said he, "who gave you leave to question me?"

The man hung back. Now that he had spoken he regretted it. Barney gave him a hard look, and walked straight at him; the man backed. Barney moved down the road, and behind him, the man who had questioned him returned with relief into the Red Lion.

Alone, Barney turned the bend of the road. It was time to run. He broke into an even jog. As he did, he tried to estimate his strength. How long would it last?

He gauged it carefully. He trotted about a mile before he came to a sudden halt. So far as he could see, the winding road was still empty. He sat down on a rock for a moment to catch his breath and listen carefully. For he was running straight toward Plymouth, and it was from this direction that pursuit would come from Mill Prison. He heard nothing. He rose, calculating that he could run for at least another half mile.

He did. At the end of that half mile, he stopped again. Beside the road was a thick hedge. He peered over the top of it. He saw well-kept lawns, and he knew they would slope down to the river. At the same moment he heard horses in the distance. It was a matter of minutes before they would be upon him.

The hedge was thick and tough. He forced his way through. Branches cracked and fought hard to keep him out, but the resilient hedge snapped back into place when he stood on its other side. He was breathing fast, and he knew his strength was waning. He was looking straight at an elderly gardener. This man said:

"These be Lord Edgecomb's gardens. Was you expected, sir?"

Barney dug in his pocket. He tendered a guinea. He smiled at the old man. "My apologies," he said easily, "for damaging your hedge."

Matthew handled the money questioningly. A troop of soldiers cantered past on the road. Matthew wondered where they were going. The horsemen galloped past, raising a cloud of dust. It floated over the hedge, and the sound of the hoofs drowned out Matthew's question. Matthew repeated it.

"Can I help you, sir?"

Barney looked at the tanned, weatherbeaten face. "Yes, you can," he said. "I've hurt my leg and I'm looking for the shortest way back to Plymouth. Do you have a dock on the river?"

Matthew nodded. "It's past the summerhouse. I'll walk down with you and show you."

3

THE RIVER WAS SILVER GREY IN THE DUSK. THE DAY WAS DYING fast now, as Douglass Harris came out onto the terrace for a stroll after supper. In the distance, down by the river, she saw two men.

One of them was Matthew. The other— She drew in her breath. Without thought she started to run; picking up her skirts with both hands she fled across the smooth lawn, past the rosebeds, past the line of yews, coming up sharp at the end of the last flower bed. He had gone into the summerhouse and Matthew was going away to his own cottage. Douglass, breathing fast from her run, stood stock-still for a moment, then she went forward again, her feet making no sound on the grass.

It seemed almost that as she went the last few feet to the summerhouse the whole day had darkened. Her feet slowed again. Dusk lay like a curtain over the lattices. The trees sighed; she heard the sound of the water, rippling. A star hung over the top of the tallest tree. Douglass stepped up the one step. She lifted her hand. Slowly she pushed the lattice door open.

The door swung gently, slowly, opening back on its hinges. She saw nothing. She stepped inside. "Oh," she gasped, catching her red underlip in her teeth. For the door had shut and Barney stood over her, close, looking down at her; she was imprisoned between the door and him.

She pressed back against the wood; she could say nothing. For the first time she heard his voice, low, with its American drawl.

"Do not cry out!"

Her eyes were enormous in her white face, her heart pounded. Once more his low voice came.

"I will not hurt you, madam."

"I know, but—" She broke off.

Everything she had heard or read about him was going through her head, spinning. She swayed, putting her hands out. She felt his arms go around her, and she grasped the lapels of his coat in both hands. "I'm terrified of you," she whispered into his chest. Slowly she raised her head, tipping it back, to study his face. "But I shan't give you away."

"No?" asked Barney. "Why not?"

He heard her draw in her breath again. "Why, because we are Whigs and sympathize with your cause."

"I see," said Barney solemnly. She meant this sincerely. "You saw me come in here?"

She nodded wordlessly, hanging onto his coat.

"Was anyone with you?"

"No," she breathed.

Barney remembered the name the gardener had used. "Are you Lady Edgecomb?"

"No. No!"

She was amazed to see him smile. "Did you drop from heaven?"

She could hardly believe he had asked the question. Her eyes grew even wider, the arms around her were strong; she became aware he was asking her another question. "Do you live here?"

"I'm visiting here, waiting for the Brussels packet!"

She threw out the explanation. She remembered the image of him this morning, in the prison yard, but this was different. Now she was aware only of the strength and dominance of him, towering over her in the dusk. "How—" Her voice trailed off.

He said briefly, "My escape is known now. They are after me."

She had seen the soldiers. She looked around at the tiny room in which they stood as if to reassure herself they were alone. In the quiet she heard no sound save that of the river.

His voice went on. "I must wait here till dark, you see. Then I go upriver, and avoid the public ferry."

"They would catch you!"

He arched one eyebrow and looked amused. "Come here and sit down."

He guided her over to the bench that ran around the sides of the octagonal room. But she stood. So Barney bowed. "You are the most natural—and beautiful—lady I've ever seen, madam, bar none. Will you sit, please?" He grinned, and set her down.

Douglass could hardly believe that he was sitting down too, alongside of her, as though he hadn't been labeled the most dangerous prisoner in England, and as if even now they wouldn't be printing reward notices for him, to be nailed on every available post. But he was sitting down, and stretching out his long legs.

"Your leg is bleeding," she cried, and made a dive for the hem of her dress which she lifted to reveal a slim length of silk stocking and six inches of lace petticoat. Barney leaned over and looked.

"Entrancing," he said.

"I'll rip off a little," she said, her head bent way over so her voice floated up to him.

"A handkerchief will do," he said, very amused.

She straightened up. She saw he was laughing. She regarded him solemnly. Then she handed him her handkerchief.

Barney bent over and rolled down his sock. He tied the handkerchief tight around the gash in his leg, and rolled the sock back up. "I was caught in the Channel. I jumped for a ship's boat, and hit my leg. I landed down here about two miles. . . . Now suppose you tell me who you are, so that the next time we meet—"

"The next time we meet?" she interrupted. She heaved a long sigh. "My name is Harris. My husband was a Yankee."

"Was?"

"He is dead."

"And you unmatched," said Barney. "What else? How old are you?"

"Twenty," she said.

She sat forward on the bench, throwing glances out the lattice to the lengthening shadows outside. Then she blurted, "Your crutches!"

"A ruse to allow me a measure of freedom."

She turned to look at him. "Oh," she whispered.

"Sit back. There's nothing to be afraid of, here. Tell me how you know about this Belgian packet. From where does she sail?"

"Southampton." She saw that this was very important. "On Thursday I'm taking it," she said. "I go to meet Joshua Harris, in Brussels."

"Joshua Harris?" he exclaimed. He looked pleased. "That makes me think of home. How do you know Joshua Harris?"

She said, "He's my brother-in-law."

He nodded. "I know now. You are the English girl James Harris married a week before he was killed in that hunting accident. It was two years ago."

"Yes," said Douglass, simply. Then she asked, "Do you know Joshua?"

Barney shook his head. "I know his name, and I've probably seen him in a coffee house, but I've never met him."

Douglass regarded him sideways, this hero of the picture, truly sitting beside her, and suddenly she smiled, a quick delighted smile. "You're famous." She went right on, fast. "Is it true that Marie Antoinette threw her arms around you and kissed you?"

He grinned. "Yes."

She nodded, as if to say that was true, then. "They say you never went to school and that you went to sea when you were nine."

He turned toward her a little. "I went to school, madam—went to sea when I was twelve."

"So did many of our most famous captains," Douglass said.

Barney said, "Please, for the love of God, do not compare me to a captain in the Royal Navy."

He got to his feet and went over to the door. It was almost dark. He swung around and looked across to her. "I must leave you now."

He had opened the door; it creaked a little. Then he turned and came over to her. She extended her hand.

[21]

He took it in his big one; she felt his strong fingers grasp hers. Then he bent to kiss it. Slowly she pulled her hand away from his.

"I'll see you on the packet," he said.

Her black lashes swept up and she looked up at him. "You will?"

"Yes. Goodnight."

He was gone, then. She watched his figure disappear. She sat still, unmoving, looking toward the river and the little landing. The lights on the boats twinkled on the blackness of the water.

She thought she sat there for more than ten minutes. Then she saw the light of a small craft pull near the landing; she heard the squealing of the pigs that must be its cargo. She got up and went softly out the door, and down to the landing. It was empty. Up the river she saw the lights and heard, growing dimmer, the pig squeals in the distance.

4

IT WAS AN ALLEY WITH NO NAME. THREE BLOCKS FROM THE CUTTE-water, it ran at right angles from a corner between two disreputable pubs. It was only thirty feet long and boasted eight houses.

In the attic of the house second from the corner Barney was dressing. It was night and he had been here for two days. For forty-eight hours he had hidden here.

The attic was a single room, stretching away to corners deep in gloom. Two men slept on a pile of rags in one corner. They would waken soon for their night's work, but now, at seven, they slept deeply.

A man was assisting Barney with his dressing, holding a piece of cracked jagged mirror so he could adjust his neatly clubbed and powdered hair.

"You look like a toff, Guvnor," the man said, and grinned.

Barney was squinting at the piece of mirror. "If you had asked for some sober clothes from the Reverend Winslow or Dr. Hindman, Willie, I would have taken you with me as my servant."

Willie looked at the back of the mirror. "They couldn't get me no clothes."

Barney abandoned the wig momentarily and looked straight at

[22]

Willie. "You're lying," he said, and started to adjust the wig again. "Hand me the hat, Willie."

Willie did so. "I ain't lying."

"The devil you're not."

Willie grinned.

"When the war is over, and I'm in port here, come aboard and see me, Willie. I'll give you a good flogging. Free. That is, if His Majesty's Navy doesn't get you first."

At the thought Willie groaned aloud. Barney held out a single guinea. Willie took it in his dirty hand. Then Barney said:

"Thank you for taking me in, Will. You ran a risk."

Willie shook his head from side to side. He was outside the law, accustomed to risks.

"And if you need help, go to Reverend Winslow. He might be able to save not only a portion of your miserable soul, but perhaps your neck."

"If he'll help a Yankee, I guess he'd help me." Willie's eyes twinkled impudently in his dirty face.

He followed Barney to the top of the twisting attic stairs. Then he bethought himself and ran back for the guttering candle, holding it so Barney could see. Willie could travel those stairs, steep and broken as they were, in the pitch dark, but Barney had ascended them only once, and descended never. He had stayed here, hidden from the hue and cry that was going on after him. Willie stood at the top of the steps. Willie felt impelled to whisper, as he saw Barney going down slowly from him:

"Be careful, Guvnor! They've got the soldiers out for you!"

Barney turned. He had assumed an expression between a grimace and a pucker. "How does this look?" he asked. "I'm pulling my mouth to larboard."

Willie said seriously, "Like you was a perishing gent who smelled somethin'."

Barney laughed. "That is how I'll look on the coach, Will. Good-bye."

Willie murmured, "Good luck." Then he repeated it. "Good luck, sir." His hand, holding the candle, was trembling a little. Then Barney was gone. Willie ran to the broken window to lean out and see him emerge into the street below. Willie heaved a big sigh. "I hope they don't catch you," he muttered.

Fifteen minutes later Barney stepped elegantly into the Exeter coach. He was the last passenger to board it. The doors slammed, the coach lurched a little, and they were off.

He was dressed in the height of fashion. From measurements penciled on a torn scrap of brown paper, delivered to the Reverend Winslow, had come these fine clothes, the cocked hat, the shining boots. Barney crossed these boots and leaned back in the dimness of the coach. So far everything had proceeded well. He had known of the Reverend Winslow—all Americans knew a few names in England of American sympathizers, who would help. But it had been a stroke of luck that Dr. Hindman of New Jersey had been with the Reverend when Willie had crept into the house. These were one of Dr. Hindman's pairs of boots.

The coach gathered speed. The driver, nicely fat, rolled on his hips as he cracked the long whip, from his high perch. The trip should be easy, for all his passengers were men, and a highwayman would find himself overwhelmed. Up ahead the coachman saw two swinging lanterns. He blasted forth a long oath, and began to shout at his eight horses. The coach came to a lumbering stop.

Two soldiers came at him, one from each side. They opened each door of the coach, one of the pair holding the lantern high to look into the interior. The other began to read aloud.

"Wanted, Benjamin Barney, American prisoner, rebel and privateer, escaped from Mill Prison." The soldier looked at the faces of the men within. Barney assumed the expression Willie had laughed at and looked straight back as he heard his description read off. The soldier looked, and looked away. Anyway, there was no one in this coach wearing a naval uniform. He sniffed, slammed the door, and yelled to the coachman that he could proceed.

The coachman's voice was heavy with sarcasm. "Thank you so much." Again the whip cracked, and the Exeter coach moved on and out of Plymouth. Barney remembered to hold his expression; he dug his chin deep in his collar. The journey had begun.

The other men had already begun to talk. It was odd, Barney thought, to sit and listen to people talk about oneself. He remembered to keep his mouth drawn down to larboard, as he had phrased it to Willie, and he remembered to keep the faint squint in his eyes. He listened.

The coach was dimly lighted. Two men sat beside him and two opposite. The one directly opposite was young, bareheaded, and muffled in a coat. The tips of his shoes touched Barney's calfhigh black boots. He was saying very little too. Almost an hour passed, while the coach lurched on through the night.

"I thought it a most perfunctory search," one man said for the fifth time.

At this the man opposite Barney spoke. "Since I am a naval lieutenant, I did also," he said. He opened his coat to show his uniform, while the others stared and Barney watched him carefully.

"I doubt if he is armed," said one.

The lieutenant spoke again: "I would say he was, by this time." His voice was quiet, and he was right. Barney began to like him. Then the lieutenant addressed him. "You say nothing, sir," he remarked to Barney.

Barney snapped, "No, Lieutenant."

He was given a brief smile. Barney did not smile back. He could feel the tension rising within; he forced himself to relax when the lieutenant suddenly said, "No, sirs." He broke into a conversation Barney had not really heard; but now he heard. The lieutenant said, "I was there." He leaned forward. "Listen, gentlemen," he said, his eyes going to the three men opposite him. There was a brief silence, then his voice went on.

"It was an afternoon last winter. The weather was foul. The winds were almost gale force; it was snowing. Do any of you gentlemen know the North Atlantic in weather like that?" He did not wait for an answer; he didn't look at Barney.

"I was serving aboard the 'Intrepid,' 74. We were out of New York. I was a midshipman last year; one rises fast in the service in wartime. Anyway, through the snow we saw a disabled sloop of war; we knew who she was, one of ours. We set as much sail as possible, and after a while we bore down close enough to hail. Captain Mallory suspected something was amiss; we ran out a few guns; we couldn't open any lower ports, of course, and came up to windward of her. You can imagine our surprise, sirs, when she fired on us."

Barney looked down at his boots. He could feel the steady beat of his heart. The lieutenant continued.

"Remember, sirs, the 'Intrepid' is a ship of the line, 74 cannon. We blasted a few shots into the sloop, and she was sinking. We threw over some irons and boarded her. There was a man still at one of the waist guns. We came up to him, in the beating snow, the deck slanting to starboard. He surrendered our own sinking ship back to us, sirs, and told us his name was Barney."

"Go on, sir," one man exclaimed, leaning forward.

"Well, you see, we hardly expected that name. He was wearing the uniform of the Navy of the United States, and he was a prize officer. I'll tell you now that another cruiser captured his captain, Talbot, that same day. But he, Barney, had joined his Navy about a month previously. Well, we took him aboard. This was the story that our own seamen told us.

"The sloop had been captured three days before, just before the bad weather broke. Barney and ten men were the prize crew. During the first day of the storm they thought she was going to sink, meaning thus certain death for all of them. You aren't seamen, so I won't explain too much. But Barney ordered the men into the tops, for the seas were washing across the decks in such a way no man could stand on them. They spent the night there, our crew having given parole. In any event, Barney saved the ship. The sea anchors held; after the wind abated a bit, next morning, he decided to make a run for it. And when one of our paroled men refused to obey the order to make sail, Barney shot him.

"Now I must make the scene clear to you. We were listening to this story, told by one of our men, on the quarterdeck of the 'Intrepid.' Barney was standing there, unarmed, of course. And when one of our officers heard that he had shot a British sailor, he turned and hit Barney. By God, sirs, I've never seen anything happen so fast as what happened then." He stopped, and he grinned, remembering.

"The Yankee acted like a coiled spring at the insult. He struck out so fast that with all of us there we didn't have time to stop it. He hit that officer so hard that he went sliding all the way to the weather rail, and then Barney leaped after him, jerked him to his feet, and sent him crashing into the hatchway. We thought he was dead. He lay there. But then he came to and when he did he was ordered by the captain to apologize to Barney. This he did, in front of all of us.

"The end of the story is short. We handed our famous prisoner to Admiral Rodney. I didn't see Barney again—and he never saw me, probably never noticed me—until I saw him in Plymouth. I heard later that he and fifty-three other prisoners had been kept five decks below the main deck in a sloping room scarcely three feet high. When they were hauled out after the ocean crossing, they could not stand, any of them. Eleven of them had died in delirium. They were

[26]

sent to Mill Prison. I'm saying now, sirs, since you don't know my name, that I don't know whether I'd turn Barney in or not, if I saw him."

There was silence in the coach. There was a little muttering. "This bloody war," one man said, and rubbed his chin, and nodded at the lieutenant.

The lieutenant nodded back. He dug in his pocket and produced his watch. "Almost midnight," he said.

Barney said slowly, "Yes. We should fetch Exeter soon."

The lieutenant said, "Fetch?"

Barney looked back at him. "I'm a sailor, too, sir."

"Yes, sir," said the lieutenant. "Aye aye, sir." He smiled and put the watch back in his pocket.

The man next to Barney said suddenly, "But there's a lot of bitterness in this war, too, sir."

"My God, man," said the lieutenant, "it is a war. But there's a deal of sympathy, too. After all, in Mill Prison, somebody supplied Barney with an English uniform. If I were the commandant, I should look for a guard who had served in America and got to like the Yanks." He grinned, and Barney thought again of Thomas Browne, who had served in America. He spoke.

"Whatever else you do, Lieutenant, don't voice that opinion any more."

The coach was in the streets of Exeter now. "We're almost there," the man next to Barney said. He sat up straighter. "I've been glad to hear your story, sir." He paused, then he too grinned. "But you know what I liked? That note to Rodney. Damme, sirs, that was like Robin Hood. Here he escapes and sends a note to the admiral."

The coach came to a stop. Barney could see the innyard out the window. Another coach with four horses was standing ready, its coachman in the seat. Barney opened the door next to him; he stepped out into the yard. The lights of the inn shone out; the horses stood quietly. Barney said,

"Goodnight, Lieutenant. I hope we meet again."

The lieutenant stepped out too. He held out his hand. "Goodnight, sir," he said. "Perhaps we shall. In fact I've no doubt of it."

Almost alongside of Barney the other coach started off with a jerk. Barney shouted, "Hey there!"

He leaped for the door of the moving coach. The horses were checked for a moment. "Southampton," cried the driver.

Barney pulled the door open. "Southampton," he answered, and almost fell into the seat.

5

"IMPOSSIBLE," SAID LORD EDGECOMB TESTILY. "COMPLETELY IMpossible he could walk up that gangplank, Douglass. Gad, I think he's bewitched you." He grabbed for his hat, settled it and his wig and frowned at Douglass all at the same time.

"Yes, m'lord," she said, meekly, keeping her eyes glued to the gangplank. There wasn't much more time.

He fixed her with a stern eye. "What does that affirmative mean? That you are bewitched?"

She smiled radiantly. "Oh, no."

He drew a deep breath. "Mark my words. He's still in a part of Plymouth, where respectable characters like myself wouldn't dare go." He smiled, ruefully. "A last minute word of advice, too. I don't approve of this trip, but you succeeded in making me think it necessary. But I don't advise you to go to the States. You'd be a fish out of water."

"Yes, m'lord," she said. She looked very fragile and alone, suddenly. She was dressed all in grey, with a rope of pearls and pearls gleaming in her ears. Lord Edgecomb glanced about the deck; the men aboard all looked like commercial men; there was a sprinkling of uniforms, for only necessary travel was permitted nowadays, with England at war with France and Spain, and with relations with Holland strained to the breaking point. The Belgian packet was almost the only means of communication with the continent. "I don't like this trip at all," said Lord Edgecomb forcefully.

He looked as though he might take her back with him. "But I can't leave till they get that equipage aboard," he said, while they both looked at the four magnificent horses and beautiful carriage that were being brought aboard. Four liveried men were engaged in the task, besides several members of the crew who had been impressed into helping.

Douglass had been diverted by the carriage and horses for only a moment. "Do you think," she said, "do you really think he cannot get out of Plymouth?"

Lord Edgecomb frowned fiercely. His gardener was mixed up in this; everyone knew that by now, and Douglass, too. "He's probably back in prison," he said shortly. "They were searching every coach that left Plymouth. You know that."

Their own coach had been stopped. She put her hand on his arm. "What will they do to him?" she asked.

"Now look here, Douglass," he said. "Don't blame me. We're doing all we can in Parliament, and every day we get a few more votes on our side. You can blame Lord Sandwich for the state of the Admiralty. They were going to try him for piracy; we stopped that."

"What will they do to him?" she asked steadily.

"When he first tried to escape and was caught, they put him in solitary confinement, in a sort of underground cell, in double irons for forty days. They threatened him with eighty days of that the next time." He caught her arm as she turned away from him. "Douglass, he's tough. Damned tough. This adventure is not new to him; it's one of many." He saw that the deck was emptying fast of all but passengers and crew. He stifled his last minute objections that rose to his lips. "I must go," he said.

Douglass extended her hand. "I'll be back soon, m'lord. I shall let you know. Thank you. Thank you very much."

Lord Edgecomb kissed her hand. He let go of it reluctantly. "Goodbye, Douglass. Don't thank me; I've done little enough—and wish I could help more. Goodbye." He bowed; he started away. At the gangplank he paused again to settle his hat; then Douglass saw his figure disappear.

She turned. She had a faint brief hope that Barney had come aboard even before herself. She would try the saloon again.

The place was crowded, and although she searched carefully, every face, Barney was not among the men who stared at her. Fumes of alcohol, tobacco smoke and Jockey Club perfume made the air of the saloon close. She came out on deck again to see that the packet was casting off.

Douglass walked slowly to the rail. She heard the shouted orders. The sails filled; they were hauling away from the dock. Douglass went fore; this was not an English ship; she flew the flag of the Austrian Netherlands. Suddenly she didn't want to see the shores

[29]

of England disappear. She walked quickly along the deck, past the carriage which was lashed down fore. She leaned disconsolately on the rail and looked out to sea.

Behind her Barney stuck his head out of the carriage window. What he saw intrigued him; he wondered what the face he couldn't see looked like under the big hat. "Would you care to sit, madam?" he enquired of the lovely back and hips.

Douglass whirled. His face was framed in the carriage window; he looked as startled as she was; he opened the door and got out.

"I'll lay you a guinea you didn't ride aboard," he said, bowing very correctly.

Douglass swept him a curtsy. "I'll lay you a guinea you didn't recognize me till I turned either!"

They stood there on the windy deserted deck, facing each other, the long streamers of ribbon on her hat blowing as were the cascading ruffles on her dress.

"You can hardly blame me," Barney said. "It's a compliment, my lady."

She checked the retort that rose to her lips. Part of her assurance left her; she was suddenly extremely conscious of his nearness. "Oh, sir," she said, low, "you are free!" Her lashes swept up and she looked up at his face. "Let me congratulate you, Captain."

Barney grinned. "You're very formal, my lady."

She said, eyes wide, "I've never had occasion to congratulate anyone on an escape before, sir. I am thrilled by your adventure."

At this he laughed. "I am delighted to have interested you."

She was silent a moment. Then she said, "I don't know quite why it is—" she paused, her cool English accent clipping off the words, "but I seem to be a trifle—" she regarded him—"a trifle shy with you."

"Why is that, do you suppose?" he asked gravely.

"I don't know why it is," she said, shaking her head. "It puzzles me. I was waiting for you, and now that you are here, I can think of nothing to say. Would it be correct for me to ask you where you have been?"

"Quite correct," he assured her. "For two days, in Plymouth, I lay in a den of thieves."

"I see," said Douglass, incredulously, her lip caught between her teeth.

He was very amused. "I doubt if you could remotely imagine, let alone see. Then last night I boarded the Exeter coach. When the soldiers stopped us, I made a face like this." He squinted at her, drawing his mouth down, and he said, in an imitation of her own accent, "My word, Lud. How genteel."

Douglass burst out laughing. Then she sobered. He had both hands on the rail and, eyes crinkled against the wind, was looking out over the choppy water. She said, "I am glad you escaped, and I think a lot of us are, even though we were very afraid of you."

He turned toward her, then, his big shoulder blocking out everything else from her sight. "Were you?"

"We were constantly warned," she said. "The newspapers published sketches of the 'Revenge,' and you, too. They gave us your description, even to the ring you always wore, on the third finger of your right hand." She looked down at the hand; on the third finger was a heavy ring, a circlet of pearls rimmed an emerald carved in the shape of a mermaid. "That is it," Douglass said. Then she thought of something. "Who gave it to you, Captain?"

Barney shook his head solemnly.

"Please tell me, sir!"

"No wheedling," he said.

She pouted a little. "Last summer at Brighton we thought we saw the 'Revenge'; the whole town was terrified." Once more she looked up at him with her great grey eyes. "But it wasn't you," she added.

"My lady," Barney said, "if I'd known you were at Brighton, I should certainly have raided it." He grinned. "But as to harrying your coast and shipping, and interfering with your mails, that was our intention."

"You took sixty of our ships, in less than six months," she said, still regarding his dark face.

"So I did, Mistress Harris," Barney said, quite satisfied to remember. "The 'Revenge' was a beautiful ship," he added.

"You must have made a fortune," she said, wonderingly.

Barney frowned slightly, his eyes swept her appraisingly. Her face flushed, and she struck her hand on the rail. Her eyes blazed.

"I am ashamed of myself if I have implied an interest in your wealth. Forgive me."

He shrugged. "It is natural for ladies to think of money."

She drew back from him. "Will you leave me now, Captain Barney?"

[31]

Barney looked down at her; he wanted to seize her in his arms and kiss the red mouth. She sensed it, and started to turn. Barney grasped for her hand, caught it, and swung her around to face him.

"I'm sorry, English," he said.

She drew a deep breath; slowly her eyes lifted to his face.

"And you have a quick temper, madam."

"I know it, Captain," Douglass said.

"I have enough for both of us. I'll see you to your stateroom, now. I have business in the saloon. Take my arm, please."

Douglass put her hand on his arm. As they walked along she kept glancing up at him. Barney said:

"Do you always have your own way?"

"No," she said, low. Then she added, "Truly I do not." She skipped a step to keep up with him, and he slowed his pace. She said nothing else as he guided her down the companionway. At the door of her cabin she stopped.

Barney pushed open the door. Once more Douglass remembered all she had heard. "You can't come in," she said breathlessly.

Barney grinned. "I might point out I didn't ask permission to come in."

Her hands were clasped tight around her bag. "So you didn't," she conceded.

For a second he hesitated. Then he said, "Goodbye, my lady."

6

BARNEY STOOD AT THE ENTRANCE OF THE SALOON, SURVEYING ITS occupants.

It was crowded, of necessity. Barney thought it more crowded than Mill Prison, and the thought brought a wry smile to his lips.

The pistol Willie had bought him rested comfortably against his thigh. Even as he was aware of it a man in British uniform recognized him. He stared, incredulity in his face, and anger too. Barney looked right back, and then began to make his way easily through the press of men. He caught various sentences.

"It is impossible to get insurance on cargoes! Impossible! And this morning the three percents dropped to 57."

Barney passed by the British major, who grunted and moved aside. Now other men were looking at him; he could almost hear his name run around the room. He paid no attention. He was almost in the middle of the saloon when he saw the group of people who warranted more attention than the rest.

On the locker under the windows was a slender, elegantly dressed woman and an older stout companion. With them was a man in the uniform of the Austrian Netherlands. Barney suspected the expensive carriage belonged to these three. At the same time that Barney saw them, the man perceived him, and he jumped to his feet, the tassels on his epaulets swinging madly.

He was a black-browed, heavy set man, and he pushed his way to Barney, heedless. "Captain Barney!" he exclaimed, when he was about three feet away.

The men between the two of them turned, startled. Barney bowed. The other cried, coming up to him:

"Allow me to introduce myself, sir! Colonel Lucas."

His accent was very thick. Hungarian, Barney thought. "Colonel Lucas," he said politely. "A pleasure, sir."

Lucas then uttered a strange emphatic exclamation. Barney was sure he was Hungarian. He smiled but Lucas did not smile back. This was no smiling matter. He said, in English:

"You escaped them!" Another strange exclamation spilled out. "We have been reading in the papers! You escaped!"

Barney had kept his smile. "Your enthusiasm heartens me, sir."

Lucas nodded. "I feel your exploit deeply. I am too intense, if that is the word." For a second he looked at Barney's face, then he realized everyone was listening to them. "Let us get away from this —canaille. Over here, Captain."

The use of the contemptuous term to indicate honest men in trade let Barney know that the major counted heavily on the impressiveness of his own European lineage.

Lucas pushed a way for them through the crowd. "God, what a mob," he was muttering.

"Wartime, Colonel," Barney said, over his head.

Lucas stopped beside the locker. The windows above it were closed against the damp wind. Barney found himself looking deep into the eyes of a woman who leaned elegantly back against pillows. Great diamonds winked in her ears; her hair was powdered and piled high, save for one long curl that nestled on her shoulder.

[33]

"Allow me to present Captain Barney, madam. Madame Roche."

She extended her hand; Barney bowed over it, released it slowly, as Lucas presented the other woman. She was a Madame Bachels; a duenna of sorts, although Barney thought accomplice might be a better word for her. He did not know what business Madame Roche could have had in England, but he suspected. He wondered how much information she was carrying in her fashionable head. She had spoken a sentence in quick Italian to Lucas; she looked up at Barney again, a smile on her ivory face. "Forgive me, sir," she said. "I use my own tongue."

"I must confess that I understood you," Barney said, looking amused. "Might I say it is also a stroke of good fortune for me to meet you?"

Lucas was about to speak when Madame Roche interrupted. "Where did you learn Italian, Captain?" she asked Barney.

Barney looked down at her figure as she reclined against the pillows. "I spent two months in prison in Sardinia. Quite some time ago. Would you like to learn some thieves' cant from me?"

Elise Roche smiled. "Captain Barney," she said, "is there no end to your versatility?" Lucas thought it was time to get a word in, and Madame Bachels took this moment to throw a meaningful glance at her beautiful companion, a look which Elise Roche interpreted correctly as saying that here was not only a man reputed to be worth millions, but open-handed at that.

Lucas was saying, "Your escape will hearten your countrymen, Captain Barney. They say there is much discouragement in America. It has been a bad year."

Barney frowned slightly.

Lucas gestured. "A bad year for you. The defection of Benedict Arnold—outright treason is always a shock to a nation. The south—your Carolinas overrun with British. The miserable failures of Count d'Estaing, your estimable French commander and ally. What a one." Lucas snorted with almost Gallic ardor. "All these serve to dampen the spirits."

Elise Roche said softly, "The captain does not seem discouraged."

Barney said, "Sometimes the tritest sayings serve. Like 'appearances are deceiving.' First d'Estaing failed so badly that he is being replaced. Had he performed in a mediocre manner we might still have had to put up with him." The boat pitched a little, and Lucas grasped for the locker.

Barney had not moved. "Second, Madam Roche, the British did well to invade our south. They are now hopelessly entangled in the Carolina wilderness and, worse for them, better for us, have brought the war home to our south."

Lucas thought the time had come to put the important question. "But, sir, what are your plans now? What are you going to do?"

Barney said, his eyes on Elise Roche, "I'm not quite sure."

"You go to Paris perhaps? And see Dr. Franklin?"

Barney said slowly, "When I was taken prisoner, sir, I wore the uniform of the Navy of the United States." He paused. "I expect I still have the right to wear it."

Lucas said bluntly, "Your Navy has no ships." He too paused, to dramatize his words. "But I can get you a ship!"

Barney balanced himself neatly against the roll of the ship. "Where?"

The answer spilled out eagerly. "There's one building at Brest, owned by a syndicate."

Barney was thinking how familiar these words sounded. Lucas went rushing on. "She will be fast, fast as the 'Revenge.' In the 'Revenge,' last year, Captain, if my memory serves me right, the damages you inflicted ran into six figures of pound sterling." Lucas' voice lingered ripely over that nice figure.

"Then last fall, even the Spanish refused me the use of Corunna."

"They were forced to! They were still neutral. But now you can have any port you want!"

"Any port, sir?" Barney enquired. "Is Lord North then thinking of committing the folly of going to war with Holland, too?"

Lucas seized quickly on a diversion. He lowered his voice and spoke in rapid French. "In strictest confidence, Captain, let me tell you that within six weeks, perhaps sooner, the Portuguese are going to forbid their ports to all belligerents in the war. This will work terrible hardship on the British, who will then have no port of call between Falmouth and Gibraltar. Think of the damages that you can wreak, operating out of Spain!" He held on tight to the locker, his swarthy face convulsed with excitement.

Barney leaned over Elise Roche and opened the window a little. "Isn't this too close for you?" he asked. Then he straightened, and faced Lucas.

"Colonel," Barney said, "we dangled prize money and Europe took the bait. Neither France nor Spain could turn down the millions in prizes we brought into their ports. Now they are at war with England; they can operate from their own ports, their warships, their privateers. To an American—to a sailor like me—the war has shifted its focus back to the States and the Caribbean. Dr. Franklin might not even give me a commission. The need has passed."

Lucas said, "We must talk further, Captain!"

Barney said grimly, "This is a sea war. I am convinced its next arena will be the Caribbean."

Lucas said, "You mean there's more money at Stasia? You'd prefer to operate from Stasia?"

"The Golden Rock?" Elise Roche asked, and immediately after uttered a long sigh. She had kept her cloak over her shoulders and she made a motion to push it back. Barney lifted it from her shoulders.

She was very white. Barney picked up an orange from the bowl of fruit on the table and slit it neatly with his knife. He held it under her nose. "Sniff it," he said.

Her eyes were half closed. "I'm faint," she murmured.

Lucas jumped to his feet. He did not look well either. "Some mulled wine, perhaps." He looked around for help. The boat pitched again and Lucas grasped for the table hurriedly.

Barney slid his arm around Elise Roche. "The Channel is behaving badly as usual," he said. "Can I—"

"Please," she whispered.

Lucas was still clinging to the table, and Mrs. Bachels was holding on too. Across the saloon, a chair crashed over; the place was emptying rapidly.

Barney rose. He lifted Madame Roche in his arms, gathering her cloak up.

Lucas had turned a deep green. Barney grinned at him, as he stood there with the slender figure in his arms. "Seek the deck, sir," he said.

He wound his way out of the saloon. A waiter scurried ahead to open the door. "It's the fourth cabin, sir. Number 82."

Barney nodded. To him the pitch of the ship was like home. He leaned down and opened the door of number 82.

The cabin was empty. And Barney suspected that Madame Bachels would stay discreetly away. He kicked the door shut. Her dark head was against his shoulder, and her eyes opened. She smiled a little.

[36]

"Put me down, Captain."

"I've a suspicion you're a very good sailor, madam."

She smiled. "Excellent, sir."

Behind them the door banged. Barney set her down, and shut the door again, latching it securely. He turned and faced her.

She said, her head tipped back to look up at him, "You wish to be respectable, now, Captain Barney?"

"No, never that," he said seriously. He had been long in prison. He had a hungry look.

She shook her head, her eyes serious. "My English is poor. I mean, you are reform. You are not a magnificent pirate any more? Why not?"

Barney disregarded the question. She shrugged her slim shoulders and turned her back on him. From an opened valise she took a silver flask. She unscrewed the top and poured the amber liquid into the round silver top; she held it out.

Barney wondered briefly if it were drugged. He reminded himself there was a price on his head; he reminded himself that the intrigues of Europe were coming closer. But he took the silver cup; full as it was, it spilled a little over his fingers. It smelled just as brandy should smell.

She had read his thoughts. "You first, then I."

He downed the smooth fire.

"You see I drink too." She poured herself some. "Why don't you stay in Europe? You are famous here. You make millions. Do you have any left?"

Barney said, "Not a penny. Not a farthing." He thrust his hands in his pockets and regarded her.

She had finished her own brandy and she poured him another cup. He took it from her. "What else are you going to say, madam?"

"You stay and make much more." She sighed a little. Then she said, "But I know you will do as you please." She smiled then.

The cabin was stuffy and warm and smelled of French perfume and powder. The bed looked soft and the brandy burned in his stomach. Barney said suddenly:

"The trouble with my life is, Madam Roche, that beautiful women divert me."

"I will give you another drink of brandy, and I can help you, too," she said.

He caught her hand and swung her around to face him. "Don't bother with the brandy." He tipped her face up with his hand.

His mouth closed over hers. With one arm he swung her feet off the floor and carried her thus to the bed.

7

JOSHUA HARRIS WAS THIRTY YEARS OLD. BORN IN VIRGINIA, OF wealthy parents, he had graduated from the University of Pennsylvania at the age of nineteen. From there he had gone to work at Willing and Co., in Philadelphia, as a clerk. Six months later, going aboard a returning merchant ship at Chester, he learned that the price of wheat had risen. Before the news reached Philadelphia, Joshua Harris had bought up all the available wheat and flour in the city. A month later he founded his own company.

In the next ten years, he had traveled all over the world on his own ships, had agents in all principal ports; he had expanded his father's holdings in Virginia, with great tobacco plantations; to this he had added a Baltimore and a Philadelphia shipyard.

He had built a mansion at Sixth and High Streets in Philadelphia; his big offices were opposite those of Robert Morris on Front Street, across from the London Coffee House, where the merchants of the city gathered. He was accounted one of the most considerable shareholders in Stephen Girard's stone-pillared bank, and one of the most eligible bachelors in the States. He was a famous horseman, and an excellent shot, and considered women as a man's pleasant diversion in his few leisure hours.

Douglass had known this much and was learning only a bit more. First that he had a deep drawl—the South, she supposed. Second that he was very handsome, with deep blue eyes and a cleft in his square chin.

"American men are big," Douglass said, watching him as he paced back and forth.

He stopped in his stride. "What?" he asked, frowning. "I have been trying to tell you, sister, that—" he stopped in front of her chair; there was a knock on the door and a man came in to clear away the supper things. Joshua waited till he had gone.

"I was listening, sir," Douglass said. "It's just that I was thinking that American men—you're not listening."

"You're not making sense, sister," Joshua said. "The point I am trying to make is this. Simply this." He drew a deep breath, as if to draw upon patience. "There is no money for you due from Harris and Company."

Douglass leaned forward. "But Joshua," she said.

He looked surprised at the use of his first name. His "sister" had been avoiding first names.

"You don't mind if I use your first name? I should like to."

"Of course not," he said hastily. "Your friendliness gratifies me, Douglass."

"You say that too politely," she said, and rose, too, walking over to the window to look out on the narrow street. She turned slowly from the window. "Then there isn't any money for me? None at all?"

"No, sister." The word "money" seemed to make his blue eyes remote.

"But Joshua," she said, coming toward him. "How can that be? When you are so wealthy a man?"

He said briefly, "But you don't have a share in me, sister. You have an eventual share in Harris and Co."

Douglass sighed. "That is true. You are so logical." She smiled then, and sat down on the couch, curling up like a kitten. "All the money goes back in the business?"

"Yes," he said, as if he were delighted she had finally understood. "After the war it will be different. Now we need every penny." Then he added stiffly, "I am sorry about James. I didn't know him very well, as you know; I had hardly even seen him; he was ten years younger than I, and in England most of his life. But I am sorry—" he hesitated—"Douglass." There was a moment of silence and then Joshua went right on. "So, foreseeing this difficulty, from your letters, I booked passage for you, as I said before."

"You have arranged everything," Douglass said. "I heard, Joshua. I am to live with you." Once more she rose, and put a hand on his arm, looking up into his face. "It is most generous of you."

"Then that's settled." He made a move to turn away.

Douglass said, "You said there was a rumor Captain Barney was returning, too." She paused. "Did you confirm it?"

"I want to see Barney now," he said. "If you'll excuse me, sister. Oh, and I hope your rooms suit you."

"They're very lovely," she said. "Truly, Joshua, I am most grateful." She looked down at her own hand on his arm. Then she said, "But I cannot even tip the maid." She smiled and fetched a big sigh.

Joshua looked grave. He reached in his coat and pulled out a wallet, from which he extracted a number of five-pound notes. Douglass looked at them with wonder.

"I know you said you'd pay my expenses, too, Joshua, but I didn't—"

"What?"

"Didn't expect that much."

He said, sternly, "Did you think I was miserly?"

"A little near," she admitted.

He frowned and explained: "Lord God, sister, it's the company's money I don't like spending now. Not my own." He thought of explaining further that when her interest on her shares could be paid it would amount to hundreds of pounds. He decided this course would be very unwise, and he smiled slightly. "Goodnight, sister." Her voice reached him as he picked up his stick and made for the door.

"Goodnight, Joshua."

He walked rapidly down the stairway to the ground floor. "Your hackney is waiting, sir," he was told.

Joshua stopped at the side of the waiting hackney. "I want you to find Captain Barney for me."

The driver grinned. "Yes, sir. I know where he is. He always stays at Fraulein Schmidt's."

Joshua got in and slammed the door. The driver jerked on the reins and the hackney started off through the streets of Brussels. Joshua was hoping he would find Barney still at supper.

He did. Joshua came striding through the door, past the small square hall, and into the dining room, with its German waiters and its rows of hanging copper pots on which the flames of the big fireplaces gleamed. Joshua didn't blame Barney for liking this place. The clientele was strictly male.

Barney was sitting at a round table with a heavy white linen cloth, near the fireplace. A wheeled cart at his side supported a chafing dish, in which the bewhiskered waiter was deftly making crêpes-suzette, rolling and powdering them, and setting them at Barney's place. And the whole room smelled delightfully of coffee. Barney looked up to see Joshua standing in front of him. Politely he rose.

"I am Joshua Harris, Captain Barney," Joshua said.

Barney held out his hand. "How is your beautiful sister-in-law?"

"Thank you, entirely well," said Joshua, dismissing that subject briefly. "Allow me to say I'm damned glad you are here."

"Thank you," said Barney. "Won't you sit down and join me in a cup of coffee? I'd seen you before, but we'd never met, I believe."

"No," said Joshua. "I'd like coffee, and I brought you a small token, let us say from one American to another." He laid an oilskin carefully on the table. Barney reached for it in delight, opened it and sniffed appreciatively. Joshua watched him and smiled.

"It's been ten months since I even had a smell of Virginia tobacco," Barney said. He raised his voice. "Two pipes!"

His waiter dived for the rack of clay pipes on the wall, extracted two, and came back to the table. Barney handed him the precious packet. "Spill any and I'll throttle you," he said genially.

The waiter bobbled his head and said, "Yes, sir." He filled both pipes, handed them to the gentlemen, and lighted them. Barney sucked in the smoke appreciatively. "Now we can talk," he said, contentedly. He noted Joshua's swordstick, with its tortoise-shell heavy knob. "Paris?" he asked.

"Paris," Joshua answered.

Joshua leaned back in his chair. "I'll come direct to the point, sir. There are rumors flying all over the city that you intend to return to the States, and resume your privateering. Also, it is said that you need money."

Barney responded noncommittally, "I've been offered a ship building at Brest."

"So I hear. However, I can do better than that, Captain Barney. I can offer you a ship already built and waiting for you at Corunna. Further, I'll obtain passage for you, which is difficult to get, aboard the 'South Carolina,' under command of Captain Gillon, sailing for Corunna day after tomorrow."

"I see," said Barney. "What is this ship?"

Joshua once more reached in his pocket and brought out his leather wallet. "She's the 'Pomona,' " he said, as he opened the wallet. "I've five hundred pounds here for you." He laid the notes on the table. "The 'Pomona' made her maiden voyage from the States last month. She is an armed barque of twenty guns. She's escorting two merchantmen. Her captain is ill. He will not be able to make the return voyage as her commanding officer."

"Pick up the money," Barney said.

Joshua frowned.

"I'm not going back to privateering."

Joshua riffled through the clean notes as he prepared to replace them in his wallet. "There is no commission in the Navy for you," he said idly. "I am one of the members of the Marine Committee."

Barney's face darkened with anger. He half rose in his chair. Then he remembered where he was. He leaned his fists on the table. "Is that blackmail? So you can get your goddamned cargo home?"

Joshua seemed to be counting the money. He looked up lazily. "No."

Barney sank down in his chair. "Suppose you explain, then, Mr. Harris."

"At present there are thirteen ships commissioned in the Navy. By the end of the year there will be nine. There is no room for you, Barney. Give it up."

Barney was silent.

"There is a possibility," Joshua went on, "of your commanding an armed vessel which has just been purchased from me by the state of Pennsylvania, for the express purpose of routing out the so-called refugee boats that harass the Delaware. These are light draught vessels manned by Tories or disaffected Americans that harry unsuspecting merchantmen after dark."

Barney's eyes narrowed. "I?" he asked, "Cruise the Delaware?"

Joshua shrugged his shoulders.

Barney said, "You have made a mess of what should have been a sturdy young Navy. There is no room for John Paul Jones. No room for me. Instead you have Gillon commanding. And Hopkins. The root of a Navy is its nation's shipping. We had it. When the British lost us they lost half their potential seamen. And what have you done with it? No wonder the uniform I wore gained no respect!"

"We have made mistakes and we are aware of them. That does not change the immediate situation, does it? The 'Pomona' is sailing soon. Are you going to command her or not?"

"No," said Barney. "I'm damned if I'll take more money for you."

"If you change your mind, let me know. I might remind you that there isn't much choice." Joshua adjusted his cape and prepared to rise, when there was a sudden diversion at the doors. Two soldiers were standing there, and the lieutenant with them was searching the room. As his glance reached Barney he started toward his table.

[42]

Joshua stood. "I fail to see how even you could get into trouble on a Channel crossing," he remarked. "But if you need money to buy your way out of this, it's ready for you. Goodnight, Captain."

He brushed by the lieutenant, who came to a stop at Barney's table. The lieutenant said, "Captain Barney?"

Barney regarded him gravely. "You are not Colonel Lucas."

"No, sir. I am Lieutenant Knippen. You will accompany me, if you please."

In a leisurely way Barney rose. His waiter came hurrying up with a concerned expression and Barney's cloak. "Goodnight, Capitaine," he whispered.

"Goodnight," Barney said.

The lieutenant followed him out of the room. They went through the big door. There was a soldier on each side of Barney as he crossed the paving to a waiting coach.

8

THE COACH RATTLED OVER COBBLESTONES FOR FIFTEEN MINUTES. Then it came to a sudden stop in front of the biggest, gloomiest stone building that Barney had ever seen.

Sentries flanked the high doors. They swung inward, and a be-whiskered German glowered at both the officer and Barney. The German took the lead, and Barney alone followed him. The lieutenant disappeared down another corridor.

Barney was led up two stairways, through a hall, past half a dozen doors. The German came to a halt in front of one of them and knocked. The door was opened, and Barney stepped inside.

Madame Bachels hurriedly locked the door after him. "Wait here, sir," she whispered. Then she, too, disappeared.

Barney was in a small room furnished with four carved chairs with needlepoint seats. A small Aubusson rug partly covered the polished floor. He had been in rooms like this before. They were anterooms where one waited to seek the favor of a woman who was close to a man in a high place. No doubt her sitting room and boudoir were just past the oak door.

That door opened and Elise Roche came toward him. Her low-cut black gown almost completely revealed her bosom. Barney did not stop to question the good fortune which brought him here to her; he took her in his arms.

"Darling," she whispered, after he released her lips. "No."

"No what?" asked Barney, kissing her ear.

"Hold me. But listen. I am to bring you to the Emperor in a few minutes."

He looked down at her face, and she said, "I remember when you whisper to me I could speak French. I speak it now. Listen. The Emperor knows you are here. I am to explain what he cannot say. I tell you more than I should, too, my sweet. Listen."

Barney listened. What she was saying was very important.

"You cannot stay in Brussels. The English have protested vehemently; they want you." She caressed the back of his head. "Sweetheart, we will not give you up to them. And I should not tell you this, but Lucas let slip about Holland. The English will declare war on Holland before the end of the year."

Barney's dark eyes glittered. "Go on, Elise," he said.

"You know that in March Russia announced an armed neutrality pact. Sweden and Denmark will sign it, to resist British aggression on the seas. To please Catherine of Russia and Frederick the Great we must sign, too. But we must also remain the only neutral nation, for the sake of the great trade which will accrue to us then. Therefore we cannot offend Britain too much, and you must go. But for the sake of our good relations with your country, we shall grant you favors. To the English, of course, we shall deny we have given them to you. Officially we know nothing about it, but there is a flying coach waiting to take you to Holland. You will sail for your own country aboard the new ship 'South Carolina.' This much we can do for you, but no more. Now I take you to the Emperor. Let me go, darling."

Barney dropped his arms.

At the door she paused for a moment, studying him. "You know to say nothing?"

He smiled. "I'm familiar with the procedures."

She said, "It is because of this perhaps you want to leave Europe. All this." She flung open the door and as she went down the hall with him, her voice was different. She was saying, politely:

"The Emperor is ill. He will receive you in his chamber."

The room they entered next was dominated by an enormous

poster bed, and the figure of the grey-haired Joseph, as he was propped on his pillows and blowing his nose. He wore a nightshirt and dressing gown. Elise Roche made a deep curtsy, and Barney bowed. The Emperor put down his handkerchief and motioned them to come closer.

Barney found it hard to believe that Joseph was in but his fortieth year and that it was this man's sister, Marie Antoinette, who had impulsively flung her arms around him and kissed him. The Emperor looked tired, drawn and old. Barney stood by the bed; Elise Roche seated herself in the chair by the bed; Joseph took her hand and measured Barney. Elise had told him a good deal about Barney.

"You were born in New Jersey?"

"Yes, Your Majesty. In a small town on the river called the Mullica, which name will be unfamiliar. But Dr. Franklin has boasted much of the oysters." Barney smiled.

The Emperor said, "I have met the eminent doctor. At my sister's court. As an American, we are sorry that we cannot extend to you our hospitality at this present time."

"The expression of Your Majesty's kindness is enough."

The Emperor made no mention of a flying coach which waited outside. "But paths will be smoothed for you. You have our interest," he added. He coughed a little, and reached for his handkerchief. The American was so full of vigor. Joseph knew he would not live much longer; he gave himself less than the nine years he was going to have. But he could wish passionately for a son like this man; and he had no children. He held Elise's hand tightly.

"You were kind to Madame Roche." He looked up at Barney and Barney was sure that there was a sudden twinkle in his eyes under the bushy brows. "She is very dear to me. She tells me that, after many years abroad, you wish now to return to your own country, that is so young. And you, you are so young, Captain."

"I am twenty-six, Your Majesty."

Joseph was silent a moment. He had been impressed by Barney's career, by the audacity of his last escape. He was impressed by the man himself. "When the war is over," he said, "seek our favor. Goodnight, sir."

"I appreciate Your Majesty's kindness, more than I can say."

He started to back away. The Emperor was still musing that he could use this man. "Seek our favor," he repeated.

"Your Majesty, you are kind."

Outside, in the hall, Barney walked along at Elise's side. She stole a glance at his face. "Now that you have what you want," she said softly, "you do not know whether you want it."

Barney nodded.

"You are leaving Europe." She opened the door to the anteroom they had talked in so briefly a few moments before. Barney followed her absently. After she had closed the door, he looked at her steadily.

"I've been here so long," he said. "Perhaps I am not an American any more."

She smiled. "I think you are."

"I have not been home, except for intervals of a few months, since I was thirteen. Five years ago I bought a small house in Philadelphia."

"You are wondering if you will like it now. I think you will."

He said suddenly, "Damn it, Elise. Are you glad to see me go?" He pushed open the door into her sitting room.

A lazy fire burned in the marble fireplace, for these stone houses in Holland and Belgium held the cold over from winter, their inhabitants complained. Over the mantle hung an original Rembrandt. The delicate chairs were imported from France; the crystal candelabra from Austria. He repeated his question to her.

It suited her. It was what he was leaving. If there was corruption, it was covered with beauty and elegance and spice of sparkling wines, intrigue and the lovely French tongue.

"You are so lovely," he said. "Before I leave—Bachels will watch the door."

She shook her sleek black head. "No."

There was danger in staying with her long. It heightened his desire for her. He seized her quickly in his arms, bending her body back so he could look down at her face. He put his lips to the white throat. "Once more, Elise," he said.

9

THE WIND WAS BLOWING STRONG. THE "SOUTH CAROLINA," NEW nervous maiden that she was, strained against her anchors.

She was lying about a league from the port of Texel, outside the jurisdiction of the port. Her rigging sang loudly, waves slapped and shook her brave paint, and the wind swept over her decks and made talking almost impossible. On the quarterdeck Captain Gillon paced and watched the shore line.

In the waist, in the shelter of one of her big guns, Douglass Harris and the American painter, John Trumbull, shouted at each other. Trumbull had just come aboard, along with two other Americans. Only he had dared the deck.

"Why didn't you bring him with you?" Douglass asked.

"We couldn't find him," Trumbull roared. "He said he was going to eat six pounds of Dutch steak and comb the waterfront for his cronies."

A cry from the lookout echoed over the deck. Aloft, he leaned over and shouted down to Gillon, "That's Captain Barney, sir! They just signaled with an oar."

Douglass caught her cloak and stood on tiptoe. Over the choppy water she could see a boat poised on the top of a wave. It disappeared and then rose into sight again.

Meanwhile Captain Gillon was losing no time. The "South Carolina" could not lie at anchor much longer, not with this increasing wind. He snapped a command to his first officer, who in turn bellowed, "All hands on deck!" which was rather unnecessary since most of the watch were already on deck or aloft. Nevertheless, the boatswain thought one sailor was too slow; as he went by the boatswain gave him a well-placed kick that hurtled him forward. The sailor spun round, the boatswain laid a warning hand on a belaying pin, and the sailor slouched on. Douglass and Trumbull watched and then they heard Barney's voice across the water.

"Ahoy, the 'South Carolina'!"

Gillon strode to the rail. Barney was standing in the stern of a longboat, waving an oar. Gillon didn't bother to answer him. Instead he roared, "Anchors aweigh!"

His voice was almost drowned out by the shouts and cheers of the men as Barney swung up the ladder and dropped onto the deck like a cat. Then he straightened up, waved his cap, and grinned widely. The first officer, regardless of Gillon, ran to greet him.

"Captain Barney!"

Barney offered his hand. "Fine ship you have here, sir."

Gillon shouted from the quarterdeck. "Mr. Smith!"

[47]

Smith turned and went aft hastily. Barney saw Douglass and Trumbull.

Trumbull yelled, "I'm your cabinmate, Captain!"

Barney bowed to Douglass, the action contrasting with his unshaven face, for a night's beard was very evident. "Keep to leeward of me, Mistress Harris, or you'll smell me out."

Douglass made a face. "Tobacco and wine."

"Dutch beer," corrected Barney. "Why are the two of you braving this windy deck?"

"It's bad below," Trumbull said. "So damned noisy. Excuse me, Mistress Harris."

Barney looked at the yellowing sky and water. He almost sniffed the air. "It'll be worse," he said.

Douglass' grey eyes were half closed against the wind. She was looking up at the mainsail, which the wind tore at suddenly. Its yards shook madly; the sailor on the footropes swayed with it, swinging there between sky and water and deck.

"American crew," said Barney. He yawned. Then he looked at Douglass. "I think you'd best go below, Mrs. Harris." A great wave punctuated his words, and spray flew over the side. All three wiped off their faces. Barney took Douglass' arm.

Trumbull followed them. Douglass said, "Aren't you going to stay on deck?"

Barney didn't answer till they were going down the hatchway. "I'm going to sleep, Mrs. Harris. I've been up all night."

Her lashes were stuck together with the wetness of the air. "All night?"

"You should know a sailor doesn't sleep his last night ashore. Is this your cabin?"

She had stopped. "Yes."

He said positively, "You could not stay on that deck." A thudding roar accompanied his words.

She stiffened. "What was that?"

A wave hit the deck. "Haven't you ever heard that before?"

"No."

Barney said, "Gillon is doing right. There's nothing for it but carry sail and lay her head into the northeast. The coast of Holland is under our lee, and British warships in the channel." He smiled. "But stay below."

Her eyes were fastened on his face and the broad shoulders. Barney saw she was not only afraid but she was looking to him for safety. He leaned down and opened her door. "Those are timbers groaning," he explained. "In heavy weather the very deck planking will open and shut from the strain. It should. A stiff ship is—" he put his hand under her chin. "What's the matter?"

"Joshua said you said Captain Gillon was incompetent!"

"Gillon's a bloody fool and so's Joshua," Barney said. He pushed the door open again for her.

Douglass looked at the door and then at him. "Are you—you can't—"

Barney said, "Will you enter, please?"

Douglass took two steps. Barney followed her and shut the door.

"Sit down," said Barney, gesturing to the lower bunk.

Douglass backed away the few feet and sat down, never taking her eyes off him. Barney took one stride and stood over her, leaning against the upper berth. "I want to talk to you," he said.

"But—" said Douglass. "You do, do you? After leaving me so unceremoniously aboard that fearful packet and—"

Barney interrupted. "Hold your fire. I'd been in prison seven months. Would you have trusted me?" He laughed at her discomfiture.

Douglass held her head high, and wriggled backward on the bunk. "What did you wish to talk of?" she inquired.

"I was surprised to see you. What made you decide this? Why are you going to America?"

Since she couldn't tell the truth, she looked thoughtful. "Joshua arranged it." She smiled up at him.

"Joshua arranged it?" Barney echoed.

"Don't you think I'll fit in, Captain?" Douglass asked, having a brief memory of Lord Edgecomb's warning.

"God, yes," said Barney. "You'll be an asset. My thought is to sink all British ships and carry off all their pretty women. Seriously, I want you to tell me why you are aboard."

She said, "It's a long story, Captain."

"I want to hear it."

"Yes," said Douglass, surrendering and summoning words. "My brother, Lord Annan, was killed last year on his ship. The estates reverted to his son, of course, and his wife—" Her voice trailed off.

"I'm sorry," Barney said.

She said, a little stiffly, "He was killed in the defense of Gibraltar."

"It was a magnificent action," Barney said.

"Even though it was ours?"

"Even though it was yours."

She was silent. Then she said positively, "I cannot endure his widow."

Barney kept from smiling. She went right on. "My husband had put all his money in Harris and Company."

Barney said, "You mean Joshua bullied it out of him."

Douglass said heatedly, "Naturally James trusted Joshua. I do, too! But my shares in the business can't pay their interest during wartime."

"There's a measure of truth in that," he said. "American merchants have all they can do to keep our credit partially stable. So he offered you his home?"

"Yes," said Douglass. "Yes, Captain Barney. But I leave this ship at Corunna."

"Well," said Barney, "that's all I wanted to know." He started to turn away.

Douglass leaned forward. She had not forgotten the storm; at this moment the ship plunged violently. "Oh," she cried. She slid off the bunk. Then she blurted, "Barney! Please don't leave me!"

He looked down at her. "I'm sleepy, Mrs. Harris." The ship pitched again, and he caught her. "That remark was not an innuendo," he said, to her averted face. He set her down on the bunk again. "When I make love to you—" he stopped. Douglass saw his boot rest for a moment on the side of the bunk and then he swung up onto the top berth. He stuck his head over and laughed at her. "Goodnight," he said. "I'll sleep here. Look out below."

His boots dropped one by one. Douglass sat on the bunk, her feet hanging over, almost touching the big boots. She could hear him stretching himself comfortably above her. There was silence in the cabin save for the myriad sounds of the ship as she groaned her way through the heavy seas. Almost rhythmically great masses of water hit the deck and roared overhead. Suddenly she heard Barney say sleepily:

"Is your dress woolen?"

She looked up, peering around the edge of the berth. He had stuck his head over again. "Yes."

He nodded, satisfied. "Otherwise I'd tell you to change it. You'd catch cold. I wouldn't look," he added, his eyes twinkling.

She sat still on the bunk. Finally she put her feet up. The noises continued. The ship shook and shuddered and protested mightily. Outside the port she could see the foaming masses of angry water that hurled themselves at the ship's sides. Above all sounded the high screaming of the wind in the rigging.

It was cold. She pulled a blanket up over her, and then wondered if Barney were covered. He was evidently sound asleep. She pushed the blanket off and got off the bunk, holding tight to it. She could not possibly stand without holding on. The cabin lurched back and forth. She stood on tiptoe and looked at Barney.

He had pulled up a blanket. One big hand dangled over the side of the bunk. She touched the tips of his fingers with hers. The blanket had slipped off his shoulders, and she pulled it up further. Standing there, hanging on with one hand, she put her hand lightly on his dark head. Then she withdrew it quickly and scrambled back onto the bunk.

Two hours later Joshua opened the door.

It had been no use knocking. Knocks could not be heard. He opened the door and stood there. As he saw into the cabin his face changed. He could hardly believe what he saw. His blue eyes blazed with anger.

"Come here!"

Amazed, Douglass obeyed. She almost catapulted toward him and he caught her with angry hands, pulling her through the door and shutting it.

"For Christ's sake," he muttered, still holding her arm tight. He glowered at her. "Do you want to seriously compromise your name, sister?"

She retorted, angry too, "I asked him to stay!"

This rendered him speechless. Finally he said, "As your brother-in-law, I—"

She interrupted. "My own brother would have been amused!"

"I am not amused! This is not England but an American ship! I'm perfectly well aware of the antics of the ruling class in England, but you can't cut those capers here!"

"I will do as I please!"

"Not with my name, you won't!"

Douglass retreated before the male wrath. "Joshua," she whispered and looked up at him.

He said, calmer, "And of all men, to pick Barney. You'll get your fingers badly burned, Douglass. You have about as much experience dealing with a man like him as you do with powder kegs."

"But Joshua," she said, "he didn't—" Another thought struck her. "You wouldn't forbid him to call on me?"

He looked surprised. "Of course not. But what makes you think he might have honorable intentions?" He smiled a little. "If he does, you shouldn't have let him enter your cabin. Poor strategy."

"I couldn't stop him."

Joshua said, "I believe that proves my previous point. It's two o'clock, sister, and they are serving a cold dinner in the after cabin."

They had reached it. "The fires have had to be extinguished, of course," Joshua went on. "I will present you to Major Jackson and Charles Adams, and then I will go back to your cabin." His grimness had returned.

Douglass cried, "Oh, no, please, Joshua."

He shook his head.

"No," she cried again. "At least wait a bit! He may waken and leave. I don't want him to know you knew he was there! Wait—till we eat! For my sake, Joshua!"

She was clinging to his arm. Joshua looked down at her, at her face in the dim grey light. Even he was having trouble keeping his balance. She had spoken in staccato sentences, her voice high to carry through the noises of the storm. The weather was worsening rapidly. He disengaged his arm, and opened the cabin door. He had not made up his mind whether to heed her. He drew her into the cabin; Trumbull came quickly to her side to take her other arm in support.

Joshua presented her to the other two men within. The cabin was not large; the "South Carolina" was a ship of war, carrying twenty-eight twenty-two pounders on the main deck and sixteen long twelves on the forecastle and quarterdecks. The cabin was grey and dim and frightening; through the stern windows only blank greyness showed. Major Jackson was saying:

"The mist is suddenly so heavy you can't see from stem to stern out on deck."

Douglass saw that he was wet.

"You've been out on deck?" Douglass asked.

He said, "Lord no, ma'am. I collared Smith, the first lieutenant, just as the hatch was opened."

"What did you find out, Major?" Joshua asked. Douglass surmised that the men knew he had gone for information.

There was an awful shuddering sound and Jackson slid halfway across the cabin. Joshua and Trumbull held onto Douglass. Jackson steadied himself and answered Joshua, his face grim.

"He told me that several of the bolts of the weather main chain plates have been started. We are not far from Heliogoland, and the northward trend of the coast. Our position is hazardous because we are drifting to leeward." He paused. Then he said strongly, "I know something about commanding men. These officers have no respect or confidence in Gillon. If they don't, the crew doesn't. I don't like the attitude of the crew." He fixed Joshua with a questioning eye.

Joshua said, "I personally voted against Gillon's appointment—it was political. Come over here and sit down, Douglass."

Almost behind her was a locker running at right angles to the locker under the windows. "Can you eat?"

She shook her blond head. One curl had come loose and bounced on her forehead. She had a white woolen shawl with a fringe around her shoulders.

"Mistress Harris," Trumbull said, "we are not sailors. It probably isn't as bad as we think." He leaned over and patted her hand.

Douglass threw a look at Joshua. Jackson said, "Where is Barney?"

The four men looked at each other. Douglass cried, "He is asleep!"

They transferred their gaze to her; she was leaning forward, her breast rising and falling with her quick breath; she added, "At least so we—so he told me—that he was going to go to sleep." She looked from one to the other. Joshua broke the silence.

"There's very bad blood between Barney and Gillon." He frowned, grimly. "Gillon is captain of this ship!"

"I don't give a damn," Jackson began.

They had begun to shout. Quick terror seized Douglass. The whole cabin stood on end, an enormous crash came from above. Douglass leaped to her feet in horrified fear.

"Call him," she cried to Jackson.

"He cannot take command!" Joshua shouted at Jackson. "Not without jeopardizing his—"

The cabin door flew open and banged back against its frame. The first lieutenant stood there, dripping wet, breathing hard. "Are all passengers here?" he cried. Feet pounded along the deck outside the door, like three or four men, running. Smith whirled. The crew were out of hand, they had succumbed to terror, he knew. Suddenly another pair of steps sounded, light.

Smith saw Barney first. He stepped out of the door, to let Barney enter. Barney towered there, he had to bend his head to miss the beams; he did so instinctively. His dark eyes went from the faces of the men in the cabin to Douglass.

Douglass stood up. The ship's roll sent her staggering to Barney. He caught and held her disheveled figure upright. He looked over her head to the others. He spoke quickly; he didn't have much time.

"I shall need your testimony, gentlemen," he said briefly. He lifted Douglass and set her down on the locker. "Mr. Smith!"

Smith cried, "Yes, Captain Barney!"

"I'm taking command of this ship. Her movements are ungoverned. Mr. Smith, where is Captain Gillon?"

"On deck, sir!"

"You can count on our testimony, Captain," Joshua said.

Barney heard him but made no answer to him save a nod. "Come with me, Mr. Smith."

"Aye, aye, sir," cried Smith, a bit of hope in his voice. They were foundering, he knew. He and Barney together flung themselves at the hatchway, putting strong shoulders to it.

A wall of water poured in. Barney waited a second to let it pour down, then he was up the companionway with Smith right after him. They had just time to bang the hatch closed and fasten it before a towering wave was upon them. Both of them again flung themselves on the hatch and hung on.

Tons of water came down on the stricken "South Carolina." Barney felt her heel over helplessly as she wallowed down the trough. He let go the hatch and dived for the binnacle head.

Storm. It was all around him, raging, shrieking. Rain swept almost horizontally across the face of the heaving seas; the day was grey-black, and great foamy white waves towered endlessly. Above all this was the tearing wind, gale force, hurricane force.

For only a second he stood by the binnacle head, before the first order was roared out against the wind. In that time he saw the men clinging in the tops, indeed it was much safer there. He saw Gillon, clinging to the grating, where he was calling down to the men at the relieving tackles, for the two men at the wheel could not possibly have held her and there would be far too much strain on the tiller ropes. He gave a glance up at the weathervane; it confirmed him; the wind had shifted to north-northwest.

"Quartermaster. Hard astarboard!"

A great wave bore down. A high scream went up from one of the men aloft. As the wave struck, the "South Carolina" turned on her side. Barney had a brief vision of the hell below decks, where the men at the pumps would be flung against the sides in the blackness. If she went over much farther, he knew she would roll completely. Barney was not at all sure at that moment that any of them would survive. Then incredibly she righted, water streaming from her, washing across the decks, she lifted.

"Mr. Smith," Barney roared. "Hands to braces in the maintops."

"Aye aye, sir," the answer came singing back.

Dead ahead towered another wave. He bellowed orders to the helmsman; this time there was only a short period of plunging before she was brought around to the wind again.

The howling squall raced across the surface of the seas from the northwest now. Under his feet the planking opened and shut. The ship shuddered, bucking like a mad thing, but she was not ungoverned. The storm canvas rattled in the wind as the squall heeled her over again.

Barney clung to the binnacle head, eyes narrowed against the pelting rain. Then he saw Gillon coming toward him.

"Get off my deck!"

Barney paid no attention. "Hold her so!" he shouted. Another enormous wave was racing toward them, foam on its lips as it curled angrily toward the ship. If he couldn't keep her from drifting to leeward, they would be dashed to pieces on the rending sands of the coast here, as it reached out into the sea.

Gillon grabbed for Barney. Barney raised a murderous fist and struck him with all his might. Gillon rolled back into the grating. The wave broke.

Barney gave no more thought to Gillon, who lay on his face on the grating and hung on. He didn't see him stumble from the deck after the wave had passed. He only knew she was riding the storm now; she was a weatherly ship; he'd known it from the minute he'd laid eyes on her. The most terrible danger had passed now; it took only a few moments of heavy squall to sink a ship. Now in between his orders to the helmsman, he could snap out more commands.

"Mr. Smith! Check the breechings on the guns! And set the storm staysails!"

Water hissed along the deck and through the scuppers. Barney thought the wind was diminishing; those squall winds never lasted too long. It was God's mercy they didn't. But the men on the pumps should be relieved; probably there was no order below decks. She was paying off now before the wind and Barney shouted down to the helmsman. This time she was brought around quickly.

The watch was obeying his every order. He was well aware that the magic of his name had enforced the discipline, over and above that of Gillon. The lookout shouted down that there was a ship. He told himself, as he stood there, by the mizzen rigging now, that it had been the only possible course open to him. Now he was enjoying the storm. He was soaking wet, hatless, but by God he was alive, and aboard. Smith came up to him.

"We were in rather poor case when I took over, Mr. Smith," Barney had time to say. "The—"

"We were foundering, Captain," Smith said baldly. "I put a new gang at the chain pumps, as you ordered." A figure was running toward them carrying an oilskin and cap.

"Officer of the fo'castle, Mr. Hutchinson," Smith said, as Hutchinson handed the oilskin to Barney. Hutchinson fastened his eyes on the famous seaman.

"You saved us from Davy Jones, sir," he said.

Barney shrugged on the oilskin. It was the way of the sea that only minutes had elapsed, and a few orders could save a ship.

At ten o'clock the "South Carolina" was still hauling to westward under reefed tops. Joshua had fallen asleep. In his cabin Trumbull wrote quickly, his pen scratching along the paper. "A squall struck us, heavier than the gale, the ship became unmanageable, the officers lost self-possession, and the crew all confidence in them, while for a few minutes all was confusion and dismay." Trumbull dipped his pen. "Happily for us, Captain Barney was among the passengers —he had just escaped from Mill Prison, in England. Hearing the increased tumult aloft, and feeling the ungoverned motion of the ship, he flew up on deck, saw the dangers, assumed command; the men obeyed and he soon had her again under control. That our danger was imminent no one will doubt." He laid down his pen. He was going to ask Barney for permission to paint him. But Joshua had made it quite clear that Barney might get into serious trouble over this. For a moment Trumbull wondered whether trouble followed Barney. He could not have done anything else, this day.

Douglass slipped quietly out of the cabin door. She was still wearing the maroon wool dress. She came out on deck, and for a moment stood in the shadow of one of the long guns.

Over her head the mizzen rose straight up, bare till its tops. The rigging sang. Fore she could see the gleaming white of the headsails as they were blown stiff, angled from the bowsprit, so white against the black seas that curled up and foamed away from the gilded lion figurehead. Lanterns shone on the lifeboats, and at the mastheads; two men were still at the wheel. She could see the figures of the watch moving about the deck and she saw Barney. He had his back to her.

She crossed the deck to him.

For a moment she caught a look of surprise that she had sought him out. Then he drew her over to the weather side of the quarterdeck. She lifted her face to his.

"You saved the ship," she said solemnly.

Barney said, "You're so beautiful, English."

She paid no attention. She was still looking up at his dark face. "We—we all thank you. The officers told us—Mr. Smith said if it had not been for you we would have foundered and been dashed to pieces on the sands there." She gestured to the east.

Barney said, "A northwest squall often follows the northeast storms." The spray suddenly flew high. He put his arm around her; he took out his handkerchief and carefully wiped off her face.

"Thank you," she said.

Barney gave a last wipe at her chin. She said, "You owe me a handkerchief." Her fingers closed over it and she took it from him, and used it on her forehead.

The wind cried a little. "Barney," she said low, into his shoulder. "Yes?"

She hesitated. "It is a different ship now because no one is afraid. But—" slowly she raised her lashes, still wet and stuck together.

He knew what she was trying to ask. She might suspect, too, that his violence against Gillon would be exaggerated and she would be right. He said only, "I shall not surrender command until eight o'clock tomorrow morning. But I shall leave the ship at Corunna."

She was well aware that all his plans had now gone awry. "I'm sorry, Barney," she whispered.

"Don't be," he grinned. "I'm going to order you below now. You are exhausted; you've kept a long vigil. And I want my handkerchief back."

Douglass stepped back. "No," she said, her fingers tight around the linen square.

He made a fierce mock scowl. "On my own quarterdeck, you dare to say no?"

She backed away, but she couldn't go far for a gun carriage stopped her. Barney loomed over her. She put both hands behind her back. "I want it, Barney."

"You can't have it."

"You owe it to me!"

He slid one arm around her hand and took her wrist, unfastening her fingers.

"I always repay my debts in my own way," he said, drawing the handkerchief from her and dangling it in front of her eyes. It blew in the wind.

"Brute," she said, leaning back on the gun, laughing at him.

"Now get off my deck. You're confined to quarters."

She looked up at him. Had he been English, she was sure he would have his own squadron by now, and a captain's rank. "What they say about you is true," she said gravely. "You are a magnificent seaman. It is a pity that you—"

This time his frown was real. "No, English." He shook his head. "I sink English ships."

A wry smile touched her lips. "Yes, of course. Goodnight, Yank." She swept him a curtsy. Then she turned. Her voice floated back to him. "Thank you for my English hide."

10

CORUNNA WAS THE NORTHERNMOST PORT IN SPAIN. THE "SOUTH Carolina" had put in at eight in the morning.

The evening before Gillon had committed the final ineptitude. He had fired on a Spanish ship, mistaking her for a Britisher. She had been damaged before she could make Gillon understand who she was. This incident had completely unstrung the Spanish authorities. Even Joshua didn't know what they would do. He had deposited Douglass at a lodging house and gone out.

The sitting room of the small suite Joshua had taken was on the first floor, about ten feet above the narrow street. It had a small iron grilled balcony, and Douglass had dragged a chair out there. She saw Trumbull coming down the street and she leaned over and called to him.

Trumbull looked up, shading his eyes with his hand. Douglass was wearing a wide-brimmed hat with a sprinkling of roses to match her rose-colored filmy gown.

"If this were the right light I could sketch you, Mrs. Harris," Trumbull said, squinting up at her. "But I'll paint you going home."

Douglass said, "You're sailing with us?"

Trumbull nodded. "We couldn't very well stay aboard the 'South Carolina.' We wanted to back up Barney."

Douglass said warmly, "Oh, I'm glad, Mr. Trumbull."

Her smile was so delighted that Trumbull grinned too. "One of America's lustiest sons, Mrs. Harris."

Douglass forgot Joshua's injunctions. "A damned elusive male, sir," she said, over her fan. In the last two days she had not seen him at all. He had remained in his cabin, where all the officers and men sought him out; he left the cabin only to walk three times around the deck twice a day. Even Joshua had been drawn into that cabin Barney shared with Trumbull.

"Well, it was a mite awkward, the situation," Trumbull said, with true Yankee understatement.

"He needed rest and food, too," Douglass said thoughtfully.

Trumbull eyed her. "So he did."

Douglass heard steps behind her; she turned. "Why, here is Joshua," she said. "Why don't you come in?"

Trumbull patted the box under his arm. "I'm off for a little sketching. I'll say goodbye."

Douglass turned in time to see Joshua disappear into his own room. He was saying, "It's hot as hell and there's not a glass of beer in this damned town. I'm going to change my shirt."

His door banged closed. Douglass called through it. "Why don't you ever tell me anything?"

His answer came back through his shirt and the door. "What do you mean?"

"You didn't tell me Trumbull and Jackson were going to sail with us!"

The door to the hall opened now, and Barney stood there. "He didn't, did he? And hasn't anyone told you not to shout?" He leaned against the door jamb and regarded her.

"Oh," said Douglass. "Yes, they have."

"You know better, then? Aren't you going to ask me to come in?"

"Yes, of course." She smiled enchantingly. "You surprised me. And I do believe you've gained another five pounds."

Barney shut the door and advanced into the room. He took her white hand and raised it to his lips. "Were you going out, Mrs. Harris?"

"My hat?" She remembered her hat. "I was sitting outside, on the little balcony. Why, Captain?"

"Because I don't want to detain you."

"You're not detaining me."

"I didn't come to see you, though, Mrs. Harris. I came to see your brother-in-law," Barney said.

Douglass set her red mouth. "Wretch," she said, and turned away from him. "I hate you, Barney," she said, over her shoulder. She sank down on a chair and carefully arranged her skirts. Joshua opened his door and came into the room.

"Captain Barney called to see you, Joshua," she said, regarding both men as though they were far away.

"So I see," Joshua said. "It would be difficult not to be aware of Captain Barney's presence, sister."

"I was wondering if you two would care for me to leave," Douglass went on.

Barney pretended to ponder this. "I guess not," he said finally.

Douglass swung her slipper.

"We will manage to put up with you," Joshua said. "Please sit down, Barney. The English have no manners." He grinned and sat down whereupon Barney did the same.

"What did you find out, Harris?" he asked Joshua.

Joshua grimaced. "The Spanish have ordered the rudders of every American ship in port unhung until the damage to that Spanish vessel Gillon fired on is paid."

"Yes, I knew that," Barney said. "Hill, of the 'Cicero,' had offered

me a lieutenant's billet, for the passage home. Now he can't sail."
He continued, "I'll come right to the point. Is your offer still open?"

"Yes," said Joshua.

Barney got to his feet and walked over to the doors that opened onto the balcony. Then he swung around. "At the time I refused you rudely. My reasons are now immaterial." His smile flashed out. "But please accept my apologies for my discourtesy."

Joshua jumped to his feet, too. "I was rude, also! I must say it's damned decent of you to say so first. You got ahead of me, Barney."

They were both silent for a minute, while Douglass watched them; standing there, they were almost of the same height and build. She kept very quiet.

Then Joshua said, "I didn't tell you. Since I'm here, and can post my bond, and grease palms, we sail as scheduled. Tomorrow morning. The tide's at seven."

"I'll go aboard tonight," Barney said. "Who's my first officer?"

"Paul. Mr. Paul. I'll go aboard with you, and introduce you." Joshua smiled suddenly. "Jesus, Captain, the men will be—I can't think of the right word. And I'll sail with you, aboard the 'Pomona.' "

Douglass couldn't stand it any longer. "Joshua," she said.

He became aware of her again. "Yes?"

Barney answered her unspoken question. "No ladies, certainly. We'll be carrying twenty guns, and we hope to use them. We shall convoy you; you'll be aboard a safe merchantman."

"I'd like to take you aboard now," Joshua said, forgetting Douglass again. "But I can't. I must go down to the port authorities and arrange everything finally."

"I'll take you," Barney said. "I've a carriage out front. Are you ready?"

Joshua nodded. Barney bowed to Douglass. "Goodbye, Mrs. Harris. Why don't you go out and sit on the balcony?"

"I think I shall, since that was my intention," Douglass said with hauteur.

"I won't be back till suppertime," Joshua said. "Barney, do you want some money?"

Douglass went out on the balcony. She heard Barney say, "I'd like you to have one of your agents pay a debt of mine. Two hundred pounds to Cornelius de Leeuw, 19 Rue Anglais, Brussels. And you might advance me a hundred pounds."

[61]

The door closed then. The sums Barney spoke of so nonchalantly made her eyes widen; below her they emerged into the street. Neither of them paid any attention to her; they were talking, as though completely immersed. She looked after the carriage as it went off down the street.

"Damn," she said, quite inadequately.

Ten minutes passed. She occupied herself in watching the people in the street below, the yelling urchins, the horsemen that clattered past. Then she saw a familiar carriage; surely it was the one that Barney had hired.

She almost rose; then she remembered. She plied her fan, eyes downcast; she threw glances down the street at the oncoming carriage. Then her eyes grew big and she put down the fan as she saw the carriage lurch over the curb and come dashing up right under the balcony. Hastily she plied the fan again as Barney stood up in the carriage, right under her, his face almost level with hers.

"Would you like to come for a ride, Mrs. Harris?"

Everyone had stopped and was looking. Douglass said, "Oh, I would, Captain!"

Barney said, "Well, put your little backside on this railing."

Douglass stood up, hesitated a moment, and then sat on the railing. Barney scooped her up. Amid a flurry of skirts and petticoats she was deposited in the seat beside him. Still standing, he reached in his pocket and tossed a handful of coins to the delighted screaming urchins. While they scrambled for the coins, they shouted his name, and the sober Spaniards stared at this display of Yankee insanity.

"La Pescaderia," Barney called to the driver, and sat down beside her.

The coach moved off with the calls of the urchins following it. Douglass was laughing and Barney, with a wide smile, put one arm around her, and captured her hand with his free one. "Hello, sweetheart," he said in her ear. "I like those big hats, but they interfere."

"It's well something does." She remembered the order he had called out. "And what is La Pescaderia?"

"The fishing village. It's quaint. Look, my dear. To larboard. A twelfth century church."

Douglass obediently looked, turning her face to his, and he kissed the tip of her nose. She drew back.

"Barney!"

[62]

He grinned. "Now look to starboard; you can see over the harbor."

She could. The port of Corunna was closely built on the east side of a peninsula that sloped down into the bay. In the blue water she could see the small islands that dotted the bay and the protecting forts perched on them. The carriage rolled on downward, descending fast. It was an open carriage and along the way people shouted and waved at Barney.

He said, as though to explain, "I sailed from Corunna all last summer and part of the fall."

"I know that," she said. "Last summer—" She had told him before. It seemed such a short time ago. She glanced at his face; last year at this time she had read in the newspapers: "Warning! This is the rebel pirate Barney." She looked at him uncertainly. Then she said, "Barney, I'm afraid I can't give you permission to put your arm around me—in public."

The delivery and the sentence seemed to amuse Barney.

"You can't give me permission?"

"No, Captain," said Douglass. Then she smiled sweetly. "But I like you to hold my hand." She looked down at the brown fingers around her white ones and at the heavy carved ring; then her eyes lifted to his face again, a bit of question in them. "If you please."

Barney sighed. He removed his arm. "With deep regret, at your command, Mrs. Harris," he said, in a good imitation of a London beau. "There's La Pescaderia."

The coach was lurching merrily over a narrow section of the peninsula, blue water on each side. The fishing village clustered around the shore, the slender masts of its vessels rising higher than the little dwellings. Douglass was surprised when the driver suddenly stood up in the seat and yanked on the reins. The coach came to a flying stop and jerked.

They had stopped in front of one of the houses next to the dirt road. A woman came running out, greeting Barney with a flood of smiles and quick Spanish.

He answered, also speaking rapidly. She kept nodding. Then he dug in his pocket and brought out a roll of bills. He peeled off a pound note and handed it to her. Through her murmured *"Gracias, señor,"* he said to Douglass, "I'm ordering fresh lobster, for the Captain's table. We keep them alive for a good long time aboard. I always get lobster here. Or did you understand?"

[63]

"No," Douglass answered, her eyes on another female figure who had come sauntering out of the house. She was barefooted and moved with feline grace toward the carriage; she kept her wide brown eyes on Barney, and she came close and leaned on the carriage, her head almost against his arm. The woman spoke to her sharply.

She didn't answer, but twisted her head sideways to look at Barney. He spoke then, his voice harsh and a scowl on his face, and she backed away; the woman smiled and waved, and the carriage turned. "Now we'll drive along the docks," Barney said.

"You had best take me back now," Douglass said stiffly.

Barney said, "What's the matter? Don't you feel well?" He reached for her hand again, and she pulled it away from him.

"How did you dare?" she burst out. "To take me there when you knew that girl would come out?"

His own temper caught instant fire. He grasped both her hands in his. "So that's it," he muttered, turning her toward him, looking at her grimly as she made a last effort to loosen his grip.

"Take me back!"

"I said we're going to drive along the docks and we are. By God, you look at me!"

Defiantly she raised stormy eyes. Barney said, "There's really no reason why I should tell you, but I've never touched her, much less slept with her. Now sit back in the seat."

Douglass flushed. She could feel the telltale hot blood in her cheeks. She leaned back in the seat; she was sitting very near him now. His shoulder pressed against hers, and he was holding both her hands. The carriage gave a lurch and turned. She heard him say:

"There is the merchantman you sail on, Mrs. Harris."

She looked out over the water, not even seeing the ship.

"And there is the 'Pomona,'" Barney went on. "Pretty thin, isn't she?"

Douglass found it with her eyes. The barque rode daintily at anchor, her painted green gunports closed, her masts rising slender and tall. Almost next to her rose a Swedish man-of-war of seventy-four guns. And out past this port would be British warships just as big; next to them the "Pomona" would be a toy. Her fingers curled around Barney's hand; she held on tight. She said, very low, "Barney."

"What is it, my dear?"

[64]

He was looking out over the water to the "Pomona." "I'm sorry," she whispered.

He transferred his gaze to her; he didn't say anything but he smiled a little.

Douglass smiled back, tentatively. Then she said, with some speculation, "Lord, how angry you were with me!"

She was very thoughtful and Barney smiled openly and a bit ruefully. "You stir my pirate's blood," he admitted. "I'd best take you back now."

Douglass could think of no appropriate answer to this. The carriage climbed the steep hill slowly.

"You go aboard soon, I think," Barney said. "And an old friend of mine, Captain Hill, is waiting to have supper with me."

"That will be nice, for you to see him again," Douglass said.

"Very nice," said Barney, laughing. "And I shan't see you again till the States."

She said, "But you will be near!"

"In case of storm I'll come alongside and pick you up."

Douglass asked, "Will you, really?"

He laughed again. "I'll promise to convoy you safely." They had drawn up before the lodging house, and he got out and assisted her. "I'll see you upstairs."

She walked alongside of him, up the steps. At the door he stopped. "Goodbye, Mrs. Harris. Bon voyage."

"Goodbye, Captain." She looked up at him. "Barney," she cried. "If they catch you, would they put you in the Tower?"

He took her hand, leaned down and brushed his lips against her fingers. Then he straightened. "They won't catch me, my dear," he said. "Goodbye."

11

"SAIL-HO! SAIL-HO!"

The cry rang out from the lookout.

Joshua Harris looked up from his writing. It was early afternoon. He flung down his pen and hurried out on deck.

Barney was already fore. Glass tucked in his belt, he was swinging up the foremast shrouds, up over the futtock shrouds to the high masthead. Joshua waited anxiously. After a few long minutes Barney slid down onto the deck again, glass in hand, and joined Joshua on the quarterdeck. Joshua started to speak, but Barney had already raised his own voice.

"We will keep on this course, Mr. Paul," he said.

Joshua looked up at the sails. The "Pomona" was carrying full canvas, the breeze was fresh and strong, and she was running free before it. The stranger was off the stern quarter. Joshua said, his accent thicker than usual:

"It is a pity, when we are so near the Delaware Capes; I was hoping we'd slip by."

Barney quoted, jibingly, "These are the times that try men's souls," and Joshua grinned ruefully. Joshua considered Thomas Paine a radical; this was another of Barney's good-natured jabs at Joshua's conservatism.

Barney was watching his convoy. There were four ships now, instead of the two he had started with. He had swung out of the normal route in the latitudes and taken a brig, loaded with fish and wines and brandies, and an English merchantman. Because of this, the crew of the "Pomona" had been reduced to ninety, or three-fourths her normal complement. Joshua knew Barney had hoped to elude the British warships that ran the blockade against American shores. He rubbed his chin. The convoy were obediently scattering. Their maneuvers seemed to satisfy Barney, for he made no comment.

Barney said, "I think she's in the corvette class, Mr. Paul." He raised a dark eyebrow, thrust his hands in his pockets, and said laconically to Paul:

"Beat to quarters, Mr. Paul."

An hour passed. Joshua remained on deck. The other four ships had scattered; the "Pomona" held her course. And the stranger was gaining.

The gun ports had slid open, the brave new six-pounders served with powder and shot; their gunners squatted before them, already grimed. The decks were sanded; rifles had been issued; hoses rigged. Barney was talking to the gunners, walking slowly along the line with Mr. Paul. Joshua turned to look at the other ship again.

She was dead astern now. He thought Barney was right; she was a corvette, with probably thirty-two guns. There was no question of her superior speed; she would be on them by nightfall with the wind

[66]

at her heels, which was what the British liked. Barney, looking pre-occupied, joined Joshua again, brushing the powder off his hands onto his canvas trousers. A brace of pistols was jammed into his heavy belt. On the horizon, only dots showed the convoy. Barney had been studying the other ship through the glass. Silently he handed it to Joshua.

Joshua raised it. Atop the mizzen the Union Jack was plain to see; on the gaff fluttered the white ensign of the Royal Navy. Uniformed marines clung to her tops. Joshua said nothing as he handed the glass back to Barney.

The officers were clustered around him. He began, "She'll hail us in five minutes or so." He was eying the water between the two ships. "When she hails, we will not waste words. We have only seconds to perform this very simple maneuver. We need one crippling hit to slow up her speed. We'll try to make it."

Joshua wiped his palms on his trousers. He tried to judge if the corvette was in range. In seconds she would be. The ship's bells struck in the silence; five times they struck. At that moment a long hail came across the water.

"What ship are you?"

The echoes had not died away before Barney had spoken. "Run up the colors, Mr. Paul. Helmsman, hard aport."

The "Pomona" yawed ship. She came about like a live thing.

"Fire!" cried Barney, eyes glued to the corvette.

The "Pomona's" ten starboard guns roared. The sound had not died away when Barney said in the same tone:

"Hands to braces! Helmsman, keep her hard aport!"

She wheeled like a gull, leaning in the water, spray flying from her graceful bows, showing her heels now to the enemy. And she had made her hit. The corvette's foretop sail had come tumbling down on her decks. Her guns had answered belatedly, and the "Pomona" was unscathed. The crew of the "Pomona" let out a yell of triumph now. It had happened so fast they hardly realized that they had been successful. They were still yelling and jeering as they drew away, faster now. Barney was saying to Paul:

"We'll wet down the sails a bit, Mr. Paul, and show her our heels as long as we can. You may send the hands to supper. We got a little taste of blood." He turned to Joshua. "Time to eat, Harris."

Joshua said absently, "I suppose so." Up overhead the flag flew.

"But she'll not give up the chase," Barney was saying in between

[67]

bites. The distant roar of a cannon bore him out. Joshua and the four officers ate quickly. But Barney seemed to be in no hurry. He drank his coffee at leisure; he seemed to be deep in thought, paying no attention to what the others were saying. Finally he put down his napkin and rose and went out on deck.

He walked down the row of brass six-pounders. Then he disappeared fore. After about an hour, Joshua saw him emerge amidships and pick his way across the dark deck. Joshua waited for him to speak.

There was no sound but the sound of water and wind; the singing in the rigging. The moon was full. In its light there was no possibility of escape from the corvette, whose white sails could be seen in its radiance, even though they were dropping farther and farther behind.

"I reckon it will be about midnight before she repairs that damage," Barney said, thinking aloud. Joshua and Mr. Paul listened.

There was a belch of fire from the corvette's fore guns. A shot splashed into the water.

"She's showing her teeth," Barney commented.

"Are we going to answer?" Joshua asked.

Barney shook his head. He motioned with his thumb. "You forgot, Harris, to provide the 'Pomona' with stern ports."

Joshua found himself clenching his hands. Then he rubbed the sudden sweat off his forehead. He swore.

"You were intent on her lines, no doubt," Barney said, but his smile was genial. He knew how fast and with what awful difficulty ships were got out of the yards nowadays.

Joshua said, "If she repairs that damage around midnight—" He left the rest of the sentence unfinished, and Barney took it up.

"Then she will hang around our stern and bang away with impunity all night."

"And she will discover we have no way of replying to their fire!"

"I fear she will," said Barney thoughtfully. Then he smiled even more broadly.

He was filling his pipe. "Now Mr. Paul, will you rout out Chips."

"Aye, aye, sir." Paul started away.

Barney's voice stopped him. "I'm not finished. I want a couple of axes. There's an old three-pounder stored below. I want that, too. We're going to chop a hole in her counter."

[68]

Paul and Joshua were silent for a moment. Then Paul cried, "Good, sir, good!" and dashed away.

Joshua's blue eyes sparkled. Then he remembered to reserve judgment. "Perhaps you can turn disadvantage into advantage?"

"Perhaps," agreed Barney dryly.

The boatswain appeared with two lanterns, then the ship's carpenter, wide awake. Joshua wondered how many of the men off duty were asleep. The English guns took that moment to speak again. They were accompanied by the usual nearby splash. But no one paid any attention. Barney was puffing on his pipe and the sound of axes began to ring forth over the deck.

At three the three-pounder was lugged into place. The splintered wood and leavings had been swept. Barney was bending over the gun, applying more oil to her rusty carriage, using a rag to wipe her off as tenderly as though she were a rare jewel he had found. The lanterns swung a little; the moon was dying down into the sea. Paul suddenly spoke over Barney's head.

"Captain!" he cried, almost despairingly.

Barney didn't move. He was looking down the sights of the old gun. "Yes, Mr. Paul."

"Sir!" Paul paused, and threw a look at Joshua. No one else was within hearing, save perhaps the helmsman. "We have no ammunition for a three-pounder!"

Barney was now squatting back on his heels. "No, we do not." He stood up, and wiped the oil off his hands on the rag. In the light of the lantern, with the smell of the oil around him like a halo and a smear of it across his face, he smiled like a delighted satan, Joshua thought. And he said:

"Now, Mr. Paul, I want fetched here a pair of crowbars, and a few stove lids, and grape shot. I'm going below and shave."

Joshua went below and shaved and dressed in old clothes. The minutes were passing fast now. The ship was alive after four hours respite. Joshua smelled coffee. He had cut his face twice shaving and was holding a handkerchief to his chin as he came into the after cabin. He drank a cup of scalding hot coffee and picked up a piece of bread.

"How much more time?" he asked Barney.

"Not long till dawn," Barney said. "Thirty minutes or so."

"You think you know what they'll do?"

Barney nodded. "You can count on the English. They fight. No distant bombardment. They'll be eager to get their teeth into us. Come along."

Joshua followed him out on deck. Joshua spoke to him as they emerged. "I, too, want to fight."

"What are you good at?" Barney asked.

"A rifle," Joshua said modestly.

"Tell the master-at-arms to issue you a rifle." Barney was looking at the three-pounder. She glistened nicely now. And alongside of her was piled the oddest and most ludicrous ammunition Joshua had ever seen. He wanted to give a shout of laughter, and Barney caught his eyes and they both grinned. "Nevertheless, those crowbars are mighty deadly," Joshua announced soberly. He looked at them harder. "Christ Almighty," he muttered, as he began to realize the amount of damage they could wreak, not only on human heads but on sails and rigging. The officers had been summoned; the riflemen were already stationed in the foretops. Joshua, standing a bit aside, listened.

The day was lightening. There was the faintest grey in the sky, and the lanterns had been extinguished. Barney's low voice penetrated the quarterdeck.

"I'll fire this gun myself," he said. "I expect, briefly, to do two things with this unexpected weapon. First, to create complete confusion among the boarders she will undoubtedly have massed fore. You can see she is going to hit us at what she thinks is a vulnerable spot, namely astern. Second, I hope to cut away the fore shrouds and rigging. This will compel her to wear, to save her foremast from going by the board. When she wears, she will thus be in position for a raking broadside." Suddenly he seemed to realize that the riflemen were already in the tops. He said, "Who the hell ordered those men aloft?"

Mr. Paul stammered. "I thought you said, sir—"

"I said," Barney growled, "to assemble all available crewmen, issue rifles and send them aft. Get them down out of there!"

The men slid down onto the deck. The last one had no sooner hit the deck than the corvette's fore guns roared. Low shots ploughed through the mizzen sails, bringing two spars hurtling down onto the deck.

"What the hell were you doing, Mr. Paul? Running a shooting gallery for the British?" Barney watched as the wreckage was quickly cleared away. The dawn was almost upon them. The corvette was narrowing the distance between the two ships rapidly now. In five minutes she would be on them. Her guns roared again, sending a section of the rail across the deck. The "Pomona" shook.

"Now you may send the men aloft, Mr. Paul," Barney said.

Joshua's hands were tight around the rifle. He began his climb. He could see now, plainly. All sails set, the corvette was dipping gracefully as she came toward her prey. As he climbed higher, Joshua saw the men massed on her forecastle; men ready for boarding. Then Barney had been right. Joshua's heart pounded. He swung over a yardarm and perched there.

Twenty feet separated the two ships. There was not a sound aboard the "Pomona." She fled on, before superior strength. But she couldn't escape. Ten feet separated the two ships. In a minute the command aboard the Britisher to heave the grappling irons would come. Joshua could see them. And there must be two hundred men massed for boarding fifteen feet from him.

There was a sudden shock as the two ships touched, prow to stern. At the same moment the most awful sound rent the air. The three-pounder strained madly as she poured forth her ammunition. The crowbars flew into the massed men almost under her nose. Then whizzing grapeshot, murderous, poured into the massed boarders. Joshua calmly sighted down the barrel of his rifle at the face of a man only eighteen feet away whose eyes were bulging from surprise and fear. Joshua heard, as though far away, the firing of the men around him as they poured lead into the men so near them. Barney had reloaded the gun; it raked the enemy forecastle again, spitting death.

Screams rose from the corvette's forecastle. It was emptying fast, as the officers shouted vainly. The corvette's jibs were hit; they tangled and fell into wrecked spars and torn canvas. All the foresails and weather shrouds were cut away. Joshua brought down an officer with his next shot. He could hear even above the cries of wounded men the orders aboard the corvette. As he was loading the rifle again, he remembered what Barney had said. The corvette was going to do just as he had said; she was being compelled to wear to save the foremast. Joshua fired again. As he did he felt the "Pomona" shake with the explosion of her own guns, in a blazing broadside that caught the corvette full in her helpless position. The sound had not died away when Barney's voice cut through.

"Hard to starboard!"

The "Pomona" heeled. Viciously she was eager to come about. Her larboard guns raked the corvette with another full broadside. Frantically Joshua reloaded. He fired once more at the receding corvette. It was his last shot. The "Pomona" was pulling away fast from the scene of her victory, leaving behind her a crippled ship.

For a moment Joshua sat there, on the yard, unable to believe it was over. He was sorry it was over. He looked reluctantly at the gun in his hands. He looked at the corvette. Was she listing, or did he want to think she was? He climbed down onto the deck. The crew were all yelling madly. They were cheering and dancing up and down. They had not lost a man; they had hardly a scratch to show for the swift encounter. They were almost out of control.

Barney let them go without reproval, as he stood there, his back to the three-pounder, his pistols in hand with smoke still curling from them. He waved them. The men yelled harder. Barney raised his voice.

"A ration of grog to every man!"

There was another cheer and then, drawn by the magical lure of grog, the boatswain could get his men to listen.

Joshua took a last look at the corvette. He realized it would be the height of folly to expose the "Pomona" to her heavy guns again. All that could possibly be done had been done. He walked toward Barney, still carrying the rifle.

Joshua didn't know what to say. Dimly on the horizon he could see the Delaware Capes. They were almost home. He heard Barney say:

"You may lower the colors, Mr. Paul." Joshua watched as the flag came slowly down. He watched as Mr. Paul handed the stars and stripes to Barney. He held out the rifle.

"I guess I don't need this any more," he said.

It was not easy to go back to being a merchant again.

PART TWO

12

ABSOLOM JONES HEARD THE KNOCKS PLAINLY, SOFT THOUGH they were. He hurried to the door. It was an early hour, too early to call. The man outside might be the bearer of an important message.

It was therefore with surprise that he regarded the morning visitor. He stood for a moment, speechless, his dark face puzzled. He scratched his woolly curls.

"*Bon jour,*" said the visitor.

Absolom blinked. "Yes?" he asked.

"I intend good morning. I speak with no thinking." The smile that accompanied this sentence changed suddenly into a sigh. She asked, "Should I come to that door?" She pointed to the back panel.

"Why," began Absolom, and hesitated. She was wearing a very plain woolen cloak of some grey stuff. Beside her on the step rested a brassbound box. "You come to see the captain? You know him?"

Her blue eyes looked into his with solemnity. "No," she admitted. Then she blurted, "May I see him?"

Absolom swallowed. He leaned over and picked up the box. "Come in," he muttered. He closed the door, and found himself alone with the stranger in the familiar hall. The big clock chimed eight. "Wait here, please."

Under the wide staircase was a door that opened on a pair of curving steps. He had to bend his head to negotiate the turn. At the foot of the steps, he paused and turned his head. She was right behind him.

"I told you to wait."

His voice had been low, but it had also been heard. Barney looked up from a plate of pink ham and omelette. He said lazily, "With whom are you having the whispered colloquy, Absolom?"

Absolom came down the last step. "What, sir?"

[73]

"Innocence ill becomes you, rascal. Who is behind you?"

At this, Absolom stepped aside. With some of the pride of a conjurer he permitted the sight of the morning visitor to come into Barney's view. "But I told her to wait, Captain!"

"Well," said Barney appreciatively.

She made him a little curtsey. Her eyes in the heart-shaped face were appealing. Her cloak was still close around her, and her ungloved hands were clasped over a worn reticule. All this he noted instantly. He cut a piece of ham and chewed it thoughtfully. The fire hissed behind him as flames whipped at green wood.

"Your name, Mrs.?"

"Ma'moiselle," she corrected. "Lucie Magnin, sir."

His dark eyes rested on her appraisingly. "I do not know you, Lucie."

"No, Captain."

There was another silence in the small white-walled room. Behind it stretched the kitchens; she could hear the activity out there, the clatter of pans, the clang on an iron stove door.

Barney spoke to the Negro. "Absolom, you may bring me another cup of coffee." He did not wait until Absolom had left the room. "Now, ma'moiselle, why are you here? What do you want from me? Speak up."

She hesitated. She was looking for the right word. "Work." That was the right word, and she smiled, her dimples showing plainly. "Work." She repeated it.

Barney grinned. He looked at her eager face. "And what can you do?"

"Anything." She nodded. "Truly."

Barney had finished eating and he began to fill his pipe. "You should have gone to see Stephen Girard," he said. "Master Girard takes an interest in French émigrés. Where have you been staying? You may speak your tongue, ma'moiselle. I shall understand you."

She answered quickly now. She said she had been staying at Denny's lodging house in Water Street. "For the last ten nights, since the ship docked."

He was surprised. "Then you sailed in our convoy?"

"*Oui!*" Again her smile flashed. "That is why I come to you. I knew your name."

"I see." He sipped the coffee Absolom had brought. Tobacco smoke was filling the room. "But I can't employ you, you know."

He blew out another cloud of smoke, frowning a little. "Have you any money at all?"

"No."

"You came to the wrong man. This is entirely a male establishment. And I don't have any respectable friends."

"Oh, sir." She shook her head.

"I should say the respectable acquaintances I have would hardly consider my word a recommendation, mistress. You'd be badly armed with a note from me. If I sent you to Mrs. Rush, for instance, she'd be sure I'd tampered with your virtue." He looked across to Absolom. "Wouldn't she, Absolom?"

Absolom grinned widely. "She might, sir."

Barney laughed outright. Then he asked, suddenly, "Are you equipped to do hair?" He waved his hand, the big pipe in it. "Can you—take care of a lady?"

She eyed him. "Yes."

"I shall employ you." He looked very pleased with himself. "Absolom, bring me pen and paper. I want to write a note." He was thinking aloud. "I'll employ you, and pay you for a year. Your mistress will be Madam Harris. You'll live with her."

"Live with her?" she echoed. She looked across at his bent head; he was writing rapidly. Another Negro was clearing away plates; Absolom was tending the fire; they were doing this while her fate was being decided. And it was done so quickly!

"Here is the note." Barney held it out to her.

She didn't move toward him, so he rose and walked the few feet between them.

She felt the note between her fingers. "This establishment—" she began.

Barney interrupted. "A gold piece for each month. Twelve of them. And Absolom will take you. 'Tis not far."

In two minutes exactly she was standing in the little court; the bare bushes shook their branches at her. In her hand was the note and in her bag were twelve shining gold pieces. "This way, miss," said Absolom.

They turned in the opposite direction from which she had come. The alley was narrow and they walked in the center of it. At the corner of Second Street, they turned left.

Absolom carried her box on his shoulder. He nodded, spoke a good morning to John Sparhawk, apothecary and bookseller, whose shop was on the corner. He spoke to everyone, waving, and making bows to people passing in carriages. Lucie decided he knew almost everyone of the fifty thousand in the city.

They passed a church, and a graveyard. Lucie crossed herself. It wasn't right to have graveyards right in the center of the city, where people lived. It was very strange.

They came to Second and High Streets. They turned right.

Absolom said, "We go to Sixth and High."

Lucie was slowing her steps, and Absolom agreeably slowed his to match. Nevertheless, the moment of arriving at their destination was not much delayed. Lucie drew a deep breath as Absolom knocked. The door opened.

"I have a note for—" Lucie stopped. She could not find the right words. Absolom came to her rescue.

He talked fast. She did not understand his accent but she found herself in a small room to the left of a hall with a beautiful stairway. Her box was on the floor beside her, and she was waiting alone.

Joshua came out of the dining room. He caught a momentary glimpse of a female figure as he went by the door. But he paid no attention, and went on.

A ship was coming in that morning; she had been sighted down-river yesterday. His chief clerk was probably down at the wharves and he should go himself. But for some reason which he himself could not fathom, Joshua Harris had, for the two weeks he had been home, varied between extreme irritability and good humor. This morning there was a scowl on his face.

He stood uncertainly in the hall. Then he turned around and made off. When he passed the room at the left of the hall, he noticed the female was still there. Once more he swung around, and came to its doorway.

"Can I do something for you?" he snapped.

Lucie had been standing at the window. She had kept her cloak on. The long minutes had passed much too slowly. The curt masculine voice made her whirl.

She made him a quick curtsey. Then she answered his question. "No, sir," she said. "I wait."

Joshua used his eyes to advantage. The girl was poor, she was French, she was lovely. And in some mysterious fashion, she was in his house. He came into the room.

"For whom do you wait, ma'moiselle?" He looked down into

deep blue eyes. Great heavy auburn braids were wrapped like a coronet around her head. In her tiny pierced ears she wore old-fashioned gold earrings. "For me?"

"Non, m'sieur." Her hands were clasped tight around the purse into which Barney had stuffed the money. She knew that gentlemen had the right to stare, but she dropped her own eyes. "I bring a message to Madame Harris."

"You do?" said Joshua, puzzled. "What is your name?"

"Lucie, sir." She looked up at him again. "I wait for madame. She has had her tea, and she will presently descend."

"She will?" Joshua smiled.

"So it was related to me, sir," Lucie said bravely. "I am going to serve her. It is contained in here." She held up the letter. Then another thought occurred to her. "I am recompensed."

Joshua was completely bewildered. "Who recompensed you, Lucie?" he asked.

"Captain Barney, sir."

"Barney?" repeated Joshua. Then he grinned. "God Almighty, I might have known. So he's back?" He turned. "I'm sure madam will be down soon."

He went out into the hall. The butler was placing the mail on a salver. Joshua said, "Marston, have the carriage brought around."

Marston, the salver in hand, said politely, "I'm sorry, sir. Her ladyship has ordered the carriage for ten."

Joshua was already halfway up the stairs when this piece of information floated up to him. "Christ Almighty," he muttered.

Marston was speaking again. "Shall I inform the stabler you want a horse saddled, sir?"

Joshua shouted, "Yes, damn it!" He continued up the stairs, and met Douglass at the top. She was carrying her cloak, masses of fur fell from it. She smelled of some perfume. Joshua regarded her for a moment. "You have a present," he announced and laughed. "You look beautiful this morning, too," he conceded.

Douglass looked amazed. "Who else is beautiful, Joshua?"

"You'll see," he said. "And Barney sent her."

He heard Douglass' steps quicken as she ran down. Joshua then entered his own room. His man was straightening it. "My boots," Joshua said. Ten minutes later he entered Bladen's court.

The court ran off Elfreth's Alley, near Second Street. Three houses faced onto its gardens. The middle one was Barney's. Joshua

[77]

stepped up the one low wide step and knocked on the white door. Absolom opened it.

"Where's the captain?" Joshua asked, stepping into the square hall, and handing Absolom his scarlet lined cloak.

"Will you come with me, sir?" Absolom said.

Joshua followed him upstairs. Through an open doorway he saw the back of Barney's head as he lounged in a big chair in front of the blazing fire, his feet propped up on a stool. He untangled his long legs and stood up as Joshua came in.

"When did you get back?" Joshua asked, as he took the proffered hand in a hard grip. "Where the devil did you go?"

Barney grimaced. "Sit down," he said, motioning to the other big chair in front of the flames. With his foot he shoved over the stool so Joshua could share it.

The walls of the room were lined halfway up with books. Over the fireplace hung a painting of the "Revenge," with the white cliffs of Dover in the background. Joshua put his feet up on the stool. "This is nice," he said. "The room."

"Yes," said Barney. "I went as far down south as I could without getting snarled up with the British. No ships."

"No. I know it," Joshua said.

"So I was meditating." Barney gestured to the bottle of rum and the glasses on the table between them. He asked, "Would you like to meditate a little?"

Joshua grinned. He poured himself a glass of the liquor and sipped it. "I wish I could give you the 'Pomona.' But I've a contract with her captain, and she sails tomorrow. Meantime I've done all I could and so has Morris. There are no ships." He shot a glance at Barney's face. "Did you get our communication?" He was pretty sure an explosion was coming.

Barney heaved himself to his feet. "Yes, by God!" He had planted his feet wide. Then, "I threw it in the fire." He sobered a bit. "I wrote that." He pointed to his desk and the open letter lying there.

"May I see it?" Joshua asked quietly.

Barney picked it up and handed it to him. He began to pace, back and forth, back and forth, as Joshua had seen him do many times aboard ship. To Barney's rhythmic strides he read.

The letter was addressed to the Delegates of the Congress of the United States. It was short. "I most respectfully show: that I have served a year as a lieutenant of the Navy, during seven months of that time being a prisoner with the enemy; that I have borne that rank aboard a ship having more than twenty guns and am at present directed to take the rank of first lieutenant on board the Saratoga, a vessel of inferior force. That one year pay is due me for former services which in the present depreciated state of the currency is not worth my acceptance. That application has been made to the Board of Admiralty and no satisfaction can be obtained from that quarter."

Joshua looked up from the letter. Barney said, "You may throw that in the fire, too!"

"No, Barney," Joshua said. "Send it." He too rose, laid the letter on the desk and faced Barney. "In 1775, you volunteered your services to the Navy, and sailed aboard the 'Hornet.' You had no commission but served as first officer. Actually you commanded the vessel. When the captain refused to fight a vessel of superior force, you, already at one of the guns, threw a match stick at his head with such force it buried its iron point in the door of the roundhouse." Joshua smiled slightly. "The captain then remained housed in his cabin, no longer even assuming appearance of command. Because of the extreme gallantry of the actions of that ship, the incident was overlooked. And the captain was relieved of his command. There was even no court-martial."

"There should have been," Barney growled. "I don't condone my action."

Joshua smiled again. "You continued to serve aboard the 'Hornet,' still with no commission. You raised the stars and stripes over her, the first time that Baltimore had seen the flag. You had the honor of receiving the first salute ever fired to that flag, at Stasia, in 1776. Still, Barney, you had no commission." He said strongly, "We need a Navy and we've got to make Congress realize it!"

Barney said, "Are you suggesting I accept a commission—the one I've been offered, aboard the 'Saratoga'?"

"No!" said Joshua. "Refuse it! Send this letter!"

Barney said, "The Gillon incident—" He broke off.

"We tried to move Gillon out. We couldn't. Too much influence. Now we are working on a single head for the Navy. Agent of Marine, Lord of Admiralty, Secretary of the Navy, call it what you will. But we want Morris. Send the letter. We'll have it published in the papers."

"I think I'll get drunk," Barney said. He sat down again, put his feet up. Then his good humor asserted itself. "Let's meditate. How is it with you since we landed?"

Joshua swallowed off the glass of rum. He twirled the glass in his fingers. "My erstwhile bachelor establishment is fouled up with females, for at least one of which I have you to blame. The household bills have doubled; seamstresses go in and out, and my butler, whom my father brought from England thirty years ago, has now come into his own with a peer's daughter in the house."

"Meditate some more," Barney said consolingly.

"And now this latest female," Joshua said, turning to pour some more rum and to look at Barney. "Where did you get her?"

"She sailed with us."

"Is that all you know about her?"

Barney considered. "She's damned pretty." Then he grinned wickedly. "If you attempt to seduce her you'll probably get your skull crushed. I can imagine the look you'll get from Douglass if you so much as mention her name."

Joshua also considered. "She's damned pretty," he agreed. "About the ship, Barney. The State of Pennsylvania will give you command of its made-over merchantman—they've pierced her for assorted guns, anything they could get hold of, and these damn refugee boats cruise around in the rivers off the Delaware, and often help the blockading British, acting as escort boats, up the river. I was thinking," Joshua said, seriously, "that it might be a temporary measure." Such a profound silence followed this remark that Joshua said suddenly, "Things are rather grim."

Barney poured some rum and drank it.

Joshua said, "It's the fifth year of the war. People are discouraged, Barney. What's making it worse is the financial situation. Washington has barely enough money to keep up the secret service, even though he does spend a good deal on it. Congress doesn't help matters when it issues worthless amounts of printed money."

Barney asked, "What do you do about that money?"

"What can we do? Ignore it. We can't use it. We do business as though it doesn't exist. That means our personal word, or bond, or barter, or British pounds. As a matter of fact, the people aren't using it either. You can't pay them with it. My barber has papered his shop with the stuff. Stasia is our trading ground. That is one of the big reasons Stasia is invaluable to us."

"Stasia, the Caribbean and the sea war. They're the important things. What I need is a frigate."

"The USS Frigate, 32," said Joshua.

"When you want something, sir, you ask yourself who's got it."

"Yes," said Joshua.

"So who has the ships?"

"The British," said Joshua.

"Yes," murmured Barney.

Joshua looked over at him. For a moment Joshua had a wonderful wild dream in which he and Barney stole into New York and made off with a British frigate. Then he sobered. Barney was filling their glasses again with an abstracted expression on his face. He said:

"I'm not the man for temporary expedients."

"A tangent in roughly the right direction is sometimes the only course."

"I prefer a straight and a true course."

Joshua said, "But how? A British ship—" he broke off, watching Barney's dark face. He wondered vaguely if he had drunk more than he thought he had.

Barney caught the look. "The hell with it," he said. "Let's go to the theatre tonight and take your beautiful sister-in-law."

13

JOSHUA REGARDED THE TIPS OF HIS BOOTS WITH SOME SURPRISE. He was still wearing the things. He stretched his legs out. Then he leaned over and took off the heavy boots. He stood slowly, yawning.

He must have fallen asleep after dinner. He had not gone down to the docks as he should have, to have dinner with the captain of the ship that had just come in, and he suddenly remembered he was going to the theatre. He yawned again; the clock struck the quarter hour. Boots in hand, he started for the hall and the stairway.

At the same minute Lucie came flying down the steps in a whirl of haste and petticoats. Since Joshua had approached the bottom step from the side of the hall, she did not see him. She hurtled into him.

"Uh," grunted Joshua, catching her with one arm and the newel post with the other. The boots clattered to the floor.

Lucie gasped in dismay. *"Mille pardons!"* She looked up at him shyly. She was gathered close in his arms. She breathed: "Did I wound you, m'sieur?"

"Not mortally," Joshua said, releasing her and the newel post. She stepped back hastily to allow him to go on upstairs, and stepped on his boot. Joshua caught her again.

"My god, girl," he said, both arms around her. "Can't you stand upright for more than a minute?" Once more he set her on her feet.

" 'Twas your footgear," she said, abashed at her clumsiness. She bent hastily and picked up the boots; she held them out. "Allow me, sir."

"Thank you, Lucie," Joshua said absently, taking the boots. Her face was lovely; so was her figure. This morning she had had her cloak on. Now the tiny white lace apron she wore accentuated her small waist. Joshua did not move and his presence held her prisoner for he blocked her way while his gaze traveled slowly down to her feet and up to her face again.

"Madame helped me fashion this dress, m'sieur," she said breathlessly.

"She did, Lucie?"

Her eyes questioned him. "You do not approve, m'sieur?"

"I approve," he said, putting his free hand under her chin and tipping her face up. He looked into eyes shadowed by curling lashes. Then he dropped his hand. Douglass was coming down the stairway. Joshua said:

"Fetch me a pair of shoes, will you, Lucie? And take these boots up for me."

He felt her fingers on his as she reached for the boots. She asked, as she moved away, "But which shoes, m'sieur?"

"Any pair," said Joshua. "Ask Partridge."

"Oui, m'sieur." She started upstairs and Joshua watched her go. Her ankles were good. Into this thought Douglass' voice came.

"I'd like a word with you, Joshua." She passed by him and went on into the drawing room.

Joshua followed her into the room he had just left. He went over to the fire and stood with his back to it.

Douglass put her black velvet cloak down on a chair. Her gown was black and a froth of lace fell over her white shoulders and arms.

"Very nice, sister," Joshua said.

"Thank you, Joshua," Douglass replied, eying first his stocking feet and then slowly raising her eyes to his face. He was looking back at her, one eyebrow lifted.

"Did you wish to speak with me?" he asked.

Douglass thought of the scene she had just witnessed. "I want to—" She stopped.

His blue eyes were frosty. "Well?" His voice challenged her.

Douglass spoke fast. "Lucie came here to meet her brother." The words tumbled out. "It had been six months since he had last written her. She finally obtained passage, and when she arrived ten days ago her brother had gone. She went to Mrs. Denny's, on Water Street, where he had been living. Mrs. Denny told her that her brother had despaired of her coming and had joined the army!"

"Well?" said Joshua.

"I just wanted you to know, Joshua." She hesitated. "She is very unworldly, having spent the last three years in a convent. She is seventeen, she—"

"Here is Barney," Joshua said. "And for your information, sister, I'm old enough to judge the innocence or worldliness of a woman."

Douglass turned. Marston had taken Barney's hat and cloak, and he was coming toward her. She extended her hand. "We were talking of Lucie, Captain." Barney released her hand. "Did you know she had been in a convent?"

"No, madam," Barney said. Standing over her, he was looking down at the shining waves of blonde hair and the curve of her white shoulder half concealed by the black lace.

"Couldn't you tell by her English that she had been educated?"

"I never thought about her English."

Joshua broke in. "Indeed, sister, it is you who have been spared some blunt English from me, because of Captain Barney's timely arrival." He swung around and then decided to see if Lucie had returned yet with his shoes. He looked out into the hall; she was coming down the stairway, shoes in hand. Joshua took them, thanked her and sat down. "Would you care for something to drink before we go?" he asked Barney.

"No, thank you," Barney said. He was amused. Douglass had risen and was standing, looking from one to the other. Barney grinned. "I've no doubt you deserved the reproof, English," he said. "How do you like it here?"

"In the colonies?" asked Douglass.

Joshua looked up from his shoes; he met Barney's eyes. Barney

[83]

bowed to Douglass. "Touché, my dear. But would you answer my question?"

Douglass flipped her fan open, and looked over it. "I find a very tolerable French influence everywhere, gentlemen. Also I must confess surprise. I rather expected to hear much talk of politics, and such like; instead the gentlemen of the city here are divided into two opposite camps—over the rival merits of two French hairdressers!"

Joshua had finished with his shoes. He stood. Once more Douglass looked from one to the other. "And, sirs, I was told I should have to conform, whereas both of you do exactly as you please! Yes, and so does Miss Goodenough next door. Being a Quaker, she doesn't even pay her taxes for the upkeep of the war!"

Joshua said, "There is a vast difference between you and Miss Goodenough, aside from her intellectual achievements."

Douglass drew a deep breath.

Joshua went on, "Miss Goodenough is seventy-seven. Are you ready to go, sister?"

"I believe so," Douglass said haughtily. "Lucie!"

Lucie had been standing in the hall waiting. She could not have helped hearing Joshua. As he came out into the hallway she was hardly reassured by the quick look she received; her hands clasped tight over Douglass' bag. Douglass came out in the hall with Barney and the four of them stood there while Joshua asked:

"Was it your intention that Lucie attend you at the theatre, sister?"

"Yes," Douglass said, handing Lucie her fan, which Lucie put into the bag.

"It is hardly necessary, sister. Not usual."

Then Joshua looked at both of them. The candlelight in the wall sconces gleamed on Lucie's coiled braids and her eyes, so soft a blue they were almost violet, were fastened on his in appeal. Joshua caught Barney's eye and Barney threw up his hands helplessly. He laughed.

"Damned if I know who won this encounter, sir," he said, as they went out the big doors with Lucie coming behind. She had never been in a theatre before. She climbed up front with the driver. Barney handed Douglass into the carriage he had waiting. "Careful of your brittle bones, Miss Goodenough," he said.

It was a few minutes after six when they arrived at the theatre, so the first skit was being presented. Douglass sat between Barney and Joshua, and Lucie sat just behind in the box, after she had carefully put madam's cloak and muff on another chair. By this time they had succeeded in getting the attention of most of the audience so that when the curtains swung closed, Lucie became aware that everybody was looking in their direction. The theatre got noisier than it had been and Lucie wondered how anyone heard what was going on or what the actors were saying. Barney's name was being called out loudly.

Then the curtains opened again. A man came striding out on the stage and almost up to their box; he bowed to Barney and a very pretty girl ran out and curtsied to him. They waved their hands for silence, and the audience, sensing something, actually became fairly quiet.

The skit began. The actor began to confide to the men about his wife. Lucie didn't understand half of what he said, but she saw Joshua smile with real amusement. She kept her eyes on Joshua, who was sitting almost sideways to her. Then the man on the stage finally broke off his harangue and started to sing. He kept gesturing to the pretty girl.

"Judy leads me such a life,
The devil never had such a wife.
How can I sing a funny song;
She's mocking me all day long, what can the matter be?"

It was a catchy tune and Lucie's thought followed it the second time he sang it. "What can the matter be?" She saw he was leaving the center of the stage and coming right over to their box. He smiled and sang:

"Barney, leave the girls alone,
Why don't you leave the girls alone,
And let them quiet be?"

The audience stamped and yelled. Lucie caught the general enthusiasm and wanted to stamp and shout too. In the midst of this Barney got to his feet and bowed. As he sat down again the girl came over to the box. She was giving orders in song to her husband.

"Put the muffins down to roast,
Blow the fire! Make the toast!
We'll have tea!"

Then she turned to Barney. She sang:

> "Barney, you're a wicked boy,
>   And you do always play and toy
>   With all the gals you see.
>   Why don't you leave the girls alone?"

Barney grinned. She was singing right to him, very close, and he reached in his pocket and brought out a gold piece; he tossed it to her and she caught it in her skirt, revealing slim silk-stockinged legs. The audience shouted approval.

"Do it again, Barney!"

Douglass held her handkerchief daintily to her nose. Barney fished out another handful of coins and started to pitch them, deliberately tossing them high. The crowd yelled louder, and finally Barney spread his hands to show they were empty.

"You'll beggar me, lads." He waved his hands and spoke to the girl. "Give them a free show, Judy!"

She pirouetted and her skirts went high. "Little bitch," Douglass said under her breath. Aloud she said, "My fan, Lucie."

Startled, Lucie found her voice. *"Oui,* madame." She handed Douglass the fan, and armed with it, Douglass remarked:

"Judy's knock-kneed, I do believe."

Barney laughed. He said over Douglass' head to Joshua, "I forgot for a moment we had a lady with us."

"Would you like us to leave?" Douglass inquired haughtily.

Barney said, "Why, no. We can return later."

Joshua heard this and dissolved into laughter. The audience had now joined in the chorus. Barney leaned close to Douglass. "Are you knock-kneed?"

Douglass snapped her fan to and raised it. "No!" she said.

Barney grinned and settled back in his chair. "An important issue resolved," he murmured.

Douglass opened the fan again and regarded him thoughtfully over it; the curtains had closed; the skit was over. She smiled at Barney. "It was fun," she said.

But she was very quiet and thoughtful as the play went on. She heard practically nothing of it. She used her fan slowly, her eyes on the stage, on Barney. She saw Joshua shift in his chair and look sideways at Lucie, look at her long. She didn't dare interfere more than she had done; he'd been annoyed enough that she had even mentioned Lucie to him. Damn him, she thought, he's such a handsome devil; she bit her lip and remembered the words of the song. She would like to comb his head with a three-legged stool, and quite unaware Joshua turned his attention back to the stage again.

Barney seemed to be engrossed in the play. She thought that probably he always gave whole-hearted enthusiasm to whatever he was doing. She was content to sit there beside him, just knowing he was there, and to catch his eye once in a while and to smile. But —she suddenly told herself to stop speculating; she remembered vividly, as though it were being enacted, the first time she had ever seen him, standing there in the dusty prison yard.

On the way home she listened to Barney tell Joshua that Humphreys and the privateer "Black Prince" had come in this afternoon, shot up a bit. "She was lucky to have escaped; she ran up Wilmington creek. A frigate of the 'Triton' class was after her."

"I have dined aboard the 'Triton,' " Douglass said idly.

A gust of wind shook the coach. "Sou'easter blowing up," Barney said. Rain sounded on the windows, hard, as the carriage stopped.

They ran into the house. "I must say Philadelphia weather is as bad as ours," Douglass said, breathless.

Lucie took her cloak. "Did you like it, Lucie?" Douglass asked.

Lucie nodded, eyes shining. *"Oui,* madame!" A vivid smile lighted her face; it was so lovely a smile Douglass glanced at Joshua. He actually looked a little bemused; then he said, "Excuse me please a moment." He started upstairs.

Douglass turned to Barney. "Won't you stay for supper?" He had followed her into the long drawing room; he looked around appreciatively.

"I wish I could," he answered.

Once more she felt her assurance leave her, when they were thus alone. "You cannot stay?" she repeated, moving away from him toward the fire. "You always leave me, Captain," she said suddenly, surprising herself with the words.

But he understood. He frowned slightly, and, looked at her. "Yes," he said. "I'm a sailor." He walked over and touched the ivory keys of the clavichord. "I've always wanted to be able to play one of these. Do you play?"

"Yes, Barney," she said, low.

He looked up from the keys. "I bought a parcel of land today. On the river, up a few miles. I have plenty of money again." He smiled a little. "The prizes were valuable. I want to build a house there; a house like this."

"You won't be able to enjoy it much," Douglass said. "Will you?"

"No. But I come home."

She said, "Joshua told me about—" She stopped. "What will you do?"

He shrugged. "I've been seriously considering either returning to France, or else joining Marion and his guerillas in the South. One or the other."

"You wouldn't stay here?" She put her hands out to him, in an appealing gesture.

"No, madam." The negative was firm and absolute.

A bit of the gay tune she had heard tonight came back to her. "Barney, leave the girls alone, and let them quiet be." He was coming toward her and she turned away from him.

He took her by the shoulders. "Is this a propitious time to ask you to drive out with me tomorrow afternoon?"

"No, sir," said Douglass. "I must take tea with Miss Goodenough tomorrow. Won't you join us?"

She laughed at the expression on his face. "I hate tea, English."

"It will be four shilling schou-schong tea, Barney. Miss Goodenough would be charmed; she thinks you are a delightful renegade."

Barney sighed.

"We'll have whiskey for you," Douglass said.

"I surrender," Barney muttered. His fingers closed around her wrist.

Douglass turned away from him. Before she could move away she felt his hands grasp her shoulders. He stood behind her.

"Let me go, Barney," she said.

"No." He leaned down and kissed the white skin at the base of her neck. He spoke in her ear. "I've made a hell of a concession, having tea tomorrow."

Douglass whispered, "You aren't going to drink any."

"No. Now I'm asking you for something."

His hands were strong on her shoulders. "You're not asking," Douglass said.

He swung her around to face him. His arms closed around her. He had tipped her head back over his arm, and she looked up at his face through her thick lashes.

He said, "I'm not trying to seduce you, wench. All I want is a goodnight kiss. Remove your hands from the front of my coat."

"Barney." She said his name very low. She placed her hands gingerly on his wide shoulders.

"Why are you so afraid of me, Douglass?" He locked her in a close embrace. For just a moment he looked down at her face and then his mouth closed over hers.

The kiss was long. Finally he released her lips.

"How was that?" he whispered.

His mouth was only an inch from hers. "Damned expert," she whispered back.

He grinned. She turned her head and he kissed the base of her throat. "Will you dream of me a little?"

"I'll try not to," said Douglass.

"Anyway, I'll enjoy my tea better tomorrow."

She laughed. "I will, too, Barney." She caught her breath and her lashes fell.

He set her away from him, but he kept her hand in his, and they went into the hall together, side by side. Even when Marston put Barney's cloak over his shoulders Barney kept hold of her hand.

He stood looking down at her. "As I said before, madam—" He smiled down at her suddenly.

"What, Barney?" she asked.

"There's a bad sou'easter blowing up." He kissed her hand. "Goodnight, Madam Harris."

14

LUCIE WAKENED IN THE GREY DAWN. SHE SAT UP IN BED; SHE heard footsteps. They were receding and she realized quickly that what she heard was the cook, Mrs. Simpson, going downstairs. Lucie got out of bed.

Her white cotton nightgown was long and full and ruffled around her wrists. The heavy auburn braids reached her waist. She went over to the window and looked out.

From her one window, she could see down into the kitchen garden; the earth looked wet, brown and soggy. From here she could see the edge of the stables, the beginning of the small orchard and the roof and chimney of the jutting kitchens.

The smoke from the chimney rose straight up. The branches of the trees were stiff and unmoving. And the storm which had beat down last night was over. Lucie knelt by her bed and said her morning prayer. She poured water in her basin and washed. Then she dressed hastily. She brushed her hair and coiled the great braids around her head. She made her bed. Then, carrying the used water, she made her silent way through the quiet house.

In the raftered kitchens, Mrs. Simpson was stirring cornbread in a huge bowl with a wooden spoon. Her helper had already put the draft on the fires in the stove. The kettle was beginning to sing; the coffee was beginning to bubble. Mrs. Simpson handed Lucie three eggshells. "Drop them in the pot, Lucie," she said, and smiled.

Lucie obeyed.

"It's a warm day," said the boy, her helper.

"What is your name?" Lucie asked him.

"John," he said. He picked up the poker and started to shake the grate.

"That don't need doing," Mrs. Simpson said. "You can go and fetch the cream. And bring me two slices of ham from the smokehouse." She handed him a shining knife, and he disappeared, after a last look at Lucie.

The warm morning air floated into the kitchen when he opened and closed the door.

"The day will be splendid," Lucie said, hardly getting the words out before they both heard the hammering noise in the distance. Mrs. Simpson stopped beating the cornbread and held her head on one side like a bird to listen.

"That'll be the front door!" She waved the spoon at Lucie.

Lucie jumped to her feet and ran. She struggled with the bolts as the pounding on the heavy oak continued from outside. When the last bolt slipped free, the door was caught by rude hands and flung open. A man stood there, whip in hand.

"Tell Mr. Harris," he said, "that a British frigate is aground up the Delaware other side of Chester!"

He swung up into the saddle, plying his whip before he got his other foot in the stirrup. "Ran aground in the storm," he shouted. "She's the 'Triton'!" He disappeared down High Street in a whirl of flying hoofs.

Lucie slammed the door shut, not bothering to lock it. She ran back through the hall and up the wide stairway. She knew which room was Mr. Joshua's. She had peeked into it yesterday. But when her flying steps carried her right to it, and the closed door faced her, her fingers dropped from the knob. She knocked gently instead.

Within the room Joshua was sleeping soundly. Lucie knocked again, louder, and there was no answer. She opened the door and ran over to the big bed.

Joshua was lying flat on his stomach. His face was turned away from her, and she looked down at the back of his tousled, short, clipped curly hair.

"Mr. Harris," she said.

Joshua rolled over and opened his eyes. He opened his eyes wider. Lucie said hastily:

"A man came. He said to tell you there is a British frigate around in the Delaware!"

Joshua sat up. "What?"

Lucie remembered. *"Non!"* she cried again. "Aground. Aground in the Delaware!"

"Jesus God," muttered Joshua. He leaped out of bed and started to get dressed. Lucie fled.

In less than two minutes he came into the kitchen, carrying his shirt and coat and a pair of boots. He dropped all three on the floor.

"Water," he said. "Boy, run and saddle a horse."

John disappeared again.

Lucie seized the kettle and half filled a basin. She mixed it with cold. While Joshua splashed and water flew in all directions the cook fetched a towel. Joshua used it hastily. He started to put on his shirt.

"That lazy bastard, Partridge," he muttered through his shirt.

He sat down to pull on his boots. "Lucie, get me my rifle. The third one on the rack."

Once more Lucie ran. She knew the gun room was right behind the hall. She had learned that this collection of firearms was his pride and joy. She seized the third weapon on the rack of rifles and ran back to the kitchen. He was standing at the open door, booted, while the boy led his horse.

Lucie thrust the rifle at him barrel first. *"Votre arme de feu!"*

Joshua grinned. He slung the weapon under his arm and gave her a swift pat on the backside. "Thank you," he said. He gained the saddle, and the boy ran to open the gate. The cook joined Lucie on the back porch to watch. Lucie said:

"*Mon Dieu,* he rides magnificent!"

Mrs. Simpson wiped her hands on her apron. "Mr. Joshua is from Virginia," she said.

Joshua galloped in headlong haste straight down High Street the seven blocks to the river. At Second he had checked his horse for a moment, but then he was sure that Barney would be down at the wharf already. At the top of the steep hill that dropped down to the river's edge and the High Street wharves, he dismounted; the cobblestones were still wet. Halfway down he hitched his horse in front of a tavern and plunged through the melee of men already gathered and filling the wide street.

The State of Pennsylvania maintained a small fleet of thirteen rowgalleys for the defense of the Delaware. The largest of these was the brig "Montgomery," boasting twenty guns, manned by volunteers. Joshua was the marine officer of the "Montgomery." He saw that she was already warped up to the wharf. Then he saw Barney.

Barney was standing with Captain Read, of the "Montgomery," and Captain Humphreys, of the privateer the "Black Prince." He was wearing the uniform he still had the right to wear. In his belt was the pair of boarding pistols that heralded action. Joshua slowed his pace as he approached them, to appear leisurely.

"Good morning, gentlemen," he said.

He heard the two other men answer him but his eyes swept them briefly before his blue ones met Barney's dark eyes. Barney said:

"The 'Triton,' 32."

"I believe," Joshua said casually, "that like Pallas Athena, she sprang full panoplied from the front of your head."

Barney grinned; the other two men look bewildered. Humphreys said:

"I was just telling Barney I wished I could take the 'Prince' downriver. But there's not the smell of a breeze. She was becalmed since yesterday!"

"Where is she?" asked Joshua.

"Past Chester," Barney said. "She ran aground during the storm; evidently she was escorted upriver by those refugee boats—you were speaking of them." Again his eyes met Joshua's and he smiled a little.

Joshua said, "Why don't you join us aboard the 'Montgomery'?"

Read interposed. "We have our full complement, Captain."

"My compliments to Captain Read," Barney said. "But I'm going downriver in a ship's boat, kindly provided by Humphreys, here. Goodbye sir." This last was to Joshua, and Joshua murmured, "Goodbye," reluctantly. He watched Barney walk away. A longboat was waiting at the dock for him. The men in it were bandannaed; they looked a cutthroat lot. Humphreys whispered to Joshua: "The worst rascals in my crew, but he asked for them."

Joshua waved to him as he followed Read aboard the "Montgomery." In midchannel Barney's boat was pulling away swiftly with the still outgoing tide.

The "Montgomery's" anchors were weighed. There was, as Humphreys had said, no smell of a breeze. Therefore the oars flashed and dipped as the brig started downriver to the sea. Joshua sat down on the arms chest aft, his rifle across his knees. The tide was still ebbing, very slowly now. It was a small aid, though, and Joshua reckoned any aid was welcome. Joshua reckoned that they had until noon at the very latest before the incoming tide would lift the "Triton" off the mudbank and let her sail unscathed to freedom.

Joshua watched the other twelve rowvessels as they ploughed along through the silver waters of the river. It looked better than it smelled, for the muddy banks stank foully. He was conscious of the smell; he was conscious of an immense disappointment, for he knew now how much he had hoped that Barney would come with them. Barney's boat was still dead ahead, so close Joshua could see the brawny scarred and tattooed arms of the men who pulled at her oars. In sudden impatience, Joshua got to his feet and started to pace back and forth on the narrow deck. His marines were clinging in the rigging. The arms chest, which he did not know if he would use, sat there like a reproach. They were passing Barney's boat now; Joshua went to the side and waved. He got a glimpse of swarthy faces, gold earrings and shining cutlasses. Barney waved a cutlass at him, and drew his finger across the blade. Joshua left the rail and went back to the arms chest. They were leaving the city behind.

Read was bustling about importantly. "Of course we should row down," he said to Joshua and the first officer. "But we must remember she's a frigate."

Joshua said, "Yes."

"It looks as though everyone in the city will be there," Read continued. The road along the river was already crowded. Horsemen galloped along, coaches lurched, and wagons struggled through the mud engendered by last night's rains.

"Everyone wants to see the British stuck on a mudbank," Joshua commented, his mind far from his words. He was more than ever conscious of a mounting excitement that had Barney at its root. He said aloud, "If we could—" He broke off, and once again jumped to his feet.

The men bent to the oars. They flashed and dipped. Still there was no wind. The improvised crew were laughing and talking, lounging on the deck, climbing aloft to see what they could see and waving to the people on the roads. A couple of them had stretched out on deck, to pass the time in snoring.

After a couple of miles Joshua could contain himself no longer. He said to Read, "Shouldn't you give the men at the oars a rest? Get fresh blood, so to speak?"

Read looked surprised. "When the time comes, sir," he said, sharply. But in a few moments he relayed the order to the first officer. One of the sleeping men untangled himself and went to relieve an oarsman. Joshua paced back and forth.

The next curve of the river should reveal Chester. Great homes along the river dominated the banks now. Their landing docks were empty of craft, and Joshua knew they were already on the scene. The men bent to the oars. They pulled past the city, its shipyards, its docks. One of the men kicked a sleeping figure sprawled on the deck.

"Get up, you lazy bastard, and you might see something," he was told.

There was activity now on the brig. Its guns were out and loaded, with shouted orders from Read. His voice annoyed Joshua. He told himself that after having sailed with Barney he was damned spoiled. There weren't many men like him in the Navy. He didn't know what Barney could do with a longboat and twenty potential murderers, but he could do something. If he were in command of the brig he could and would do something.

The "Montgomery" had at least maintained its lead dead ahead of the other smaller craft. Astern came the other twelve galleys, slim, rakish, a little fleet of them. And then suddenly a shout went up from the lookout. "Sail-ho!"

This electrified all the rowgalleys since the cry had echoed out over the river. They seemed to pull harder and gather speed. The curve of the river came nearer and nearer, and then Joshua saw the "Triton."

Joshua jumped up on the arms chest to see better. He swore. There she was, all right. She was no mirage—the "Triton," 32.

Joshua's experienced eyes told him she was not only lovely but fast. Three great masts towered over her upward, courses, tops, royals furled. The stiff set of the standing rigging and the slack curves of the running rigging made a picture against the pinking skies.

Her crew would be upward of three hundred men. She was single decked, built for cruising, for spying out the enemy, for quick capture. Ensnared with mud, she listed. Her runout starboard guns pointed slanted up; the larboard guns stuck their muzzles listlessly down toward the river's slow moving water; they were eighteen pounders. On forecastle and aft long nines bristled. Now the incoming tide had swung her around about; she presented her stern to the oncoming rowgalleys; her rakish bow held fast in the mud.

The "Triton," 32. Joshua felt his excitement rise. His mind whirled with plans. If they could capture her, could he finance her for privateering? If he and Barney threw in together all the money from the recent prizes, and— He broke off his calculations sharply. He had instead a picture of Barney standing on that quarterdeck with the stars and stripes on her gaff; into this came Douglass' cool voice: "I've dined aboard the 'Triton.'" British oak, copper bottomed, fitted with brass guns, gleaming; in Barney's hands she would be quick deadly menace!

The reality of her was upon them. Uniformed figures moved on her decks. Loud voices and jeers went from ship to shore, and ashore there were crowds of people. Across the rolling fields, in the distance, came still the sound of the bells of the little country churches, ringing, tolling out their warnings. The British are here.

Coaches and wagons of every description were on the scene, fires had been built; hawkers were selling coffee and hot chocolate and lemonade. Flags waved gaily. On the river the thirteen rowgalleys began to slow their oars; and over this merry scene the sound of gunfire was almost startling.

The "Triton," incensed and harried by these paltry vessels, shook with the recoil of her stern cannon. Joshua knew they were beyond the range, but these were the guns which would keep the frail galleys at their distance. Nevertheless, Read roared out an order to fire.

He wasted ammunition. The British jeered loudly, the cries plain to hear. "Come no further, Yankees," yelled a topman perched high in the "Triton's" rigging. "You might get hurt."

Read was standing next to Joshua. The "Triton's" guns were indeed formidable. She towered upward, bristling with armament. All thirteen galleys ceased their rowing, and spread out a little. Then began a sort of serenade, military in sound but not in action.

The rowgalleys were not close enough to have their shots do anything but fall helplessly into the water. Every once in a while the "Triton" would answer their shots with a sullen roar of disgust as her stern cannon belched fire. The British kept up their jeering. They didn't like being stuck on a mudbank; what had been deemed a daring maneuver was funny, and to allay their discomfiture they hurled verbal insults. Their officers didn't try to quiet them. The Americans shouted back; for a while they contented themselves with rude language for the British; then they turned eyes on their compatriots.

The rowgalley, the "Montgomery" in the van, danced out of range. Five hundred men were held helpless on the rest of the galleys. Suddenly a loud voice addressed the "Montgomery."

"Scared of guns, lads?"

This was taken up instantly. Taunts came across the water; the British, the Americans, outdid each other in calling names at the rowgalleys. After Joshua had been dubbed a number of cowardly bastards for ten minutes he stood it no longer. His accent was very thick as he finally spoke to Read.

"This is nonsense!" His blue eyes were cold with contempt and Read stepped back from him. Read looked from one to the other of the faces of his officers.

"What would you suggest, sirs?" he asked.

"I'd suggest either we attack, or go home," Joshua said grimly.

Read looked around at the ship Joshua suggested they attack. Once more he reminded himself with his own eyes of her size. He turned back to his officers. The ship was silent; the jeers sounded louder than ever; the volunteer marines, the men at the oars all were silent, looking toward the knot of officers on the quarterdeck.

"My dear sirs," Read was saying. Joshua's jaw set; he pushed Read aside rudely, and went to the rail. He raised his voice.

"Lads," he said.

They looked back at him, some of the oarsmen half rising to their feet, hands still on the heavy wood, when suddenly Joshua saw Barney and the longboat.

Almost as if the "Triton" realized Barney's presence, her stern guns fired. The sound died away, the smoke curled up slowly, and Barney's voice cut through in a crisp command:

"Back starboard!"

The longboat was coming alongside the "Montgomery." Barney was standing in the stern.

"Bow!" he said. Then, "Way enough!"

The oars dipped once more.

"Stand by to toss! Toss!"

The crisp orders, the immediate obedience, the sight of the boat, its oars vertical now, as it came alongside, handled so well, were immediate reassurance. Barney grasped the ladder and swung aboard, landing on the deck like a cat. He looked around lazily.

"Well, lads," he said. "Who would like a little fighting today?" He grinned, and pulled one pistol from his belt. He cocked it and snapped back the lever holding the layment; the dagger-like blade flipped forward. "Who would like a pocketful of prize money to spend tonight?"

They said his name, they answered him in low voices and with smiles; their eyes followed him as he went slowly aft.

Joshua, like everyone else, watched Barney. He knew, and the other officers knew, that Read was Barney's target, and they stepped away from Read, leaving him alone in the circle formed to face Barney. Joshua wondered for one wild moment, as he saw Barney's face close, whether he would kill Read.

"Captain Read." Barney's voice was low but like the crack of a whip.

The murderous boarding pistol, one of the pair, was leveled at Read's midsection. Barney said, "You'll note, you sniveling coward, that I can either skewer you with this or put a bullet through your guts. Get off the decks!"

Read, nor anyone watching, did not question for a moment but that Barney would do as he had said. Without a word Read backed off, his eyes bulging with fear. He stumbled, and then dived into the door of the roundhouse. Barney shoved the pistol back into his belt, and surveyed the knot of officers. That was that.

"Maybe the British'll do for him what I didn't do. We'll give them a chance," he commented. "Mr. Harris, if you'll present these officers to me, we can get started."

"Certainly, Barney," Joshua said, in his excitement forgetting the names of every one of them. He tried to be calm. "I am the marine officer, sir, and—" a name flashed before him—"this is Mr. Hendrickson—" he heard his voice go on. By the time he had finished things were already happening.

The master of arms had run fore, keys jingling from his hand; the quartermaster stood tense at the wheel, waiting. The gunnery officer was snapping out orders; Barney was addressing the crew.

"Men," he said, his voice ringing across the deck, "we can tell the British to load their guns now. We're ready to receive their lead."

They shouted and cheered; a wave of sudden cheering came from them.

"Remember," said Barney, "to obey your officers' orders quickly; the quicker it's done, the fewer of you'll get killed."

This sobering note had just been sounded when Barney said to the first officer, "We will commence rowing now, Mr. Hendrickson."

Joshua heard another voice take up these orders. Almost in a daze he heard, from amidships:

"Stand by the oars!"

They were clear.

"Give way together!" Joshua watched them dip into the blue water.

The first inkling the people ashore had of the coming action of the Pennsylvania brig "Montgomery" was the flash and dip of her oars. They stared for a moment in amazement; she was pulling toward the stranded "Triton," sure enough; from midchannel she was making for the enemy as fast as she could be rowed. Men with glasses leveled them in excitement, and a silence prevailed suddenly.

The other rowgalleys had seen the longboat pull alongside the "Montgomery." They had seen Barney board her. Their commanding officers, taut with excitement, realized instantly what Barney was going to try to do—silence her heavy guns and ready her for boarding. But they were too frail to venture closer now; they waited.

Aboard the "Triton," Captain Rodgers watched the first dip of the oars. He had made ready for this attack and now it was coming. The danger was obvious. Boarding. So the hammocks and nettings were well triced, and all precautions possible taken astern, the quarter from which attack would certainly come. Marines were stationed at the rail, rifles in hand. The best gun crews were on the stern cannon. Nevertheless, his place was right here, alongside of them, and here he intended to stay. At his side a lieutenant was looking through his glass. He blurted:

"That's Captain Barney, sir!" He thrust out the glass. "He's atop the binnacle head—his favorite place to watch from—he did that on the 'Revenge'!"

Captain Rodgers answered curtly, "When I want your information, Mr. Carr, I'll ask for it."

But he knew now that the coming attack would be a determined one. Every man jack aboard was armed and ready. The stern cannon could be loaded and fired every fifty seconds. The "Montgomery" would have to be sunk, and Barney with it. Even as he thought this the cannon roared.

Since there was no wind, the smoke was long in curling up and away. By the time it had risen the sponges had been rammed into smoking muzzles, the guns brought to bear again from their recoil, and loaded once again with powder and shot. Through the veiling smoke came the first cry of a wounded man from the "Montgomery." Rodgers squinted through the smoke; hanging in the mizzen weather shrouds he saw the damage the first shots had accomplished.

When he saw it he blasted forth a long oath. Her foretop had been carried away; even now it was being tossed overboard, along with cut trailing rigging. And a section of counter had been stove in, splintering the first two oars. It was probably one of the men on those oars who had cried out. Rodgers yelled:

"I don't want her dismasted; I want her hulled! Lower your sights!"

The guns boomed forth again. The "Montgomery's" oars dipped regularly; she was coming inexorably onward, over the rippling silvery river. Rodgers could hear the boatswain's voice calling the strokes. Suddenly he saw she was going to come about to deliver her first broadside; then she would present a better target.

"Hold your fire," he growled.

The "Montgomery" came about. Her ten starboard six-pounders let fly; at the same moment the "Triton" fired. Before Rodgers could see what the "Triton's" guns had done he was more than aware of what the "Montgomery" had accomplished. One stern cannon was knocked from its carriage, and a stern port smashed in; blood marked the deck.

[99]

But the "Montgomery" had been hit badly. Heavy shot had ploughed across the afterdeck and through the roundhouse. She'd been hit below the water fore. She had staggered under the blows.

Barney had jumped down from the binnacle head. He was amidships now, directing the firing and the helmsman. "Hard aport! Wait till the aftermost guns bear!"

The matchsticks flared noisily, sizzling. The crews bent over the gunsights; the "Montgomery" came about and as she did another roar of British cannon tried to stop the maneuver.

The "Montgomery" shook. She shuddered from stem to stern, like a mortally wounded thing. Splinters flew, ploughed up from decks and bulwarks; a spar crashed to the deck alongside of Barney; he leaned down and tossed it overboard, sailing it over the heads of the rowers. The guns fired; he watched through the smoke; they found their target. Barney raised his voice. When the smoke cleared he gave a shout of triumph. Another of the "Triton's" guns had been hit; it had spun around crazily, and a whole section of her counter had been stove in.

"You'll make mincemeat of her, lads," yelled Barney. But worse punishment was coming and he knew it. The rifle fire had begun now. In between the heavier guns the peppering sound of the muskets kept up a staccato tattoo of deadly sound. The men stationed on the pumps below were working frantically to keep the water from rising so fast in the wells; the wounded were being dragged from the decks to partial safety. All this while the "Montgomery" was making straight for the enemy.

Barney jumped up to the binnacle head again. The distance between the two ships was narrowing fast now. They would make it; he was sure of it; they would make it. The "Montgomery's" fore guns spoke as fast as they could be loaded, fired and reloaded. Another broadside should do the work.

"Hard astarboard!"

The musket fire rained like hail onto the decks. Joshua, standing at the rail, concentrated only on his aim. They were drawing nearer and nearer, splintered oars rising and falling. He could not see that astern other rowgalleys were following in their wake. He did not hear the wild crazy cheers that came from shore. He heard Barney's voice, but he was not conscious of what he said. He only knew to load and fire and reload, and to do his own job as fast and as accurately as possible. He aimed at the heads of the men he could see.

The mizzen crashed to the deck alongside of him. Someone cleared it away. Joshua reloaded and fired at the white cap on a man on the frigate's deck. The "Triton's" last shot hit the "Montgomery" fore. Tangles of mast and rigging hit the deck, her bowsprit was torn off like a splinter. Then the "Montgomery's" starboard guns fired with deadly result. The last stern cannon on the "Triton" spun crazily. Her last heavy shot had been fired.

The deck was slanting under Joshua's feet. Now Barney himself had taken a wounded gunner's place. The "Montgomery," listing badly to port, was brought around to bring the starboard guns to bear upon the stern quarters of the "Triton." Her broadside crashed in the enemy counter, spewed across her afterdecks.

"Direct your men's fire to the enemy quarterdecks and tops, Mr. Harris," called Barney. The first officer had taken the wheel; the helmsman was being borne below. The surgeon appeared, ran fore to Barney.

"Sir!" he cried. "I've forty wounded!"

Barney spoke to two gunners; they raced after the surgeon. Two more followed them, and alongside the longboat was drawing up in a hail of bullets that came from the "Triton." They swarmed aboard, as Barney directed them fore to take position for boarding. Only twenty feet separated the two vessels.

The "Montgomery's" starboard guns had been reloaded. Once more they fired; tilted upward of necessity, they hurled their cannon balls at the enemy's stern. Joshua kept on loading and firing. They were close enough now.

"Your targets are heads and chests," he yelled.

There was now no cheering from ashore; no time for either combatant to waste time in jeers. The Americans ashore could see the other rowgalleys creeping nearer and nearer to the "Montgomery's" sinking stern. Her incredibly gallant action was leading them like a magnet to the quarry she had readied. And her splintered oars still dipped as she narrowed the distance between her and the "Triton."

Joshua didn't see the irons swing out and bite deep into the "Triton." The deck now slanted badly, and he braced himself. It was slippery with blood. A man slipped down to deck beside him and lay still. Joshua dropped to his knees on the sloping deck and turned him over. He had been killed instantly. Over the sound of the fire of small arms then came Barney's voice.

"Boarders!"

Joshua realized suddenly that more men were surging onto the "Montgomery's" deck, as she formed a frail wooden pathway to the "Triton." She was kept afloat now only by the irons that held her to the frigate; she would never sail again. But now she served like a bridge to enemy decks. Joshua yelled to his men to cover the boarding. He seized a cutlass and ran fore.

The rigging and tangled foreyards and shrouds were massed with men. At their head was Barney, climbing fast, a pistol in each hand and his cutlass held in his teeth. He was the first over the side onto the "Triton's" deck, leaping down, both pistols blazing fire. Then he used the murderous cutlass, as he and the twenty men first on the decks cut a swathe for the others to follow. By the time Joshua dropped to the "Triton's" decks, Barney was at the rail. Joshua rushed forward, swung over the rail and dropped down amidships at the same time Barney did. Behind them came more.

From the shore, the people could see that the galleys were discharging men as they raced across the sinking "Montgomery" to the "Triton." They saw victory being slowly gained as the fighting surged forward on the frigate's decks, as the British slowly retreated, as the Americans swarmed upward into the rigging to pick off one by one the men perched up there who were firing down upon their number. The boldest of them did this, climbing upward in the face of fire to bring down the topmen, to sway high in the shrouds to silence the enemy rifle fire from aloft.

Inch by inch the decks were gained. Joshua, at Barney's side, fought his way forward with him. He knew he had been hit, but he could keep swinging the cutlass. Then suddenly he realized he and Barney were looking across a few feet of cleared deck, facing a knot of men at the forecastle rail.

Barney said, "Have you struck?"

Behind him posed the invading force, eager for victory, not yet realizing it had been won. But a sudden silence pervaded the scene. The British captain held tight to the forecastle rail, because without its support he could not stand. He said, in the stillness:

"Lower the colors." His eyes met Barney's; three officers were at his side, and his remaining crew clustered on the forecastle. He drew his sword from its sheath; the sunlight gleamed on the blade and the silver hilt. With a savage gesture he threw it; it sailed like an arc into the muddy river.

"I should never surrender it to a damned rebel, Barney!"

Joshua heard no more. Blood was streaming from his leg. He staggered and Barney caught him as he fell.

15

DOUGLASS SAT VERY STILL IN THE CARRIAGE, HER HANDS CLASPED tightly in her lap. The driver had stopped the carriage at the top of the steep hill where Joshua had dismounted that morning. They had not been able to go any further because of the densely packed crowds.

The city bells were still tolling. At the wharf was the "Triton," her great masts dwarfing the other craft. Proud she looked, and stately in capture. On her gaff floated the stars and stripes.

Douglass had been waiting here for half an hour. She had not spoken, so Lucie kept silence too. But Lucie moved restlessly in the seat, whereas madam sat in cold silence, not moving even a finger. For the tenth time Lucie prayed a silent slow prayer that M'sieur was safe. They knew that Barney was unhurt; word had already circulated through the crowd that he was on the quarterdeck of the "Triton," that he had aimed a pistol at Read and taken command. They knew that Read had been killed later. The crowd was shouting at Barney; they called his name. Then Douglass suddenly saw that the crowd was parting, ahead of the carriage, and the first wounded were being carried from the "Triton."

The hammocks swung between their bearers. The sight dampened the cries of victory. Then Douglass saw two uniformed men carrying a chair between them. She flung open the door of the coach and ran toward them.

Some of the people near called out, in jeers. Douglass paid no attention. She came up to the British captain just as the two officers set him and the chair down opposite a coach.

"Captain Rodgers," Douglass cried.

He looked up at her. "Lady Annan," he muttered incredulously.

"Sir, you are hurt!" He had taken the hand she held out; the two British officers looked at her with certain longing; their captain was kissing her hand. He was saying:

"My dear, how do you come here? It is under miserable circumstances that we meet." He smiled a little. "But the wound—it is not much."

"Where are you going, Captain Rodgers?" Douglass asked.

"To a certain Quaker lady: Miss Goodenough. Lieutenant Barney has arranged it. We have given our parole. And I am forgetting the amenities. Your ladyship, allow me to present Lieutenants Mr. Mitchell and Laux. And my surgeon, Mr. Wilkes."

"I am charmed, gentlemen," Douglass said. "It is good fortune that you will be residing next door to me. I shall look forward to the pleasure of your company."

Around them, the people crowded and stared. The damned British were as cool and unconcerned as though they were chatting on the Strand. The captain was once more kissing the lady's hand in farewell. "I trust we part for a very short time, then."

Douglass smiled and swept them a curtsey. "Adieu, then." She turned slowly and went back to the carriage, the people making way for her grudgingly. In a sort of daze, the coachman jumped down and held the door for her. He slammed it.

"We shall return home now," Douglass said, her head high.

Lucie stifled a cry of protest. The carriage swung around and started back toward Sixth Street. Once more Douglass maintained silence. The two carriages left the mob behind; Douglass did not see that another carriage followed them closely.

They drew up in front of the house in a matter of minutes. Douglass stepped from the carriage. Lucie followed more slowly, keeping her eyes on the wide street. At the doorway she heard Douglass instruct Marston to send two hams, a case of brandy, eggs, apples and a wedge of cheese next door to Miss Goodenough. "And you will kindly ask Miss Goodenough if she is in need of anything further, Marston."

"Yes, madam," Marston said. Then they both turned as Lucie let out a cry.

"Mon Dieu!"

She ran out the big doors, dashing toward the coach which had stopped out front where theirs had just driven off to the stables. The door flew open and she heard Joshua's voice.

"For Christ's sake, I can walk!"

"Don't try it, sir," said the man whose back was to Lucie. "You'll hurry the bleeding again."

Joshua's face was set with pain. His trouser leg had been slit, and it flapped as he stumbled out of the coach. Lucie saw the heavy bloodstained bandage around his upper leg. Another man seized him from the side. Douglass had also come flying down the path. She took one look at Joshua; her quick mind came to a rapid decision. There would be few doctors available.

"Lucie! Prepare his bed! Marston, show the men where to take him. Oh, Joshua," she cried, then she took to her heels. She ran straight to Miss Goodenough's parlor, coming to a stop before the surgeon, Mr. Wilkes.

"Come, please, sir!" she said. "We need you! Desperately. Please!"

Without a word he took up his bag, which he had set down in the hallway. Douglass fled back along the brick sidewalk with him following.

The men had carried Joshua upstairs and laid him on his bed. Partridge and Marston were with them; they removed his boots; they were preparing to undress him, and Lucie picked up the bloodstained boots and carried them out into the hallway, shutting the door behind her. Then Douglass came flying up the stairs with Wilkes behind her. Lucie spoke up.

"I can aid you, sir. I aided the nuns!"

"We'll see," he said. He entered the room, with Douglass after him. Lucie saw him bend over Joshua and start to unwrap the bandages.

"Get the fire lighted for the iron," he said as he took out his scissors to slit the bandage. He dropped the bandages in the slop bucket; he lifted Joshua's leg. Then he laid it down again on the bed.

"Fetch linen," he said to Lucie. And to Douglass, "The bullet will have to be removed. It looks like a large calibre; it may be embedded in the bone."

Joshua had closed his eyes in the pain of having his leg lifted. Now he opened them and regarded Wilkes with suddenly narrowed eyes. "Who the hell are you?" he asked.

"Mr. Wilkes, Joshua, the surgeon of the 'Triton,'" Douglass said breathlessly.

"The bullet, sir, did not come out—it's still there; I deeply regret to tell you." Wilkes leaned down and fished in his bag. Lucie came back with linen. She folded a sheet in fourths and slid it deftly under the injured leg. She paid no attention to the surgeon or the other

[105]

men. She filled a basin with water, and started to bathe Joshua's face in the cool water. Then she took scissors and started to rip out bandages from an old soft sheet.

The surgeon was wiping the blood away from the wound; it was not welling up so fast now. "I shall have to probe," he said.

Lucie poured some brandy into a glass. She held it to Joshua's lips. "Drink it, sir," she whispered.

He gulped it down. He saw the glitter of the instrument in Wilkes's hand. He set his teeth.

The pain was excruciating. It came in terrible waves. Then it stopped. He sucked in a breath. "Jesus," he muttered.

"I haven't got it yet," Wilkes said. At the same moment the door was flung open. Barney stood on the threshold.

His eyes briefly took in the scene. Then he stepped forward and took Wilkes by the back of the collar. He yanked him past the bed, to the doorway, to allow the man who had come with him to step to Joshua's bed. For a second Barney looked as though he were trying to control his anger. Then the violence blazed forth. "D'ye break your parole so easy?" With angry hands he flung the Britisher backwards into the hall and laid him flat on his back. Barney swung around.

"Joshua!" he said, coming over to the bed. "I've brought you the best surgeon in the city, Dr. Hindman. I pray to God you haven't suffered too much at the hands of that bloody incompetent! Lucie, give him some brandy!"

Dr. Hindman took Joshua's hand and stood over him, feeling the pulse. "A little brandy, Mr. Harris," he said, "and then we shall look at your leg. Barney, you're exciting my patient! I don't need you, nor you, madam."

Once more Lucie spoke. "I can aid you, sir. I am trained."

Dr. Hindman smiled. "You are, Lucie? I'll be glad for your help."

Joshua's eyes glittered with pain and excitement. "Barney, the 'Triton,' 32! I can finance her!"

Barney said, "I've already given your boys at the yards the order to get to work on her!"

Dr. Hindman said, "Barney!"

Barney grinned. "That intelligence will calm him down. There's nothing more to be done now for him to worry over. I'll go now, Doctor."

"I'll throw you out," Hindman said, smiling, but keeping his eyes on Joshua's and his fingers on his pulse. Joshua was sipping the brandy Lucie held to his lips.

"It won't take long," Barney said comfortingly. He turned to Douglass. She looked white and shaken. He stood aside for her to precede him, and closed the door behind them. "I've had bullets dug out of me, sweetheart," he whispered. "It hurts—but that passes, too."

She did not answer. Wilkes had got to his feet. He backed off from Barney. Barney said levelly:

"When a man disobeys an order he gets punished." He motioned him to the stairs.

Wilkes went. He went slowly down the steps and toward the big doorway. The two men who had brought Joshua home were still standing out front, and a crowd had gathered because they knew Barney was in the house. Barney called to the two men.

"Throw this man in jail," he said curtly. "He's broken parole." He closed the big doors and turned to face Douglass.

She was looking at him incredulously. She whirled away from him, and into the long room at the right. In the silence the clock struck three.

Barney took a long stride to come through the archway into the drawing room. Four feet away she stood, facing him, her great grey eyes in her white face regarding him; they dropped from his face past the wide shoulders to the big belt with a pair of pistols.

Barney stood and looked at her. Her eyes were on his hands, and he looked down at them. One hand was still marked with blood. He pulled the pistols from his belt and laid them on the polished top of the clavichord; the murderous layments were held back in place now against the long barrels. He took a step toward her.

"I'd like something to drink, Madam Harris, if you will."

She brushed past him; he smelled faint perfume. He heard her tell Marston to bring brandy and whiskey. She turned back to him.

"Is that what you want?" she asked.

Barney went over to the window and sat on the deep sill. He waited till Marston appeared with a tray which he set on the coffee table. Marston left the room. Then Barney said, "I'd prefer whiskey, if you please."

Douglass said, "Won't you help yourself, sir?"

"Yes, if you don't want to do it for me." He went over to the coffee table and poured two glasses of whiskey; he brought one over to her. He tossed his off and went on, slowly. "It was the fault of bad seamanship. Then, as a final foolish gesture, Captain Rodgers refused to surrender his sword. Rather than surrender it to me, he threw it overboard, silver and all."

"I'm proud that he did!" Douglass said.

He stood over her. "He might better have destroyed these."

Douglass stared at what he held in his hand. Her heart beat fast. "They are—"

"Yes, English. The codebooks." He put them back under his coat. He went over to the coffee table and poured another glass of whiskey. "He'll be court-martialed and broke, probably. Are you ready to join me? To the day's events!"

Douglass hurled her glass into the fireplace; against the bricks it shattered. "Join you?" she cried. She rose to face him.

"Sir," she said, "Mr. Wilkes came here expressly because I begged it of him!"

Barney frowned.

Douglass thought he understood. "It was not his fault, therefore."

"Not his fault?" Barney repeated. "Madam, when a man gives his word it's no excuse that he breaks it for a woman. In fact, it's less excuse. You'll pardon that line of reasoning, I'm sure."

Douglass said incredulously, "You won't have him released then?"

"No, madam," said Barney. Then he said, "But I will not have him placed in a dungeon, with irons on both legs and wrists. Nor will I starve him!" He took her hand and swung her around to face him. "I have my real prize in the codebooks! Ah, here is Dr. Hindman." He dropped her hand.

Dr. Hindman said, "You cannot see him now, sir. But the bullet was removed quickly. It was not in the bone." He opened his palm. "You see, it is still in its original shape. Madam, he will probably be feverish; he has lost much blood. Miss Lucie is competent. I shall myself return this evening, even if it is late. I go now to the hospital, where Captain Barney has sent all the wounded. And if you should need me, before I come, send a note."

"Thank you, Doctor."

"I'm ready, Barney. Goodbye, madam."

"Goodbye, Doctor," Douglass said.

Barney bent over her hand. "Your obedient servant, madam," he said. "Please tell Joshua I'll call tomorrow, and if he wants me, send word."

Douglass stood by herself in the empty room. She went slowly toward the hall. On the top of the clavichord lay the two gleaming pistols. She stopped.

She ran one finger over the long barrel. Then she withdrew her hand quickly and went upstairs.

16

THE DOOR TO JOSHUA'S ROOM STOOD OPEN. A LOW FIRE BURNED IN the grate and atop the mantel the clock ticked in the silent room.

The bedcurtains were hooked back; the candles flickered; the clock struck gently three times. Douglass changed her position slightly. Then she saw Lucie.

Lucie slipped into the room. She was fully dressed, in her grey gown and tiny white apron. "Madame," she whispered.

Douglass threw a glance at the sleeping figure of Joshua. She rose and drew Lucie out into the hall. "What is it?"

Lucie said, "You must sleep, madame. I have wakened and dressed. I will take up the vigil."

Douglass said, "It is three. I had been thinking; I did not realize how late it was."

"I will watch over him, Mr. Joshua," Lucie said.

Douglass nodded. "He is asleep." She started away. "But call me, Lucie, should you need me."

"*Oui,* madame. I have turned down your bed."

Lucie tiptoed back into the silent room. A chair had been pulled up to the bed; Lucie sat down in it.

Joshua lay full length in the big bed, one arm flung out as though he had pushed the pillow aside and fallen asleep in that position. Lucie leaned forward and touched his hand. It was not too hot; she leaned back in the chair and sighed with relief, keeping her eyes on him. She could look her fill; he was sleeping quietly. She could hear his breath; his chest rose and fell evenly. Then suddenly he moved, a quick restless turn; the quick movement must have hurt his leg. He spoke; then his eyes opened.

He lay still; he became aware of the presence of someone else, and turned his head to see who was in the room. He frowned at her.

"Lucie," he muttered. He raised himself on one elbow cautiously, looking around the dimly lit room. "What time is it?"

"A half after three, sir."

"I'm hot," Joshua grumbled irritably, and pushed back the top blanket and grimaced, for he had moved his leg.

Lucie cried, "I do it!" She took the top blanket off, and folded it back. She felt his eyes on her, and she straightened and looked back at him.

"I was dreaming," he said, frowning at her.

"*Oui*, m'sieur," Lucie said.

"Did I speak aloud?" he asked, keeping his frown.

She nodded, catching her lip in white teeth. "*Oui.*"

"Well, tell me what I said!" Joshua gave a grunt as he started to sit up and feel for a pillow.

Lucie was torn between answering his question and helping him find the pillow; with his eyes on her she found difficulty in doing anything. But she lifted the big pillow and shoved it behind him. Joshua leaned back against it and rubbed his hand over his forehead to push the short hair back. "Well?" he asked.

"You said, sir—I am trying to recall exact—you said: 'Now that you have the ship I can't sail with you because of this goddamned leg!'"

Joshua said forcibly, "What a silly damn dream!" Then he smiled a little. "My language sounds incongruous on your lips." He drew a deep breath and tried easing his leg into another position. "Cramped," he said. Once more he looked up at her. "What are you doing here, Lucie?"

"Madame and I—" Lucie said. "We watch."

"Oh, God," said Joshua. "What are you watching? If there's anything I hate, it's women fussing."

Lucie's eyes regarded him. "I do not fuss, sir."

Joshua smiled. "Don't you?"

She hesitated. "I don't think I do." Then, "What does it mean—fuss?"

He laughed.

"I think I know," she said, gravely. "But perhaps I do not understand the male mind. Do you want your man?"

"Lord, no," said Joshua; he was amused. "Go on, Lucie. Explain further."

She said, "You fight and receive a bullet. I make you comfortable and do what you ask."

"Direct and simple," said Joshua, "and there may be some merit to such a program. A pity I can't take full advantage of it."

"What, sir?" asked Lucie.

He grinned. "I'm thirsty. First I ask for half a glass of water."

"*Oui*, m'sieur," she said, turning away. Joshua peered past her.

"Hold," he said, as he watched. "Enough. *Assez!*"

She turned to look.

"Pour a trifle out and now fill it up with whiskey," Joshua said.

"*Oui*," murmured Lucie, filling the glass. She brought it over to him and watched him as he tasted it. "Does it suit?"

"*Oui*," said Joshua.

She said, "You mimic me."

"*Oui*," he said. He looked at her. "Damn it, you're a beautiful female. Your accent is music to the ears; you have me at a disadvantage immediately with it. Say something else to me."

She leaned forward, the candlelight shining on the auburn braids. "What do you wish I should say? No, I intend—what do you wish to say *about?* Is that right?"

"Where were you born?" Joshua asked.

"In Normandie. Near the sea. We have great rocky coast. It is very beautiful there."

"I know," said Joshua. "Do you want to go back?"

"No, m'sieur."

"No?" He drank the rest of the whiskey and water. Lucie took the glass from him. He yawned. "I don't know why I'm so sleepy," he said. "I was going to smoke a pipe."

Lucie said, "You had laudanum."

"Laudanum? How long did Dr. Hindman say I'd be confined in this damned bed?"

"He did not say. Captain Barney said to tell you he would call tomorrow."

"I think," said Joshua, "I'll stay drunk for two days and then get up."

Lucie dimpled.

"Do I amuse you?" Joshua growled.

"*Oui*," said Lucie. "You are so mad because somebody shot you." She held the glass, and she turned to put it down on the table. She came back to the bedside. "Now what you want, sir?"

Joshua smiled and looked sleepy.

Lucie said, solemnly, "Is it fuss if I straighten the linen?" She waited for his answer.

"I guess not." He slid carefully down flat on his back again. Lucie bent over him, to smooth out and turn down the sheet.

"La," she said.

Joshua reached for her with both hands. "I couldn't resist," he began, looking into her dark blue eyes; he caught her head between his hands and pulled her down for a kiss on the red lips so near his. "Um," he said, releasing her. "That was nice." He smiled as she straightened up quickly. "Wasn't it?" he asked, catching her hand in his.

"*Oui,*" she said. She sat down.

Joshua kept hold of her hand. His eyes closed. Lucie thought he was sound asleep. When his voice came, she jumped.

"What are you thinking about?"

His blue eyes were open again. She said, "I was thinking that was how a kiss worked, m'sieur." Her heart beat fast.

He grinned. "We'll work it again sometime, Lucie," he said.

She was silent. The next time she looked at him he was asleep.

17

IT WAS THE THIRTIETH OF NOVEMBER, A COLD GREY DAY IN BOTH New York and Philadelphia. In New York harbor, aboard the flagship "Sandwich," Admiral George Rodney dipped his pen and began to write.

"The occurrence of consequence is Lord Cornwallis' retreat in North Carolina. The whole expedition appears to me to have been an ill-concerted measure and could only tend to weaken the army and give the rebels the opportunity of destroying our troops by detail."

He leaned back in his chair and frowned. Then he continued. This was an important letter, for he must make clear to Lord Sandwich the state of the war in these colonies.

"The Highlands of Hudson River, which cut off communication between northern and southern provinces here, was the post which

Arnold was to have betrayed to us. The rebels would have been undone had the scheme succeeded. At all events it must," he hesitated
and underlined, "it must be recovered. I offered every assistance but
was told it was too late."

"The damned fools," he muttered aloud in the silent cabin. His
anger enabled him to proceed strongly.

"The evacuation of Rhode Island was the most fatal measure that
could have been adopted. It gave up the best harbor in America
from whence squadrons in forty-eight hours could blockade the
three capital cities. France has wisely taken advantage of our mis-
conduct, and has made it now impregnable. I now come to the third
evacuation—Portsmouth and Hampton, a post which commands
the Chesapeake. I fear again this will hamper the actions of the fleet
here immensely. Now I myself shall proceed immediately to my station in the West Indies."

He stood up. Retreat in Carolina; the loss of Portsmouth and
Rhode Island! His mouth was bitter.

In Philadelphia that day the newspapers printed a newly written
poem alongside the war news from Carolina. They boxed it on the
front page, for Captain Barney was recruiting a crew.

> "Come all ye lads that know no fear,
> To wealth and honor we will steer,
> In the Athena privateer
> Commanded by bold Barney.
>
> She's new and true and tight and sound,
> Well rigged aloft and all well found,
> Come and be with laurel crowned,
> Away and leave your lasses."

Barney looked up from the paper. "I could have done better myself," he said. "And it gets worse."

Gouverneur Morris smiled. The paper lay on the table, and Gouverneur tapped it with his finger. "Seems now to be incontroverti-
ble the British have bitten off more than they can chew in Carolina.
God, that's a bloody campaign, Barney."

Barney said, "Cornwallis could be completely cut off by sea power
—he would be forced to surrender." He motioned to a waiter, got

[113]

a pipe and regarded Gouverneur through a cloud of smoke. They had just finished breakfast; they were sitting at their ease in the London Coffee Shop, favorite meeting place for the merchants. Robert Morris' and Joshua's offices were across Second Street. Gouverneur produced a watch from his waistcoat pocket.

"We have a few minutes," he said. "How is the recruiting going?"

Barney said, "I've bought the best gunnery officer in the States out of debtor's jail. Twenty of the British crew volunteered—I took them, for they were mostly topmen. The marines—" He grinned. "They're mostly Bucks county backwoodsmen. Lord, how they can shoot. They don't waste bullets; they shoot to kill, sir. Ever since they've been ten and allowed the use of a rifle, they've had to account to their fathers for the amount of bullets expended. They've got to have some game to show for those bullets. That's one thing the British can't understand; an American rifleman shoots to kill. Habit, sir." He drew on his pipe. "I'll make marines out of them."

"I'm sure you will," Gouverneur said, taking a pinch of snuff and brushing it off his elegant pink coat with its row of gold buttons. When he pushed back his chair and stood, his wooden peg leg was in violent contrast to the elegance of his dress. He had a habit of tapping the peg for attention. A servant came dashing over with his cloak and hat. Gouverneur allowed him to place the cloak on his shoulders, and tipped him well.

"Intelligence reports that Rodney is sailing soon for the West Indies, Barney," he said. "You know there's nothing better than Washington's secret service."

"If you know what the enemy is going to do—" Barney flung out his hands.

Gouverneur could walk very fast on his leg, and he swung out the door. The few loungers on the wide wooden settee out on the brick pavement stared at the two men. They crossed Front Street. It was such a dark cold day they could see the oil lights shining through the windows of both Morris' and Joshua's offices. But it was with surprise that they saw Joshua himself.

He was using his cane, and he descended the one step down from his door with difficulty. He had negotiated it when he looked up and saw the other two men.

"You shouldn't be here," Barney said.

Joshua explained with a variety of oaths that he had stayed in bed three days. "And I've been conducting business with three clerks

[114]

—two men and one bottle," Joshua ended. "I've had a hell of a time."

Gouverneur tapped his leg. "I know all about it, sir. But the stories I could tell you, of sympathetic ladies—which of course I am honor bound to keep to myself—those stories would tempt you to part with one of yours." He grinned, and threw open the door to Robert Morris' offices, which he shared. The two men were not related, even though they bore the same name. But they were carrying the burden of financing the war for the United States. The three of them entered Robert Morris' private office.

All three of them had nothing but admiration and affection for Robert Morris. Gouverneur and Joshua, born of wealthy and old families, differed thus from Robert Morris, who had made his own way, orphaned at sixteen, the son of a port agent for a British merchant firm. "Robert Morris," Joshua had said, "is a damned genius, a financial wizard. No one else could have done it; the United States of America owes him an eternal debt. When the treasury is worse than empty we can borrow as a nation, because Morris pledges his word."

As for Barney, he felt a kinship with Morris. Both men had lost their fathers early through accidental gunshot. Morris had sailed more than once around the world; if ever a man knew the value of a Navy, he did. "Where our ships go, so must our Navy; trade is the lifeblood of a nation, and it must be protected." He had taken time to write this to Barney. He had ended, "I will add, for myself, that if you continue to act with the same bravery and devotion, you shall always find me a friend ready and happy to serve you."

"Joshua," Robert Morris said, repeating Barney's words, "you shouldn't be here."

"I brought the bond," Joshua said. He had sat down gratefully before the fire. He produced the bond of which he had spoken. He handed it to Barney. "Read it, Barney," he suggested, a little wearily.

It was very familiar. "Know all men by these presents, that we, Joshua Harris, merchant, and Benjamin Barney, mariner, of the city of Philadelphia, are held and firmly bound to the Treasurer of the United States of America in the penalty of twenty thousand Spanish milled dollars or other money the equivalent thereto, by force of arms, to attack, seize, or subdue, the enemies—" Barney read fast. He finished and looked up at Robert Morris. "Privateering again," he said.

Morris nodded. "Some day, Barney—" He broke off, and stood up. "I've been immured here, behind this desk, too long." He walked across to the fire. "Let it be a consolation to you, sir, that your summer cruises last year financed the whole of our diplomatic services abroad for all the years of the war, and are still financing them; that they helped most materially in drawing our allies into this war, and that from accounts sent me you have charmed the court of France with your forthright personality."

"Thank you," Barney said.

Morris picked up the bond. "Now you shall be, as soon as this is signed and witnessed, in possession," he read, "of the 'Athena,' of thirty-two guns, with a crew of three hundred and forty officers and men." He paused. "Every prize you take, every dollar that comes into the treasury, is much needed. Do you know what I'm going to do now? I'm going begging, for pay for the troops."

Gouverneur explained. "From door to door." He stumped over to the nearest chair and sat down, regarding his leg.

Barney said, "Are those buttons gold, Gouverneur?"

Gouverneur looked up and nodded. Barney reached in his pocket and handed over his knife. Gouverneur started to saw off the buttons. While he sawed he talked. "Christmas coming, and the troops haven't been paid for months; they're grumbling and I don't blame them." He laid the buttons one by one on the desk, and then looked at his coat. "Damn you, Barney," he said, "you're so practical."

Barney grinned. He was in the presence of three of the wealthiest men in the United States and none of them had a cent in cash. "I can raise a little cash," he said.

All three looked as though he were a wizard. "How?" asked Joshua.

"Simple," said Barney. "My little house is clear. I'll go over to Girard and borrow in Spanish dollars on it. As much as I can get."

"I'll give you a note for it," Morris said.

"Also," said Barney, "I've got a number of captured weapons— fifty guinea dress swords, and such—duelling pistols. There are many men in the city who'd pay high for them."

"Yes, there are, sir," Joshua said. "Do you have many, Barney?"

"Chests of 'em," said Barney.

Gouverneur burst out laughing.

"That damned Rodgers," grumbled Barney, "tossed his silver-hilted one in the Delaware but he surrendered a matched set of fowling pieces with silver mountings. When you remember I took sixty ships last summer and spring alone, sirs, you realize a lot of men have handed me whatever weapon was handy when they surrendered."

"A parade of 'em," said Gouverneur, still convulsed with laughter. "I'll take over the selling of them," he said to Robert Morris. "Let's get this bond signed, and have a drink to it."

Morris smiled. "Get the whiskey, my friend," he said. "He's been working day and night, Joshua," he continued as Gouverneur went over to his desk and got out a bottle of whiskey. "Why don't you take him with you, Barney; inspect the parade of surrendered dress swords, and take the rest of the day. Have some fun."

Gouverneur was pouring out four cups of whiskey. He looked up from his task. "I'd like to talk to Barney," he said, "about France— and such like. I'm angling for diplomatic service after the war." He passed the cups to each man.

Joshua and Barney each signed the bond. Gouverneur scrawled his witnessing signature. "From this moment on," he said, "the 'Athena'! Who named her?"

"Joshua did," Barney answered. "He says she sprang from my head."

"Fully panoplied," Robert Morris quoted. "Perhaps she did, Barney."

Gouverneur raised his glass. "Allow me a bit of romanticism: To the goddess and to the ship!"

18

AT THREE THAT AFTERNOON THE CHILL LATE NOVEMBER WIND blew hard off the river. Lamplight from the shops shone out into the city streets. Lucie passed the Cathcart's bookshop and apothecary at Second and Elfreth's Alley, and even though she was thoroughly cold, she stopped for just a moment to try to read the recipe on the open page of a new cookbook.

Just as she stopped, Joshua opened the door of the shop and came limping out into the street. "Lucie," he said, surprised.

"M'sieur!" she exclaimed.

The wind blew the ends of her gay knitted yellow scarf, which matched her knitted mittens. Her cheeks were pink with cold. "You look pretty as a picture," Joshua said. "I've the coach. I'll take you home."

"Thank you, m'sieur," she said. But she didn't move; she looked up at him. "Are you feeling—" she searched for the right word— "fine? How is your leg?"

She was very concerned, and Joshua smiled. "You're keeping me standing on it."

"*Mon Dieu!* Forgive me, m'sieur!" She looked around for the coach, flew across the pavement and opened the door. She called up to the coachman, "Why you not have this ready open, for m'sieur?" As Joshua got in, she said, "He is bastard?"

Joshua sat down in the seat and laughed. She eyed him questioningly, and was about to close the door when Joshua leaned forward and caught her hand.

"Get in," he said, and pulled her down on the seat beside him; he was still chuckling. "Lucie, Lucie," he said reprovingly.

She clasped her hands. "What did I do?"

"Where did you hear the word bastard?" Joshua asked sternly.

She glanced at him. "From you, sir."

"Oh, lord," said Joshua. "Never repeat my words, Lucie." He smiled. "My language is too full of liabilities for you." He added, "You must have heard a great many words from me, lately. I expect I was a rather irritable patient, wasn't I?"

"Terrible," said Lucie, truthfully.

"Here come these rolled r's at me again," Joshua said. "They say women are better patients than men."

"*Oui,*" said Lucie. She sighed and gave him an angelic smile. "But I rather take care of you."

"Would you?" asked Joshua. "What were you doing down here?"

"Walking, m'sieur." She didn't meet his eyes.

"Walking?" Joshua looked at her. "You're shivering with the cold, Lucie." He put his arm around her and drew her close to him, turning her face to his with one hand.

At his nearness, Lucie found words more difficult. "What were you doing?" she asked low, looking at the collar of his cloak.

"I was going to buy a book to read tonight, but I decided I didn't have enough money."

Her eyes widened. "Enough money?"

He said, "Cash is short, Lucie. I can't expect you to understand my finances, but all the gold we have—" He explained how Gouverneur Morris had taken the gold buttons off his coat.

Her eyes were studying him as he spoke. "I have gold, sir," she said.

Joshua smiled. "You do, Lucie?"

"*Oui*," she nodded. "I have sixty pounds in gold!"

"Sixty pounds?" Joshua exclaimed.

"*Oui!* Five pounds a month for twelve months. Captain Barney paid me in gold!" She lifted her face to his. "I give it for the troops."

Joshua kissed her quickly, and drew back a little to study her face. "You'll have a note for it, Lucie."

"A note?" she whispered. "What is that?"

"I mean you'll get it back; I promise," Joshua said, his mind not on his words.

"I don't want it back, sir; I was saving it for my dot—my dowry." She drew a deep breath. "Now I do not think I ever marry."

"What?" asked Joshua. He looked deep into her eyes.

She said, "When George ask me to marry him today, I knew I tell him no."

"What?" Joshua growled. "Who is George?"

Lucie looked amazed. "Your clerk."

"How did you meet—" Joshua broke off. For the last three days, George Griffiths had been in and out of the house. "He worked fast, the bastard," Joshua announced; then he grinned. "Don't repeat that, Lucie. So you turned George down?"

She nodded, wordlessly.

"Why?"

"Because," she whispered.

Joshua kissed her. When the coach jolted to a stop in front of the big house, the coachman jumped down to open the door. He closed it again. But Lucie had heard it close.

The sound of it made her open her eyes. She withdrew her arms from around Joshua's neck and laid a mittened hand against the side of his face. "We are home," she whispered, drawing away from him a little. She traced one finger along his face, and Joshua kissed her again, for a moment holding her close. Then he released her, leaned forward and opened the door of the coach.

Joshua gave the coachman a brief stare. Lucie got out and walked at his side into the house. Within the fires were burning and there was the smell of woodsmoke. Even Marston smiled at her today. She looked up at Joshua as Marston divested him of his cloak.

"I go to madame, now," she said.

19

DOUGLASS WAS WAITING. AS SOON AS LUCIE APPEARED, AND AS SOON as she had shut the door, Douglass grasped up her red cape. "He has gone?" she asked.

"*Oui,* madame." Lucie unfastened her own cape and removed it. "He has gone to the cockfights and then to the theatre and supper."

"The theatre?" asked Douglass. She went over to her mirror, regarding her piled curls, so lightly dusted with powder. She picked up a filmy veil. "The theatre? The little singer, Judy, probably!" She set her full mouth. "Goodbye, Lucie. I shall be back before supper."

Marston was surprised to see Douglass go out alone and on foot. He wondered where she was going, and then decided that probably she was only going next door, to visit with the English captain and his officers. He shut the big door after her.

Once in the street, Douglass walked fast, her cape flying behind her. She had seven blocks to walk and she walked them quickly. At Elfreth's Alley she slowed her pace.

It was very narrow, cobblestoned, with a tiny sidewalk about two feet wide. She gathered her cape close and walked along; she could look into the houses, through the many paned windows. Toward the end of the block she paused; at right angles Bladen's Court ran from the alley, and Douglass stepped around the corner quickly.

A giant tree sheltered one of the houses under its spreading limbs. She passed a stone-walled well, and stepped up the one step to a white doorway. She lifted the brass knocker.

Absolom answered the door. Douglass entered. She drew a deep breath; she was standing in his house.

She looked around the white panelled hall; a lazy wood fire burned and the stairway went up around it. A pair of beautiful chairs flanked a French table with a mirror atop it; she caught a glimpse of herself, and she realized Absolom was saying:

"Captain Barney is not at home, ma'am. May I take a message?"

Douglass knew very well he was not at home. But her voice was unsteady as she said, "I will wait." She gave a glance to the empty room at her right. "I'll keep my cape," she added. She could not push aside the feeling that any moment she would hear Barney's tread, and that he would be there, looking at her with his dark eyes. She said, "I will wait, in the study!"

She knew of the room from Joshua; he had spoken of it and described it to her.

Absolom was confused. "But ma'am. The captain has gone to the theatre—I mean the cockfights, too, ma'am, and—"

"He may return." Douglass turned her eyes on him, and Absolom wilted.

"Yes, ma'am. I'll take you up. There's a fire lighted."

Douglass sighed, and made for the steps. She climbed slowly. Upstairs the same white panelling marked the pretty hall. In the room to her right again she saw indeed the fire was lighted; she could hear it crackling, and it threw a warm glow over the room.

"I shall light the lamps, ma'am," Absolom said.

Douglass watched the room come to life. As the light sprang up she saw the cushioned window seat, the round globe in its polished wooden frame. She saw his desk; on one wall were a pair of magnificent duelling pistols, and a gold-hilted sword. Next to them hung a barometer.

In front of the fire was his padded chair and stool, with his table beside it. And over the fireplace, the painting of the "Revenge." Douglass stared up at it, the white cliffs of Dover, and the "Revenge." Absolom was looking at her, and she turned to him. "I shall wait a few minutes."

He turned and left her. She did not even hear his "Yes, ma'am." But he was gone and she was alone in Barney's study.

Her fingers were icy. Her heart was pounding in her throat. She leaned over and picked up one of his pipes, and then set it down again. Once more she looked up at the "Revenge." Then she went over to the desk and opened the first drawer.

The papers rustled under her fingers. Charts; charts and legal papers. The second drawer yielded nothing but letters, and she closed that one hastily. She listened. The whole house was still.

Gradually her hands grew calmer. She searched through the two remaining drawers: nothing but more charts, writing paper, sealing wax. She closed the last drawer and stood up. Then determinedly, she picked up the biggest lamp.

She walked across the hall on tiptoe, and peered into the room directly opposite the study, across the hall. Within another fire burned, and thus this room must be his bedroom. She entered it.

She set the lamp down on the bedside table. It had one drawer, but there was nothing inside it at all. Once more she picked up the lamp, and crossed the room to the highboy, with the shadow following her. She listened again. There was no sound. So, one by one, she opened the drawers.

The highboy contained nothing but clothing. She shut the last drawer. At the foot of the bed was his sea chest.

She left the lamp on the highboy. Her red cape glowed like the fire in the fireplace. She looked down at the chest. Double bronze nailheads made an oval on its top, in which a B was scrolled. The nailheads rimmed the lid, and the bottom, and the whole chest glistened with polish. A bronze key, with a chain, was in the lock. Desperately she turned the key in its lock and lifted the lid.

Barney had already laid within it a few things that he wished to take. Charts of the Caribbean, marked and revised by his own hands, with the native names for small bays and coves. Douglass drew one out, and opened it, folded it and put it back again. She leafed through the charts, when a sound in the distance startled her. She knelt there, by the open chest, frozen. Had she heard voices and the tread of feet? She didn't move a muscle; she listened.

She had heard a voice. But it was outside. She breathed a little easier when suddenly she heard the sound of a door opening downstairs, and she heard the familiar voice say:

"Come in, gentlemen."

Douglass rose to her feet so quickly it seemed that the whole room tipped on one end. She stood there, paralyzed, not stirring. Downstairs she heard what seemed to be at least four different male voices; then there was a sudden quiet. She knew with certainty that Absolom was telling Barney a woman waited for him.

The silence ended abruptly. She heard a deep laugh. Then a voice said, and it was Gouverneur Morris, "You lucky dog. With this money shortage I'm going to have to find a wench who loves me for myself alone. Is she beautiful, Absolom?"

Absolom must have nodded. "Look at his eyes shine," another voice said; then Barney's cut through.

"I'll be back in a few moments, sirs. Absolom, get the gentlemen something to drink."

"Don't hurry, Barney."

He was coming upstairs. The tread she had imagined when she had first entered the house was real now. In desperation she fled across the room to a white door and flung it open.

"Oh, lord," she whispered. It was a closet. She shut the door, her cape had slipped off one shoulder, and it fell to the floor, just as Barney came to stand on the threshold of the room.

"Barney," she whispered.

He towered there. His dark eyes looked back at her; his cloak swung from his shoulders; he was wearing his calf high boots. His dark eyes looked back at her, then they went to his open sea chest, to the single lamp burning on the highboy, and then they came back to her again, standing there in the middle of his bedroom, his gaze going slowly over her until it reached the cape on the floor.

He did not speak to her. He took one step and closed the door behind him, pushing it shut. The latch clicked.

His voice came at her. "And to what do I owe this pleasure, madam?" He unfastened his cloak and removed it, tossing it on his big fourposter bed.

She did not answer. He came toward her.

"I want the truth," he said.

"All right!" She looked right back at him now. "You shall have it!

"You know why I'm here!" She leaned over and picked up her cape, slinging it over her arm. She faced him again. "I didn't get what I came for! So you can go back to Judy now!"

"By Christ," Barney said, trying to control the rising wrath, "be careful! And answer my question!"

"I'll answer it!" Imitating him, she flung her own cape alongside of his on the bed. The filmy veil was still about her hair, and she drew it down over her bare shoulders, slowly. "I came for the code-books!"

The heavy muscles along his jaw set ominously as he forced himself to keep his hands off her until this wave of anger passed. "You know, English," he said, "my sea chest is my most personal possession, and you've had your little fingers in it. Wilful fingers, I should say." His voice was very low, and as he spoke he felt the hot anger being gradually controlled. His eyes went from her to the closed door to the smooth made-up bed.

She was replying passionately. "Wilful hands, mine? What of yours? How you held those codebooks in front of me, challenging me with them? Didn't you know I would try to get them back? Didn't you know that when you did it, Captain Barney?" She threw the name at him.

He approached her slowly.

"Had you been in my place, you would have tried!"

"I?" He looked down at her and there was the vestige of the old smile on his face. "Do you imitate the crude rough Yankee, now?" His fingers closed around her slender wrist, tightening, and he lifted her hand and put it against his chest. "Here are the codebooks," he said.

Her grey eyes blazed; he looked at the rise and fall of her breast. He added, "Want them?"

She tried to wrench her hand away. "Ah, I hate you, Barney," she whispered. "You flaunt them—you, the victor. Well, that's done, Barney. You won."

"Yes."

She turned away, forgetting the fingers pressing her hand; she turned, and was brought up short by those strong fingers.

She asked wildly, "Then why don't you go on to the theatre now?"

He looked at her beautiful head and the bare shoulders. "Because you intrigue me much more."

She lifted one hand to touch her hair. "Go seek out the little Judy; she'll suit you better!"

"Her real name is Marie."

Her lashes flew up; her body was tense. Barney dropped her hand and went over to the fireplace, leaning his elbow on the mantel. His eyes searched her.

The angry jealousy that she felt was accompanied by the blinding flash of realization that this man was the most important focus of her life. It was he she had followed here; he for whom she had deserted England; he for whom she dressed and lived and breathed. She said:

"Yesterday—I mean three days ago—you expected me to congratulate you on a victory."

He answered this. "Yes!"

"Even supposing I had no conflicting loyalties, you offered physical insult and violence on my countryman, who was present at my request—nay, my urgent pleas."

"He broke parole," Barney said. "And you should have depended on me."

She looked over at him. "On you?"

"Yes, madam. I knew Joshua was hurt. Instead of waiting for me, you go dashing for aid from your British friends!"

"And I am not permitted British friends?"

"No," he said.

"Oh," she cried, "but I am not your property!"

"Not yet. By God, I've been very patient, madam. I—"

"Patient?" she repeated incredulously.

"Do not interrupt me. I'll talk now. I should never have told you about the codebooks; it was an action born of anger." He walked over to her. "But I never thought you would attempt to steal them! Meddling in men's affairs is a dangerous business; you are guilty of a treasonable act, and we have been at war five years and every effort has been made to gain an honorable victory. Fortunately for you no one but me knows. I see you are still unconvinced, English!" She had turned away from him, and he reached for her, turning her around to face him. She drew a long breath and tipped her head back to look up at him.

Barney said, "There's a loaded pistol in my pocket, for I usually go armed. Had this room been in darkness, I might have used it, without knowing who you were. I might have seized you and knocked you across the room. We'll test the truth of that. You wouldn't have sent one of those paroled officers here, would you?"

"No," she said. "You might have—"

"Killed him, I'll end it for you."

She turned her face away from him.

"Brutal words, Douglass, but this is a war, and men feel deeply about it. Let me warn you not to tell Joshua, or you will find out to your sorrow that such a sortie into betrayal will not be condoned. You are only a woman and you do not understand."

"I do understand!"

"By Christ," he said, "if I thought you did, I'd—" His hands tightened on her shoulders. "No. You did it to get back at me; it's a personal matter between the two of us, and I will handle it. Now."

"No!" cried Douglass. "I did it for England!"

He looked down at her grimly. "Did you?"

"As the last thing I would ever do!"

"You'll retract that, shortly. You came here to me alone. You

[125]

were married for a week, to a boy. Why don't you admit you came as a woman, seeking to give yourself completely to me? Well, then, I'll be back in a moment." His hands dropped from her, and he went to the door. He left it open and she heard him going quickly down the steps. With a quick gesture she snatched up her cape from the bed; she too went to the door, crossed the hall, and set her foot on the topmost step.

Below her, in the hallway, was a jumble of men's voices. She heard not a word of what they were saying, or of Barney's voice explaining briefly that he had forgot a previous engagement and that they would have to excuse him. Douglass was halfway down.

"Rendezvous?" Gouverneur Morris said. "I am—" he broke off. Douglass was halfway down the stairs.

She had snatched up the cape so quickly that it trailed from one hand, its whole brilliant length behind her on the steps. The filmy veil floated about her shoulders. Her face was white and her grey eyes fastened on Barney, as step by step, in the silence, she descended toward him.

Gouverneur Morris, stifling an exclamation, stepped aside from the foot of the staircase. He was struck by her vivid beauty, and he noted instantly the appeal in her eyes as she came to a stop before Barney.

But Douglass, standing before him while these men stared, knew that it was Joshua who protected her; she knew as she looked back at him that had it not been for the name she bore, Barney would keep her here openly.

"Sir," she said, low, while Barney took the cape from her hand and put it around her as though to shield her from the openly appraising eyes of the four other men.

"Thank you, sir," she said. She turned her head slowly to smile at his guests, and she made a brief curtsey. "My apologies, gentlemen, for detaining Captain Barney."

"No apologies at all are necessary, Mistress Harris," Gouverneur said quickly, bowing.

Douglass put her hand on Barney's arm. He opened the door for her. "Ah, no, sir," she said. "My coach awaits me. I go the way I came."

She slipped past him. There was no coach but he wouldn't know it, and besides that, it was only four-thirty, and not late; it was best for him not to follow and he would know it. She ran across the court and out into the alley. Halfway down, against the brick walls, she stopped.

Her hands were trembling a little as she adjusted her veil over her hair. The narrow alley was empty. Back in Bladen's Court she could imagine what the men were saying, but what would Barney reply, and what was he thinking?

"Oh, lord," she whispered aloud. "What have I done?"

She leaned against the wall, while her mind tried to encompass the brief thirty minutes just passed. She was alone; the loneliness of a strange land, a strange city, a narrow empty street pressed around her.

Within the window of 109, into which she could see, the cabinet maker, a jolly man from whom she had bought a set of carved chairs, put his feet up on the settle and opened the paper. He had told her proudly that his son had been with Washington since the winter at Valley Forge. She caught her breath suddenly as she realized what that man would think if he knew what errand had brought her to Elfreth's Alley. Was Barney right? The image of Joshua's face floated in front of her. She gathered her cape closely about her and walked rapidly down the alley, alone.

20

MARSTON LET HER IN THE HOUSE. SHE DID NOT EVEN SEE HIM. "Mr. Joshua?" she asked.

"In his room, madam."

She went slowly up the stairway, past her landing, and around to the big front room. From its doorway she saw the back of Joshua's head, as he sat in his big chair in front of the fire.

"Joshua," she said.

"Yes?" He turned his head to look. "Come in, sister," he said, smiling.

She approached him uncertainly. Was that the last time he would ever smile at her? "Are you weary, after your first day out, Joshua?"

"A little," he admitted. He had propped his legs up on the stool, and laid the book he had been reading across his knees. His smile faded. "What's the matter?"

"The matter?" asked Douglass. She saw that his man was in the room, taking clothing out of the drawers of the highboy. Joshua followed her glance.

"I forgot to tell you," he said, "that I am sailing for Stasia to-morrow."

That was like him, she thought.

He frowned a little. "Leave us, Partridge," he said shortly.

Partridge did so, immediately. Douglass watched him go; then she bethought herself, and she went over to the door and closed it. When she returned to Joshua's chair he was eying her with narrowed eyes.

"What's the matter?" he asked, curtly.

"I wanted no one to hear us," she said.

"So I assumed. Your action speaks plain enough." He laid the book on the table. "Well? I'm waiting."

How to begin, she wondered wildly. She sank down into a chair, a straight ladderbacked chair. "Sir," she said bravely, "I have to tell you first. I would rather—than have you hear it elsewhere. I went to Bladen's Court!"

"What?" exclaimed Joshua; then he was silent, his blue eyes icy.

The words tumbled out. "I waited for Barney upstairs. When he came home, we quarrelled; he left me for a moment to go down to tell his friends to leave. I—I went down after him."

She looked across at his face. "They knew me, of course. I spoke to them. One of them was Gouverneur Morris, and one was Captain Humphreys and the others are two whose names I forget."

He said grimly, "They won't have forgotten yours. And why did you go there? You omitted that salient fact."

"To see Barney," she whispered.

Joshua sat forward. "Tell me the truth! That is a lie!"

"Joshua," she pleaded.

"I wish to know why you went there," he repeated, "and I want the truth!"

"Joshua," she said. "I went—I went to get our naval code-books!"

He had been leaning forward. He swung his legs off the stool and stood up, forgetting the injured leg; a knifing pain went all the way to his head, and he grasped for the top of her tall chair. Resting his weight on the good leg, he put his other hand in her thick curls and turned her face up. He spaced each word evenly.

[128]

"How do you know about the codebooks?"

"Joshua," she gasped. The low voice and deadly calm did not deceive her; he was pale with anger.

"From your dear friends next door," he muttered, answering his own question. Blue eyes narrowed, he slowly unfastened the fingers of the hand he had in her hair. Because she was afraid of him physically, she cried out and put her bright head in her hands.

Joshua raised his open hand. "You would, would you?"

"Joshua," she cried, "it wasn't the men next door—" She stopped. "What is the use?" she whispered, through her fingers, her body braced for the blow that was coming.

But it didn't come. He stepped back. And through his mind went suddenly and vividly the struggles that had confronted Barney and himself not only to lay hands on a ship but to finance her; through his mind went the whole day just past, when men were making every conceivable effort to win—"You'd jeopardize it all, would you? You can look at me, madam! You don't need to hide your face! Much as I'd like to—" He took another step backward to his chair, and sat down heavily.

Douglass shivered with relief, and raised her head slowly. But when she saw his face, she knew it would have been better if he had struck her. "I wouldn't have minded, if you had," she said tearfully.

"I might have broken your goddamned neck," he said. Then he smiled grimly.

"Oh," she said. But the punishment that was coming was going to be worse—she was sure of it. Her eyes fastened on him.

"I confess I find this difficult to credit, madam. Not only aid and comfort to the enemy, but outright treachery!"

These words, almost calm, did not deceive her either. She moistened her lips.

"You would have stolen—from three hundred and fifty American officers and men, including Barney, what may offer them some slight protection against the whole damned British fleet now stationed in the West Indies! Rodney sailed from New York today, with eight sail of the line, and numerous escort ships. He meets with more, at his West Indian station. You wished to add to the odds?"

"Rodney sailed?" she asked and fear smote her. "I did not know," she whispered, and she looked at him with her grey eyes and waited, because he was speaking.

"Doesn't that please you?" he asked, with sudden force. "Well, I shall send you to join him because that's where you belong, and God forbid me from keeping you here against your will!"

It was her turn to stare unbelievingly.

"You—you are sending me—back to England?"

"Indeed not," he said. "I have no money for passage! Another of my vessels leaves next week. I shall make arrangements for you to sail on her, as far as Stasia."

"Stasia?"

He smiled grimly. "The men at Stasia won't bother to enquire about your politics, madam!"

"Stasia?" She rose and steadied herself on the chairback.

"It is hardly my fault," Joshua said evenly, "that the most lawless port in the world is the only one by which you can reach England. See the British resident, upon arrival, or seek aid from the Governor. As a distressed English refugee, you should arouse deep sympathy in the breasts of the men in port."

She flushed deeply. "I want to say one thing—"

His smoldering anger burst through his tones. "I don't want to hear it! Now get out!"

There was nothing for Douglass to do but go.

Joshua stared into the fire. She had deliberately worked against all for which he had striven for so many years. It flashed across his mind that last year the Cabot firm in Boston had had twelve vessels; now they had none, through the activities of the Navy she was so interested in aiding. A blasting oath came from his lips and he stood up. He limped over to the table as fast as he could and poured himself a glass of whiskey, which he drank off standing there. How had she dared?

His leg hurt. Then the gross ingratitude occurred to him. Partridge, coming down the hall, heard his master swear again. Partridge saw that Lucie was standing at the door, ready to knock.

"Don't!" He shook his head warningly, but it was too late. Within Joshua heard Partridge.

He limped to the door and flung it open so that it crashed back against the frame. While the sound died away, Joshua glowered down at Lucie. "You come from madam?" he growled.

"*Oui*," said Lucie, shaken.

"Is she too afraid to come herself?"

"*Oui*," Lucie faltered.

"She shows wisdom. By God, my decision is final! Convey my message!"

"*Oui*, m'sieur," said Lucie. "But that is not what I came to ask." She drew a breath. "*S'il vous plait, m'sieur.*"

Joshua's leg was now paining him considerably. He saw the bed was nearest, and he went over slowly and sat down, stretching out the leg, his hands touching around the wound gently, rubbing the aching muscles. "What is it?" he muttered.

She looked at him. "I am sorry sir," she whispered to his bent head.

"What for?" Joshua muttered again.

"That your leg hurts, and that you and madame—"

He looked up. "Get on with it! What do you want?"

Her face was white. She was the daintiest woman he had ever seen. From the small slippers with their ankle ties, to the top of her shining head, she was lovely. "I'm sorry, Lucie," he said gruffly. "Tell me. What is it?"

The curling lashes swept up as she raised her yes. "I sail with madame?"

There was silence. Joshua didn't answer. In trepidation Lucie waited. Finally he said, "Yes."

Her knees trembled. Was he sending her away, too? He was speaking further, and she listened fearfully.

"Madam"— he grumbled over her name even— "should be accompanied. But you will be escorted from the ship—you do not sail with me, you know. I sail tomorrow. But I will leave orders that you are to be escorted to the Governor's house. There you will be safe. There I shall see you. If I am not in Stasia when you land, wait. Do you understand?"

Her relief was great. "*Oui*, m'sieur. I wait."

"*Un moment,*" he said, and smiled a little. "In Stasia, a woman does not go about by herself. Most especially in Lower Town. That is for men. Men only."

"*Oui*, m'sieur. I shall not."

"Remember." He said, then, "*Au revoir,* Lucie. Goodnight."

"Goodnight, sir," she said softly. Then she was gone.

She had left the door open. Joshua saw Partridge peering around the edge of it. "Partridge," he snapped. "Fill me a pipe. And bring me that bottle."

PART THREE—STASIA

21

IT WAS TEN MINUTES BEFORE SIX A.M. MR. SCULL, FIRST LIEUTENant of the "Athena," stood on the lee side of the quarterdeck, hands clasped behind his back. On the weather side, men were holystoning the deck; the quartermaster, both brown hands on the wheel, was within a yard of him, and Mr. Jerrell, just turned twenty and a junior lieutenant, was at his side. This much was usual; the rest wasn't. With misgiving Mr. Scull heard Barney's voice come singing down from his position atop the fore topgallant masthead.

"Three points to starboard, Mr. Scull!"

The wheel swung. Jerrell and Scull both turned their heads to look at the shoreline. Scull muttered, "Jesus God, we're running right under those goddamn guns."

Jerrell shoved his cap back on his head. "If we don't get away with it, we'll be sunk, sir."

A soft Scottish brogue answered him as Mr. Macgregor came up from behind. "Ye never said a truer word, laddie." He thrust his hands in his pockets and rocked back on his heels to survey the rocky shore that rose from its white line of breaking surf. Slowly his eyes lifted from the rolling waves up to the walls of the white fort that overlooked the entrance to the roadway. "You can take it from me," he said softly, "that we're within range." He patted Jerrell on the shoulder. "Watch for the puff of smoke from those big babies." He went on down the gangway, coming to a stop before two runout guns. He looked down at the heads of the crouching gunners.

"You're not nairvous, are ye?" he jibed. He stood there, watching, not hearing Barney's soft tread. Barney came to a stop beside him, looking out over the blue water at the ship that was trying so desperately to escape them. Barney gave a brief glance to the shoreline himself. They were running between this quarry and the high-perched fort, cutting off the English ship from the sanctuary of the harbor to which she was running.

Macgregor said, "This man is Limey, sir. He's usually better dressed since he had mutiny on his mind."

Barney looked down at Limey's hunched shoulders and the badly scarred back. He was one of thirty English seamen who had volunteered, out of prison, to serve aboard the "Athena." Two days out, Limey had been betrayed by a fellow Englishman, who reported that Limey was plotting to retake the "Athena."

"Limey don't talk much," Macgregor went on. "It takes the cat to make him talk. Then he speaks quick enough."

Barney knew that this was not true. It had taken severe pain and a long time to make Limey tell the names of the men who agreed to throw in with him to try to recapture the "Athena." He had stood the flogging long and without a sound until finally Barney had had to stop it. Barney still felt traces of his own perturbation as he had approached left quarterdeck and the man tied to the grating, as he had taken the bloody whip from the seaman who had wielded it.

"Limey," he had said low and crisply, hoping the man could hear him, "I don't like to see a man flogged to death. I'm going to give you plenty of chance to die at your post behind your guns. I want the names of the men who conspired with you; they'll get twenty lashes apiece. Otherwise I shall be forced to use this treatment on all your fellow Englishmen. Are you ready to talk, Limey?"

It was with terrible relief he had heard a muttered, "Aye, aye, sir."

Barney addressed him now, via Macgregor. "Mr. Macgregor, I want a shot across her bows, near, very near."

Limey glanced up at Barney, who stood right alongside of him. He sighted down the gun, he elevated her a little, the muscles rippling across his naked back. The gun roared.

It was a perfectly aimed shot. It arched up very slightly, clearing the bow of the trapped merchantman as a good tennis shot clears the net.

"Excellent," said Barney warmly. Limey straightened up, sat back on his heels; he gave another look at Barney's face, saw the smile, and smiled too.

"Thank you, sir," he murmured.

"You scared the hell out of her," said Barney.

[133]

It had. She was coming about obediently, in the face of the "Athena's" eighteen-pounders. Her flag came down. And the guns of the fort remained silent.

"Very satisfactory morning's action, Mr. Macgregor," commented Barney. He went aft slowly, to take his place on the quarterdeck. He noted that Scull and Jerrell were still glancing around at the fort.

The distance between the two ships was fast narrowing; the "Athena" was looming up alongside her prey, her guns bristling as she bore down.

"She's the 'Falcon,' sir," Scull said, squinting through the glass. "She's hoisting out a boat, sir!"

She *was* lowering a boat. It pulled rapidly to the "Athena" as the "Falcon" itself hove to and rested quietly beside her captor. Barney said, "I'll lay you a guinea the word her captain says is: 'This is piracy!'"

Scull grinned. The boat was alongside. The English captain's head appeared next and then all of him. He strode toward the quarterdeck and up to Barney.

"This is piracy," he announced grimly.

Scull could not suppress a smile. Barney bowed. "Indeed?"

The Englishman gestured to the fort. "Under the guns of Fort Oranje," he said. "In neutral waters, sir!"

"If we had been within range, the guns would have fired, sir," Barney said, lazily.

"That is a lie!"

Barney sighed. "Sir, it could also be a difference of opinion."

Jerrell tried not to smile. There was nothing he liked better than to hear his captain's conversations with prisoners of war.

"We shall put it to the test," Barney went on. "The Governor will decide."

"The Governor?" asked the Englishman with sudden passion.

"Yes," said Barney. "We shall lay the matter before Governor de Graaf. I believe he may decide we were without the jurisdiction of a neutral port."

"You damned Yankee pirate," the Englishman growled. Now cold, he said, "I am Captain Johns, sir."

Barney bowed. "Captain Barney, and my officers, sir." He introduced them quickly, while Johns endeavored to control himself. When finally Johns felt he could speak without passion, he said:

"This was a flagrant violation of the law. We were in neutral waters."

"We shall lay the matter before the Governor, sir," Barney repeated curtly. "Mr. Scull, you may take possession of the 'Falcon.'"

"Aye aye, sir," said Scull, looking alert.

Johns clenched his hands. "I am ready to give my parole, sir!"

Barney swung around to look at him. "It shall be accepted at six o'clock this evening."

The other flushed a deep red.

"Until then," said Barney easily, "I shall be forced to regard you and your officers as prisoners of war."

Johns laid his hand on his sword at this Yankee impudence. "You have the gall to let the matter go unreported all day? And to hold me aboard?"

"Escort the gentleman below, Mr. Jerrell," Barney said. "And to relieve your mind, sir, I'll report it." He bowed and turned his back. He was damned hungry; he had had no breakfast. He would see to that now.

Jerrell came out on deck again and went over to the rail. He had never seen Stasia. The great cofferdams stretched their arms on both sides to protect the blue roadway in which at least a hundred and fifty ships of all nations rode quietly at anchor. Even from here he could see that the beaches themselves were jammed with crates; he knew that less perishable goods were stored on the beaches temporarily, as they were in process of being moved from one ship's bottom to another. Mr. Jerrell reflected that here warring nations traded, so their mercantile houses did business they kept on making money and paying taxes for the upkeep of their wars. It was very complicated. He turned blue eyes on Macgregor.

"I'm glad I'm just a sailor, sir," he said.

Macgregor rolled the fat cigar in his mouth over to one side. "You could retire for life on what you've made this voyage, laddie."

Jerrell said, slowly, "We had only two guns loaded."

Macgregor grinned. He shook his head and gestured toward the fort. "Captain was taking a chance the fort wouldn't fire on the stars and stripes if we fired only once."

"Then the Englishman should have known we could never have come to actual blows?"

Macgregor thought that a foolish question. He sucked on his cigar and made a face. "We outbluffed him."

[135]

He was squinting across the water at the "Falcon," whose courses were set now. "Scull's sending a boat back," he remarked.

The officer of the watch, Mr. Lang, had already noted it, and stopped in the middle of a shouted order. "Avast there!" he bellowed, and went over to the gangway. The "Athena's" crew was all on deck; the men hung over the sides to watch. Two wooden boxes were handed aboard.

"Well, bring 'em aft," Lang shouted. "Hands to braces! Bo'sun, where the hell do you think we're going to anchor? Here?"

The courses were unfurled and caught by the strong wind; the "Athena" heeled. "Hard aweather!" roared Lang, harassed. He knew this would bring Barney out on deck. He glanced up at the tops. One man sat perched unconcernedly on the end of the mizzentop yardarm. "Get down on deck, you bastard!" The two seamen stood holding the boxes. "Set them down!"

"Mr. Scull said, sir, these here were for the captain, sir."

"Set 'em down," Lang shouted. Macgregor lounged over and looked. He leaned down and opened the little hinged door at one side of the box; he withdrew his hand hastily.

"He bit me, by God," he said, looking at his finger, while the occupant of the box scuttled out the open door. At this moment Barney appeared.

"What's going on, Mr. Lang?" he inquired, looking around the ship. "Can't you get sail up without sending my breakfast on the deck? And what are those boxes?"

Macgregor grinned. "Turtles, sir."

"Turtles?" growled Barney, and saw one. "By God, Mr. Lang, are you running a circus out here?"

"No, sir," said Lang hastily.

"I opened the box, sir," Macgregor explained. "That's Lord Sandwich over there." He pointed to the turtle who faced them, his tail waving. "He's got 'Lord Sandwich' carved on his shell, sir. He's a present for his lordship, I guess. Mr. Scull sent them, sir. Shall I see who this one is?" He gestured to the other box.

"Mr. Macgregor," said Barney, "get that goddamned turtle off my quarterdeck. Mr. Lang, if you spill another cup of coffee on me, you'll get no shore leave."

Macgregor said, "Aye aye, sir." He started toward the turtle. Barney had stopped in his stride. This promised to be good. He grinned.

"Well, Mr. Macgregor, maybe the turtle will reverse the usual order and have you for dinner."

"He already has a bite out of me, sir," Macgregor said, approaching the big snapping turtle warily. He reached out for a belaying pin.

"No you don't, Mr. Macgregor," snapped Barney. "I want him alive."

"Aye aye, sir," muttered Macgregor, eying the turtle, which stared back. Macgregor made a feint at the turtle, which snapped viciously. Macgregor made another pass at it; this time the turtle withdrew his head. Macgregor dropped the belaying pin and grabbed for the turtle; he almost succeeded in shoving it in its box before the turtle decided to bite again. Macgregor yelled, and slammed the hinged door.

"Not many men get bitten by Lord Sandwich, sir," he said, regarding his hand.

Barney laughed. "On second thought I've decided to let you discover the identity of the other turtle, Mr. Macgregor. Find out and report to me." He started away.

"Yes, sir," Macgregor said, wiping the blood off his hand, while Lang said:

"I'll thank you not to drip blood on the deck either, Mr. Macgregor."

Macgregor raised his fist. "Go to hell, Lang," he said good-naturedly.

Jerrell, who had stayed out of the way, came to his side. "I'll help," he said.

"Lord North," they both cried together, as they slammed the door closed again. Macgregor got to his feet. "Here we are, putting into Stasia, with both their lordships aboard."

"Get the heads'ls off her," shouted Lang. He turned and flashed a smile at Macgregor and Jerrell. "Stasia tonight," he said.

22

THE TOWN'S OFFICIAL NAME WAS ORANJESTAD, BUT NO ONE EVER called it that; they called it Stasia, and Upper Town, and Lower Town.

The whole island was but three by six miles. It was an extinct volcano, whose black crater, cold, thrust upward almost in the center of the island, and was called the Quill, or Signal Hill.

Its rocky wooded slopes descended directly into the blue seas; the trade winds fanned it. Its coastline was deeply indented with bays, and they bore names that reflected its conquest and reconquest.

On top of the island, in English Quarter, and Corcoram, and White Cliffs, were the spreading homes of the wealthy merchants. The road dipped down to the sea from the town that perched precariously on the slopes.

The houses were wooden, and painted white. In Upper Town was the Dutch Reform Church, the hospital next to it, the Fort that overlooked a steep cliff; lodging houses; houses of planters, few as they were, government workers, officers, more merchants. There was no Negro quarter. Most of the seven hundred slaves on Stasia were household servants and attached to the houses of the rich, for there were few plantations to work.

Douglass' chair was carried by two slaves from the Governor's mansion, which stood high on the hillside in English Quarter. She passed along under the shadow of the Amsterdam Fort, down a narrow tree-lined lane, past white fences and white houses, crowded close, past the hospital; the bearers swung through another tree-bordered lane and emerged. She was looking down the street into Lower Town.

The way down was so steep that great ships' anchors were sunk in the road; tackling was used to raise merchandise, and the anchors were used to fix purchase to. Great warehouses stretched, literally a mile long. Below her were the shops, exactly a mile of shops. Enormous auction houses; from here she could see over the tops of them. Way below was the beach, jammed with crates; like two great arms the cofferdams protected this cupped trading post and the shipping cradled between the man-made walls.

The sea was not so heavy today. A good stiff breeze in Stasia meant lighter surf; even the sailors didn't know why. Douglass' bearers stopped. She could go no further, for Lower Town was male, except for ladies of pleasure.

She peered from the window with undisguised curiosity. The street, descending rapidly, was busy; uniforms and dress of every nation in the world were represented here. They said you could smell the tobacco smoke that rose from Lower Town; Douglass was sure she could.

Tavern signs, shop signs went down like steps. Men passed in and out of them; laughter floated up to her, the crack of a pistol shot punctuated the air. By one of the big anchors a drunk lay, and men went on around him, unnoticing. Up this street Barney would come, for it was the main road from the landings.

A woman in a chair with four bearers went past Douglass and down the steep street. Douglass had a glimpse of diamonds blazing in her ears, on her hands and around her neck.

"I wish I had fifty guineas," yelled an English voice, after the chair.

The woman put her head out. She had a French accent. "It would cost you one hundred, Limey."

Douglass leaned out of the chair to listen, but there was no more dialogue. The woman was carried around the nearest corner. Douglass became aware that a man in the uniform of a French naval officer was looking at her. He stared. Douglass retreated into the chair again. After a while she peered out; he was gone.

Still there was no sight of the man for whom she waited.

Joshua also might be along. She had not seen Joshua since the night he had told her he was sending her to Stasia. She wished passionately that an opportunity would offer itself by which she could prove to him that she wished only to return to the States with him, but he would be skeptical now. The trouble was that unless he came soon, and would listen to her, she would be sent back to England before she could even speak with him. She moved restlessly in the chair. She had left Lucie behind, at the Governor's mansion. If Joshua came up the street, she wanted to talk to him alone.

She kept her thoughts on Joshua. Her real hope was to see Barney. There were so many men in the streets that it was hard to see more than forty feet down the dirt road. She clasped her hands tightly over her reticule. Suddenly, in front of her very eyes, a street fight exploded.

In less than two minutes, at least fifty men rushed out of the nearest taverns; they battled savagely. A window shattered; a couple of shots rang out; yells sounded. And at the second sound of gunfire, Douglass' bearers fled.

"Come back," she cried helplessly, watching them take to their heels. Impelled by fear, she thought that perhaps running was the safest thing for her to do, and she opened the chair door and got out into the street.

A Spanish sailor hurtled almost to her feet. He stumbled, got up, drawing his knife, and plunged back into the fray again. Douglass saw one man hurled back against an anchor. Agilely he flew over it in a backward somersault. "Yank, Yank!" came the cry for aid, and after it, "Athena! Athena!"

Douglass knew she should run, but she held onto the chair door, paralyzed with wonder, with amazement. Two more pistol shots cracked through the air; she shrank back. The fighting had surged both up and down the street, and just as she was about to take to her heels, another man was spewed out of the melee almost at her feet. He got up on all fours, then stared at her.

"Oh," she gasped. "Are you hurt?"

He shook his head. "Goddamn Limeys," he said breathlessly. "We got more Yanks now." He stood up; he was covered with dirt. Suddenly he reached for her.

"Let me go," cried Douglass, struggling wildly.

She almost got free. In quick succession five more shots sounded. While they rang out, Douglass found herself seized hard by one arm, and swung around. Then, across ten feet of cleared space, she saw Barney running toward her.

"Barney!" she cried.

Barney was right beside her, a pistol in each hand. She gave a quick glance at his face. "Oh, no!" she cried, fearfully, catching at his arm, clinging to it. "No, Barney!" she repeated wildly. The sailor was rooted to the spot right before her eyes. "Do not harm him!"

For a second Barney looked at him. Then there was an amazing rapid-fire change of expression on his face: anger to puzzlement to amusement. He took her by the arms lightly, looking down into her face. "Sweetheart!" He smiled. Her little flowered parasol, attached by a loop on her wrist, swung between them. A disarranged curl fell over her forehead; her sash was undone.

"Are you all right, Douglass?" he asked. "Good God—" He broke off, and shook his head incredulously. His eyes took her in again. Then he said, "I can't believe it's you. Turn around, sweetheart, and I'll tie your sash."

"I'll tie it, Barney," she whispered. But for a moment neither of them moved.

Then Barney dropped her arms. He watched her as she tied the sash. She looked so sweet; she had fastened her black-fringed eyes on him. When she had finished tying the bow she clasped her hands and waited.

He smiled and took her arm. He looked around as if to get his bearings. "We can't stand here, Douglass. Is this your chair?"

"Yes, Barney." She caught her lip in her teeth. She thought of something else to tell him. "I didn't really go into Lower Town. I was waiting. And my bearers fled!"

Since no harm had come of the adventure, Barney looked amused. "Please get in the chair." He helped her in, and spoke to the two men who were standing patiently, waiting. "You may put the box in here, Wolf."

The box Wolf was carrying was shoved in. Barney got in too and closed the door. The two sailors picked the chair up. Once more Barney surveyed her. "Before we do anything else, ma'am, like kissing, you might tell me where you live."

Douglass caught his eye. "At the Governor's," she said. "But—"

"No buts," Barney said gravely. "The Governor's, Wolf," he called. He stretched out his legs, turned toward her a little. "Wolf is my coxswain."

The chair swayed gently. Douglass sank back into the cushions; Barney's arm brushed hers. She knew what his next remark would be; and it came quickly.

"I gather you know I'm amazed to see you here, Mrs. Harris."

"And I can't believe it's you either, or that I'm me!"

"Bad grammar. Speak up."

She said simply, "Joshua is sending me home."

He shook his head slowly, remembering. She was looking at him as if he could do something about it. "I warned you not to tell him, Douglass."

"I couldn't help it, Barney!" The words flew out. Then she was quiet, remembering herself. Once more she fastened her eyes on him. "Joshua told me to tell him the truth."

Barney smiled ruefully. "So you did." He sighed. "And that is that." He reached out and took her hand, turning it over in his big one. It looked white and fragile next to his; he flexed her fingers back and forth in his. "What else, sweetheart?"

"I sail for England."

"I see," he said. He raised an eyebrow, keeping her hand imprisoned in his. "When?"

[141]

"When?" she repeated. "Why I don't quite know, Captain." She spoke fast, trying to still the rapid beating of her heart. "I—the British resident—I talked to him. My cousin's cousin—Lord Edgecomb's cousin—he owns part interest in a merchantman, the 'Falcon.' I sail on her."

At this Barney looked very amused. His brilliant smile flashed out.

"Yes," said Douglass uncertainly. "Why do you laugh?" Then since he didn't seem disposed to answer and was still smiling, she asked, "And what is in the box?"

"A snapping turtle," Barney said.

"Oh, lord," she exclaimed, drawing her legs away.

Barney laughed. "I'll save you from the turtle. The turtle has 'Lord Sandwich' carved on his back, but instead of going to England, he is a present to the Governor."

Douglass tried to maintain her decorum. What was he smiling at? "Did you have a successful voyage?" she asked, her cool voice clipping off the words.

"A bad storm hit Rodney. Nine-tenths of the fleet was disabled, including the flagship, 'Sandwich.' Cordage was badly needed but American, French and Spanish merchants had bought it all up, fast. So Rodney sent to England. In the meantime, the 'Athena' roved about almost unchallenged. Besides that, through the clever intelligence of the Marquis de Bouillé, we got a false report credited; we spread the rumor that St. Vincents and Kingston had been leveled by the hurricane that almost leveled Barbados. Rodney proceeded on that false information and spent two weeks maneuvering only to find the island impregnable and its fortifications prepared for his attacking forces. Tomorrow I send five more prizes back to Philadelphia, including Lord North, the snapping turtle, for Robert Morris."

He paused, then continued:

"Douglass," he said, "Robert Morris' turtle sails on the 'Falcon.' "

She turned slowly to look at him.

"We captured the 'Falcon' this morning. Will you write and tell your cousin's cousin I'm sorry?" He grinned. "Tell me, Douglass, do you have any money?"

She lowered her lashes. "No." Then she said, "You took the 'Falcon'?" She watched him. "Truly?"

He nodded. "I'm afraid you're fair game, and on Stasia, too. You came straight to the pirate's lair. I even have a den to carry you to."

She raised her eyes. "Don't joke, Barney."

"I have a house at White Cliffs," he said. "I'm going to take you there tonight."

"You can't," she whispered.

He said, "I shall never forget the way you looked at me when you came down those steps at Bladen's Court, Douglass. You were asking me to let you go; you were asking me to keep you with me. Let's get it straight, ma'am. Here on Stasia the same situation has developed, and this time I'm not going to let you go. Listen to me a moment."

She didn't answer and he looked over at her. "I must see the Governor now, to persuade him we did not violate Dutch neutrality." There was another cogent reason, but he didn't tell her. "After that I have a little business to transact. At seven, then, I'll call for you and take you to the reception tonight; we must put in an appearance."

She had drawn away from him, and she seemed to be regarding the field of sugar cane that stretched along the road.

"It's the Governor's birthday," Barney continued. "The Dutch put a lot of store in birthdays. I want you to look your most beautiful tonight. I suggest you have a siesta, too."

Out the window she could see the spreading lawns of the Governor's home. She felt the strong clasp of his fingers over hers.

His voice came again. "Do you know what a siesta is, ma'am? It's a nice long nap."

They were swinging quickly toward the pillared mansion, up the long drive. Three carriages stood in the crushed stone oval; liveried slaves flanked the wide white doors. The chair was set down, its door opened.

Barney got out and drew her with him.

One of his two men, jersey damp with sweat, reached in and retrieved the box.

"His lordship, sir," he said.

"I'll take him in, Wolf," Barney said, digging in his pocket and bringing out a roll of notes. He thought that not only had Wolf had unexpected labor in carrying this chair, but precious minutes of his leave had been expended. Barney gave him two five-pound notes.

"One for each, Wolf," he said. "It's a long climb."

"Jeez," Wolf said, touching his cap. "Thank you, sir."

Barney took Douglass' arm and guided her through the big doors.

Within, the wide hall stretched and another pair of latticed doors opened for them.

Barney said, "Which way is your room?" He was carrying the turtle under one arm.

"This way," said Douglass, very low, her steps beginning to slow; her heels tap-tapping on the polished inlaid floors. Closed white doors were passed, then another pair. "Here," said Douglass.

Barney reached down and opened the door. Within the room it was dusky, for the blinds were drawn against the noonday sun. Barney said, "Goodbye, then. But don't try running away."

He was smiling, and she looked up at him with her wide eyes.

"Don't try it," he continued. "I'll sail in pursuit."

"Would you, Barney?" she whispered.

He nodded. He took her in his arms. "What do you want, sweetheart?" he asked. "I'll give you the whole damned world. What do you want?"

"Nothing but you," she said. She leaned back in his arms. "Don't bring me anything!" She felt his arms tighten. He kissed her, her eyes, her cheek, her lips. Then quickly he lifted her in his arms and carried her to the bed and laid her down. He straightened and stood over her, looking down. "I warn you," he said.

With a sudden movement, she rolled over on her stomach, putting her head in the pillows.

"You'd better get some sleep now."

He turned around, picked up Lord Sandwich, and opened the door. From the bed she was watching him. "Goodbye, sweetheart," he said.

23

"WHAT I CAN'T UNDERSTAND, BARNEY," THE GOVERNOR SAID, "IS that the British captain hasn't put in an appearance."

The Governor, Count de Graaf, was standing in the center of his big study. He was short and powerfully built, with blue eyes and an almost bald head hidden under an elaborate wig.

"Well, I'll explain that, m'lord," said Barney, smiling wickedly. "He didn't want to give me his parole before six o'clock."

"You bastard," said de Graaf.

"It must be a new rule in the British merchant marine," said Barney. "Odd, isn't it?"

"Very," said de Graaf, grinning. "What's in the box, Captain?"

"Happy birthday from Lord Sandwich," Barney said. "Lord Sandwich wants you to have this turtle, that was going to be a gift to him. Not wanting to depend on his lordship's generosity too much, I intercepted it for you."

De Graaf laughed. Barney lifted the hinged door and the turtle stuck its head out and stared. The spectacle amused de Graaf; the turtle eased out and onto the polished floor. "Lord Sandwich," de Graaf read. He chuckled. "You crazy Yank," he said. "I'll eat him with relish."

"I captured Lord North, too," Barney said. "I'm sending him to Morris. I thought you'd prefer the lord of the Admiralty. Hold the box, m'lord, while I shove him from the rear. You should have seen him bite one of my officers this morning. I came out on deck to complain and found turtles." He snapped the door to, and stood up. De Graaf still looked amused, and Barney was most satisfied with this gift. De Graaf was so enormously wealthy that it was almost impossible to bring him anything.

"I think I'll postpone eating him for a while," de Graaf said. "We will have a tank built for him in the gardens and show him off. Now sit down, Barney, while I give you hell."

Barney sat down; de Graaf went back behind his desk. He picked up an inlaid gold paperweight and banged it slowly on the desk. "This island," he said slowly, "is not dubbed the Golden Rock for nothing, Barney. It's worth its weight in gold, like this." He lifted the weight and set it down. "I will give you one figure, of which you are perhaps unaware. The rent on the warehouses—the rent alone—is bringing in one million, two hundred thousand pounds sterling per annum. In the history of the world there has never been a trading port like Stasia."

"Granted, m'lord," Barney said. "That is why I would look to its fortifications."

"What?" asked de Graaf. He paid no attention. "The beaches are piled high with tobacco, rum, sugar, cannon balls. All your American correspondence goes through Stasia. Where would you trade if it weren't for Stasia? At all costs, Barney, its neutrality must be protected!"

"True, m'lord."

"Will you have a pipe?" de Graaf said absently, picking up a long clay pipe and beginning to fill it. Barney rose and picked out a pipe, scooping up some tobacco from the open jar.

De Graaf put the unlit pipe in his mouth. "We certainly do not need to talk about the value of Stasia to the American war."

"No," said Barney. "But I would like to talk about Fort Amsterdam."

De Graaf frowned. "Well?"

"I passed it today. The guns stick out through masses of prickly pears. Visibility from the fort is, I should imagine, about five yards. You've allowed houses to jam in around it. More than that, the cliff wall is crumbling. If you fired one of the twenty-two-pounders, its recoil would send it dashing down the side of the cliff into Lower Town."

De Graaf lighted his pipe. "We are neutral. We don't need guns."

Barney said, "You're neutral? There are two parties to neutrality."

"The verdom English," said de Graaf, "would not go to war with Holland, too." He thought a moment. "No. It would be too stupid."

Barney leaned forward. "Lord North," he said, "is stupid."

De Graaf thought this over. "True," he conceded in turn. "But—"

"But what, m'lord?" Barney blew out a cloud of smoke and thought about Douglass.

"No, it's impossible," de Graaf announced. "You've been away from the islands, for a few years—since '77. All are interdependent. British St. Kitts can't exist without maize from the States for its slaves. And so forth. But more than that, Barney. The British are hard pressed now; the fleet is too spread out. Do you suggest that they are willing to widen the war still further? Such a diversionary action might lose them the war on your continent!"

"I believe it would cost them that war," Barney said.

"And that would be agreeable to you?" De Graaf bit on his pipe.

"I'm an honest man, m'lord," Barney said. "We've been in this fight five years." He looked down at his hands. "According to intelligence given me by a certain Colonel Lucas, of the Austrian Netherlands, and a woman whose name I won't mention, I was told that England would declare war on you before the first of the year. It is now the end of January—just about time, m'lord, for the British

[146]

fleet commanders to receive the signal to attack, to raise the enemy flags." He got to his feet and went over to the window. "The wealth here is fabulous, m'lord. It should be protected!"

"Barney," de Graaf said slowly, "we have received such reports for four years."

Barney turned. "I know it. That's why I put little credence in it at that time. But once more—the sight of Stasia—the bulging wealth. And as a tactical campaign, it recommends itself. For it is so damned important to us, that I am not so sure that a great many military men would not recommend its seizure. It will work incredible hardships on the French islands, which succor the French fleets. It will strike at the heart of American trade. And all our ammunition is transshipped here." He was frowning. "I passed a warehouse with literally tons of cordage. The British are crying for it."

De Graaf grinned. "Forget the British. You are in Stasia. You stay long?"

"Not as long as I'd like," Barney said.

"Now about this other matter, Barney, which you diverted me from. What happened this morning? The British resident has been crying in the antechamber for two hours."

"That is because the 'Falcon' is a rich prize. She's loaded to the gunwales with rum, spices, brandies, silk, jewels. She was stopping here before the run to England. I caught her. Johns, the British captain, surrendered after one shot. If he had really believed we were within port waters, wouldn't he have stuck to his guns? Risked getting shot up a bit? Waited for the fort to fire?"

"Clever," said de Graaf. He too rose. "I'll use that argument. If he were in close, he impugned my honor and Dutch honor by not depending on us." Then he smiled. "It's been a long time since I bearded the British."

Barney's mind went back almost five years. He could see the wash of the heavy seas over the "Hornet's" decks as she hoisted her flag and as the topmen took in the royals and tops. He could see again the many ships in the blue water of Stasia's roadway. Over the crying of sea birds, and the sound of wind in the rigging had come the first boom of a saluting gun. There had been thirteen of them fired —the first salute to the stars and stripes ever offered by a foreign power.

Barney took the hand de Graaf held out in a strong grip. "By God, sir, I shall never forget it."

The Governor said, "I'll see you tonight, sir."

Barney made his way out slowly. At the big doors, he stood for a moment, absently, while he loaded both pistols and replaced them in his pockets. Then, shaking his head to offers of a chair, he struck out rapidly for the town.

His prizes had already been given into the hands of the auctioneers; their contents would go on the block tomorrow. That meant tomorrow night, at midnight, for the auctions were open till twelve —there was so much business to transact at Stasia—he could weigh anchor.

The uneasiness that bred in the back of his mind was subtle. The lure of Stasia was so apparent. He could sail at midnight tomorrow, and maybe it was the best plan. De Graaf's words were idle, Barney was sure. He wished there were something he could do about it, but the Dutchman was stubborn, and resisted advice. There should be batteries at a number of places; Barney catalogued them in his mind, for he knew the coastline well, and knew each bay even to its stretching fingers. Because of the high rocky walls Stasia could be made invulnerable; sweeping heavy fire could envelop an attacking naval force. As he passed under the shadow of Fort Amsterdam, and saw the heavy guns through the prickly pears, he was suddenly sure that he would sail tomorrow at midnight. He was passing the cliff wall, underneath the guns of this fort that overlooked Lower Town, when behind him he heard an imperative warning cry.

"Look out!"

Instinctively Barney ducked to one side. He was just in time to avoid the whistling blow of a heavy club, which grazed his shoulder and then fell to the ground. Its wielder was already showing his heels up the narrow tree-lined lane. Barney drew his pistol from his pocket, cocked it, raised it. He fired at the same time that the man who had warned him reached his side. Two shots rang out.

The smell of powder was acrid. Down the lane the man fell forward. Barney and his companion ran up to him. The man lay face down on the dust. From the sight of his striped jersey, it was plain that both bullets had found their mark.

Barney said, "Two good shots. Thank you for warning me, de Bouillé." He leaned down and turned the man over. "Seen him before, sir?"

Francis de Bouillé frowned and shook his head. The dead man wore gold loops in his ears. "Renegade sailor, hired assassin, Barney.

Using a club because it doesn't make a noise or because he has pawned his pistol."

Barney said, "If I could get my hands on the man who paid him—" He broke off, loaded the pistol again, and shoved it back in his pocket while de Bouillé did the same. "I was hoping you'd know him," he added.

De Bouillé grinned. "We never use French spies, and the man looks French. However, de Borotra has a standing offer to these renegades. Probably fifty guineas on your head, Barney. Cheap."

"Go to the devil," Barney said. "When did you get here?"

"I'm paying a visit, Barney," de Bouillé said.

"Having a good time?" Barney inquired. Then he asked, "How is Mr. Ross?"

De Bouillé grinned widely. "I say nothing, Barney. I stop in his store once in a while."

"Let me ask you if you have heard anything about British designs on Stasia."

De Bouillé looked surprised. "I need keep no grave face with you. We've heard nothing but the usual. What do you know?"

"War," said Barney. "From a Colonel Lucas."

De Bouillé scowled. "Hungarian: I've met him in Paris. Not to be trusted at all, Barney; not at all, and not very clever, either. Probably carrying false information. Unless, of course, someone who really knows told him." He smiled a little. "We do know the English are up to something. Fleet's ready to sail; we hear to Martinique. Preparations have been made—but we may be wrong. Intelligence has been perfect so far this year; in fact it's been so damned good, and we fooled Rodney so badly last month, that he is going to be foxier than usual. Would you come in here—" they were passing a tavern the officers frequented—"and have a glass or two?"

"I wish I could," Barney said. "When do you leave?"

"I'm using native canoes this time. I leave day after tomorrow, at night, Barney. I'll see you in Martinique, then." He stopped, looked at Barney and then down the dusty street. "It's a far cry from Paris, isn't it?"

Barney bowed elaborately. *"Mes regardes á votre père, M'sieur le Marquis."*

"You may reach Martinique before I do. In any event I'll see you tonight. It would be *lèse-majesté* to miss the Governor's birthday reception. Confidentially, Barney, I've asked my father for my release from this duty, which I took for fun. I want to rejoin the fleet. We do not know exactly when de Grasse comes, you know. Soon, we hope. I want you to meet de Grasse, and he desires the pleasure, immensely."

"A pleasure for me, too, m'lord," Barney said. "Au revoir."

Once more he went on down the street. He was in Lower Town now, descending rapidly along a warehouse that seemed to be fast sliding downhill. Through open doors he went into one of the largest auctions.

The smoke was so thick it was hard to see and even harder to breathe. He passed by naked blacks, ready for the auction block. The cries of the auctioneers and the answering voices of the bidders sounded. Barney was reminded of Joshua; he could imagine him here, leaning tall and elegant on his cane, calling out in his accented voice. The thought made him smile, but he didn't see Joshua; he saw British, American, French, Greek, Irish, and Armenian merchants. At the door of the Armenian office he paused a second to look out again over the thick press of men. He remembered de Bouillé's words. It was a damned far cry from Paris.

24

BARNEY KNOCKED ON THE WHITE DOOR. IT WAS OPENED FOR HIM, and he stepped in, closing it softly. He had never seen her look so beautiful.

She was dressed in white, yet the shimmering white satin was no whiter than her bare shoulders and arms. As she walked toward him, the gauzy poufs of the gown floated away from the slim shiny sheath.

Her eyes were deep grey pools fringed by blackest heavy lashes; the faintest flush on her cheeks glowing pale beside the warm red of her lips. He bowed.

"I should have brought a bodyguard, Douglass," he said with sincerity. "They will snatch you away from me."

"I'm not afraid of that, Barney," she said.

He took her hand; it felt cool. He stepped back to see her better.

She faced him. "This afternoon—you did not by any chance see Joshua?"

The answer was brief. "No."

And even if Joshua were here—"You do not understand, Barney," she said, across the five feet that separated them.

He crossed the five feet quickly, towering over her.

"I think I do," he said.

"I only want you," she whispered.

He looked down at the curve of her lips as she spoke, the shadowed eyes. Then he said, "Douglass, if we don't leave now, we never will. I would prefer you to be in my house." He opened the door and they started down the hall. He heard her ask, in a small voice:

"You mean tonight?"

"Yes, tonight, too. But I mean I want you to stay there. It's safer. I have four men to look after the grounds, and two women, one a cook. They came with the house." He guided her through the huge doorway to the ballroom.

It looked like fairyland. The carved ceiling and walls were decorated with orange and citrus branches in bloom. The room opened into the gardens, and on the royal palms crystal lamps hung in up-going spirals. The brilliant red and gold and blue of dress uniforms vied with the magnificent dress of the women. Music played.

"The Armenian there measures his income in millions," said Barney. "He runs two auctions, and owns Lord knows how many vessels. He'll eat a bit of supper and then disappear to gamble somewhere."

Douglass stared at the jewels on the woman beside him. The Armenian bowed to Barney as they went by. "Cards later, sair?" he asked.

Barney said, "My regrets," and smiled. The Armenian surveyed Douglass broodingly, studying each feature.

Barney steered her over toward two men, standing at the edge of a little indoor grove of potted fruit trees; they were drinking champagne and the candlelight winked on the glasses. He said, "Those two are the British resident—whom you know—and a British spy, de Borotra. I want a few words with them."

Douglass heard herself acknowledging their introduction. She listened to their talk. The British resident was saying:

"I detected your fine hand in Governor de Graaf's decision on the 'Falcon' case, Barney. It seems that Johns impugned Dutch honor when he lowered his colors."

"Myself, I thought he impugned English honor," said Barney levelly.

There was a moment's silence in which Douglass caught her breath and waited to see what would happen next. Barney had said that de Borotra was an English spy, and yet his Spanish accent was heavy. "Cowardice," said de Borotra, "in one man reflects on all men, let us say." He sipped his wine.

"Two shots in the back of a fleeing man mean something to you, then," Barney said. "In case you have not yet discovered it, de Bouillé and I disposed of your hired assassin."

"My dear Barney," said de Borotra.

The resident said, "On my honor, sir, I know nothing of this!"

"You bloody the fingers of only one hand, sir?"

There was another silence. Then de Borotra said to Douglass, "How long are you and Barney staying with us on Stasia, madam?"

Douglass said honestly, "Why, I don't know, sir," and she was surprised when Barney flushed, angered and protective, said to the Spaniard:

"There may come a time when I'll have to dispose of you myself, sir."

De Borotra acknowledged this with a slight bow. "Hurry then, Barney. We have a further charge against you now. Wearing a British naval uniform in wartime is a crime punishable by hanging."

"That's why I issue this warning, sir. Stay off the streets till I leave, or you'll never have the pleasure of watching me kick my heels." He bowed and Douglass found herself walking away with him. Her fingers pressed against his arm.

She whispered, "Will he?"

"Yes," said Barney grimly. "I've given that warning to one other man. I meant both of them!"

She stopped. In her wide grey eyes was the same look he had seen there before, questioning, unsure. He said harshly, "I'm a rough bastard for you, am I not?"

The room seemed to recede and there was nobody in it but him. "Barney," she said, "did you—"

"No, but only because I haven't had the chance. This is no place for you!" He glanced about. He saw de Bouillé and the Governor and Lady de Graaf. "There are the only three people who are fit for you to consort with! I want you to meet Lord de Bouillé; he is

an old friend." Then suddenly he smiled. "I do know a few respectable people. And sometimes I behave myself. Rarely, though."

Douglass heard herself congratulating the Governor on his birthday, greeting Lady de Graaf, and being presented to de Bouillé.
De Bouillé bent over her white fingers. He looked at her with undisguised admiration. He murmured in French that he would be
happy if she would dance with him. Barney and de Graaf stood
together and watched them move away.

"So stunned he forgot his English," said de Graaf. "I did not
know that you were friendly with Madam Harris."

"I wanted to speak with you about her," Barney said. "I'm taking
her with me tonight."

De Graaf muttered, "You lucky dog."

Barney had told the truth without thinking. Now he amended
his words. "Madam wished me to tell you how much she has enjoyed
your hospitality," Barney said. "I am lending my house to her because I believe it is safer. I have convinced her she will be in less
danger there."

De Graaf laughed. "I expect you're very convincing, sir."

Barney did not smile. "Just a matter of her safety, m'lord," and
de Graaf looked askance. Then he shrugged his massive shoulders. A
passing servant stopped and offered a silver tray with glasses of
champagne. Barney took one and watched Douglass.

He found himself waiting impatiently for the music to stop. She
was engrossed in the steps, except every once in a while she would
look up at de Bouillé and smile at something he had said. When the
music ended, de Bouillé released her hand reluctantly; her head
was tipped back and she was saying something to him. Barney
walked toward her fast, coming up to interrupt a sentence. She
turned to see him beside her.

"I would have returned madam to you, sir," de Bouillé murmured, one black eyebrow raised with a smile.

"I'm sure you would, m'lord," Barney said.

His eyes met Barney's and his smile widened, whereupon he
turned away. Douglass said, "Why you didn't give me time to say
goodbye?"

"No," said Barney.

"I liked him," she said.

He said abruptly, "I hired a carriage, Douglass. Later, Lucie will
join you."

They were near a huge four-shelved sideboard laden with sweet-meats from four continents. Douglass studied it.

"Did you hear me?" Barney asked.

"Yes," she said. "I was wondering if I wanted to walk around the garden."

He looked into her eyes. "Do you?"

"Barney," she said. "I don't know."

He took her arm. She walked at his side. He was conscious of the other men's eyes on her; it seemed to take more than a long minute to walk the sixty feet across the ballroom into the wide deserted hall. But once in the hall, she stopped, dropping her hand from his arm.

He made a move to recapture it. She stood back against the wall; gradually she raised her eyes. "Barney," she whispered.

He didn't answer; he waited for her to go on.

"I wanted to tell you something."

"Yes."

She spoke fast then. "When I came to take the codebooks that night," she made a gesture, "I never thought it might deprive you of aid in danger! It was Joshua who said it. I—" She reminded herself thus that it had been that headlong act which had brought her here to him.

"I knew that." He waited a moment. "Is that all?"

She nodded.

"Then come, darling," he muttered, taking her hand. The doors were open, and he took her down the two shallow steps.

Down the line of carriages one swung out and started toward them. She said, low, "Is it far?"

"Scarcely a quarter of a mile."

The carriage was coming closer.

"Is it on the sea?"

"On the top of White Cliffs," he said.

The carriage door flew open. She got in, sitting straight. Barney sat down beside her and they started down the drive.

For a moment he studied her. The time before she would belong to him could be reckoned in minutes. Because he was only too well aware of his passion for her, he said, almost curtly:

"There is a maid at the house. Will you want her services?"

They had turned out of the grounds and were rolling rapidly down the high road across the top of the island. The carriage lamps swung. In their dimness, her grey eyes looked back at him.

If she answered he never heard her. He took her in a close embrace, locking her in his arms against him. When the carriage rolled to a stop, he lifted her from it.

A long flight of stone steps was cut into the rocks. The wind cried a little. Far below, the sea pounded and the restless water stretched. In his arms he bore her easily up the steep steps to the house on the rocks.

25

"M'SIEUR!" LUCIE JUMPED TO HER FEET. "I HAD NO IDEA IT WAS you, sir! You didn't speak and so I didn't recognize your voice."

Joshua nodded and shut the door. "I knocked," he said, looking around past the bed and a table with a lot of bottles on it and silver backed brushes.

His first feeling was vague relief that Douglass was not here. Guilt had nagged him considerably lately. He looked at Lucie.

She was wearing a gay blouse and matching ruffled skirt. Her hair, instead of being braided, was massed in waves on top of her head. She had stood rapidly at his entrance, and the filmy material on which she had been sewing had slipped to the floor in a pool of color at her feet. Joshua leaned down and retrieved it, looking at it critically as it dangled from his hand.

"What on earth is it, Lucie?" he inquired.

"A peignoir, m'sieur," she said; her eyes shone deep blue.

"It looks like a curtain," Joshua said, holding it out. "You can see through it," he added, and looked at the swell of her breast and the tiny waist. "Enchanting idea," he commented, and smiled a little. "You've changed your hair. Did you miss me?"

She looked across to his tall figure; he was very tanned. "I assure you," she began, "vastly."

Joshua grinned. "You're sounding just like a lady of fashion, Lucie." He imitated her. "Oh, but vastly!"

"You puzzle me," she said gravely. "Should I not?"

Joshua deliberately misunderstood. "Should I not puzzle you, Lucie?"

Her delicate brows drew together. "No, sir. I meant should I not—" She stopped. She smiled enchantingly. "You jest."

"*Oui*," said Joshua. "But if you are going to be so damned fashionable, you might ask me to sit down."

"Oh," she said. "I beg your pardon! Please sit down."

"You sit first," Joshua said, smiling down at her.

"Oh," she repeated. She sighed and sat, then looked over to him. She said, "I missed you vastly."

He laughed. "I'm glad you had kind thoughts. I imagine madam did not think thus." He regarded the tips of his shoes. "One thing a man should learn, Lucie, is never to take what a woman does seriously. I should have bounced her over my knee and whacked the hell out of her." Having thus delivered this, he felt better. "I suppose she told you, didn't she?"

"*Oui*," said Lucie.

"The trouble was that I lost my temper completely."

"*Oui*, I know," said Lucie very soberly.

"Well, Lucie, where is madam?"

Lucie hesitated.

"Well?" Joshua said.

Lucie took the wrong stitch. "Madam is with Captain Barney."

Joshua pondered this. "I gather from the tone of your voice that your sentence is supposed to have deep import. It's almost noon. Out with it, Lucie. I gather you mean madam did not return from the ball last night."

"*Oui, m'sieur.*"

Joshua got to his feet and went over to the long French windows. He swung around. "Has madam communicated with you?"

"No, sir." Then she said, "She loves him, sir! So much!"

She could not tell what he was thinking. Finally he said, "I came for two women, and have only one." He came back to her. "Some disposition will have to be made of you, Lucie." Then he added, "I have your gold for you. But I can't leave you here. Impossible." He glanced around the luxurious bedroom. "God Almighty," he said to himself, then he looked at Lucie again.

She said, "Madam will let me know, sir."

"I'm aware of that, Lucie. It's whether you should be permitted to follow madam, and—" He broke off.

Lucie tried in vain to keep her mind on the sewing. She said, "Oh, sir, what are you thinking?"

[156]

She was surprised by the vehemence of his answer. "God knows! I can't be developing morals at my age. I'm thirty, you know. How old are you, Lucie?"

"Eighteen. I'm old enough."

He laughed. "I'm sure you are. But I thought you were seventeen."

"I've had a birthday, *m'sieur.*"

"You did?" Joshua smiled. "When?"

"On Christmas day."

"That settles it," he said. "You're a Christmas present."

She stood up. "Please tell me what you're thinking."

He said, "If I did, you'd slap me. If you did, I'd toss you on that bed there. Does that answer your question?" He looked down at her. "Red-haired women have such white skin. Now listen to me, Lucie. I'm no man for you. You're too damned sweet; my intentions are not honorable. I'm going to send you back to the States and you can marry George."

He thought her eyes turned deep purple. Slowly she shook her head. "No," she said.

Joshua looked at her closely. "You wouldn't enter a convent, would you?" he asked anxiously.

"No," said Lucie. "But I do not marry George!"

"You'll change your mind when you get back home," Joshua said.

She said, "You decide everything for me!"

"Damn it," said Joshua. "Shall I let you decide, then?"

"*Oui!*"

"All right," he said angrily. "Decide."

She turned away from him. "I must think," she whispered. "But most of all, I must pick my own man." She put her hand on his arm; she looked up into his eyes. "Madam did."

Joshua removed her hand from his arm. "Look, Lucie, I have no business fooling around with you; you're in my care. I'm going to take you home with me and find you a good husband. And that's that." He picked up the swordstick he had laid down on the bed. "Now, you may decide what you wish. We sail tomorrow."

He went to the door and opened it—was just about to turn and say once more to be ready at twelve, but instead he bumped into de Bouillé. Both men apologized hastily. Then they looked at each other.

They both said their names at once. Then de Bouillé bowed, and announced he had a message for *Mademoiselle* Lucie. Joshua was about to go on, when he decided he had better stay. He followed de Bouillé back into the room, as de Bouillé handed the note to Lucie.

"Captain Barney gave it to me," he said. "I believe I've heard Barney mention you are one of his very good friends. I, too." He smiled.

Lucie was reading rapidly. She looked up from the letter. "Captain Barney says, sir, that I am to go to madam tomorrow and bring her things! And stay with her!"

There was deep silence. De Bouillé looked from one to the other as both Joshua and Lucie faced each other. Finally Joshua said, "You may pack madam's things. You may pack your own. You're going to sail with me, and go back home! That is final! Come on, sir." He strode to the door, and de Bouillé followed him. He followed him down the long hall, and outside. Once there, de Bouillé permitted himself to smile.

"Would you care to ride down to Lower Town with me? I thought—a little dinner, a little wine?"

Joshua grinned. "I've been looking forward to a free day for some time, sir. I'd be glad to go."

26

DOUGLASS WAKENED SLOWLY. HALF AWAKE, SHE REACHED OUT with her foot toward the other side of the bed. She felt nothing but smooth linen.

She sighed. "Barney," she whispered.

There was no answer. She turned on her side, opening her eyes. He was not there. But she was suddenly conscious of rapid footsteps. Quickly she rolled over and buried her head in the pillow.

The door opened gently. She waited. But the steps went past the bed and to the windows; she heard the sound of the blinds being raised. She sat up.

Brilliant sunshine flooded the room. A small Negress turned from the windows; as Douglass regarded her she made a small curtsey. "I am Esther, madam," she announced. "It is after one o'clock."

"Oh," said Douglass. Her hair fell over her bare shoulders. "One o'clock?" she repeated. "Oh, you should have wakened me before! Suppose—" she looked at the white door— "suppose he had come?"

Esther smiled. "He will not come yet, madam. Captain Barney left a message he would be back at two."

Douglass heaved a sigh. Then she smiled back at Esther tentatively. She said, "What do I—" she paused. "First I would like a dish of tea, Esther."

"Yes, madam." They were both silent for a minute. Douglass looked helplessly at her; she felt that Esther knew more about what she should do next. Then she recovered herself. "Will you fetch me hot water, Esther? And hand me a big towel, please."

Esther complied, getting the towel from the washstand drawer. Douglass wrapped it around herself and stood up. "I'll wait on the balcony for my tea," she said.

"Yes, madam." Esther disappeared. Left alone, Douglass crossed the room, and went out on the small stone balcony that overlooked the sea.

The sun glittered on the rolling expanse of blue water. The island of Saba rose from it, green and rocky, with its white rim of breaking surf. There was no harbor at all on Saba. Last night it had loomed up dark out of the sea. Last night . . .

She drew a deep breath. The wind blew her disheveled curls. The sudden sound of the door again made her stand bolt upright.

But it was Esther, with the tea. She set it down on the little table; Douglass herself sat gingerly on the edge of the chaise longue and held the towel with one hand and the cup of tea in the other.

It was hot. But she drank it hastily, gulping it down. Through the open doors to the bedroom she could see a big Negress helping Esther with the preparations for her bath. They laid a grass mat down first, and then put the tub on it. Douglass went back into the bedroom.

By the time she had pinned her hair up on her head the bath was ready. Douglass closed her eyes while Esther soaped her back. But when she had stepped out of the tub, and had finished drying herself on the big towel, she looked at Esther helplessly again.

Esther came to the rescue. "I washed and pressed your petticoat and underthings, madam."

Douglass donned them hastily. But her hair was still unbrushed and—"I cannot wear that ballgown," she announced. It was only two o'clock.

She was sitting at the table, while Esther took the pins out of her hair. She began to brush it. She said, over Douglass' head, "There is a robe, madam. When I finish your hair I will get it."

Douglass nodded. "Pin that part up loosely, and let the back curls go." She surveyed it when it was done. It met her approval. Esther held the lacy robe up for inspection.

Douglass put her arms in it and looked at it. She made a slow decision. "I don't think I'll wear it," she said. "I am dressed enough. I am all covered up," she added.

"Yes, madam," Esther said. The big Negress returned and helped take the bath things away. Douglass went out on the balcony again, and sat down on the chaise longue. She sat there for five minutes, stiffly, when she suddenly and determinedly eased over onto the pillows and propped herself up. She had just finished getting settled when she heard Barney's steps. She turned.

He was standing about ten feet away in the doorway. He had paused to take in the picture of her lying there; then he came toward her.

She was lying in the center of the chaise. He came to a stop beside it. "Good afternoon, Douglass," he said.

"Good afternoon," Douglass said.

Barney grinned. "I'm not going to eat you, wench. Your eyes are as big as stars." He laughed, and sat down on the edge of the chaise. Then he said, "Move over, darling."

She hesitated. Barney looked a little puzzled, and a little amused. Douglass moved slightly, and Barney stretched out beside her and took her in his arms, tipping her face up to his. "What's the matter, sweetheart?" he asked. He looked into her eyes. He kissed her lips. When he released them he buried his head on the curve of her throat. "What's the matter?" he murmured.

She held him tight. "Nothing."

"Tell me," he said.

"I love you, Barney," she whispered.

He raised his head, and kissed the tip of her nose.

She leaned back. "But why did you leave me?"

He smiled slowly. "So that is the matter?" He pushed her back against the pillows with his hands on her shoulders. "It was an action born of strict necessity—my leaving. I had to attend an auction." He was looking down at her face as he spoke, his fingers in the thick curl on her shoulder.

[160]

"You are so beautiful."

She lowered her lashes. "I'm not dressed, even."

He slipped his arms around her.

"You're too much dressed. I feel a lot of hooks back here."

He watched her flush a little. "They're just the fastening of the petticoat at my waist."

Barney grinned. "That's cheering news. But what's this strap?" He pulled it off her shoulder.

Douglass tried to pull it back up. He caught her hand. "All I want to do is kiss this little hollow in your shoulder and the strap covers it up. And there was a robe in the closet."

In between his kisses he heard her answer.

"I didn't want to wear it, Barney."

He raised his head again and looked at her.

"I was afraid," she whispered, "that you might remember—someone else who wore it. Barney—" She stopped.

"No one else has worn it, darling," he said easily. It was not much of a lie—he couldn't even remember the last time he had been here, it was so long ago.

"Even so," she said, low.

He looked at her steadily. "No compromise, sweetheart?"

She knew what he meant. "Only for you," she answered. Vaguely she realized that he did not understand. She thrust the thought aside. It was impossible to think. She loved him. "Are you hungry, darling? Dinner is probably ready. Are you hungry?"

He nodded. He held her close but his eyes were closed and he pulled her up a little to put his head on her breast. "Sleepy," he said. "I was up at dawn."

She put her hands on his dark head and ran her fingers through the thick hair. In less than a minute she was sure he was asleep.

His head was heavy. The dark lashes lay against his tanned cheek; she traced one finger along the black brows. His big hand still lay on her arm. She didn't move, for fear of wakening him.

In the distance was the crying of the sea birds. The surf pounded. Occasionally she could smell a whiff of cooking. Every sense was alive and alert. The sight of the sea, the feel of the tropic sea air and heat on her bare arms and shoulders; the weight of his head and arm, the sound of Barney's rhythmic breathing; the look of his face in sleep. She closed her eyes, too.

He startled her when he spoke. He hadn't moved. He asked, "Am I too heavy?"

Her eyes had flown open.

"I am too heavy," he went on, lazily, and moved his head over onto the pillows beside hers. He stretched out. From the pillows he regarded her. "I'm used to taking quick naps, darling," he said, as if in explanation. "Douglass, I sail tonight at one."

She repeated, "Tonight, Barney? Tonight?"

"At the stroke of midnight, I shall be gone from here, darling. That's the trouble with getting mixed up with sailors. I think you should—" He broke off, frowning a little.

She waited what seemed to her a long time. "What should I do, tell me!"

"Don't hurry me." He took her hand. "This is a difficult problem, where to stow you."

"Sir," said Douglass, "I can stow myself."

He chuckled. "On the contrary. I had already despatched a note to Lucie by de Bouillé, telling her to attend you here tomorrow, and pack your things."

Douglass frowned, slightly. "You did?"

"Yes, ma'am," he said positively. "I did. Don't you want me to take care of you?"

Under his dark eyes, she answered, "Yes, Barney."

He intended to return to Stasia soon, in a week or less. But of course he couldn't tell her that. In the meantime—she was looking at him with her grey eyes, her red mouth was too near. He turned over and began to kiss her, and his passion for her mounted swiftly now. As he felt at her waist to unfasten the hooks, he remembered what he had been saying. "Darling," he whispered against her mouth, "wait for me here. Wait for me here."

27

THE PALEST SIGNS OF DAWN WERE IN THE SKY. THE LANTERNS AT the mastheads of each ship had been extinguished for twenty minutes.

On the deck of the ninety-four gun flagship "H.M.S. Sandwich,"

Admiral Rodney stood motionless behind the helmsman, noting absently that the date on the open log was February third. The breeze was cool this morning, and he felt the rheumatic twinges in his left leg shoot their darting pains up into his thigh. He set his lips.

To his side his officers were silent and watchful. The van of the fleet, under Admiral Samuel Hood, was dead ahead, the cool morning wind bellying the white sails.

All ships were cleared for action. The war on the Caribbean would blaze forth today, February third, 1781. It was singularly fitting, Rodney thought, that British guns would open it, and this fleet strike first and fast, seizing the offensive and thus keeping it within his capable and careful hands.

He had memorized the map of the harbor of St. Eustatious. In ten minutes the dawn would reveal it to his eyes. And it might not be necessary to fire a single shot to complete this morning's action. Already the van had passed under the guns of the sleeping fort; within the harbor the merchant ships could hardly resist, and the few ships of war and privateers—they would be helpless before already runout guns of the fleet. Yesterday at St. Lucia, he had embarked a company of marines.

Mist was rising now. But the skies were lighter. Mist floated over the grey water, curled around the dim shapes of the ships at anchor, curled around the distant upright Quill, as it thrust upward like a standing sentinel. Like sultry smoke, the mist gathered and blew.

He drew from his blue coat a sealed envelope and handed it to the officer who waited. There were two other officers with him, and since one of them was Rodney's son, Rodney smiled briefly at all of them. Rodney watched as they stepped into their waiting boat.

Then he walked to the rail. The boats pulled away fast. The roadway of Stasia was completely blocked off. The town was under the British guns. If there was powder stored in those warehouses, terrible destruction could be wrought, and the whole island could be shaken to its foundations. The Quill, which Rodney could see plainly now— even that might shiver and shake.

The twinge of rheumatic pain knifed up his leg again. Nevertheless he began to take his morning walk, up and down, across the weather side of the quarterdeck.

Governor de Graaf struggled into his dressing gown, put his feet in his slippers. He opened his door.

Red-coated British marines formed a barrier. He stalked past them, smoothing his hair. In his study he found three British officers, in their blue uniforms. One of them handed him an envelope. De Graaf tore it open.

He already knew what it must contain. Therefore he had difficulty in reading it. He forced himself to assimilate the words.

"We, the general officers commanding in chief his Britannic Majesty's fleet and army in the West Indies, do, in his royal name, demand an instant surrender of the island of Saint Eustatious, and its dependencies, with everything in and belonging thereto, for the use of his said Majesty.

"We give you one hour from the delivery of this message to decide. If any resistance is made, you must abide by the consequences."

And the heavy signatures. G. B. Rodney. J. Vaughn.

Governor de Graaf raised his eyes from the single page. Anger and shame blotted out thought. His great shoulders hunched; he crumpled the paper and threw it on the floor.

Then he set his heel on it. "I trust you have a copy?" he sneered.

Young Rodney took a step forward. "How—" he began angrily.

De Graaf cut him short. "I expect to be addressed as Your Excellency!"

John Rodney was speechless with anger. He looked at the British seal, crushed under de Graaf's shoe. "Do you accept our terms?" he ground out.

De Graaf smiled. His voice was silky. He drew his watch from his pocket. "Using the words of Admiral Rodney himself," he said mockingly, "I have one hour, sirs." He kicked the note with his foot. "I suggest you read it." He started for the door, and at the doorway he turned. "Now get out!"

He held the door open for them. One by one they filed past. De Graaf, shaking with anger, watched their blue backs walk away from him. He had an hour. But what was he going to do with it?

Joshua woke slowly. Thirst wakened him. He started to sit up and felt a throb of pain in his head. He sank back again and closed his eyes.

He opened them slowly. The ceiling at which he stared was unfamiliar. Forgetting his head, he sat up and felt for his wallet. Its bulk reassured him; he realized he was fully dressed save for his shoes, and he turned his head to see who was in bed with him.

He saw the back of de Bouillé's head. He, too, was dressed; he was sound asleep, sprawled out. Joshua tried to remember where they were.

While he was remembering thirst again assailed him. He got up and went to the elaborate table on which stood a pitcher of water. He poured a glass, and drank it; he poured another glass. His head ached.

But now he knew where they were. A very high-priced bawdy house. As Joshua looked at de Bouillé, he grinned. He said aloud: "I hope to God they didn't charge me fifty guineas for you."

De Bouillé stirred. He opened his eyes. When he saw Joshua he tried to sit up and sank back. His eyes closed. "And I was going to have fun." He groaned, and turned over. "I remember picking a Ma'moiselle, and it wasn't you," he murmured in the pillow. "Do you suppose twenty-eight is too old?"

"Considering it carefully, in the light of what daylight there is," Joshua said, "I seem to remember vaguely we were very drunk when we got here."

"Don't make excuses for us," de Bouillé said, trying again to sit up and succeeding. He made a terrible grimace and held his head.

Joshua decided to go over to the window to look out and see if they were where he thought. He squinted through the glass, and then pushed the window farther open and stuck his head out.

It was barely dawn. But it was light enough for him to descry immediately the red coats of British marines, marching double file, past the corner fifty feet down and they were followed by three British officers.

They filed past the corner, muskets over their shoulders, and Joshua turned from the window. "De Bouillé," he said calmly, "the British are here."

De Bouillé swung his legs off the bed. "What did you say?" he asked.

"You heard me," said Joshua. He inclined his head to the corner. "They're marching up the main street—a detail, ready for action, back toward the beach. They were accompanied by three officers."

De Bouillé had been drinking a glass of water. He sat down on the bed and reached for his shoes. "Let's get going," he said, standing up.

Joshua was already at the door. "I remember seeing Captain

Black, last night!" He raised his voice. "Yanks!" he shouted. "The Redcoats are here." He opened the nearest door and flung it open. A woman's cry answered him, but Joshua had found Black the first try.

"Black," he shouted.

Captain Black sat up in bed. "Are you still drunk?" he wanted to know.

"The British are here!" Joshua said. "Come on!" He started down the hallway, flinging open doors as he came on them. Black appeared in the hall behind him, wearing his trousers only. "Are you serious?" he roared at Joshua, twenty feet down the hall.

Joshua turned. "Yes!"

De Bouillé was standing at the top of the stairway, loading his pistol. "Come on!" He started down the steps.

Black dived back into the bedroom for his pistols, and his belt. Fastening it, he ran down the stairway after Joshua and de Bouillé, and following them was another American they none of them knew. He caught up to them in the street.

"Are you sure?" he panted. He had snatched up his shirt and was putting his arms in it.

"I'm Rourke, first mate of the 'Salem Belle'!"

The four of them stood there in the empty street. With a single thought they raced for the next corner, where they could see over the harbor. What they saw was enough.

"Rodney," Joshua said.

"What a sight," murmured de Bouillé. His quick mind was recapitulating. While the others stared at the line of battleships that completely blocked the harbor, and had under its guns the only fort, he said, "What you saw, Joshua, was an ultimatum being delivered to the Governor! Presumably we have about thirty minutes left of the probable hour they allowed him!"

Black said, "There is no escape by way of the sea!"

"No," said de Bouillé. "You two go to the beach and rouse the crews; we'll go through the town and arouse the Americans here! Then make for the Governor." He swept them all with his black eyes. "We can offer to defend the town. We can offer our services!"

Without a word Black and Rourke started down the steep street fast, raising their voices as they went. As their cry of "Yank. Abandon ship!" rose up from the beaches, and echoed over the water, the Dutch town of Oranjestad, Upper and Lower Town, was roused by the cry used five years before by an American named Revere at Lexington. Joshua couldn't think of any better words. He shouted, "The Redcoats are coming!"

De Bouillé took it up. They raced through the streets banging on doors, and from the taverns, the bawdy houses, from side alleys and poor lodging houses, the Americans poured. Half dressed, but carrying what weapons they had, they responded to the old battle cry.

Doors banged and stood open; windows flew up. Gunfire sounded. By the time Joshua and de Bouillé reached Upper Town, they had at least three hundred men with them, and more coming.

"To the Governor!" de Bouillé shouted.

Five minutes had passed.

At the top of the long street, leading down into Lower Town, Joshua paused for just a moment, to see the men behind him streaming up the hill, and coming from the side alleys. From here, too, he saw that already boats were pulling from the American merchantmen in the harbor, loaded to the gunwales with men. There was only one American privateer—Black's vessel. As Joshua watched, he saw the first line of battleships moving closer for the beginning burst of fire.

"Horses," cried de Bouillé, motioning the men on.

He and Joshua ran through the garden of a lovely home, making for the stables. Within, they each seized a horse, and, saddleless, galloped out, through the garden. And once more, from astride a flying horse, came Paul Revere's cry.

"The Redcoats are coming!"

De Bouillé repeated it in French, in Dutch. It was shouted out through the narrow ways, as they also yelled encouragement to the men who were following, afoot and ahorse.

Every stable was looted quickly of its animals. From hastily opened windows, British officers and seamen got into the fight. Musket fire sounded; Limeys rushed into the streets and hurled themselves into the fray. But the Americans didn't stop to fight now. They pushed onward, toward the goal Joshua and de Bouillé indicated. They quickly disposed of whoever tried to stop them, leaving dead and wounded behind, of enemy, of their own number. They pushed on.

Meanwhile the relentless hands of a watch were ticking. De Graaf had laid it on the bureau; he was dressing in Lady de Graaf's bedroom.

[167]

"Accoutre yourself finely, my dear," he said over his shoulder as he surveyed the neatly clubbed wig that was being laid on his head. As always, he reached up and settled it himself.

The whole mansion was alive with sound. Lady de Graaf turned to her husband as her maid hooked her gown. "M'lord," she asked. "What—"

He picked up his watch and put it in his waistcoat pocket. "We shall surrender in style," he said, and then, ears alert like a hunting dog's, he dashed suddenly to the window. Across the spreading lawns, down the road he saw two flying horses; he heard the sounds of more horses, and men. He jumped immediately to a conclusion.

"The Americans!"

He stood rooted to the spot. More horsemen rounded the curve and attained the level heights of the top of the island. He saw the figures of men, running.

"The Americans!" he repeated. He crossed the room fast, seizing his wife by the hand. "We'll greet them!"

Lady de Graaf gathered her skirts in one hand and ran too, at his side. He passed the great front doors which already stood open, and were flanked as usual by the liveried slaves. He went past them, and around and up the great state stairway, to its landing.

On the landing were latticed doors opening out onto a curved balcony. De Graaf led his wife to the rail, between the white columns that rose on past and up. By the time they reached there, Joshua and de Bouillé were galloping down the drive. Slowly de Graaf took his watch from his pocket. Then he replaced it.

"We have ten minutes, m'lady," he said quietly.

She had no notion of what he was going to do. At his side was his dress sword. As Joshua and de Bouillé stopped under the balcony, still ahorse, he bowed to them.

"Good morning, gentlemen."

Both men slid to the ground. Both bowed to the Governor and his wife. Then Joshua's Virginia accent said breathlessly:

"We have come to help defend the island!"

"There are more of us, m'lord, m'lady," said de Bouillé, catching his breath.

"So I see, m'lord," de Graaf replied. The men were coming across the lawns; the running men had left the road and cut through the fields of sugar cane, the lawns of other homes. They were streaming fast, leaping hedges, while down the drive pounded the horsemen.

De Graaf stood silent and motionless, unable to speak. He glanced at his wife and saw she was biting her lip, and that there were tears in her eyes. "Don't do that, my dear," he whispered.

She turned toward him and smiled, putting her hand on his arm. But she still refrained from asking him what he was going to do. Surely there could not be any time left!

But there was. Only five minutes had passed. And about fifteen hundred men were massed in the gardens, and down the driveway Captain Black came, ahorse.

He brought his mare to a flying stop under the balcony. "I've garrisoned the fort," he cried. "With three hundred seamen!"

De Graaf reckoned quickly; there were eighteen hundred to two thousand Americans on the island, and most of them here. They would fall into British hands. And it was his fault. He looked past the garden, to the road. The sun shone now, on the marching marines, who were coming for his answer.

He raised his voice. "Yanks."

Cheering interrupted him, as the men waved their muskets, or whatever weapon they had managed to seize in their mad flight to the mansion.

De Graaf raised his hand for quiet. In a moment the men would spot the British marines, coming inexorably onward.

He said, "First I must tell your Captain Black that Amsterdam Fort is completely indefensible. Its guns cannot be fired." From three days ago de Graaf could hear Barney saying, "The visibility is five yards. The guns would crash through to Lower Town."

There was a swelling murmur from the massed men; then it died away, but one voice had said clearly, "Let us try it!"

De Graaf answered this. "I cannot! There are women and children in the towns, the islands. Fort Oranje could not hold out against the heavy guns of the fleet. The British have asked surrender of St. Eustatious and all its possessions, goods, inhabitants. It shall be surrendered to them."

The British marines swung smartly into the drive. The Americans saw them. And de Graaf roared:

"Hold your fire!"

Lady de Graaf held tight onto the balcony rail, watching this curious scene with incredulous eyes.

De Graaf shouted: "They cannot be harmed; they bring a summons!"

Slowly the Americans moved aside to let twenty Redcoats march solemnly onward, looking neither to left nor right, sun glinting on their shouldered muskets; in perfect formation they came steadily toward the mansion.

American trigger fingers itched. The three British officers walked easily through the press of men.

The officers stood beneath de Graaf, with Joshua on one side and de Bouillé on the other. Silence prevailed, as the marines were halted by a sharp command from their sergeant. In the silence de Graaf's voice came again.

"I accept your terms," he said evenly. "As the Governor of St. Eustatious, Saba and St. Maarten, I hereby surrender these islands with everything in and belonging thereto, in accordance with the summons received this morning, one hour ago. Fort Oranje and Fort Amsterdam have been notified."

His voice died away. Then he said, "Now, Yanks! Do what you will! Get going! And remember, though we were friends before, now we are allies!"

De Bouillé and Joshua acted instantly. "Rush 'em!" yelled Joshua, hurling himself forward at the first marine, his pistol raised as a club. Before the marine could shoulder his musket, he was felled. Joshua grabbed the weapon.

The twenty marines, engulfed, went down in a matter of minutes. De Bouillé had knocked one officer to the ground. He put his foot on his stomach and leaned down to draw the sword from the scabbard. "We always were at war, sir," he reminded, jabbing the Englishman with the point of the weapon. Then de Bouillé grinned. He released his prisoner. All the British were disarmed now; a couple lay face down. De Bouillé raised the sword high.

"Every man on his own!"

It was exactly seven o'clock. At Fort Oranje, in accordance with instructions sent thirty minutes before by de Graaf, the flag came down. At Fort Amsterdam it came down, too. The Americans within essayed the streets, spreading out through Lower Town, entering taverns, bawdy houses, shops, warehouses. And the first detachments of British marines marched up from the beaches.

What happened next in Lower Town was to make Admiral Rodney livid with rage. His troops, supposedly, were under order to seize and padlock all stores, shops, warehouses, of this surrendered island. His marines and the overseas regiments were well-seasoned troops and the first file of marines passed smartly up from the beach. A musket shot felled one of their number, and their lieutenant whirled. The shot had come from the tavern he stood before. He spoke to a sergeant, motioning him to take ten men.

The sergeant approached the door of the tavern and threw it open. A bottle of whiskey caught him full on the head. He dropped. After the bottle came a heavy bar chair.

One of the marines grabbed the chair and heaved it through the window, taking frame and glass with it. The next second it flew back out the door again, and the marine went cautiously to the window and fired. He hit a barrel of beer, and it started to flow forth.

"Free beer, free beer," jeered the Americans within. "Come in and get it!" This was followed by another bottle.

The marines formed a line to rush the door. They pounded into the tavern amid flying bottles and chairs. Tables fell over. Glass littered the floors. There was no time to load muskets; the marines used them like clubs, the sailors used chairs and bottles.

From the Governor's mansion, through Upper Town, more Americans had come, slipping down into the maze of Lower Town before the British could stop them. Only a brief half hour had passed, and it was but seven-thirty, but there were eighteen hundred sailors hiding out in Lower Town. Fifteen minutes later, as more marines landed, the whole of Lower Town was involved in a savage battling brawl, into which all parties plunged with vigor, aided by flowing whiskey, beer and rum, by the screams of the women in the fancy bawdy houses, where whole cases of champagne bubbled and fizzed off British or American heads. It was to last all day and into the night, and the damage ran into thousands of pounds. Not a window was left unbroken. It raged through the streets, the alleys, the houses, the bars. British officers lost control of their men within forty minutes. The brigs were not going to be large enough to hold the culprits. Nobody was going to know what to do with them. They made away with enough liquor to keep the fleet in rum for years. And nothing could stop it; like wild conflagration, five thousand men turned Lower Town into a mad barroom brawl. All that could be said later was: the Yanks started it.

But up at the mansion, de Bouillé and Joshua knew nothing of what was going on in Lower Town. De Bouillé had explained hastily:

[171]

"I have a canoe at Tumbledown Dick!"

De Bouillé had started around the side of the great home, through the gardens; he looked around for Joshua. "Where the hell did he go?" de Bouillé muttered.

Joshua was already at the French windows that opened onto Lucie's room. The door was locked. He crashed in a pane of glass with his elbow, and put his hand in and opened the door. When he saw her, he said:

"Thank heaven! I have found you." He was breathing fast. "Come with me," he said.

Without another word, he took her by the hand and out on the balcony; he lifted her over the rail and set her down on the other side just as de Bouillé came running up. He panted:

"I didn't know where you'd gone!"

"I want to take Lucie to Douglass," Joshua said. "She'll be safe there!"

De Bouillé nodded understandingly. "Come on, then," he cried. He knew very well the British marines would be swinging up over the top of the hill at any moment. "Through the sugar," he said.

They ran across the lawns. The sugar cane waved in the distance. They began to hear the sharp crack of musket fire.

"Crouch down, Lucie," Joshua said. Bent over, they entered the field of sugar cane. "We can cut through to the road, down near madam's."

Ahead of him, de Bouillé jogged. Joshua said, "Do you have any bullets left?"

"Two," de Bouillé called back. They had expended some during the sporadic fighting before they reached the mansion.

Joshua was better armed. He had taken from the British marine his musket, his powder and shot. Although he had no time now to think ahead, the very possession of the weapon and powder and shot was satisfying. He carried the musket over his shoulder, and as they ran, crouched, through the rows of cane, he felt no immediate apprehension of the future. He wanted to give Lucie into Douglass' hands, because the British would treat Douglass with respect, and, as her maid, Lucie would be out of danger.

He watched her as she ran ahead of him, lightly, her little feet flying; occasionally she would look over her shoulder and smile breathlessly. He hadn't given her time to say a word, but she had

[172]

realized there was no time to explain and she had been ready to depend on him.

"Hold on," he said.

She stopped, and he came up to her. Cautiously he put his head up over the cane and looked to see where they were. He frowned; he had misjudged, all right; they were still a good long way from their goal. But he could see that there was an open stretch of long lawns ahead, between the road and them, over which they would have to pass to cross the road to Barney's. Joshua called to de Bouillé, who was about fifteen feet ahead, and he also stopped to get his breath.

Joshua said, "Look ahead there."

De Bouillé did. He sat down on the ground, and looked over to Joshua. Then Lucie said, "I could go alone."

"No," both men said at once.

De Bouillé knew that this field of cane stretched all the way to Signal Hill. Then there was a narrow pass, just wide enough for one man, and then the road to Tumbledown Dick, if it could be called a road. It was a narrow defile between sharp rocks, leading a mile down to the sandy small beach in the bay called Tumbledown Dick.

Then there was the sudden sound of musket fire, near by. Joshua got to his feet again and peered over the waving cane. Up the road came a company of marines, scarcely a hundred yards away.

De Bouillé said, "We take Lucie with us!" He got to his feet. He felt no fear about taking her; he was a good sailor, and his boat a triangular sailed sturdy craft; he had sailed much in her, and he knew the waters, the small islands well. "This way," he said.

They started to run again, cutting diagonally through the field of cane, away from the sea road, through to the middle of the island where the Quill rose, black. They passed under its shadow, and through the pass, squeezing through, for it was grown with bushes. Then they started down the mile long steep defile to the beach.

Little streams plunged down the side. They leaped them; they waded through. They hastened, as fast as they could, for as de Bouillé got closer to the beach, he began to have a vague fear. He increased his pace.

Lucie was between the two men, with de Bouillé ahead and Joshua behind. She did not know how far she had come. Suddenly she stumbled. Joshua stopped. De Bouillé watched him help her up. He realized instantly she had been keeping up too fast a pace. But he could not wait. "You stay here! I'll go on down to the beach. Come as soon as you can! I'll wait, once I'm there."

He did not stop for an answer, but disappeared around a sharp bend in the path. There was no danger from the British here; they would not penetrate into this wilderness now. Joshua set Lucie down on a patch of ground under a tree that leaned its branches over the path. He flopped down beside her, full length, putting his head in his arms.

After a moment he raised his head. She was lying flat, breathing fast. "We ran you too hard," he said.

She shook her head from side to side, and smiled.

"Don't talk," he said. Suddenly he frowned a little, and propped himself on one elbow and looked down at her face. "Perhaps—" He was about to say that perhaps he shouldn't have brought her. "I had no idea the troops would appear that fast, Lucie," he said. "Will you be afraid, in a small boat? I'm a good sailor, too."

"I'm not afraid. With you."

"We got you dirty," he said. There was a smudge on her cheek, and her round white arm was scratched, and bleeding a little. Joshua took out his handkerchief and wiped her cheek off. "We'll bathe your arm in seawater," he said, turning her arm over to see the end of the long scratch. Suddenly he looked into her eyes, he could feel the warm earth beneath him; a little bit of sun pierced through the trees and shone on her disheveled hair. With a quick movement he rolled over and, his shoulders pinning her down, he began to kiss her; lying there with her, his mouth on hers, he felt her response. With a muttered ejaculation, he drew away from her.

"Lucie," he said, low; he couldn't resist, and leaned over and kissed her again, a long kiss; then he pulled her into a sitting position, and to her feet. "We have to go on, now," he whispered, taking her in a last quick hug. She fastened her fingers in his as they started down the path again.

Joshua watched her as she walked by his side. Finally he said, "I hope to God the boat is there."

"*Oui*," Lucie answered, and he smiled. The path was steeper, they pushed through onto the small beach almost before they knew it. They saw de Bouillé coming toward them, from around a great rock. He said simply:

"Somebody got here before we did. The boat is gone."

[174]

28

"THERE IS ONLY ONE THING TO DO," JOSHUA SAID BRIEFLY, "AND that's find a place to camp out here in the woods for a while. We'll be relatively safe from the British; they won't come hunting us yet."

De Bouillé nodded. "I'm going to reconnoitre along the beach, and see if there are more men; there must be."

They had been sitting on the sand. The sea stretched lonely and vast. There was no sound but the sound of sea birds and surf.

The bay at Tumbledown Dick was narrow and deep, cut between fingers of cliff walls. This little beach, sandy and shelving, would make it ideal for swimming. Way up, almost over their heads, the cliff leaned over, and trees grew, as though from the sky. Joshua said, "Do you have your watch?"

"Yes," said de Bouillé.

"I'll meet you here, at three, then, for a swim, if you cannot find us in the forest." As he spoke he wondered at his use of that term forest, and yet it was the one that came to mind, for this windward side of Stasia was a deep wilderness, rocky, overgrown, full of tiny little bays, on which the surf pounded. Over to his extreme right, a small stream plunged down the side of the hill. He picked up the musket, which he had laid carefully across his lap, and slung it over his shoulder and stood up. He helped Lucie to her feet. He stood there a moment, and she said:

"You have plans, then?"

"Yes," he said.

He wasn't looking far into the future. He knew only that there were certain things that must be done, and it might take some time. As they walked away from de Bouillé, who waved goodbye, and struck down the beach, Joshua said:

"First I want to follow that little stream. If we could find a place to camp near fresh sweet water, it would be best."

"*Oui*," she said. "Then I could bathe."

He smiled. "You won't stay here long, Lucie. Only long enough for the hue and cry to die down, and then I can sneak you to madam some night."

He had no way of knowing this was going to be impossible. "We have plenty of powder and shot," he went on, "but I want to try and fashion a bow and arrows, and shoot some of this game. I used to do that when I was a boy, in Virginia."

She looked up at him. "Did you, sir? You never say anything about yourself." She eyed him a little. "Speak more of it, please," she asked.

He smiled. "You're a sweet wench. There's nothing to tell except we used to play Indians. I used to be good with a bow and arrow. We'll see if I've lost track of it. We have to eat, you know."

She said gravely, "I had not truly had time to think much."

"No," said Joshua thoughtfully. "As a matter of fact, neither did I. I think you had better remove your shoes and stockings and tuck your dress up, and we'll wade in and out of this stream. Walking in the water will be easier in some places."

He sat down himself, and she sat at his side. She removed her shoes, stuffed the stockings in them, and tied the laces so they swung over her shoulders. Then she bethought herself. Finally, face puckered and intent, she said, "I have it!" She pulled a hairpin out of her hair, and gathering her skirt tight around her knees, thrust the pin through the material. Joshua nodded with approval.

"Fine," he said.

The water was cold. It felt good. They waded in and out, climbing upward always. In less than half an hour they reached a tiny pool, surrounded with leaning pines. To the right was a level piece of ground, sprinkled deep in pine needles.

"Excellent," said Joshua warmly, not believing such luck. He stepped out of the water, and looked around. An almost perpendicular hill went up, about thirty feet away. He walked over toward it. "There might be caves," he explained, his voice floating back to Lucie.

She could hear him thrashing through the thick growth of the hill, and he disappeared from sight. After about fifteen minutes she began to grow apprehensive. She could hear nothing, and she got to her feet.

She started to walk in the direction in which he had gone, when she suddenly heard his voice, coming from the hillside. "Come here and look," he called.

In relief, she ran in the direction of his voice, pushing through the bushes and trees; suddenly she was face to face with him; he was pleased.

[176]

"Look," he said proudly, indicating a cave in the side of the hill. "It's dry and warm," he announced. "I've been in."

"That's why I didn't hear you, then," she murmured, looking into the cave uncertainly.

He said, "You weren't frightened, were you?"

"A little," she admitted. She amended the statement. "Just a very little!"

He did not smile. He said, "If I ever leave you again in a certain place, do not leave it! You would get lost. Wait for me." He swung the musket off his shoulder and unfastened the gleaming bayonet. "You can sit down, while I cut this growth away to let the sun in, for dryness. It will take some time."

Sun slanted through the pines. Joshua took off his coat and shirt, hanging them on a tree limb. He worked fast; the sweat began to pour off him. But gradually he cleared the thick bushes back. Lucie had gone into the cave to explore. It was not large, but it was dry and warm. Joshua said, in between sawing away at the plant branches:

"In the tropics it is imperative we find a dry place."

"I see," said Lucie.

"I think you had better start gathering pine needles, for a bed of sorts. I'm trying to think what you could use to carry them in, I guess my coat would be best. Take it over there." He gestured with the heavy knife.

He had already cut quite a swath toward the little level plot alongside the pool. *"Mon Dieu,* you are wonderful," Lucie said simply.

Joshua paused a moment to look at her. "There's a smudge on your nose."

She felt for it, brushing her fingers against her nose.

He grinned. "Are you hungry?"

She shook her head. "I gather needles."

For more than an hour she passed to and fro, from the cave to the pine grove, while the sound of Joshua's sawing and crackling filled the air. They spoke little, each intent on his own task, but occasionally their eyes would meet as both paused a moment to straighten up and stretch a little.

"I'll be stiff," Joshua said ruefully. "It's been a long time since I played Indian."

"I remember you said you were thirty."

He raised an eyebrow. "Perhaps you'd better forget the rest of that conversation. I may retract it."

"Oh?" She did not quite understand, but pushed the curling hair off her forehead and regarded him. "Well, m'sieur, I am finished." She went to the door of the cave, and disappeared for a moment. Then she stuck her head out. "Come see," she called.

He laid down the knife gratefully and came over to her side. She threw out her hands. *"Voilà!"*

"Merveilleux," Joshua said, going over to the thick bed of pine needles. He lay down carefully, stretching out. "Why, it's fine," he said. "Soft! My lord, it's thick; there must be a billion—two billions!"

"Ten billions," said Lucie. "I'm sure. I'll be stiff too."

"Come here and try it," he invited.

She drew a deep breath and looked at his recumbent figure. "I do not know," she said. "Perhaps—"

"Are you addressing me or yourself?" Joshua wanted to know.

"You will grow a beard," she said next.

"True," said Joshua, laughing. "I'm sure I haven't the faintest idea what is going on in your head, and you don't either."

"Yes, I do," said Lucie. "I should make another bed."

He laughed outright. "In one cave? Unnecessary, wench." He got to his feet and came to her. "We won't talk about it now. I'll feed you first."

Lucie turned away and started out the door. Joshua patted her backside, and she turned around quickly. "Now I'll make a bow and arrow," he said solemnly.

But first he went over to the pool and splashed water and stuck his whole head and shoulders in the cool water. Dripping, he emerged, and told her to sit down under the pines and watch. "After you have rested a while, you can dig a little firepit, which I shall line with stones," he said, whittling away on what was going to be an arrow.

"Oui," said Lucie. She looked at him and then down at her hands in her lap.

It was almost three when de Bouillé splashed through the stream, and stood in the little clearing. He was sniffing appreciatively, for Lucie was turning a browning bird on an improvised spit. A lazy fire burned in the stone-lined pit, and two big stones edged it to support the spit. "My lord," said de Bouillé, noting the bow and arrows under the big pine, and the plaited vines that tied the bird onto the tough branch.

"I plaited the vines, but m'sieur thought of it."

Joshua had fallen asleep at her side. He slept deeply, and de Bouillé regarded him affectionately. "I have news," he began.

Almost as he said the word, Joshua stirred. He lifted his head, saw de Bouillé. He turned over on his back, and looked up at him lazily. "You found us," he said.

"Yes," said de Bouillé. "I followed the stream." He sat down. "I have news," he repeated.

Joshua yawned. "Out with it, man." He too sat up, hooking his arms around his knees and regarding de Bouillé.

"Well, first, there must be four hundred of us in this forest. It's a dense wilderness. What officers there are have rounded up their own crews, and all resources have been pooled. They're catching fish for tonight. The big problem, of course, is going to be food. Considering the terrain, I think it most unlikely that the British will bother to send men in here after us. They will think hunger will force us to surrender." He was silent for a moment, and then he smiled. "Let that be, for the present. A few men have sneaked in from Lower Town. I gather the biggest brawl in history is going on down there; they're completely wrecking it. As far as I can gather, they're all drunk, and the British have completely lost control of their troops."

"Good God," said Joshua. "I can just see it."

"No, you can't," said de Bouillé. "Listen. This one man was one of four Americans from the 'Salem Belle.' He and three pals barricaded themselves in a bawdy house, with the women screaming upstairs. For a long time they held off the attacking marines, throwing chairs out the windows at them, bottles of champagne, tables —everything. Finally the British forced them back into the dining room, one Yank passed out—two got hit on the head, and this man crawled into the kitchen and passed out himself. When he came to, the five marines were sitting in the dining room drinking. Before the Yank realized what was happening they got involved in a brawl with more marines. He left about a dozen marines completing the job. The house was shaking to its foundations. He stood in the kitchen doorway and fired everything in the kitchen at them, ducking behind the door after each shot. Then he left in a hurry."

"*Mon Dieu,*" said Lucie.

De Bouillé rose. "We're having a meeting tomorrow morning sir. On the beach at Tumbledown Dick."

"I'll be there," said Joshua. "Won't you stay and have dinner with us?"

De Bouillé had picked up the bow. He said, "We're cooking a mess of fish. I will bring you some tomorrow morning, and we can cook it for breakfast, together. I will tell Captain Black about your bow and arrow. I have seen how it is done, now."

"I'll see you in the morning, then," Joshua said. He was very pre-occupied. Lucie kept on turning the roasting bird. Joshua stared at the ground, and drew patterns with a twig in the loose dirt. The sound of de Bouillé's steps died away; the quiet was broken only by the birds and the sighing wind in the trees.

Lucie tested the bird with a sharp stick. "It is done, I think," she said, low.

Joshua roused from his revery. "Good," he said, and she was relieved to see him smile. He speared the bird with his pocket knife, laid it on a clean flat stone from the pool, and disjointed it expertly. Once more he speared a brown leg, and presented it to Lucie.

They ate in silence, hungrily. They quarreled a little over who should eat the last two pieces. "But no," Lucie said. "I have enough. You are much bigger."

Joshua ate them both. "I feel guilty," he announced, through mouthfuls.

She shook her head firmly. "You have bigger appetite than me."

Joshua swallowed. "*Oui.*" Nothing was left of the bird but clean bones. Joshua piled them neatly. "Savages use bones for lots of things, but I'll be damned if I know what."

"They put them in their noses," said Lucie.

Joshua grinned. "I doubt if this wishbone would become you." He stretched out again lazily. "For some reason I feel good."

"You have accomplished much." She hesitated. "Are you going to close your eyes?"

"What?" asked Joshua.

"I wish you would close them." She was going toward the little pool. "I am so hot; I wish to sit in the water." She stopped. Then she said, "Please don't look."

Joshua laughed. "I won't." He turned over on his stomach; the grave way she had asked him not to look continued to amuse him, and he chuckled. All the same this was not a laughing matter, this situation. Right now he saw no way out for himself and de Bouillé and the other Americans. But perhaps tomorrow, in the meeting, they could think of something, some way to lay hands on boats or make them. He was puzzling over this, how he could hollow out a log, when he heard Lucie say:

"You may look."

He sat up and turned, wondering what he would see. He saw her face and shoulders; they rose above the clear water; she had evidently bathed her face for water dripped off her, and stuck her long eyelashes together in points. "Oh, I am happy," she said.

"Are you, Lucie?" he asked.

"I sit here long time."

"Not too long," he admonished. "It grows late, and the evening air is cooler, and we have nothing for towels."

She considered this. *"Oui,"* she said. *"C'est vrai.* I emerge soon then." She paused. "I tell you when I emerge."

"You mean I may look, then?"

She shook her head. "No," she answered.

Joshua laughed, and after a moment she smiled, too, dimpling. Then she said, *"Allons!* I emerge."

Joshua obediently turned over on his stomach and put his head in his hands. He waited what he thought was a long time. Finally he felt her hand on his shoulder. "I am here," she said.

"So I see," said Joshua, sitting up.

She was dressed in her blouse and petticoat; the low necked underblouse showed her rounded white shoulders and soft arms. She held one arm up. "The scratch is better."

She was unpinning her hair. It fell around her shoulders in shining waves of auburn. "Was it not good fortune I had two combs in my coiffure?"

"Very," said Joshua, watching, fascinated, as she combed out the long hair. "Are you Circe?"

"She had yellow hair," Lucie said. "Mine is red."

"And red is better?"

"I think so." She smiled. Then she sighed. She threw him a sideways glance. "Is it time to go to bed?"

Joshua said, "Yes."

She watched him as he got to his feet. He leaned down and pulled her up. She looked up at him. "I hung my dress in the cave."

They walked toward the cave. As they approached the entrance she said, "You're sure it is time, m'sieur?"

"You're sleepy," said Joshua.

"*Non.*" Her voice was uncertain. They were at the low doorway. "*Nous sommes arrivés,*" she whispered.

"Yes," said Joshua.

She looked up at him with enormous eyes. Then she entered the cave. He had spread his coat across the top of the pine needle bed for her head. She lay down and put her head down on the coat. She was lying way over to one side of the bed. "I leave you much room, m'sieur."

His back was to her. He was wrapping the lock and stock of the musket in his waistcoat. He said over his shoulder, "I want to protect this."

"I see," murmured Lucie.

He turned then and saw her lying way over on the pine bed. He smiled; he came over to the bed and knelt down. "Lucie," he said. "Today is really no different from yesterday. At least that's what I'm trying to tell myself. I don't get any better with time."

"No?" asked Lucie.

He was about two feet away from her. "Listen, wench," he said, "I'll sleep outside."

She drew a long breath. She sat up. "If you sleep out there, you will catch cold. It may rain; it dews! If you get the fever, what will I do?"

"I seem to be suffering from some kind of fever now," Joshua said.

"*Mon Dieu,*" whispered Lucie, leaning forward to touch his hand. Then she said, "I should have made another bed!"

"That would make no difference, Lucie. Honestly." Her hair fell over her shoulders; her great blue eyes fastened on him. Joshua said, "I told you yesterday I was going to take you home and—" He stopped.

"Marry George?" Lucie asked.

"I can find you a better husband than George!"

"You can?" She studied him. She touched the side of his face. "You do grow beard."

Joshua took her by the shoulders and laid her back on the bed, with her head on his coat. He himself settled down beside her carefully, stretching out full length, flat on his back. "I've changed my mind," he said.

His voice seemed to come from a great distance. Lucie lay still, not moving. He took her hand and placed it palm down over his lips. "Lucie," he said, low, looking up at the ceiling of the cave, "if I sleep here, I want to make love to you, very much." He turned over and looked down at her face.

Lucie looked up at him. "You always explain everything. But you don't need to. I understand."

Joshua grinned. "You do?" He paused, while her lashes fell. "What do you understand?" She didn't answer, so he put his hand under her chin. "Tell me."

She hesitated. Then she said quickly, "I cannot! I love you, m'sieur!" She turned her head away.

Joshua turned her to him. "Lucie," he said urgently. He held her close and kissed her. After a moment he whispered against her lips, "You love me, Lucie?"

She opened her eyes to look at him. "Yes," she said.

29

LIEUTENANT MACKENZIE SAID, "BUT SIR, THE SITUATION AS IT EX-ists is this. We have filled the hospitals, and the private homes in Upper Town. The jail is full; the ships' brigs are full. My thought is, sir, to make them clean up the mess. The streets are ankle deep in glass, for one thing!"

General Vaughn said gravely, "There might be merit in such a plan."

"The jails won't hold 'em, sir!"

"Disgraceful," said Rodney coldly. "They ought all to be pun-ished!"

Vaughn said mildly, "It's hardly possible, sir, to punish five thou-sand men except by docking their pay. What I don't understand is how they had time to drink so much."

Mackenzie looked surprised. Then he remembered that he had come up through the ranks; General Vaughn had not. "If there's flowing liquor around, sir—" Suddenly he smiled. "By God, sir," he said, "it took twenty men to get five out of one bawdy house, after they had chased the Yanks out."

Rodney asked, "And how many Americans were taken prisoner?"

"About fifteen hundred, sir. In various stages of drunkenness." He tried to keep his face straight. "There are five hundred more of them, sir, on the island."

"And what is your plan concerning them, General?"

"Well, sir," Vaughn said, wondering how to sum it up quickly. "You see, Major Calcott and Major Watts are both badly injured. Watts got hit by a bottle of champagne. Lieutenant Mackenzie is the engineer officer of the regiment; we intend to leave him here at St. Eustatious. He has already drawn up plans for the defense of the island, and I'll show you his submissions. Briefly, heavy batteries at a number of strategic spots. As for the Yanks, we have thrown up an outpost at White Cliffs, and at Signal Hill. We believe hunger, fever, so forth, will compel them to surrender. It is a wilderness back in there, sir, dangerous to infiltrate, unless there's need."

"I agree," said Rodney.

Vaughn sighed with relief. "That's all then, Lieutenant."

"Thank you, sir." The lieutenant saluted. It was nine o'clock at night, and he had been besieged with duties which were not ordinarily his province at all because most of the five thousand officers and marines were either drunk or wounded. He thought that he could stand a stiff drink of rum himself, to say nothing of the champagne which had flowed like water all day, and unfortunately was still flowing. They had not yet gathered up all the malefactors in Lower Town; there were some hardy Yanks and British marines who were still going strong in a few sections. He was going back now with a fresh detail to try to rout them out.

Within the big cabin, John Rodney faced his father. "According to your instructions, sir, the Dutch flag has been left flying. Governor de Graaf refuses to give us his parole, and insists on being regarded as a prisoner of war."

"He will be so accommodated," Rodney muttered, and Vaughn said nothing.

John Rodney continued. "We are trying to estimate the dead— roughly about two hundred men, marines and seamen. The Americans had few of their number killed, less than thirty. The damage is going to run into thousands." He flung out his hands. "We can

[184]

hardly estimate it yet. But we confiscated many of the merchants' books. And now we have most of the shops and stores under our control. But there was looting."

He waited for the pronouncement he was sure his father would make. His father said, "At least we have been the instrument of bringing this nest of villains to condign punishment! They deserve scourging! This island has long been an asylum for men guilty of every crime, and a receptacle for the outcasts of every nation!"

"That is true," Vaughn said, and relieved John Rodney of answering. "We have been examining some of these merchants' books you brought, sir." He tapped one. "These two British merchants have been sending 'grain' and 'fruit' to Stasia, dealing with a merchant, Joshua Harris, of Harris & Co. There isn't that much fruit in England! 'Fruit' is cannon balls, 'grain' is gunpowder! And there is a warehouse full of cordage! We couldn't buy it!"

"Lower Town," said the admiral passionately, "is a nest of vipers that has preyed upon the vitals of Great Britain. Everything will be padlocked, including food, and doled out to the residents of Stasia. And everyone on the island will be treated as prisoners of war!"

John said, "It is an immense capture, sirs. Two million pounds sterling in the warehouses alone!"

"And had the Dutch been as attentive to their security as they were to their profits, this island would have been impregnable!"

"Condign punishment shall be meted out to every man who was engaged in these nefarious activities," Rodney said. "As for you, John, yesterday there sailed a rich convoy of thirty sail, under the protection of a sixty-gun ship. I have detached Captain Reynolds, of the 'Monarch,' with the 'Panther' and the 'Sybil' to pursue them as far as the latitudes of the Bermudas."

John's ship was the "Panther." "Aye, aye, sir," he said.

The admiral was closing the interview. "I am allowing you an hour's leave, sir," he said. "Now is the time for you to do your duty and make your fortune!"

30

THE WIND WAS STRONG AND GUSTY FROM THE SOUTH-SOUTHEAST.
Spray flew from the "Athena's" bows as she climbed the Atlantic
combers. Barney said crisply:

"Tell her we are the 'Triton,' number forty-one. Ask her who she
is."

The British signal book was in his hands. The signalman worked.
The answer came back. "She's the 'Sylph,' His Majesty's cutter
'Sylph,' sir, number 103."

"One-oh-three," repeated Barney, turning the page. "Correct.
Tell her to keep under our lee." On the page opposite the name
"Sylph" was her number and her captain. "Commander Carr,"
Barney said aloud, watching as they bore quickly down on the
"Sylph." Macgregor came running out on deck, buttoning his
British blues.

"You look lovely, Mr. Macgregor," Barney said.

Macgregor wanted to say that the captain did, too, but he didn't
quite dare. Instead he said gravely, "Thank you, sir. Blue certainly
becomes Jerrell, there. It matches his eyes."

Barney turned and raised the glass in his hand to his eye. Abaft
the starboard beam were three sails. There wasn't much time here.
He had certainly found part of the fleet for which he was searching.

He went down the gangway, and amidships. The guns were run
out and loaded. The matchsticks already sizzled. The ship had been
cleared for action since the enemy sail had been sighted an hour
ago. And the cutter "Sylph" was almost within hailing distance.
Barney said, "The first man who fires, or gun crew who fires a gun
before the order will be flogged as soon as he can be hauled to the
nearest grating!" He turned on his heel and went aft again, once
more raising the glass to study the three ships. At the time they had
been spied, they were sailing full before the wind, on a north-northwest course. Now they had kept on the same course, but had taken
in some sail, and the nearest ship had backed the maintop.

"She's hanging around to see what's happening," Barney said to

Scull. Macgregor had gone fore and was along the line of guns.

Scull knew the first sound of gunfire would bring the enemy ships upon them. To Scull they looked like a line of battleships and two frigates. He pushed the thought aside and concentrated on his task orders, which were to bring the "Sylph" under his lee, in a completely indefensible position. He kept glancing from the weather-vane, to the "Sylph," to the helm. At least the "Sylph" was obeying orders which she thought came from His Majesty's ship "Triton." The "Athena," sails set, bore down on the cutter.

The distance between the two ships narrowed fast. In Barney's hand was the brilliant red flag that meant no quarter. He dug in his pocket and came out with his watch. What would happen next would happen fast, or not at all.

"Commander Carr!"

The cry came back immediately. "Aye aye, sir!" Commander Carr had been watching the "Athena" for some time; he had seen the uniforms of her officers; her signals had been correct. The next words he heard, from only fifty feet away, were incredible. First he heard his name repeated.

"Commander Carr! You have been sadly tricked! This is the United States privateer 'Athena'!"

Carr stood stockstill on his own quarterdeck. And the ship "Athena" was even closer now; thirty feet, then twenty. He heard,

"Captain Barney speaking. You'll note the red flag, sir. If there is any resistance whatsoever, we give no quarter. You have three minutes."

Barney held up the watch. Commander Carr saw the eighteen-pounders only twenty feet away; he saw the sizzling of the match-sticks. He was helpless, completely helpless. The relentless voice went on.

"You have two minutes, sir, to surrender, else I will sink you with all hands."

Carr cried, "You give us no quarter?"

"None," said Barney, his voice coming over the twenty feet. Carr saw his face, plainly; he saw the watch upheld; he smelled the matchsticks burning and pointed right at him was an eighteen-pound cannon. He faced it, looking right into the muzzle.

"Oh, God," he muttered.

"You have one minute," Barney said, the red flag fluttering from his hand. "Else I sink you, sir. With all hands."

Carr could not stand it any longer. He said, his voice strangled, "We surrender. We surrender!"

The "Athena" was almost touching the "Sylph." "Irons," cried Barney.

The men were ready. The irons swung out. The "Sylph" was boarded in a matter of seconds. Lang, the marine officer, swung over to her quarterdeck, pistols in each hand. "Don't touch that flag," he roared, as a British sailor started to haul on the ropes.

Men swarmed aboard. Barney was taking no chances. He watched with approval as Lang and Jerrell and Macgregor took charge. In less than two minutes the English crew were mustered on deck. Their knives flew overboard. Barney leaned on the rail and spoke to the commander, who stood on his own deck, dazed.

"You hadn't even broken out your arms chests, had you, Commander Carr?"

He didn't wait for an answer. He turned again, and raised the glass. The other three ships were still on the same course. It was possible he might get away with this. By the time he turned back to the "Sylph," Macgregor was swinging aboard the "Athena" again, and coming aft to report.

"Crew confined, sir; Mr. Lang and prize crew ready, sir, to take over. Mr. Jerrell is escorting the captain and officers aboard the 'Athena.' "

"Very good, Mr. Macgregor," Barney said briefly. He watched Carr come aboard, followed by his officers. They came slowly up to Barney.

They offered their weapons. Barney motioned to Scull. "Take these men below, Mr. Scull." They looked abashed and hopeless. Barney said, "Fortunes of war, sirs. I'll send you in a couple of bottles of rum. Drown in it. Just a moment, Commander. What ships are those?" He gestured.

Carr knew. He spoke without thinking, for he was praying they would sense something amiss. But as his eyes took in the "Athena" —she looked British! He answered Barney's question. "Those are His Majesty's ships 'Monarch,' 'Panther' and 'Sybil'!" He turned. "You'll excuse me, now, sir!"

"Gladly, sir," said Barney. As Scull herded them below, the three younger officers kept glancing back at Barney.

"Yes, that's he, sirs," Scull said. He couldn't help grinning widely. He added, "I'll send the rum Captain Barney ordered."

[188]

When he returned to the deck, the "Sylph" was already hauling away, Lang waving from the quarterdeck, and the British flag still flying bravely. Not a shot had been fired.

Aboard the "Monarch," Captain Reynolds was frowning deeply. Across the heaving water, he watched for signals from the "Panther," who was relaying them from the frigate "Sybil." When he received the signal he was even more puzzled as to the correct decision.

He was under orders to intercept the Dutch convoy, of thirty sail of merchantmen. Convoying them was a sixty-gun Dutch ship. The "Monarch" herself boasted seventy-four cannon; the "Panther" thirty-six; the "Sybil" thirty-two. But Reynolds had not an hour to lose. The Dutch had left Stasia thirty-six hours before he had; he could not pursue beyond the latitudes of the Bermudas. He would have to beat to windward, and consume precious time in order to see what ship was hauling away to the south as fast as she could. He swore under his breath. But he thought his duty was plain, because he was pretty sure he knew what ship that was. He gave a brief order to the signalman, to be relayed via the "Panther" to the ship nearest the stranger.

The signal was read quickly. The "Sybil's" captain, Rutherford, looked up at weathervane and sails. He gave a brief order. Then he said, to his first officer:

"Hands to dinner, Mr. Jowett."

High on the mizzentopgallant masthead Barney fixed the glass on the "Panther." He saw the signal. He saw the "Sybil" change course. He lowered the glass and came down onto the deck.

Once there he consulted the signal book. He left it open, on the binnacle head. He looked up at the weathervane, and the set of the sails.

"Hands to braces, Mr. Scull," he said. "I want to change the trim of the sails. Lay your course north-northwest. We'll need the wind at our heels."

Macgregor had been watching the "Sybil." He blurted, "I thought we had fooled them, sir!"

Barney said, "If we'd kept on our course, she would have been able to come about and have the weather gage, Mr. Macgregor."

Macgregor swallowed. "Is she—"

Barney tapped the signal book. "If I'd had those orders, I'd do just as she did." The thought made him ponder. Macgregor looked down at the book, and where Barney's finger pointed. He read three brief words: "Engage the enemy."

Barney's voice was going right on. "Hands to dinner, Mr. Scull."

There was time to eat. What was coming was a ship-to-ship battle, between ships evenly matched. But by the time they met, he would still have the weather gage; he had it now; and he would keep it. It would probably mean the difference between defeat and victory.

He paced the deck, back and forth, back and forth. The crew came up from dinner; they were talking and laughing. It made Barney smile a little himself. He had trained them well, but baptism by fire was coming now. It had been years since a British ship of the line had hauled down her colors. The battle about to be joined would be bitter, long and bloody. And only a few of his crew were aware of it. The officers knew, well enough. Except perhaps Jerrell. Barney found himself hoping nothing happened to him. Then he said, "Perhaps you had better escort our prisoners to the cable tier, Mr. Macgregor. And remove that uniform, sir. I doubt if you'll need it again today."

Once again he looked down at the signal book. "Engage the enemy." He closed the book. He decided he had better get out of British uniform himself. Carrying the book, he made his way to his own cabin.

31

THE MAGNIFICENCE OF THE SUNSET WAS FADING IN THE DARKENING sky and the "Athena" was alone on an empty sea. The battle which had lasted four hours was over.

It was difficult for Mr. Scull to hear the first order Barney gave him, almost the same second as the "Sybil" had exploded and sunk. The vision of it was imprinted on Scull's mind; the mighty roar, the flash of a sheet of fire, extinguished quickly by the lapping water that had seized the "Sybil" and drawn her down. And Scull couldn't hear well because his ears were deafened by the continuous gunfire. Barney repeated sharply:

"Hoist out a boat to pick up survivors!"

"Aye aye, sir," said Scull, wondering dimly if they had a boat. "Lower a boat to pick up survivors," he bellowed.

All eyes in the "Athena" were on the empty waves where the "Sybil" had been just a few seconds ago. The sight of a man in the water brought forth a yell; the boat crew, acting instinctively, worked fast.

Marines still clung in the tops and held muskets motionless along the rail; the gun crews sat back on their haunches, ears ringing; they wouldn't need the cannon balls piled beside them; stale smoke and powder smelled acridly.

The boat was lowered, pulled away. Voices called out to the boat crew, in instruction. Topmen clambered high to look out over the waves for a sign of other men struggling in the water. All their energies now were directed at saving the few survivors who had been shooting at them, and who were now at the mercy of their mutual foe, the restless sea.

Barney let them go. He let them watch. There would be no rest for men tonight, but they could watch until the last of the "Sybil's" crew had been picked up. Then they could eat. He heard Jerrell's voice, fore, telling the cook to hurry and get fires started. Barney was conscious of the sound of the pumps. His eyes went over the "Athena" slowly, marking her hurts; damage below had been sustained, but it was still under control. Macgregor and Scull had lost their cabin; there must have been at least a hundred shot holes in the mizzentop; spars, yards, the foretop royal, half the bowsprit, were gone. Martinique was about a day's sail. They must try to make it.

His own head still rang with the sound of the guns. He tried to segregate the different phases of the action just past; it was the speed of the "Athena" which had weighed in his favor, the speed gained by having the weather gage, which had allowed him to seize the offensive and force battle when he chose. The gun crews had worked well. From a broadside every minute and a half, they had reduced it later, under fire, to twenty seconds less, he was sure. He watched the cruising boat.

There were few cries now from the "Athena." No more men's heads could be seen in the darkening seas. And a sudden silence prevailed aboard, as it was thus borne in upon them that of a gallant ship and a crew of three hundred and fifty, this handful of men remained, dragged from the sea. They surveyed their own ship.

More than fifteen minutes had passed. Jerrell stuck his head into the hatchway; he smelled coffee. He asked a question which was answered in the affirmative. He went aft, fast as he could.

Barney nodded in approval as he relayed his message. "Hands to supper, Mr. Scull," he said.

"Aye aye, sir," Scull answered.

"Mr. Jerrell, see to those Englishmen. Send them to the surgeon, then fore to supper. But I want to question one of them. I'll leave it to your judgment, sir, to pick out a man."

"Aye aye, sir."

"And Mr. Jerrell, after that I want you to see the surgeon and get that arm rebandaged."

"Aye aye, sir," said Jerrell, and flew down the gangway; the boat was pulling up alongside again, while Macgregor's voice suddenly pierced across the decks.

"Goddammit, what are you doing with those hoses? Leave them rigged there; do you think you're going to leave the decks this way?"

Barney noticed Absolom at his elbow. He was carrying a cup of coffee. He knew Barney wouldn't leave the deck now.

Two hours later Barney asked Scull and Macgregor to have supper with him. Scull, bending his head to enter the aftercabin, after washing up hastily, could hardly believe the last six hours had been. There was cold chicken and pork, and a big bowl of fruit on the table, and Absolom moved about as imperturbable as ever. Scull grinned at him.

"Looks good, Absolom," he said.

"Thank you, sir," Absolom said, serving him coffee from the captain's heavy silver pot.

The three men sat for just a moment in silence. Then Macgregor said, "I know that the purpose of naval action in wartime is to sink enemy ships, sir, but it always gives me a shock to see her go—that last bit of mast."

Scull said, "But even if we hadn't hit the powder magazines, she wouldn't have lasted much longer, sir."

"Yes," said Macgregor, "but did you notice, sir, that the firing improved?" He broke off; he and Scull were doing all the talking.

Barney smiled. "Go right ahead, Mr. Macgregor."

He listened to them as they recapitulated the battle past; putting in a word here or there. In a few minutes, Mr. Jerrell knocked.

"Bring the prisoner in, Mr. Jerrell," Barney ordered.

Jerrell did so. "This man is John Butler, foretopman of the 'Sybil,' sir."

Barney nodded. "You may join us, Mr. Jerrell." He transferred his gaze to John Butler, from his bare feet to the top of his still wet head. "I see you received dry clothes, Butler."

Butler said, low, "Aye aye, sir."

Barney turned to Jerrell again. "Has Butler had anything to eat?"

"Aye aye, sir," said Jerrell.

Barney's face was impassive. He wanted information. "Absolom, give Butler a tot of rum."

"Thank you, sir!" Butler was enthusiastic. He took the glass and cradled it in his hand.

"You may drink it," Barney said with a smile.

Butler tossed it off, looked around at the three other officers hastily, and leaned forward and set the glass down on the table. "Thank you, sir," he repeated.

"Where did the 'Sybil' sail from, Butler?" Barney asked.

Butler blurted, "From Stasia, sir."

Barney refrained from looking at any of the three officers, and hoped devoutly they were not exchanging knowing glances. He said, "You took Stasia? When?"

"The day before yesterday, sir." Then he shifted uneasily.

"Considering your ordeal by fire and water, Butler, I'm going to allow you another tot of rum," Barney said. "First, I want you to tell me in your own words what happened at Stasia."

Butler hesitated. The temptation was too much, and he was too weary to refuse. Besides that, Barney was looking right at him. He said, "We took the island, easy, sir, except the Yanks were loose in Lower Town, and Jeez, what a mess, sir. The marines and them was tangled up in the taverns all day, throwing bottles."

"Drink your rum," Barney said.

"Thank you, sir!" Once more he drank it in a gulp, and set the glass down; once more he looked at Barney, as if to make sure he was really here, and alive. His eyes gleamed.

"Admiral Rodney is at Stasia?"

"Aye aye, sir, but Admiral Hood sailed. I saw the 'Barfleur' myself, sir."

"And the Americans on Stasia. Are there some still at liberty?"

"They say so, sir. They said three hundred or more."

Barney said, "All right, Butler. That's all."

The rum had worked, Barney thought, as he wiped his mouth with his napkin and absently watched Absolom pour him a cup of coffee. Then he gestured to the rum. "Help yourselves, sirs," he said. "We have a night ahead of us."

But he didn't give them much time. He was on his feet himself. Suddenly his smile flashed out. "I must have been more engrossed than I thought," he said. "I'll be damned if we haven't left those British officers in the cable tier!"

He doubled the lookouts that night. Admiral Hood had sailed. It would have been useless to ask Butler Hood's destination; it was useless to ask the British officers. But Hood would have a whole fleet. The course had been set to windward of Stasia, giving the island a wide berth. During the night as much work as possible was done. The rising morning sun saw part of the crew holystoning decks already scrubbed but still stained; the gleaming white of new canvas contrasted with the old suit of sails. New spars had been placed, and running gear rereeved. But below the pumps still worked constantly, and even so there was two feet of water in the wells.

Macgregor and his crews worked on the gun carriages; the burial service was read and ten more men wrapped in hammocks slid over the side into a bluing and vast sea. There were more than a third of the crew wounded; some of them would not recover. The price of victory was high.

The English sailors had given their parole and worked side by side with the enemy, in dried-out clothes. Everyone moved methodically about the many tasks; they were all lucky to be alive, and unhurt. Jerrell wore his bandage with covert pride.

Barney was badly worried, but gave no outward sign of it. It had been a bitter battle and the effects were lasting throughout this day. The winning had been exciting; the battle itself sobering, and officers and crew responded first to one and then to the other. Macgregor, for instance, had lost his temper over a triviality, and had not Barney appeared immediately, an innocent man would have suffered. Macgregor cooled down, and remained cool. It seemed to Barney sometimes that Absolom was the most dependable of them all.

He was worried because of the known fact of the presence of Hood and his fleet. The "Athena" could not run fast from anything. Nor was there sanctuary near, nearer than Basseterre, on Guadeloupe, and that course would certainly bring him into contact with Rodney's cruisers out from Stasia. Whereas he could set his course now for Martinique, in more safety, and Martinique was where he wanted to be. If any man would know what had happened and what was happening at Stasia it would be the Governor of the French island, the Marquis de Bouillé. Stasia itself, across the water, unseen, lured him, but he postponed thinking about it until he knew all the facts. But Douglass would be safe; even though she was in English hands, no one would harm her.

But during the long day, only one sail was sighted. Barney supposed she was a merchantman because on their sighting, she had changed course and fled. He could not give chase; she might be an American vessel making for what she thought was the security of Stasia.

He was not one to waste time in regret. The blow he had expected had come. He had thought perhaps good could be wrested from it; Stasia was quite a pie, and once the British had their fingers in it, they would be occupied for some time counting their profits. It was such an immense capture they would have to give time and energies to holding onto it. The spy system on Stasia was so well established, and the methods used heretofore so devious, that Barney smiled when he thought of Rodney trying to stamp it out. And what would they do with all they had captured? Short of sitting there on it, they would be compelled to send it home to England or to other British islands. Anything that floated was to Barney already half his. As long as he was able to cruise.

In the first ten minutes of the first dogwatch, at eight minutes after four, Mt. Pelee was sighted. It was a hot day, with a fair wind, and a cloudless sky. Mt. Pelee beckoned. By morning they should be putting into Fort de France. Five minutes later a second call came from the lookouts; the call Barney had feared. It rang out over the ship.

"Sail-ho! Two points off the starboard bow!"

Scull snapped out an order to Jerrell, who dashed fore with a glass. From the masthead Jerrell bellowed down to deck.

"Four sail; five!" There was a pause. "Seven!" Then, "Three sail on the starboard quarter!"

Scull whirled to see Barney standing alongside of him. "There's hardly need to relay the message to me, Mr. Scull," Barney said laconically.

He went fore, and began to climb to the foretopgallant masthead. Jerrell obligingly swung over and sat on a yardarm.

Barney swung the glass slowly. He said nothing. Jerrell blurted, "I can see ten, sir!"

Barney answered this. "Nineteen." There was no doubt about it; they had found Hood and his fleet. Hood was blockading Fort de France. Barney glued the glass to his eye. Why Fort de France? Why, indeed? De Bouillé had said there were four frigates there, when he had sailed five days ago. Surely Hood wouldn't waste nineteen ships, blockading for four. Barney frowned. He swung the glass. Jerrell said, "I saw three on the st'b'd quarter, sir!"

The silence lengthened. Jerrell squirmed. Five minutes passed. Then Barney called down to deck. "Mr. Scull! Get the courses in!"

Jerrell leaned over to look way down to deck. The boatswain's voice floated up. "All shorten sail!"

Quite some time passed before Barney was sure of his first surmise; what intelligences Hood had had were correct, then.

Barney said, "Mr. Jerrell, I'm going to leave you up here for thirty minutes with my glass." He handed it over as Jerrell swung back to the masthead. "Report to me in thirty minutes," he said.

He started down to deck. His mind raced ahead. Now he would be free to cruise! As soon as he could get the "Athena" ready for the sea again— His mind raced with plans. He gained the deck and went aft. Scull turned from the rail, glass in hand. Barney grinned.

"Looks like we've picked up quite an escort, doesn't it, Mr. Scull?"

Scull nodded. "Aye aye, sir!"

"It'll be quite a sight, when we fall in with them."

Scull said, "I can't believe it, sir!"

Macgregor was talking to himself, as he looked. "The whole French fleet," he was repeating. "The whole goddamned fleet!"

32

"THIS CAME THIS MORNING," THE MARQUIS SAID, FLINGING THE letter down on the polished table. "Read it, sir!"

Barney picked it up and read:

"H. M. S. Sandwich.
St. Eustatious
March 4

"I have received the honor of your Excellency's letters, and am sorry to find that a man of such high rank should descend so far as to use intelligences which he confesses came to him in an indirect way.

"British admirals are responsible to none but their sovereign and their country, and were never known to insult an open and declared enemy. But, perfidious people, wearing only a mask of friendship, and traitors, and rebels to their King deserve no consideration and none shall they ever meet with at my hands.

"I must again repeat to your Excellency that I can no longer permit flags of truce to pass between the King my master's islands and those of the French. This communication I am determined to prevent, and I have given orders to all my cruisers to seize and detain all flags of truce but such as General Vaughn and myself may be honoured with from you, without exception." It was signed G. B. Rodney.

Barney looked up. "This spoils your intelligence system." He couldn't help smiling.

The marquis was in no smiling mood. "That sanctimonious devil," he said, "has refused to exchange prisoners, and the French merchants on Stasia! According to him, they come under these," he tapped the letter, " 'perfidious people'! I have replied. I have replied thus," said the marquis calming down a little. He read aloud from the letter he had just finished writing.

"I am satisfied that a British Admiral ought to be responsible to his King and Country. To both, I owe reprisals; they shall be forthcoming. You have set the example and I shall pursue it." He looked up at Barney over the letter to punctuate this. He went on.

"I repeat once more that you may act as you please towards our flags of truce. To quiet your apprehensions on that score, I shall send no more. In the future the interpretations of our sentiments shall be our cannon."

"Very much to the point, m'lord," Barney said, crossing long legs.

From outside in the gardens came the sound of hammering as the construction of a dance floor under the palms went on. Six hundred people had been invited to a reception for the Comte de Grasse and his officers tonight. The marquis laid the letter down.

"You will miss the festivities, sir," he said. "I am sorry," he added, abstractedly. Then he went on again. "There can be no possible doubt but that François was caught on Stasia, and now lurks somewhere in the hills with the Americans. Mr. Ross, in his last communication," the marquis grimaced, "supposed there to be from three to four hundred of them, but they surrender daily—starved, feverish. Rodney has arrested Curyon and Gouvernier, and sent them as prisoners of state to England, for treasonable trading with the enemy. All goods, including those of French merchants, have been confiscated; the food is even doled out to each household! When they are deported, they may take only household goods and household slaves with them! Rodney is also after the Englishmen who became Dutch burghers, to enjoy the trading air of Stasia." The marquis smiled. "All canoes have to be drawn up on the beaches before dark. Fort Oranje now boasts forty ten-pounders. Batteries are being constructed—we're not quite sure where."

"I don't wonder Rodney stopped the so-called flags of truce," Barney remarked.

The marquis said, "We must keep communications open. The situation now is that we can watch Hood, and his fleet, since they retreated to St. Lucia. We must devise means to watch Stasia. I have requested Captain Connor to attend us. He waits." The marquis crossed the floor and opened a door; Barney waited for the sight of the man who was to accompany him on his next mission.

Connor was Irish, with freckles and hazel eyes. A scar marked one cheek; adventurer and professional soldier, he commanded the marquis' garrison of some five hundred men. He wore a resplendent uniform, dark blue with red facings, with a line of white down neat trouser leg. "Captain Connor," Barney said, bowing.

"As soon as you two have said hello, we will get down to business," the marquis said, and went over to the wall and unrolled a magnificent map of the islands which covered almost one whole wall. Barney and Connor, drawn to it, moved slowly together till the three of them stood in front of it. The marquis, with a long wand in hand, looked at both of them and smiled with satisfaction.

"You are two aces I have against the British, sirs," he said, and his smile was delighted. "Now. *Attendez!* Here are we." The marquis loved his maps, and he loved strategy with Machiavellian fervor. He was enjoying himself this morning; it was with some regret he realized his correspondence with Rodney was at an end. However, the bullets would come next, as he had promised. "Here are we, and de Grasse, and twenty some ships of the line, besides my four frigates. Here is Hood. Close." He pointed to St. Lucia. "Hood is kept under surveillance at all times."

That surveillance was good, Barney knew. Good and accurate. It was going to allow him to proceed with assurance that he was not bearding Hood and the fleet at Stasia at the same time.

The marquis went on. "Here is Stasia, Saba, and St. Martin—a stone's throw from St. Kitts and Nevis. In British hands. We watch from Guadeloupe."

"One moment," Connor said. "Once we take Stasia back, we are free to include St. Kitts and Nevis in the same bundle, my lord. They go together."

"Later," said the marquis. Then he said, "You understand, I have no say—" he gestured— "as to the doings of the fleet and le Comte de Grasse. I tell you confidentially we must do all this out here in the islands ourselves. The fleet serves as a balance wheel only."

"A big one," said Barney, and Connor nodded. "May I smoke, m'lord?" he asked, and knowing the answer would be in the affirmative, got out his pipe. He filled it abstractedly.

He said, "The damage done by the Yanks to those British regiments is going to be of great value."

"Now the regiments which General Vaughn is leaving on Stasia are the thirteenth and the fifteenth." The marquis walked over to his desk, and got out a small notebook. He opened it. "Six hundred and twenty men, Colonel Cockburne commanding. Harris, surgeon, Captains Bathe, Rigerson, Lieutenants"—he read down the list— "Mackenzie, engineering. He's good." The marquis squinted at both younger men. "Let's leave that for a moment, and look once more at the map."

Connor puffed on his pipe. Barney took his eyes from Stasia and followed the marquis' pointer. "Curaçao has fallen, yesterday, but we have reason to believe it is about to be succored." He grinned. "We can count on the Dutch to retake it shortly. We cannot retake Stasia till Rodney and the fleet leave it. But we can strike a blow by removing the Americans; and we must try to establish a system by which we can learn when the convoys leave."

Barney pointed to the map of Stasia. "I propose to use Tumbledown Dick for the evacuation; the bay is deep, the beach shelving and sandy. At Jenkin's Bay, I can anchor within a stone's throw of what beach there is, but there is a precipitous cliff wall reaching right down into the water. On all sides. More necks would be broken than those I'd save."

Connor said, "Tumbledown Dick is best, I think, sir. For the first landing." He smiled contentedly. "The second time, Jenkin's Bay."

Barney eyed him thoughtfully. "Yes, Captain Connor."

The marquis looked at both of them. "A *coup de main*—by way of Jenkin's Bay? But, sirs, that cliff wall is three hundred feet down, and straight down!"

"In ancient castles they used scaling ladders. On shipboard, we use rope." Barney said, next, "What I noted about your men, sir, was that they wore uniforms almost exactly like the British—red coats with yellow reveres. Did the similarity ever strike you? Well," he ended, "all that later. First get the men off. We will approach the island from the north, m'lord. We'll slip out tonight."

Joshua woke suddenly, sitting upright. The late moon, hovering halfway down the incline of the star-sprinkled skies, threw its light palely in the cave and on the sleeping girl at his side.

In its white light her face had an ethereal quality. She slept with one bared round arm under her head; her long braids tumbled over one shoulder. Joshua reached down and covered her legs carefully with her skirt, tucking the material around her bare feet, and pulling his shirt over the bare arm. He felt her hand.

It was cool. In sleep now, her face looked thin, too. The long lashes covered the darkish blue signs of fatigue. In sudden anxiety he felt her forehead; it too was cool. Propped on one elbow, he looked at her and slowly the long lashes lifted and her eyes opened.

She said, "Joshua?" She sighed a little, and moved slightly toward him; he put his arms around her and drew her close. For a moment neither spoke.

Then Lucie said, "What wakened you, Joshua?"

"I don't know," he said. But he did know. "You looked so sweet."

"I was dreaming." She smiled at him.

"What?" he asked, kissing the edge of her cheek.

"I was dreaming we were having supper again tonight."

"I could have eaten it twice," he said.

"I know. But I was listening again to you and François talk, and it was nice to hear you. It is nice to have such warm regard for another, is it not?" She traced her finger along the side of his face. "As it grows, it gets smoother."

"*Oui,*" said Joshua. He was silent.

Lucie glanced at him. "Food did not waken you, then?" She asked the question as if she knew the answer.

She did. "No," he said.

"You want to tell me?"

"I was thinking."

She said soberly, "Please tell me."

He held her a little away. Then he said, "You cannot stay here longer. I am going to give myself up, and take you with me."

"Ah, no!" She twisted away and sat up. She repeated, "No, please!"

He stretched out full length and frowned up at her. "Don't cozen me, wench." Then he took her hand, and turned it over in his. "Thin little hand," he said. "I can't stand it any longer, Lucie. It's impossible." His voice was strong. "Tomorrow I take you into the town, and surrender you into the care of the British."

"Please, Joshua!" she said.

"There are a few times when I arrive at decisions and do not alter them." He sat up himself and kissed her. "I love you, sweetheart." He pulled at one braid and stretched out again. "But I can't stand it any longer, Lucie!"

"I do not argue," she said, whereupon Joshua laughed. "I do not argue because I know it is useless," she added, and curled up beside him with her head on his shoulder.

Joshua said, "I may be able to bribe our way out. At first I hated to give up."

His arms tightened around her. "I don't want to do it, darling! But I must. If something happened to you," he spoke slowly, "I should never forgive myself. Never."

The moonlight shimmered. "But," she began, and then stopped. "What will they do to you?" Her eyes fastened on his bearded face; he could see the rise and fall of her breast as she waited for the answer.

"Probably nothing," said Joshua comfortingly.

She didn't believe him. She said clearly, "I love you so much."

He caught her close. "Listen, darling. Even if we are separated, it won't be for so long! We'll be together again. It won't last long! It can't, can it?" He tipped her face up. "If you squeeze even one tear out, I'll beat you, wench, so help me God." As he stopped speaking, he heard the crackle of a branch under a man's foot. He set her away from him, rolled over and seized his knife. He went to the mouth of the cave, the knife held down by his side.

"Who comes?" he called.

"It is I," answered de Bouillé breathlessly, and Joshua saw him, then, running across the clearing as though the devil himself pursued him. De Bouillé couldn't speak for a moment.

Joshua felt a wild surge of hope. He stared at de Bouillé, coming out of the cave to stand in front of him. "What?" he said.

De Bouillé pointed. "The 'Athena,'" he said. "Barney's come."

Lucie came out of the cave, dressed in her torn blouse and skirt, braids swinging. They each took her by the hand and smiled down at her. Nevertheless, when she passed the clearing and the firepit, and came to stand on the edge of the little pool, she turned for a last look. Now at night in the moonlight it was peaceful and lovely—she would never see it again. This part of their life together had ended. There had been so much good in it.

Joshua caught her eye. He squeezed her hand and smiled. Now that it was over he could forget the anxiety. "Now you go home and marry George," he said, and chuckled.

De Bouillé looked puzzled, and Lucie said, "That is one of m'sieur's private jokes, and it really has no merit as humor."

Joshua grinned again, and picked her up in his arms. "I carry you, wench," he said. "You can't get your feet wet at night."

He splashed ahead with her, de Bouillé coming behind. They both knew the way by heart, to the beach, where they swam every day; in fact they both had explored this wilderness together, sometimes taking her along with them, on a hunt for game.

"If I never see a wild fowl again, or a fish," de Bouillé muttered from behind them.

Joshua held Lucie tight and safe in his arms as he carried her easily through the water. When they came to the sandy path, he set her down carefully.

Trees brushed at her with impatient fingers. For the last descent she gathered her skirts in one hand and held to Joshua with the other. She heard voices.

The other men were gathering. The news had been spread fast through the forest. Then suddenly they were at the small sandy beach. And there, riding just a few hundred yards from shore, was the "Athena." She had already put out her boats, and for the first time in many months Joshua heard Barney's voice, coming across the water in a crisp command.

"Hold water!"

Joshua saw the boat was waiting for the oncoming breaker behind it.

"Stern all!" cried Barney.

The oars were backed. The boat waited, and then the breaker seized it like a toy and lifted it and Barney yelled "Oars!" and the men pulled fast with the wave, and in the next second, it seemed to Joshua, it was flung on the beach and right before their feet. The men jumped out and pulled it to safety on the white sand.

Whereupon Barney leisurely stepped out of the boat. He stood there a moment, hands on the big pistols in his belt, and looked around. "Well, gentlemen," he said, and Joshua saw his flashing smile.

Joshua and de Bouillé each took Barney's hand in a strong grip. "Nice to see you again, sir," Joshua commented.

Barney grinned. "Bunch of jolly tars landlocked, I see." He bowed to Lucie.

Lucie said, "You came just in time!" She put out her hand and Barney took it. "François and Joshua—they say nothing! But they thought you would come!" She stopped breathlessly, looking up at Barney's dark face, seeing past him the rolling waves which used to be empty. Now the "Athena" rode out there.

"You did come, sir," Lucie repeated, eyes shining. "And they waited long. *Ecoutez;* they call your name!"

Barney looked around the rapidly filling beach. He waved his hands.

"They were starving, sir," Lucie whispered to Barney. *"Vraiment!* Before they surrender!"

More boats had pulled into the beach. Scull and Macgregor and Connor came running up, and the boat crews emptied out of the boats and ran up to the groups of excited men on the beach.

"They call your name, sir," Lucie said. "But not quite like in the theatre! They do not dare make noise!"

Barney smiled down at her. "You remember the theatre?"

"I never forget," Lucie said. "I had your note; Joshua came next day to the Governor's, and we escaped through the plantation, through the sugar cane. François had a boat here, but when we arrived, it was gone."

Suddenly all that had gone before was recalled; once more they stood together as though the fates had spun, and the tangled webs of their lives enmeshed. And around them the men gathered.

Barney called, "We take the sick first!" Then he said, "Mr. Scull. Carry on. Get these men aboard." He turned to Joshua and de Bouillé. "I'll be back soon, sirs."

33

THE HOUSE WAS WELL LIGHTED. BARNEY CLIMBED RAPIDLY UPWARD toward it. He knew the climb well, for he had often used this way of coming down to the surf to swim. Nevertheless, it might be difficult for Douglass, so he had taken the precaution of bringing a length of rope which was coiled and hanging from his waist. He drew himself up over the last big rock. There he paused, listening, his dark eyes seeing the lighted windows. For the first time it occurred to him she might not be alone.

Above his head the stone balustrade of the small balcony afforded a good handhold. He pulled himself up, as he always did, set his foot in the edge of the stone, and vaulted lightly over onto the stone floor. He edged carefully to the wall alongside the open door, just past the oblong of light that was thrown out here from the bedroom within. He pressed back against the wall; he could see into the room sideways.

The balcony looked just as usual; just as it had the last night he had been here. Way below, from the beach, the surf broke with a constant thunder; Saba rose black from the sea in the distance. Over that distant thunder he now heard the murmur of men's voices from the open windows of the next room; his ears and senses told him sharply of the danger. He stood unmoving, his breath coming swiftly and shallowly; there were at least six men in the big room.

He could see Douglass. She was sitting in front of her table, and Esther stood behind her, repinning the curls on the top of her head. The vision of her he had carried now was replaced by the reality; for a second he forgot that she was not alone and almost stepped forward into the doorway when he was brought up by the sound of laughter coming from the long windows to his right.

Sharply the scene presented itself. It was etched on his mind as though it were a play, and he quite outside of it. For the man at her side must be Admiral Hood.

There was no conversation to overhear, for the moment. A number of things went through Barney's mind, as he pressed back against the stone walls. His hands had dropped to his loaded pistols, resting on the butts. He thought that Hood must have come over to Stasia for brief instructions, and perhaps because some of his ships were more disabled than the French thought. Barney knew that the gold braid on the magnificent uniform was real; he thought with cynicism that the British Navy had reclaimed its own.

Hood was completely at ease; Esther's fingers still pinned and repinned the shining piled curls while Hood took a turn around the room. Then he came back into Barney's sight again. Douglass' eyes met his in the mirror. It was hard for Barney to realize only seconds had passed and that the scene had conveyed so much without a word being spoken. Douglass smiled at Hood; she too was at ease, her cool voice sounded now.

"Sir George said that he thought it would be best for me to wait, since I am safe now."

Sir George was Rodney, Barney knew. Hood was saying, "The house is remarkably comfortable—I must say it surprises me that the Yankee has such good taste. His antecedents are completely unknown, you know."

"I know," said Douglass softly.

"He is the friend of your brother-in-law?" Hood questioned.

"Yes," she replied.

"Your experiment of living in the colonies didn't work, Douglass. You might have known." He eyed her sharply in the mirror.

"Yes," she said again. She rose, sweeping her skirts to one side with one white hand.

Hood took her other hand and put it in the crook of his arm. She walked to the door with him. Barney saw her go away from him, and then the door opened; he heard for a moment the more distinct sound of voices and then that door closed too, shutting out the voices and the last sight of her.

Barney let his whole body relax slowly; he let his hands drop down to his sides, and he stepped to the balustrade.

[205]

As he did so, Esther sensed him. She stood in the center of the room, her head on one side, listening. Barney froze against the wall again. His big chest rose and fell fast as he waited for Esther to leave the room, too.

It seemed a long time; actually it was a scant two minutes. But as he waited there alone, in such a situation that even the sharp cry of a surprised woman might mean disaster or death, the folly that he had committed in coming here was made plain.

It flashed across his mind that it was similar to the madness of the anger which had caused him to hurl a burning heavy matchstick at his captain; and this time it was worse, it was premeditated. Let him deceive himself not at all; he had all along thought of climbing here, and taking away with him the woman he wanted. Surely it was as mad an action as the fit of anger which he had allowed himself and which might have ruined his career; it served to emphasize also to him, in these brief ticking seconds, while Esther listened, uneasy, and he waited—it emphasized his own reckless seizing. He told himself grimly he was twenty-seven years old, and should know better, and that if he didn't soon, he wouldn't live much longer, anyway.

Esther had gone. He, thinking now of time, realized with guilt that he had left Scull in command of a dangerous operation—dangerous not because of the operation itself, but because of the discovery which might ensue. With quick, steady hands he hitched the rope over the stone balustrade and swung down it as fast as he could, feet just touching the rocks once in a while as he slid. He landed on the beach sooner than he thought; he stood for a moment, then he turned and walked rapidly in the direction of the "Athena" and Tumbledown Dick. The rope dangled. Then guilt once more assailed him and he began to run. Scull was efficient, so was Macgregor, but they were unimaginative.

It took him thus only seven minutes to reach the outskirts of Tumbledown Dick, and he slid down the steep wall of rocky cliff, again reaching the bottom before he expected. He landed on all fours, and picked himself up, brushing the loose sand and dirt from his legs. He was back; the ship was safe; there was a handful of men—around fifty—left on the curving white beach. He stood, to catch his breath; they had not perceived him yet, even though he was but a hundred feet away.

The ship was safe; the men were safe. The other events could be summed up quickly. He had behaved like a damned fool, and he had lost to the British Navy the woman for whom he had committed this rash act. For a moment he could not believe it, any more than he had believed it when he saw it with his own eyes. It was too easy to remember her voice, whispering, "I love you, Barney." The danger he had been in had not prevented the anger and jealousy, but muted it beneath enforced caution. Now he thought cynically that it had been his own fault for leaving her where the British might reclaim their own; he'd taken a chance on that, he'd known it at the time. Now too she was lost to him. He frowned, and thrust away the image of her, and walked toward the beach in even long strides. There was no use thinking about her now; he would admit only that she intrigued him more than most women did; the adventure was ended and over. He saw Macgregor, and smiled a bit to himself when he realized he had never been quite so glad to see that square face before.

Macgregor said, "We have almost completed the mission, sir!" Proudly, he waved his arm at the five boats that were now pulling toward the "Athena," crammed to the gunwales with men. The moonlight obliquely paved a path across the water to the frigate. Macgregor, looking at the ship, said, "Isn't she beautiful, sir?"

"Yes, Mr. Macgregor," Barney said. "Yes, she is. Carry on, sir."

His feet sank in the sand as he walked over to Joshua and de Bouillé. Lucie sat on the big rock, and Connor crouched at its foot, talking. As Barney came up, he looked past de Bouillé to Joshua; their eyes met. Joshua said, "Barney," and then without another word, both of them walked away a few feet to the wet sand, the water curled in near them with a little sucking sound.

Joshua said, without preamble, "Connor's been telling de Bouillé. We're going to stay."

Barney looked at Joshua; he was conscious of the sound of the water, and the men's voices and of Lucie sitting there on the rock, with Connor crouched beside her.

"You're going to stay?" he repeated.

"I know every inch of this forest, and the beaches. I've climbed down Jenkin's Bay many times. Jenkin's Bay is the only bay that is not visible from Signal Hill; and after this, after they discover what happened tonight, they will leave the picquet at the Hill all night— you can be sure of that."

"Yes," said Barney, "but—"

"Connor's been telling us how vital it is you get information on the fleet and convoy movements. Both de Bouillé and I are able to judge, with a good glass, what's going on. Connor also said you would use the cutter 'Sylph,' the 'Athena' and sometimes native canoes, from Saba, Guadeloupe."

"Yes," said Barney.

"Of course they will not know these men have been evacuated for some time, Barney."

"Yes," Barney repeated.

"It is a very simple matter to keep the harbor under surveillance; there are numerous advantageous spots." Joshua suddenly added, "Why so glum? We'll let you know what's happening and you can catch 'em." He grinned and Barney smiled, too.

"It's a damned important job you'll be doing," he said.

"I know that," said Joshua briefly, and Barney couldn't help smiling.

A returning boat was dragged in almost at their feet. This job was almost done. Joshua turned, and Barney nodded. It was time to say goodbye.

Connor and de Bouillé were still talking. Joshua came up and lifted Lucie off the rock. Barney, looking at all of them, said, "Connor told you we brought the chest of provisions?" He glanced around and saw the big chest, fifteen feet away. "Now unpack it; so you don't leave it all to be found. And move daily. That is important. Never stay in one place. I shall be back in three days. At that time I will arrange for the next rendezvous. I will come always at night, of course." He wanted suddenly to say more. He wanted to say something reassuring. "We brought muskets, pistols, rum, lemons, bread, pork—" He broke off. They would find what he had brought. He glanced at Lucie.

Lucie was standing between de Bouillé and Joshua. She put out her hands and touched each one on the arm. "Take care," she said. She caught her lip in her teeth.

Barney knew that was what he had been saying, too. Lucie dropped her hand from de Bouillé's arm and put it in his hand. He kissed it. *"Au revoir,"* she said.

Joshua gathered her close in his arms, tipping her head back for a long kiss. "Let them look," he whispered. "I love you." He kissed her again, holding her tight, and then he set her back.

Barney said, "I'll take you, Lucie."

"The devil you will," said Joshua, picking her up. Barney looked at his bearded face, and the slight figure of Lucie in his arms. "She's my gal, Barney," Joshua said, carrying her toward Barney's boat, and wading out into the water to set her in the sternsheets as Barney climbed in from the other side. Joshua kept his arms around her; he leaned close. "Don't marry George," he whispered. "How about waiting for me?"

"I love you, Joshua," she said. "Take care."

"Don't forget what I told you about my agent in Martinique."

"I won't."

"Take care of her, Barney." He stepped away.

"I'll keep her safe," Barney said.

The boat was shoved off. Joshua waved. "Goodbye," he called. He heard her call back. She looked so little sitting there with Barney. Wolf, Barney's coxswain, jumped in last, and the oars dipped and rose. The boat pulled from shore.

Joshua stood at the water's edge. He watched the boat. It reached the "Athena" without incident, but it was too far to see figures mount the ladder to her decks. Alongside of him de Bouillé watched, too. The last men were leaving, calling goodbye in low voices, touched a bit with awe, for they knew what the two men must be staying for. Macgregor came over for a last word.

"I'll be thinking of you, lads," he said, and held out his hand. Joshua took it and grasped it hard. De Bouillé did the same. Then Macgregor jumped in the last boat. He waved as it pulled away, humping over the first line of breakers and bouncing down the other side of the wave in a splash plain to see. The spray flew up.

Joshua turned then from the sea. The big chest lay on the lonely beach. The tide was coming in faster now; he knew soon it would reach the big rock. De Bouillé said, "While you put Lucie in the boat, Barney told me a last instruction."

"Yes?" asked Joshua, since de Bouillé had paused.

"If one of us is caught, the other is not to go to his aid. Someone must be left to tell the news, and besides it would be useless gallantry." De Bouillé paused again. "Those were his exact words. Then he said, 'For you are but two.'"

Joshua said, "I see." He regarded de Bouillé for a long moment. "It makes sense." He went over to the chest and put his hand on the sturdy handle. "Let's get this up to the cave and unpacked. I'm starving."

PART FOUR

34

THE ROPE DANGLED. IT WAS LOOPED AROUND THE STONE, AND THE knot looked to Douglass like a figure eight from which it fell all the way to the beach. Had it been five months since she had first come out in the morning and seen it hanging there?

She sat down on the chaise longue. It was two o'clock and the sun did not yet strike with dazzling blindness this small stone balcony. This was her favorite spot. The sea sparkled endlessly; Saba with its collar surf beckoned; the rope swayed and trembled in the wind.

It had been a message from him, she knew. Every day for a month after she had found it, she leaned way over to look at the dangling end, to see if there were something tied to it—a note, any kind of a message but this silent one. She heard Esther coming through the bedroom.

Esther said, "Admiral Hood, madam."

Douglass said, "I am sorry. I want to see no one, Esther." She turned back to the sea again.

There was silence again. She leaned back on the chaise. Then she heard a man's footsteps, coming across the bedroom. She stood quickly. She regarded the intruder's figure.

"You shouldn't, Samuel," she said. She backed away. "You intrude!"

Hood made a gesture, took her hand. "I had to see you," he said. He looked at her, and then around the balcony. "Sit down, Douglass," he said. "Please."

She obeyed slowly, watching him as he went over to the balustrade and looked across the blue tropic seas, as if he were deciding how to frame his next words to her. He ran his hand absently over the rope.

"How did this get here?" he asked.

She said, "I don't know." But she did not look at him. "It looks like a figure eight, doesn't it?"

"No," he said absently. "It's a bowline, not a figure-of-eight. A bowline, Douglass, is one of the most common and useful knots known to seamanship. It forms a loop, of any length, and the heavier the pull upon it the tighter it jams. It's used for lowering men over a ship's side, and so forth."

"Lowering men?" she repeated, leaning forward.

He turned from the sea. "Have you been lowering a ship's company?" He smiled a little, and dropped down into the chair opposite her. "Lean back, Douglass. I've news for you."

She said, "A man could have lowered himself down it?"

"Of course," he said. "And it looks as though a man did—from the condition of the knot—it's tight; it's had weight." He contemplated her, frowning a little. Then he said strongly, "If he came, you missed him; or we were here." His jaw set and he got to his feet. "How long are you going to hang onto this silly dream? That the legendary Barney will descend upon the island and carry you off singlehandedly?"

Her red mouth set rebelliously, and her grey eyes shone. "How dare you, sir?"

"Douglass, let's quit play-acting. You haven't fooled me for a long time. As a matter of fact, one of the reasons this house is under guard is because I expected he might turn up. We missed him, too, if he came, and this indicates that he did. But he won't come now."

Douglass looked at the rope. Hood continued. "Put it out of your mind. There are heavy batteries at Tumbledown Dick, English Quarter, White Cliffs, Gloucester and Townsend. And I didn't come this morning to talk about Barney; I came to talk about you. There is almost nobody left on the island save the plantation owners, and the Dutch merchants. You have no place here; we're going to send you home."

There was silence. Then Douglass said, "But I don't want to go!"

"You've been saying that for three months. Your position here is no longer tenable, and for a matter of fact neither is ours. I can tell you that frankly. It's no secret. Our every move is watched and reported. Yesterday we got word that the big convoy, the first one, under Commodore Hotham, was intercepted by a swarm of well-informed French privateers. That's been happening to all of them.

"Let me tell you, Douglass, your legendary Barney is too busy preying on our commerce. It's almost incredible. It's as though someone were at his elbow telling him that such and such a barquentine left Stasia, bearing north-northeast, carrying cannonballs, whereas the information about convoys is relayed fast to every French and American privateer—in the whole damned world, I think! The capture of Stasia was supposed to cut off the rebels from the sources of their supplies, and to punish the Dutch; instead, it looks as though we're supplying the rebels free! We've been busy as bees mopping up honey, instead of fighting the French!" He got to his feet and paced across the balcony. "And the admiral's last order is that every national save the Dutch are to leave."

Her golden head was bent a little; the long lashes shadowed her eyes. "Sir," she began.

He cut her short. "The answer is no." He looked down at her and sighed.

"Oh, Douglass, forget him. Give him up."

"I don't think I can."

"What if he were dead?"

"I—I—well, I think I should want to die too. There is no such report, is there?"

"No, unfortunately. But there have been reports . . . It's been five months now. There have been reports . . . What if he has found himself a new love, a mistress?"

There was a flash of anger in Douglass' eyes as Hood went on.

"I do not know this. I do not believe it. But Barney was not born for one woman. His mistress is always and only Adventure. Call it what you please—Glory, The Sea. That's what he is wedded to. Everyone knows that for him women are only passing excitements. How many he has had! So many who loved him and tried to hold him! They've had no better success than we. We have him, he seems to be ours and then, as in Plymouth, he is gone."

Douglass may not have been listening to all this, for suddenly her smoldering eyes changed and she said:

"Passing excitement. He was only a passing excitement to me. Very exciting, but passed now forever.

"Yes, he could have come, could have sent word if he wanted to. Good, I'm glad.

"I was never serious. It could never have worked—he off on his pirated vessels somewhere at sea and I in that Philadelphia. I don't like the country at all. I'll be glad to get home to England."

"And the company of Englishmen. You could almost take your pick of my officers. Captain Reynolds wants to marry you, and Captain Henry—"

She raised her eyes. "The fleet leaves?"

"I can't answer that. But your sojourn here is almost ended. Be ready to leave on a moment's notice." He still stood over her. Now he sat down beside her. "I'm sorry." He took her hand in his. "Maybe the more beautiful a woman is the more trouble she gets into." He smiled. "Why don't you marry John Reynolds?"

Douglass stood up. She walked to the balcony and the dangling rope. Then she turned. "Perhaps I shall, sir." Then she added, "In England, of course."

35

DE BOUILLÉ GLUED THE GLASS TO HIS EYE. HE WAS LYING ON THE bare ground, his toes dug into the dirt loosened by his own restless movements.

He was hot and sweaty. The sun had boiled down on him for the last four hours, or almost four hours. Soon this vigil would end, and he visualized Joshua peacefully asleep in the cool darkness of the cave. "Lucky bastard," said de Bouillé to himself cheerfully, for there was big news today. His half-shut blue eyes gleamed when he thought of the report already written.

Joshua had begun it, at dawn, and begun it ominously.

"Eighteen men hanged this morning for mutiny." That was marked six-thirty.

The next entry came at ten. "Cofferdam below fort blown up."

The roar of it wakened de Bouillé. Now he could see the incoming tide washing up over the destruction. He winced a little as he watched. There was no doubt but that the English were systematically destroying the harbor. And there was no doubt that they were provisioning the fleet for sailing.

He had made his last entry. With dirty fingers he rolled it up and tucked it into the oilskin packet. This he placed under the big rock, carefully. Joshua would come soon, in fifteen minutes precisely, and until then it rested safely, hidden well, in case; it was a precaution they always took.

De Bouillé yawned. By his side lay his loaded musket, and at his hand his pistol. The sun glinted on the barrel. He looked at his watch, squinting at the hands in the brilliant sunlight. Only ten minutes more. He almost fancied he could hear Joshua coming, when he realized suddenly, with a tenseness that held him crouched low there, supine, that it was not Joshua at all.

The first thing that flashed through his mind was that the packet was safe. He had already laid down the glass. Slowly he raised himself enough to crawl, drawing his legs up under him. The big rock over which he had peered to watch the harbor might serve as protection. He eased himself around it, still almost flat on the ground, dragging the musket with him. Once around it, he reached out for the pistol.

He told himself that now he must try to see who had made those noises. He wet his lips. Hunched over, he looked around the big black rock.

Right below him the Quill sloped down into a mass of thick trees. This spot could be approached through that cover, and that was why it was one of Joshua's and his favorite spots to watch from. Now he fancied he saw the branches of those trees move. But it was not fancy. De Bouillé saw plainly the flash of a red uniform.

His heart thudded. In one quick second he realized that if he lay here longer they might not find him, for a while. They might not. But de Bouillé knew that through those thick trees, Joshua was coming, soon. Slowly de Bouillé raised his musket.

He sighted down it carefully, ready. Lips slightly parted, one eye closed with the sweat trickling down his dirty face, he waited for the next flash of red, and when it came he fired. De Bouillé reloaded fast, reflecting grimly that he had not only surely made a hit, but had warned Joshua. Joshua, hearing the musket shot, would stop in his tracks.

Now there was, suddenly, no sound at all. The musket was ready to fire again, and again de Bouillé was searching through the green of the trees for the flash of red. At the same time he saw the red again, he heard the sound of another gun, and a bullet zinged off the rock, spattering him with fragments of stone. De Bouillé fired in the direction of the sound. He would have time to reload again certainly. With steady fingers he tamped the powder down, when suddenly the trees disgorged his foe.

De Bouillé fired. He dropped the musket, raised the pistol. A bullet whistled past his ear. He aimed the pistol at the nearest figure, running toward him. The man dropped. De Bouillé snapped the weapon open.

He felt a stinging pain in his arm. Before he had loaded the pistol the blood was running down over his hand. He wiped it off his fingers onto his breeches, endeavoring to cock the weapon with one hand. This he did. He was able to fire it once more. He raised it slowly, at a man who was almost on top of him.

"You son of a bitch," he said distinctly, as he leaned back against the rock and watched two more British marines coming. Three pistols spoke at once. De Bouillé heard no more.

Down the trail, under cover of the trees, the sound of musket fire stopped Joshua dead in his tracks. Barefooted, naked to the waist, and browned a deep mahogany by the sun, Joshua edged silently behind a big tree.

Another burst of fire held him motionless. It was not far away. With ease he began to climb the big tree.

He ascended high into its branches. His ears had told him plainly that at least ten muskets were being fired. While it did not yet occur to him that de Bouillé had deliberately fired to warn him, it did occur to him that there were far too many men on this hunt for Joshua to give any aid, even though he had been under orders *not* to give aid. Joshua, sitting grimly athwart a high branch, waited.

There was no more sound of firing. Because of the wind, he heard no voices. If he climbed even higher, he could see. This he did.

He clung to the top of the swaying pine. He counted fifteen redcoated soldiers. Between four of them they were carrying de Bouillé, like a sack.

Joshua brutally forced himself not to think, not of de Bouillé. He had only one duty, and that was to stay alive to give the news to Barney.

Undoubtedly they would leave men around the rock, hidden there, later, perhaps in the darkness. Joshua slid down from the high perch, choosing a branch about thirty feet off the ground. Sitting there, his feet dangling over, he would wait till darkness. Then in the familiar forest he would make his way to the cave and then to Jenkin's Bay.

The afternoon sun slowly began its descent. Long minutes made grueling hours. Through the trees there was only silence, the twittering of birds, the sigh of the summer wind. From time to time Joshua moved, to give relief to his aching muscles, cramped by his position. From where he sat he could see the sun sinking into the sea. The wind began to have the night smell of salt and wet. Tonight might be misty.

If de Bouillé were not dead, what would they do to him? He was still wearing the remnants of a French uniform. Joshua could hear him saying, plainly, smilingly, "They might not hang me, but they'd string you up for sure, Yank."

Joshua muttered, "God damn it to hell!" He stared unseeingly out across the vast Atlantic, empty, rolling. The night colors of the sunset touched the highest of the piled clouds; slowly the majesty of it began to fade. When the colors were gone, when the sea was grey with coming night, he left his perch. Silently he retraced the steps that had brought him here so many hours ago. With precision he took exactly three hunks of biscuit and the water flask. He swung the lantern over his shoulder. Then he went down to the beach to wait.

36

IT WAS MIDNIGHT. THE BLACK WATERS OF JENKIN'S BAY SWIRLED with foam as they beat against cliff walls.

The cliffs were three hundred feet high, and descended in ruthless swiftness to the waters they enclosed; the crash of surf was endless and angry.

From no height on Stasia could the waters of Jenkin's Bay be seen; this promontory of rock was so well guarded by nature that Lieutenant Mackenzie had reported it impregnable, therefore no bluntnosed guarding batteries marked its topmost rocks. It was exactly midnight when the "Athena" nosed cautiously into its restless waters; mercifully they were deep, deep right to the walls. Even so the leadsman in the chains called out the fathoms, chanting. Astern the "Athena" came the Marquis de Bouillé with his accompanying frigates, four of them.

Joshua was dressed in short canvas trousers and a shirt of Barney's. He leaned on the rail. It was so familiar.

He heard the muted commands of the officers, of the bo'sun, of Barney, as he and de Bouillé had often heard them from the tiny strip of beach where they had waited so many times, swinging their lanterns to guide the "Athena." There were no lanterns on the beach tonight.

It had been six days.

The surf crashed as always. Way up, the trees towered. This bowl of rock shook with the boom of endless beating waves.

"In with the tops."

Around Joshua's waist was a coil of rope. The boats were ready. Over his head he saw the tops furled tight; he heard the orders fore and the splash of anchors. It was time.

He went down the gangway to the lee boat, and got in. Barney hopped in beside him. The boat was swung quickly over the side.

It hit the water sharply and neatly. Barney's coxswain, Wolf, had landed him on this beach many times. Tonight it was accomplished as swiftly and well as it always was. In three minutes Joshua stood on the tiny beach, for there was only a strip of beach about ten feet by twenty here, at the base of the cliffs. He turned to Barney. "We —we always climbed up this side." He gestured.

"Good luck," said Barney.

Joshua moved away, his figure disappearing from sight in the blackness. He was barefooted, as always, and he made no sound. But, nevertheless, Barney strained his eyes to see and his ears to hear.

Barney paced back and forth on the strip of sand, pausing occasionally to listen. A loosened rock hurtled down to the beach, bouncing against the cliff as it came down. His body tensed. Then there was no further sound. He turned to stare at the bay.

The five frigates were peacefully anchored. Barney knew they could not be seen from any height on the island, not here, within these enclosing walls. On the beach the men were unloading the rope ladders, laying them neatly atop one another. A lighted lantern burned.

Another fall of rock made Barney tense again. He listened. No more sound, and he could see nothing.

Atop the cliff Joshua pulled himself over the last outcropping, once more dislodging a loose stone. He hung tight to the big boulder, seeking for another toehold. He found it, tested it, loosed the one hand, and put his weight on the left foot. It held! He was up and over.

As he walked toward the place Barney had chosen from the detailed map, he uncoiled the rope. He fastened the rope to a tall pine, some fifteen feet back from the cliff wall, fastening it with the knot Barney had instructed, a bowline. Then Joshua approached the sheer wall; he tossed the weighted rope down.

The belaying pin bounced against the rocks as it came down. Barney leaped for it. Swiftly he tied to the rope the topmost rope ladder. Then he gave three hard tugs. It began to ascend as Joshua hauled it up.

When the end of the rope ladder dangled right at Barney's feet, he waited for about two minutes. Then he tugged on it again, and felt the answering pulls. He put his foot in the first ratline and began to climb. In two minutes he stood on the top of the cliff with Joshua.

"Your knots held, sir," he said, and grinned. Then he leaned over the cliff. "Lanterns, Wolf," he called softly.

Wolf obediently swung the lantern, back and forth, back and forth. And, seeing it, aboard the French frigate Captain Connor gave a quick order. Then he turned to the Marquis de Bouillé. "We are ready to commence landing operations, sir."

Four long rope ladders swung over the sides of the cliffs at Jenkin's Bay. Boats pulled from the ships to shore and back again. And hand over hand, in the long hours of the night, uniformed French soldiers swarmed onto Stasia. They formed into small companies at the top, drawing back from the steep cliffs to let more of their fellows gain solid earth again after swinging between air and water for three hundred feet. Not many men could be landed at one time, because the boats had to be well crewed. The surf was heavy. And only one man could climb the swaying ladders at one time. It took four hours to land four hundred men. But at four o'clock, Captain Connor was able to say to the panting marquis, "I am able to report that only three men were lost in a difficult and lengthy landing operation, sir!"

They were landed, all right, Connor thought. From the height he could hear faintly the sounds of anchors being weighed, as the foremost frigate weighed anchor; the rest would follow suit. In the morning they would be in the roadway at Stasia, appearing out of the night. His own men were moving off; every minute of the next hours had been well planned. He smiled as he came up to Barney and Joshua, the smile crinkling the scar on his face.

"We'll go ahead of the troops now, sirs," he said, looking delighted.

"It is roughly a mile," Joshua said, in muted tones. "Roughly a mile to Signal Hill, and then another mile to Tumbledown Dick. We can send a detail to man Tumbledown Dick."

They were moving up a dirt trail, rocky, steep. "This is formed by torrents of water," Joshua explained. "At Signal Hill only one man can walk abreast."

With them were a few picked men. They went single file; they carried no muskets, they hoped not to use pistols. They carried knives. With Joshua ahead, they climbed upward still, toward Signal Hill.

It didn't take them very long. Late moonlight infiltrated the scene. They slipped through the pass, and onto the bit of level land with the sugar cane stretching in the distance, here on the top of the island.

The small garrison was sound asleep. Signal House was a low barracks. Two sentries paced back and forth; within thirty men slept peacefully. Connor and one of his lieutenants moved forward like swift lightning. Before the surprised sentries had time to sling the muskets off their shoulders, Connor and his lieutenant sprang, knives in hand. Then the rest of the men moved out of the shadows to surround the building.

Connor flung open the door and ran down the center of the long room with Barney and Joshua and the rest of the men behind him. The garrison woke to look into leveled pistols. No resistance was possible. They were tied quickly, and the doors closed again, leaving each helpless on his cot, with five armed guards. Connor ran back to the pass, to hear the reassuring sound of more men marching. They appeared through the pass, formed into a line of four men abreast, and began the march down to the town.

It was five o'clock. The dawn was breaking over Stasia. In Upper Town, Colonel Cockburne's orderly roused, yawned, and sat up sleepily. The colonel always rode at daybreak, a brisk canter before breakfast. He rolled out of bed.

In Upper Town, Mrs. Bachels, widow, was already dressed. She went over to her window to look out. She stared. Then she ran out of her own room and to her son's door. She knocked.

He answered sleepily. She called, "I see the glitter of arms on the road to Signal Hill! Get up!"

In a few minutes he appeared. In response to her admonition, he ran downstairs and out into the garden; she followed him. He disappeared up the winding road toward Signal Hill.

He didn't return. In desperation she dashed down the road to the nearest house, forgetting her cows that needed milking. She knocked on the door of the house where Lieutenant Mackenzie was quartered. When the front door flew open, she said, breathless, "Tell the lieutenant I saw the glitter of arms on Signal Hill road! I sent my son William, and he has not come back!"

The lieutenant, too, rolled out of bed. At the same minute he did so, Colonel Cockburne rode out the lowered drawbridge of Fort Amsterdam, and clattered across it for his morning ride. Lieutenant Mackenzie saw him pass by, shouted to him, but could not make him hear. Mackenzie, dressed now, dashed downstairs and down the hill to the church.

A red flag raised over the church steeple was the warning signal, in case of danger. As he entered the church he heard hoofbeats behind him. He had the flag half raised when he heard a voice behind him.

"Halt or I fire," Connor said grimly.

Instead, Mackenzie yanked on the ropes. Connor raised the pistol and fired. Slowly Mackenzie's hands fell from the ropes; he swayed and crumpled. Above, the red flag slowly drifted downward. A loose end of it clung to an edge of the slanting roof.

Connor had commandeered Colonel Cockburne's horse; the colonel himself had ridden straight into the arms of the marching French. The colonel was not even armed. He could not believe it.

"A *coup de main*," he muttered. "But how?"

Joshua did not bother to enlighten him. The troops marched past steadily, at double pace. Joshua said, "The Frenchman you captured! De Bouillé! Where is he?"

The colonel was thinking he would face court-martial for this. "In the hospital," he said.

Joshua and Barney ran, followed by the twenty marines Barney had picked for tonight. They ran down past Mrs. Bachels, and past the church, and into the white hospital next to the church.

It was another long low building. Sixty-one men were its patients. The sixty-first was guarded.

Joshua did not even bother to disarm the guard. With twenty marines behind him, there was hardly need. De Bouillé slept flat on his face, as always; it flashed through Joshua's mind that the entrance of twenty-two men had failed to disturb de Bouillé's slumbers. "He can sleep through anything," Joshua said, as he stood over the bed and looked down at de Bouillé's dark head.

De Bouillé rolled over. His eyes flew open. Then he sat up slowly. His chest and one arm were swathed in clean bandages; they had shaved him and he looked thin. But the smile on his face made up for it. He held out a bandaged arm and hand. " 'Allo, Yank," he said.

Connor's men were marching across the drawbridge; the first intimation that the unwarned garrison had of imminent attack was the actual presence of enemy troops within the fort. Exactly three shots were fired, and then the flag that had just been raised was hauled down. Connor despatched a detail of his handsomest flaxen-haired English and Irish troops, with a lieutenant in charge. "Inform the Governor that he is a prisoner of war."

That detail of troops marched through Upper Town and up to the mansion. The still unsuspecting people thought them English. So did the Governor. When the lieutenant told him politely, in his English voice, that he was a prisoner of war, the Governor didn't believe it.

"You are reinforcements for the island, that we sighted last night!"

"Exactly, Your Excellency," said the lieutenant. "But in French pay." He grinned. The prize money would be big.

And at that same time, Connor's other details had reached their objectives. The posts of Gloucester, Townsend, Fort George, had been manned by French troops; and the still sleeping English officers were routed out of their comfortable quarters in the various homes of Upper Town. Stasia had been recaptured.

37

BARNEY GALLOPED UP THE STEEP ROAD, REACHED THE LEVEL AND pounded down past the waving sugar cane; through it was the road they had used this morning. He reached the low white house in a cloud of dust.

He raced up the steep steps.

The door was unlocked. He walked in. Then he waited a moment and listened. Hurrying footsteps in the distance told him by their sound they were not hers. Barney said, "Madam Harris?" He took a step forward.

"Madam has gone, sir."

The two men looked at each other. Finally the Negro spoke. "How, sir? You are back?"

"We've recaptured Stasia—you are in French hands now. Where is Esther?"

"Madam took her."

"I see." Barney walked past the white-coated servant, into the bedroom, through it and out onto the balcony. He saw the rope.

He went over to it. He reached down and untied it; he hauled it up, coiling it neatly as he did so. When it was all in his hands he looked down at it.

Why had she left it there? He went through the bedroom again. The closet door was open and empty. The servant was still standing where Barney had left him.

"When did madam leave?"

"With the last convoy, sir. Four days ago."

Barney didn't say anything. He laid the rope down. He went out the door and closed it firmly behind him.

Halfway down the hill back to Upper Town, he reined in. She was gone, then. She was four days gone; she was somewhere on the high seas, and every French and American privateer knew the sailing time of that big convoy. Suddenly a vivid picture of her came into his mind and he could see her plainly—beautiful, willful and alone, in a convoy inadequately guarded.

The horse ambled to a stop. From here Barney could see into the harbor; he could see the "Athena"; she was putting out a boat, and it was for him. He urged the horse on again.

Joshua and de Bouillé and the marquis were waiting for him, in a small room in the hospital. De Bouillé was saying, "But of course I am recovered. I was going to be hanged tomorrow."

The marquis, who had remained unnerved by the three-hundred-foot climb up a swaying rope ladder, twitched his mustaches. "You are sure, François?"

"Sure I was going to be hanged? I've no reason to distrust the word of the English." De Bouillé grinned.

"Non, non," the marquis said. "I meant—you want to go on with Barney, then?"

"The business in the Caribbean is done, my lord. The action moves to America."

"We descend on St. Kitts tomorrow, and Nevis the day after," the marquis said, as if to lure him.

"But I am a sailor, sir." De Bouillé looked over at Barney. "Barney sails now. I recover completely aboard. The sea will cure me."

Barney smiled now. De Bouillé said, "Where is de Grasse, sirs?"

Barney answered, "The fleet sailed for Cap Haitien."

"And that is where you go?"

"Yes," Barney said. "Lucie awaits Joshua there."

Joshua seemed lost in thought. Head bent, he was frowning a little. Then he looked up at the marquis. "I leave you, too, my lord. Again my deep gratitude for your care of Lucie."

"A pleasure, sir," the marquis said, a little sadly. He looked from one to the other. "I lose you all," he said. "I offer nothing but a few island invasions."

Barney said, "We'll be back, my lord." He got to his feet and started his pacing. "There's something brewing!" He spoke to de Bouillé. "We know—Rodney is at Antigua now. He's split his forces. Hood has sailed for America. There's something brewing," he repeated, and Joshua felt the old excitement; he looked up. De Bouillé squinted at Barney.

"Go on," he exclaimed.

"All I know is that the Comte de Grasse has asked me to meet him in Cap Haitien." Barney flung out his hands; then he grinned, pushing his cap back on his head. "The 'Athena's' ready."

The marquis stood, too. "And it is all done here. All done, and all

[223]

ended well, thank God." He turned to Barney. "Do not let François overdo yet, please. Order him to rest."

Joshua said, "We both will, m'lord, I promise you."

The marquis kissed Joshua on each cheek. "My warmest regards to your ma'moiselle. I wish you to be most happy."

"Thank you, m'lord," Joshua said.

The marquis next approached Barney. "This is my country's custom, to show affection," he said gravely, as he kissed Barney's cheek. "I wish you every success, sir."

"Thank you, m'lord," Barney said, too.

"And François." The marquis fixed him with a stern eye. De Bouillé gave his father a quick hug. "You old rascal," he said. "I'll be back."

The marquis went to the door. The hot sun burned through the drooping trees. The white steeple of the church thrust up into the blue, blue sky. In the quiet he could hear the thunder of the surf on the beaches. He heard Joshua say, "For God's sake, lean on us." He and Barney had taken de Bouillé by the arms. There was a carriage coming down the road.

It came nearer. The marquis stood in the doorway, watching. He saw Barney wave his hand at the carriage. "Avast there!" he shouted. "A coach for his lordship, varlet!"

The coachman reined in hastily, staring. Barney leaped for the door and flung it open. "Enter, my lord," he said, bowing deeply. The marquis heard them all laughing as the surprised coachman drove off with his three passengers. They waved out the window. *"Au revoir,"* they called. *"Au revoir."*

38

THE BARGE OF THE COMTE DE GRASSE WAITED. BARNEY STEPPED IN, with de Bouillé beside him. They were both silent.

The crew of the boat were magnificently uniformed. Commanders with money always maintained such a boat; Barney had himself, in Europe.

He was thoughtful, and de Bouillé, sensing his preoccupation, did not speak, either. De Bouillé didn't know what Barney was thinking about, but he himself was thinking of Lucie and how she looked in the little dim church just a few minutes ago. He heard again her words as he had kissed her. "François," she had said earnestly. "When the war is over, when it is all done, you must come! Promise me!"

"I will," he had said. "I promise." He looked out over the blue water, not seeing the brave fine ships riding at anchor. He felt almost well; weariness crept up on him quickly, but that would pass very soon. And he had had the honor to be attached to the Comte's ship. Still, he was leaving—he had said goodbye to Joshua, he and Lucie would leave soon for the States. Soon he would bid Barney goodbye, too. He caught Barney's eye.

Barney said, "It comes from being in a church." He grinned.

De Bouillé said, "I'll miss the goddamn Yank. I speak better English now, *n'est-ce pas?*" He crossed his legs and leaned back.

"I was thinking how lovely Lucie looked; I was thinking—" Barney stopped. "I don't know what the devil I was thinking," he ended, but he knew. He was remembering a few brief words Joshua had said. Barney could hear every one of those words, delivered as only Joshua could deliver them. "It was both our faults, Barney," he had said. "Mine for sending her to Stasia; yours for allowing her to remain there. I should have looked after her better." He had paused. Then he went on. "And so should you. That sums it up, in my estimation."

"Well, rouse from your abstraction," de Bouillé said. "There is 'Le Robuste.' And unless I miss my guess, sir, you're going to receive a captain's salute."

He was. De Bouillé smiled with pleasure as he mounted the ladder behind Barney. The men stood at attention; the pipes twittered; the hot sun beat down, and de Bouillé, at his side, said formally, "I shall escort you to le Comte de Grasse, sir."

Barney said, low, as they went aft, "And you look as though you know what's going to happen, sir."

De Bouillé shook his head. "Well, perhaps a little," he conceded. He introduced two Swedish officers who had come to greet them. Their French was execrable, Barney thought, making polite replies, as they openly stared at him. Barney knew many Swedish nobility sought glory and battle with the French fleet.

The ship was a beautiful one. "Le Robuste" boasted only sixty-four cannon, less than most fleet commanders used, but this ship—Barney wrenched his thoughts from her. De Bouillé was saying, "Le Comte de Grasse will receive you on the stern gallery, sir."

Had it not been for the Haitien heat Barney would have had the illusion he was in Brest. The presence of the fleet, the babble of French voices, the very sight of le Comte de Grasse. Barney and he had met in Martinique. De Grasse bowed. De Bouillé excused himself. And Barney found himself using his French.

"I assure you it is a pleasure, my lord."

De Grasse begged him to be seated. He went on to say that it was pleasant out here, a little breeze and shaded, and Barney complimented him on the ship. De Grasse smiled.

"I'm really an old soldier, you know, sir." He smiled faintly. Then he added, "Perhaps that's why I receive orders with better humor from the military branch." His eyes sparkled. "I apprised you of the receipt of your return communication this morning, that you held the 'Athena' in readiness for sailing."

He did not expect an answer—none was necessary, so he went right on. "Speed is of the essence. We know that Hood sailed. Last night I received despatches from General Washington. I have considered them, and I have written my reply. Two days ago I received despatches from France and from Rochambeau."

Rochambeau was the commander of the French armies in America. Barney knew that what he had suspected four days ago in Stasia was true. Something important was brewing. What Washington needed now was money and sea power. Was he going to get it? And suddenly he heard de Grasse say, "But first I must convey to you the respects of His Majesty, King Louis the Sixteenth. He has empowered me, sir, to offer you the rank of Captain in the Royal French Navy, with the command of the sister ship of 'Le Robuste'— the ship 'Le Gloire.' "

It took only a few seconds to say the words. Had they actually been said? Barney's eyes studied de Grasse; the words echoed around in his head. Then he jumped to his feet.

"You overwhelm me, sir!"

He stood there, with de Grasse watching him. He stood motionless; he had indeed spoken the truth. He wondered whether de Grasse knew, could possibly know, what such an offer would mean to a man who had been born in a little white frame house with a dock hanging on thin legs over the Mullica river, in New Jersey where the mosquitoes bit so badly. He said aloud, "Sir, there have been times when I didn't have enough to eat." He grinned, and threw out his big hands. "I don't mean in prison, either, sir." He walked across the gallery and back again. "Forgive my pacing, m'lord, but it's long habit. I'm trying to think."

De Grasse was thinking this forthright manner was what had charmed the court. "And rightly so," he announced. "Look, sir, as an old campaigner I know what you mean."

"And it has taken me a few minutes to assimilate this. His Majesty does me great honor." He sank down into his chair again.

"Consider, sir."

De Grasse's voice came through Barney's thoughts. This was what he had always wanted. With these cruises this year he had made and piled up thousands of unspent dollars. With high rank, with money, with a magnificent ship and later perhaps a squadron—and Paris to come back to. A command in the French Navy was reserved for nobility, but—

This was what he had always thought he wanted. Was it possible he was going to turn it down? And that the decision was going to be so easy? It crossed his mind that sometimes a man knew little about the changes that went on within him, until the new values suddenly made themselves plain, for it was wonderfully clear now what his answer would be.

But in his pocket was a letter from Robert Morris, just received. Morris was Agent of Marine, now. Morris was in charge of a handful of ships, of a brand new struggling Navy; at this moment in his oil-lit offices he was probably trying to scrape up some money to buy one more. Barney said:

"But it is plain to me, sir, that even though my services are not at present enlisted in the United States Navy, they should remain available." As he said it, he knew he had put it bluntly; he wondered how de Grasse would take it. His admiration for de Grasse rose because de Grasse nodded gravely.

"I understand your position, sir. I did not know what answer you would give. It was suspected that in time of war we should receive a negative from you. Therefore, we wish it made plain the commission remains open to you, sir, at any time."

"Thank you, sir," Barney said, and would have continued.

"Now on to the other matter. My methods may seem unorthodox to you, sir." He looked questioning.

"Indeed not," Barney said. "I like them."

De Grasse laughed. "We are far away from court orders, nevertheless there are a batch of them. There are two places for attack on the American shores. The Chesapeake and New York. Therefore, and with Rochambeau's urging and Washington's, we have picked the Chesapeake, with Cornwallis as our target. I've raised the money from Havana merchants. The court also wants me to send a convoy home. This order I'm going to disregard. I'm taking every available ship to the Chesapeake; therefore, I'm entrusting to you the despatches for Washington." Once more he gave Barney no chance to reply. He went right on. "His army is poised, ready to strike at either New York or Carolina—they want to know only where *we* will be. A fast frigate has already been spared to apprise de Barras, in Newport. He is taking the wide route, to avoid the British, carrying with him our siege artillery. Thirty-five hundred soldiers have been spared by the Governor of Cap Haitien, here, upon condition of the Spanish fleet anchoring at this place, which assurances I have just yesterday received. It is my wish that these despatches be received by Washington no later than the fifteenth, for I intend to anchor in Lynnhaven Bay, just within the capes of the Chesapeake, on the thirtieth of August, with twenty-eight ships of the line. De Barras is under orders to sail the twenty-seventh; Washington is ready to march. Cornwallis will be trapped and we should have his surrender in six weeks or so. How long will it take you to make the voyage?"

"Five days, with good winds," said Barney.

"Good," said de Grasse. "You will not meet with Hood. I expect Hood to reach America at least a week before I do; he will probably poke his nose in the Chesapeake, see it empty, and sail on to New York. He will return with reinforcements; by that time we shall be in possession of the bay—and can seek battle when we choose."

It was the eighth of August. De Grasse held out a sealed oilskin packet. "Here are the despatches. I have picked the fastest frigate here, and to my mind the best commander, to carry them. Good luck, sir."

"Thank you, sir," Barney said.

De Grasse shrugged his shoulders. "Someone, much more famous than we shall ever be, had a word for it: 'The die is cast.' "

On deck de Bouillé said, "Even you are a bit dazed."

"Granted," said Barney. Then he smiled.

"We shall have Cornwallis bottled up; we'll have him tucked away by October."

Barney grinned. "You've got it settled, haven't you?"

"We have a commander now, Barney."

He had accompanied Barney to the ladder. They shook hands. *"Bon voyage,"* de Bouillé said. Barney repeated it. He went down to the waiting boat.

The bowmen pushed off. De Bouillé leaned over. "Tell Joshua I see him on Lucie's birthday."

Barney echoed this. "Lucie's birthday?"

"Oui," called de Bouillé. He was laughing. "Christmas!"

39

"I THINK YOU'D BETTER CALL HIM," SCULL SAID. "SHE'S ACTING damned queerly." He transferred his gaze from the ship he could see across the water to Jerrell, who was watching the strange ship too. "Well, then, sir," snapped Scull. "Move!"

Jerrell ran. Scull once more lifted the glass to his eye, listening for Barney's step. When Barney stood beside him he talked fast.

"She's changed course three times in the past half hour, as though no one knew whose orders were being obeyed, sir. And now she's trying to get to windward, and put that prize of hers, whatever it is, between her and us. Damn it, sir, I could understand her wanting to run, but why didn't she do that first?"

Barney had been in the act of dressing for supper. When Jerrell had knocked on his cabin door, he had yanked on a pair of canvas trousers. They had sighted the two ships an hour ago—they had looked like a privateer and her prize, making for the port Barney had left two days ago.

Scull repeated, "I just didn't like the way she was acting, sir."

Barney frowned. There was little likelihood of English ships being in these waters. The big convoy had passed a week ago. "I expect my original surmise to be correct—that she is French." He paused, and Scull waited. He was not surprised at the next order. "Beat to quarters, Mr. Scull. We'll see what's happening aboard her."

During the next ten minutes the ship was cleared for action; Barney had strapped on his heavy belt and thrust two pistols through it, and they had sailed near enough to see that indeed the one ship was a prize; she bore the marks of battle plainly.

The colors had been hoisted. On the privateer the French flag fluttered.

No sooner had the flag gone up to the masthead, than Mr. Scull tried a hail.

There was no answer. "She's trying to avoid us, sir!"

She had changed course again. Barney said, "Try her again, Mr. Scull."

Once more she refused to answer the hail. The "Athena" was bearing down on her fast. Barney took the glass. In the deepening dusk the glass was almost useless. "Ready me a boarding party, Mr. Scull."

The two ships were very close. Rapidly the water narrowed between them. But even when the irons were thrown, and the two ships jarred together, there was no sound from the Frenchman.

Barney and fifty men landed on the privateer deck almost at the same time. No hand was raised against them. Two officers came forward toward Barney; they were both very young and uncertain. Barney said:

"Why didn't you answer our hails?" He looked around at the almost deserted deck. Fifteen of his own men stood behind him. The others had already overrun the forecastle and were in possession of it.

"We didn't think you were English, sir! The captain gave orders to keep on our course toward Cap Haitien. Then he sent up a command to try to avoid passing near you, and—"

"Captain who?" asked Barney grimly.

"Captain Landais, sir."

Barney said nothing for a moment. Then, "What prize is that?"

"An English merchantman, sir. A straggler from the big convoy from Stasia."

"Where is Captain Landais?"

"Having supper, sir. We are not to disturb him."

Barney said, "Show me to him."

The young Frenchman hesitated. Then he said, "Follow me, sir."

Barney motioned to his men to stay where they were.

The Frenchman knocked on a dirty door. A voice answered.

"I gave orders I was not to be disturbed!"

[230]

The Frenchman licked his lips. "Sir, we have been boarded. The American captain wishes to speak to you."

"Open the door," growled Barney.

There was the sound within of a chair scraping back. In a moment the door was flung open. Landais, resplendent in blue satin, peered out into the passageway. His face changed. He cut off an oath; almost furtively he backed into the cabin again. Barney stepped in and kicked the door shut.

Landais and he were only about seven feet apart. The lamp swung overhead, lighting the table and the remains of a meal. And across the table Douglass sat, as though carved in ivory. The wine glass she had been holding spilled and ran across the bare table. Landais followed Barney's look at her, and Landais laughed.

"You interrupt," he said, bowing.

Douglass' eyes had not wavered from Barney's face; now they went slowly and carefully over him. All the remembering was hardly a patch on his actual presence; the towering vitality of him, as she saw him now, dominating the small cabin. The scene was almost incredible.

It was Landais who spoke first. His voice was soft and sibilant.

"Captain Barney, I submit you have no business aboard my ship."

Without taking his eyes from Landais, Barney reached behind him and unlatched the door. He spoke to the officer. "Have the lady's effects put aboard my ship." He closed the door again. "Landais, I take the woman."

Douglass felt her heart pound. The hot blood stained her face. "No, Barney, I will stay here," she cried, taking a step around the table, toward him.

"Be quiet," he commanded. He repeated his statement to Landais, as though she had not spoken at all. "I take the woman."

Landais wiped his blue satin sleeve across his face. It was very hot in the tiny cabin and sweat was pouring off him, running down into his collar. "How high will you pay?" he asked, his voice sneering. "You pay high?"

Douglass took another step toward Barney. He saw her from the corner of his eye. He reached out and took her by the arm and almost swung her back toward her chair. "Stay there!" He himself stepped nearer the door. Then he resumed his calm. "I pay nothing, Landais."

Landais looked at Douglass. "She does not want to go?"

[231]

As Landais regarded her, Barney did too. She was sitting on the edge of the big armchair, leaning forward, lips parted. Barney could see well enough her perturbation; the grey eyes on him were full of questions. On her white arm were the marks of his fingers as he had pushed her back from him.

"Douglass," he said. Then he tore his eyes from her and a flame of anger came into her grey eyes.

"I do not go with you!"

Landais laughed almost silently. "She wants to stay with me," he jeered. He was edging backwards, and Douglass suddenly saw that whatever had been said or gone before between these two men was just a prelude, and that both men were waiting for an act, a move, on the part of the other.

Barney's eyes were glittering as they watched Landais. Now, in a flashing second Douglass understood why he had pushed her away from him. The danger in the little cabin, the tension of it, the violence of it, stood her on her feet. The two men didn't move, but she did. She moved back, against the paneling. Her knees trembled, her face was dead white. If she could have got to the door— Then she suppressed a cry as Landais' arm moved in a lightning gesture. A thin knife whirred through the air toward Barney.

At almost the same moment Barney had drawn the pistol from his belt. He dropped down to one knee, twisting his body sideways, and from that position Barney fired.

Douglass put both hands over her mouth to suppress the cry she was afraid she might utter. The shot reverberated; the smoke curled from the long barrel on the pistol held so mercilessly in the big brown hand as Barney had fired. And Landais slipped slowly to the floor, his hand reaching for the table; he slipped and teetered and fell in a heap.

The door was flung violently open. The young officer stood in the doorway. He stared down at the figure of his captain.

Douglass couldn't see Landais because the table was between his body and her. All she could see was his legs. She heard the officer say:

"You killed him!"

Douglass cried out and then was silent. Barney asked, "Are you the first officer?"

Wordlessly the man nodded, taking his eyes from Landais' body and raising them to look at Barney.

[232]

Barney said, "You may write it in the log that I shot him, after he had thrown his knife." Barney touched the gleaming knife with his boot. "And that I am taking this woman, Madam Harris, with me, to insure her safety. Were there any other female passengers?"

"No, sir," he muttered. With a last look at Barney he turned.

In amazement Douglass watched him go out the door.

Barney stepped over Landais' legs to reach Douglass. Back against the paneling she waited for him. It would take him only a few seconds to reach her; only four strides would bring him right to her. Without a word he swung her up in his arms.

For a moment he thought she was going to resist, but then he felt her go soft in his arms, her golden head back against his shoulder. He carried her out on deck.

When he saw his men waiting patiently, he wondered how long he had been in that damned cabin. He told himself it could not have been many minutes. He saw Esther.

"Help her aboard, Wolf," he ordered. He saw Absolom rush to the rail to help swing the slight figure of Esther onto the "Athena's" deck. He handed Douglass down to Macgregor; she stood beside Macgregor for just a second, as Barney jumped down beside her, and possessively, as though it were the last time he could, he lifted her in his arms again. Standing there on deck, with her in his arms, Scull and Macgregor stood on each side, peering at her face. Then Scull blurted:

"You killed Landais, sir!"

Wolf had tossed Douglass' boxes, heavy as they were, down onto the deck as though they were toys. Barney said:

"Tell Absolom to clear my things out of my cabin. And cast off, Mr. Scull!"

"Aye aye, sir," said Scull hastily.

Douglass kept her eyes tight shut. She heard the sound of Scull's voice; she heard the sounds of the ship as men hauled on sheets and braces, as the "Athena," freed, steadied and gathered way again. Barney carried her easily.

He set her down gently on something soft. For a second she felt the touch of his arms still around her, leaning her back. For the first time in six months they were together again.

She was regarding him as though he were remote and strange. They watched each other silently. Douglass sat up straighter;

Barney had laid her down in a reclining position and she, with a movement of her hips, sat up farther against the pillows.

She was in a cabin with a table big enough to seat about six people for dining. There were chairs, and the cushioned locker on which she sat. Three feet away from her Barney sat in his own chair. His face was grave; while she watched he ran his hand over his chin absently.

"This is the aftercabin," he said, breaking the silence. "I eat here."

She made no answer; she remembered his way of getting things straight. He would begin at the beginning and tell her where she was. Then she said, "I never expected—" She stopped.

But he knew what she meant. There was a certain amount of fatalism in both of them. "But I did, madam. Somehow." He smiled faintly. He thought that was as good a starting point as any. He continued with the line of thought. "Although you have Joshua to thank for this—this interruption of your voyage home to England. It was Joshua who stayed on Stasia, to relay information about the convoys."

She said slowly, remembering Hood's words on the balcony at Stasia, "So that was how you did it? We wondered. But Joshua—" She could hardly believe it.

"And Joshua and Lucie are married," Barney said.

Real astonishment showed in her face, and vast relief. "I couldn't find her! She had disappeared."

He nodded. "You were on the other side of the fence. But Joshua rescued her—that morning the British struck."

"And they are married?"

"That couldn't happen in England, could it? In your circle?"

He was emphasizing the difference between them once again, she knew. She too smiled. "Hardly," she admitted, but then, "Yet it might!" she said.

"Let it go," he said. "We retook Stasia, madam."

She leaned forward, eyes on him. She didn't speak for a moment. "But the heavy batteries?" she exclaimed. "How, then?"

"Jenkin's Bay," he said.

She knew well the sight of it. She remembered the foaming angry water hurling itself at the base of the cliffs. "That precipice? Lieutenant Mackenzie explained—he thought it didn't need batteries."

"You knew him? He was killed."

[234]

"Oh," she whispered. "I'm sorry." She lifted her head to look straight at him. "He was charming, clever, brave."

"He was shot trying to give the alarm, and raise the red flag, madam." Now he, too, was silent, and finally he said, "And how has it been with you? Since the night of February 2nd?"

"February second?" she repeated.

"The night I left you," Barney said evenly.

She made a little gesture with her white hands; she drew in her breath swiftly, and in her wide eyes was the old look, questioning. Then her lashes fell. "I?" she asked. The flicker of a smile crossed her face. "Perhaps you know more about what happened on Stasia than I do, sir, with the fine intelligence system you had. But speaking practically, the Navy fed us. Fed everyone. They doled it out, to all. Actually, some were given less than others. But Samuel saw that we had plenty."

"Samuel is Admiral Hood?" His dark eyes were veiled.

"Yes, sir. He is my godfather, you see."

He didn't answer. Douglass continued. "In any event, I should have been well treated, as an English refugee, on my way home, you understand, sir. Naturally they would look after me. The house was guarded."

"I didn't know about the guards," Barney said.

She looked up, frowning slightly, feathery brows drawing together. "You certainly did not worry about my being in English hands, sir." She said it as statement of fact.

"I did not worry, no," Barney said. He crossed booted legs in the white canvas trousers. For a moment each of them was conscious only of the other's immediate presence; that they were together. Then Barney said, "Now you go home, to England? What are your plans?"

She said, low, yet clearly, "I am going to be married."

His hands tightened on the chair arms, then relaxed. "To whom?"

"Captain Reynolds."

Barney said, "He meets you there, on your arrival?"

She looked puzzled. "Why, sir," she said, as though she were reminding him, "John could not assure me of that. I do not know when he will get back. It was he who sent the 'Sybil' to engage you. He could not use the 'Monarch'; he had orders to intercept the Dutch convoy."

"Oh, yes," Barney said. "He was successful, I know."

[235]

"He gave the Dutch admiral full honors, when he was buried at sea," Douglass said.

"You do not need to defend Captain Reynolds to me, English." She said, "I was not defending him."

"You were, madam," said Barney. "There is one more matter I wish to speak of. Tonight. On Stasia I told you there was one other man to whom I had given a warning. That man was Landais; I shan't give him the courtesy of calling him a captain. I'm sorry I spoke roughly to you in his presence; but that's the only language he understands. Please accept my apologies."

"I see," said Douglass, unconsciously imitating his way.

"He did not harm you, did he, Douglass?"

There was urgency in the question.

"No," she answered. Then repeated it. "No!"

Their eyes met. Then Douglass said, "I would like to retire now."

He nodded. "My cabin should be ready at any minute, madam."

"Your cabin?" She hesitated. "That is most kind of you."

"A courtesy I am glad to extend."

"Thank you," she said.

There was silence again. Then Barney said, "You'll excuse me if I smoke?" He picked up his pipe after her polite reply, and began to fill it. Macgregor knocked on the door.

"Come in," Barney said.

Macgregor said, eyes on Douglass, "Sir, your gear has been stowed in our cabin, Scull's and mine, sir."

"I'm aware whose cabin I'm using now, Mr. Macgregor!" Barney's voice snapped out at him. Then he said, "Allow me, Madam Harris, to present Mr. Macgregor."

"It's a pleasure, I vow, madam," Macgregor said, bowing, but this time keeping one eye on his captain, whose temper seemed very uncertain.

"I'm a nuisance, sir, I know," said Douglass. "You are being moved from your cabin. How can I thank you?"

"We couldn't ask for more than to have you aboard, ma'am."

She smiled and said, "And now, gentlemen, I think I shall retire. Goodnight, Mr. Macgregor. Goodnight, Captain."

40

THE NEXT MORNING WHEN DOUGLASS CAME OUT ON DECK, SHE SAW that amidships a knot of men were gathered around the carriage of one of the heavy guns. Douglass let her eyes rove over the "Athena."

"You have doubled the lookouts," she said. "Why?"

"Captain's orders, ma'am. We seem to have doubled our crew, too."

"Every man jack aboard's on deck, ma'am," Jerrell said, his blue eyes crinkled with laughter.

"They were never so interested in those guns before, the bastards," Macgregor said. "Excuse me, ma'am."

Jerrell's mind went ahead rapidly. She couldn't stand here long. "Couldn't we get you a chair, ma'am?" he asked eagerly.

Macgregor walked to the gangway, and ten men ran forward toward him.

The chair was brought and Douglass sat down in it.

Barney had heard her light unmistakable step on the companion. He had put his pen down, and filled and lighted his pipe. After fifteen minutes had passed, for that was the amount of time he had allotted—after those minutes had passed, he followed her. He came out on deck.

Lang, who had been leaning over the back of Douglass' chair, straightened up. Jerrell cast a hasty look at the helm and stepped away from the chair, and Macgregor moved backward because it was obvious Barney was coming to stand in front of the chair. The first realization Douglass had of his presence was Macgregor moving from in front of her and Barney standing there instead.

"Good morning, madam," he said.

"Good morning, sir," she answered.

He paid no more attention to the other officers than as if they were not visible at all. He said, "That's a pretty thing on your head, English."

She was wearing a dress copied from the costume of the milk-maids in Covent Garden, and a little cap made of filmy material that was tied around at the back of her head with a bow. Barney went right on. "But it doesn't protect you from the sun, madam."

"I had not thought of that," Douglass said. "It matches the dress."

Barney noticed Lang. "Mr. Lang, have a fresh piece of canvas rigged over this chair."

"Aye aye, sir," Lang said. He disappeared.

Douglass was looking up at Barney's face. "The 'Triton'—the 'Athena,'" she corrected hastily, "is a beautiful ship, sir." She asked then, "How is the wind?"

"Holding fair, ma'am." He smiled a little.

"What are those things?" asked Douglass, pointing.

"Carronades, madam. I hope we don't have to use them with you aboard."

Macgregor said, "I had the morning watch, ma'am, so as the captain says, I'm a bit sleepy." He patted a yawn, apologized and left them. Scull hurried after him. Mr. Jerrell stood over by the helmsman.

Douglass said, "What are the names of the topsails?"

Barney, standing beside her, answered, "The tops'ls take their names from the mast on which they stand. Now, these questions—"

"You don't need to be so formal with me, Douglass, do you?" His dark eyes met hers.

"I thought, aboardship, it was courtesy to the captain." Her lashes fell; she glanced to each side; there was no one near.

He said next, "Is my presence disturbing to you?"

She made a little gesture; the wind blew the tiny lace apron on her milkmaid gown, and she smoothed it back into place. Then she looked up at him again. "Why, no, indeed, sir. Why should it be?"

"It is largely my fault the others left."

"Indeed, sir?" Douglass repeated. "Well, I have never sailed aboard a ship of war before, except for the Frenchman."

She was looking up at him. In the background rose the mizzen-mast; she heard the singing of the rigging; the voices of the men fore; the sky was clear blue and the sails white against them as they bellied out with wind. Barney's eyes were crinkled against the sun and wind as they looked down at her; he bent toward her a little; at the mention of the Frenchman he had muttered an oath, for which he said abruptly he was sorry.

"You're safe now, English. I'll explain about my officers. They want me to have a clear field. That is, they may not *want* me to, but they think they had best offer it. But I'm not going to stay here long."

"It's your ship?" said Douglass.

"I want to give you a chance to get accustomed to me." He smiled suddenly. "And besides, I have duties to perform. I'm writing my reports. I'll leave you now, and they'll be flocking back, to entertain you. Only be careful, madam, and remember their susceptibilities."

Douglass smiled. Then she remembered. She had no reason to trust him. "I shan't play any havoc with your officers, sir. And it will only be a few days—only one more day after this."

"True," said Barney; he raised an eyebrow and looked undaunted. "I'll have to work fast."

She said clearly, "You don't have to work at all, Captain."

"It's a matter of choice, Douglass," he said. He bowed and turned and left her.

She had dinner alone, in her cabin. She picked up a book at random; it was a hot day, and she lay on her cot reading. At six there was a rap on the door.

Eagerly Esther, who had been given quarters near Douglass' cabin, flew to open it. She smiled widely when she saw Absolom.

"The captain's compliments to Mrs. Harris," Absolom said, "and he requests the pleasure of madam's company at supper tonight."

Douglass spoke quickly. "Please convey my regrets to the captain. I am not feeling well."

The door closed. Douglass lay on the cot, waiting. Her refusal would not be the end of the matter, she was sure.

She tried to read. Outside, on guard, Wolf waited, ears pricked to see what would happen next. Absolom was back in less than two minutes.

"The captain says to tell madam that she will be ill if she shuts herself in her cabin. The captain says he will call for madam at eight."

Absolom, Esther and Wolf listened for the answer. Finally Douglass laid the book down on the cot. "Perhaps the captain is right, Absolom," she said coolly. "I shall expect him at eight, then."

The door closed. Wolf would inform in forecastle of what had happened. Within the cabin Esther heard her mistress say, "You may unpack and press the white lace dress, Esther, with the satin basque."

At eight exactly she was ready. Wolf had been relieved; there was another man at the door who kept his eyes resolutely ahead as Barney entered, but tried hard to hear.

But Barney's voice was very low.

"You look lovely, Douglass."

"Thank you," she said, frostily.

"I've asked three officers to dine with us."

"Oh," she said, then because she thought there was no use dissembling, "I am glad of that, sir."

Barney looked at her steadily. "And even when you are ill, it is not good to confine yourself in your cabin, English. You are not ill now."

Barney had invited Scull, Macgregor and Jerrell. Douglass had met them all, and they had been waiting. Barney seated her to his right and Macgregor was on her other side. Barney had provided wine from his own stock and that made the officers doubly happy. While Barney entertained them at supper quite often, tonight it would be special. Douglass and the prospect of rare brandy later removed whatever tension there might have been, for although they did not know the exact reason for this voyage, they suspected. Rumor ran rife that they were carrying important despatches—the most important of the war, Macgregor had said weightily. It accounted for Barney's snappy temper, too, and it accounted for the route chosen, doubled lookouts, no prizes.

"Why don't he tell us?" Jerrell had asked Scull, and Scull had said, "Why do you need to know, sir?" Whereupon Jerrell had replied, with a glance at Macgregor, "I'd appreciate the confidence."

Scull had grunted, "You're too fresh, lad." He looked at Jerrell now, across the table, his blue eyes alight in his tanned face. "Roast chicken, sir," he was saying in tones of deep approval.

Macgregor said, "The stomach is very important to the young, madam. Mr. Jerrell's young enough to be still growing, I do believe."

Jerrell looked over at him, and then to Douglass. "Never believe him, madam."

"Oh, I don't, sir," said Douglass matter of factly, and Macgregor laughed. She went on, "I warrant you're older than I am, Mr. Jerrell. I am twenty."

"I've a year on you, ma'am," Jerrell said with dignity.

Barney was looking at Douglass. He eyed her now, and she caught his glance, and looked down at her plate. She began to eat again.

"So you are twenty, are you, madam?" Barney said. "Regardless of age, your sex turns them into the semblance of gentlemen."

"You make me sound very depressing," Douglass said. "But I should have to go a long way back to make a change."

Jerrell grinned. "That reminds me of the time we took two ships at once. And two enemy captains later began to quarrel on deck about which one of them should have done what. And then Captain Barney said, in that way of his, 'Well, gentlemen, suppose I set you back on your ships and we'll try this over again?' "

Douglass laughed; she looked at Barney and for a second their eyes held, a look of deprecation and boyishness in his dark ones. But Jerrell's remark had started the flood of reminiscences. They began to talk, to regale her with the incidents of a voyage which would soon be over. Incident after incident was related, as though they were bringing her up to date on the voyage of which she was now a part.

"That was the day we used the British codebooks," Jerrell said. It was long after supper. The brandy had been served. Macgregor was peeling an orange for Douglass. She said:

"Then you did use them?"

Barney nodded. "Yes, madam, I did."

"Oh," said Douglass. She realized the other men were wondering how she knew about them; they were waiting to see if they would find out. She swept them with her grey eyes, and when they rested on Macgregor, he leaned forward in response.

"Yes, ma'am?" he asked.

"Mr. Macgregor," Douglass said. "I don't believe I can eat the orange. It has turned so hot."

"Storm coming, Madam Harris," Barney said.

Douglass heard herself saying that she had enjoyed their company and they had been vastly entertaining; with their leave she would retire now. At this Barney rose.

For a moment no one spoke. Douglass looked up at him. The whole ship knew by this that she had refused the captain's first invitation. Macgregor had said, "By God, she's the first gal who ever said 'no' to Barney." He rose, too, and stood on the other side of her. With some misgiving Macgregor heard her say:

"I'm sure Mr. Macgregor won't mind escorting me."

Macgregor looked over her head at Barney. But Barney was looking down at Douglass between them. "I suggest the deck, madam," he said.

Douglass had risen. Barney went on. "You haven't been well this afternoon. Air is what you need. I prescribe it. A little walk on the deck." He pulled back her chair, and took her hand, tucking it in his arm.

Out on deck Douglass stopped after the first three steps. Alongside the carronade, alone as they were, she said, "I didn't want to walk, sir."

He drew her to the rail. "I know you didn't. There are the storm clouds, madam."

They were piled black in the skies to the south; a crooked belt of light split them suddenly. Overhead the stars still twinkled.

Barney said, over her head, "You're giving no quarter, are you?"

"I don't understand you, sir," she said, idly, capturing an errant curl that blew across her forehead; she tucked it back in place.

"I could make it plainer."

"Let me make something plain, sir. I do not want your company."

Barney said, "I see." Then his eyes twinkled. "But I have to eat too, madam."

"You left me, and then after waiting a while for you, I decided that you had left my life. It was exciting to be with you. But there was and there would always be too much waiting. And no certainty that the waiting would ever end, that you would ever come back. Only your promise, an easy currency for you with which you have paid off others . . . Well, all right, you have paid me off, too. The matter is ended. No, I have decided. It is futile to talk any more."

"Douglass, my promise is good. Now, listen. I went back for you—"

"I have put you out of my mind. Please do not insist on coming back."

"I came back for you as soon as I could and Samuel Hood was with you. I thought I had lost you, I thought you didn't care, but I went back again and found that you had gone. Do you still exclude me from your life? Do you still hate me?"

"I don't blame you for being angry with me. I will speak plain, too."

A crash of thunder punctuated his words. He added, "It is still quite distant or I shouldn't be standing here. You are not afraid, are you?"

She told the truth. "Not with you, sir."

He smiled. "Sweetheart," he began. Then he said, "I didn't mean to say that, madam, and I had this carefully thought out. Give me five more minutes, Douglass."

She leaned back against the gun. "This is quite futile, sir."

"You didn't love me in Stasia, then?"

"I believe that was fully six months ago, Captain Barney."

Thunder rumbled again. She leaned away from him; he waited till the thunder rumbled to a stop. Then he spoke soberly.

"Douglass, you know my passion for getting things straight. What was between us has to be cleared away. You are fortifying yourself behind a mask of polite strangeness; I have to break through it somehow. Are you through with me, for good, do you think? I love you, Douglass. Let's get it straight, ma'am; I've always loved you, from the very beginning."

He heard the swift intake of her breath. She turned her head to look out over the sea, as a bolt of lightning ripped the black clouds.

"Get the courses in, Mr. Scull," Barney called. He took her arm. "You'll have to go below now, sweetheart. Wind coming up. Feel it?"

She made no answer. She walked along beside him; at the door of her cabin the man on guard opened the door.

"The waits," he said. "Soon, if this voyage is successful, there will be no waits. I cannot tell you why, but if I get through to port when I expect to, the war will be near its end. I will stay in Philadelphia—"

"Stay there if you wish. I will not. I do not like it nor its strait laces. I do not like its ways."

"Ah, Douglass, then we'll make our own ways. We'll go where we want—it's a big country—and we'll do what we want."

"No," said Douglass. "That's wrong. You, perhaps. Not I. Not we."

"Tomorrow night," said Barney, "I'm going to ask you to marry me. It is my earnest hope, ma'am, that your answer will be in the affirmative." He turned and went to the door. "I'm quite sure you would want at least a day to think it over. Goodnight," he said quickly, and left her.

41

THE NIGHT WORE ON. THE GREAT ROUND MOON SET. THE WIND WAS variable, swinging around almost every point of the compass. At exactly four-thirty it sprang up from the northeast.

Macgregor reminded himself it was August, and therefore it could be the herald of a gale. Yet it was still light and tremulous, just enough to bring a mist that would hang deep over the shores of sandy barrier beaches of New Jersey and Delaware, and shroud the bay in drifting wisps of fog.

There would be no dawn this morning, worth seeing. Gradually the grey day would lighten and that would be all.

The mist, though, was light too. It dampened his hair. He took a turn around the deck.

The helmsman waited for him to resume his place near him, so they could talk. Macgregor swung back to him; the ship's bells rang out clearly in the stillness; the watch had two hours yet to run. The helmsman was just about to ask Macgregor a question when Macgregor uttered a sharp exclamation. Through the grey mist he saw a shape.

He let out a volley of oaths addressed to the lookout aloft, who at almost the same moment perceived it too.

The cry came. "Sail-ho!"

Macgregor was already fore and in the shrouds, climbing like a cat, swinging up over the futtock shrouds to gain the masthead.

"Well, four eyes," he growled. "You dumb sons of bitches." He saw what he did not want to see, and he muttered, "Christ Almighty."

He slid the last twenty feet down. The junior officer of the watch was poised at the gangway. "Call the captain," Macgregor shouted as he ran aft.

Barney was sleeping fully dressed save for shoes and coat. He rolled out of his bunk, pulled on his shoes. His mind noted the greyness of the dawn; visibility would be cut down. He shrugged on his coat. In two minutes he was standing on the quarterdeck, glass to eye.

Looking almost directly to the northeast, over a heaving sea, with the mist already only wispy, he saw clearly the proud outlines of a ship of the line. Sailing before the wind, with mainsail and headsails trimmed for a broad reach—his mind flew ahead.

A fight! "Oh, no!" thought Barney and then realized that for the first time in his life he did not want to fight. The despatches? Douglass? It didn't matter why he didn't want to fight, it was clear that he would have to. The warship was sailing at an angle to her course; soon she would jib, then on the other side of the course she and the "Athena" would meet. He asked himself the first question he always asked. How much time?

He reckoned it. He lowered the glass.

"Mr. Scull," Barney said, "summon all hands. And raise the colors."

He walked over to the rail and waited. As they mustered, fast, he looked down at the rows of faces. Behind him were the officers, and up the masthead went the flag.

There was a moment's silence. Somehow, despite everything, he felt an exhilaration that made his heart beat fast. He looked at his men. He glanced around at the flag; they were prepared to keep it flying.

"Men," he said simply, "in thirty minutes or so we meet the enemy. We are carrying despatches, perhaps the most important of the war; they must get through in time, they must not fall into enemy hands." A cheer went up. He cut it short with a command. "You may clear for action, Mr. Scull!"

For a second he stood there; then he turned on his heel; there was another matter to attend to, an important one.

He found Wolf on guard at Douglass' door. "You're relieved, Wolf," said Barney. While Wolf said "Aye aye, sir," and darted away, Barney paused before the closed door. Then he knocked.

Esther opened it. Barney stepped in, and closed the door behind him. Esther slipped to one side; Barney forgot her, so did Douglass. They stood watching each other gravely.

Douglass was dressed in a loose filmy dressing gown. Her hair was undone; she stood like a beautiful statue, watching him; then suddenly her voice came through the quiet.

"Barney!"

His face changed. She had spoken his name the way she used to. His eyes shone. He went across the five feet of deck between them, gathering her into his arms tight. He kissed her cheek, the tip of her nose. "Oh, Douglass," he whispered, holding her even closer. "I was so afraid you didn't love me!" He found her lips, then.

Finally he held her away from him. Neither of them spoke. Esther sighed and smiled and looked at both of them but neither saw her at all. Douglass had laid her hands on his shoulders, feeling the cloth of his coat beneath her fingers. He said, "I was so afraid you could not forgive me. I wouldn't blame you."

She shook her head and whispered, "I love you. How much time, Barney?" She smoothed the cloth of his coat with light fingers.

He answered honestly. "Fifteen minutes." He took her in a close strong embrace. "You'll come to no harm," he whispered before he kissed her. She put all her love for him in those kisses, he knew.

He felt her arms around him. He released her lips, pressing her head into his shoulder. He spoke into her soft curls. "Please don't be afraid, Douglass. I'll keep you safe. Don't be afraid." In his mind was the picture of the British warship.

She tipped her head back to look at him. "I'm not afraid."

He said, seeking the right words to reassure her, "Let's get this straight, madam. I'm not going to lose you now. Not to the whole British Navy."

"You'll win. I want you to win," she whispered. "But please be careful!"

He grinned, and hugged her.

"Don't get hurt," she added.

"I'm a damned bridegroom, almost, ma'am," he said. "And you have to get dressed. I'm leaving Absolom with you. He'll take you to the cable tier, where you'll be safe."

Her eyes searched him. "But you might need Absolom!"

"Those are orders, sweetheart. Goodbye." He kissed her quickly.

Her arms slipped from around him. "Goodbye," she said.

But at the door his voice came again, with a shade of tension. "Get ready, Douglass. I'm giving you only three minutes. Then I want you below."

He closed the door. He would try to keep her safe, but he knew this would be his hardest fight. And never before had he had so much to gain, so much to lose. He ran to his own cabin, grabbed up his heavy belt, the pair of boarding pistols. Then he dashed for the deck again.

The roll of the drums had echoed and died away some minutes

ago. He was aware of the sound of the ship being readied for action. He lifted the glass to his eye.

Standing there, with the enemy ship captured in the round glass circle, he saw her to be a heavy cruiser, boasting probably forty-four guns, to the "Athena's" thirty-two, and probably at least twenty-five per cent more crew. He felt the wind on his cheeks; he snapped the glass to, glancing up at the weathervane, and over to the enemy ship again. Then he looked across the decks.

The gun crews clustered around their run out cannon. The decks were already sanded. Long hoses were rigged to the pumps. There had been barely enough time to get cleared for action, and it was just as well. There was no time to be afraid.

The boys dashed madly across the decks with gunpowder and shot for the guns. Marines lined the rails; topmen clung to their perches. And the two ships were now ready.

"Looks as if she's going to close for action, Mr. Scull," Barney said. He had come to stand behind the helmsman.

"The wind's increasing, sir," Scull said, as the "Athena" rolled.

"How far do you reckon she is, Mr. Scull?"

"About three-quarters of a mile, sir," Scull answered.

Macgregor bounded up onto the quarterdeck, waiting for his orders. "You may fire only when I give you the order, Mr. Macgregor," Barney said impassively. The water was narrowing fast between the ships. The warship was holding fire too. The tension would lift as soon as the guns fired. It couldn't be long now. Barney started down the gangway at a fast clip.

The gun captains and crews watched him as he went past. Fore, he raised the glass. With the wind off her quarter, she was bearing down for the kill.

He strolled leisurely along the port guns. The gunner's boys watched him with awe. As he mounted to the quarterdeck again the English guns fired for the first time.

The fore guns had spoken, like the bark of a bulldog, for no hits were sustained.

"Look at her roll," Scull yelled. Firing with accuracy was almost impossible at the distance.

But the tension on the "Athena" was growing, as the size of the enemy ship was all too plain. Barney cursed the slow minutes. Every nerve in his body jabbed at him mercilessly, and he stood stock-still, behind the helmsman, waiting. Waiting was all he could do, for he intended to deliver the first broadside at close range, and between then and now the "Athena" would be punished hard. He forced himself to relax. If an opportunity arose, he must be ready to seize it calmly.

"Keep her small with the wind, Mr. Scull," he said.

"Aye aye, sir," breathed Scull.

A roar of guns punctuated the air. A shot skimmed across the decks amidships, knocking a gun from its carriage, instantly killing two men, Barney heard Macgregor yell, "Axes! Clear away this wreckage!"

The "Athena" held on her course. The men were already frantically working to remount the guns, and the two men were being dragged across the bloodied deck. Then the Britisher came about for a full broadside.

"Here it comes," breathed Scull.

It came with a thunderous roar. The whole ship shuddered. A section of rail hurtled at Barney's feet. The foretop royal crashed down onto the deck. Two port guns spun around madly. Barney leaped for the rail.

"Get them lashed quick, Mr. Macgregor," he shouted, even as men dashed to drag away the wounded. "Quick!" Barney shouted. If they loosed and went skidding around the deck they would be worse than the charge of a maddened elephant.

Behind him Scull was yelling for the deck to be cleared. The English ship was wreathed in the smoke of her own guns, and now from below could be heard the sound of the pumps.

The warship had changed course; her sails were set now, as the two ships bore down on each other.

"Oh, Christ," Scull swore. "Here she comes!"

"Hold her thus!" shouted Barney, as the warship bore down. They would pass within fifty yards. "Mr. Macgregor!" he shouted. "Hold your fire till the foremost gun rests square on your target!"

The prows of both ships were on a line now, across the heaving water, almost in a line mast for mast. Both captains intended to deliver their broadsides at the same time. But the Britisher, with the wind at her heels, foam swirling from her wake, still held the weather gage. In the next moment the "Athena" fired.

She rocked and trembled. No sooner had her guns fired than she was answered.

The heavy shot whistled like a dreadful wind, tearing and plunging through sails and timbers. The "Athena" reeled, smoke completely enveloped her. Slowly it lifted to let Barney's eyes see the damage.

Even as it lifted he shouted, "Stand by to come about!"

After his voice came Macgregor's; with relief Barney heard him yell, "Stop your vents!"

The sponges were rammed into smoking muzzles. Wounded men were being dragged away to the masts, to wait there until they could be carried below. The foretop mast was hanging uselessly; already it was being cut away, and the "Athena" was coming about.

His crew was working like the best trained crew in the whole damned world. The "Athena" dipped; men tugged on sheets and braces. Eyes narrowed, Barney watched the enemy ship, as she too came about and was bearing down again, guns loaded, ready to fire, ready to board.

Barney looked up at the weathervane. He jumped to the side of the helmsman. A great rolling sea on the stern quarter came boiling at them. "Helmsman," he said, "execute my next order by rule of contrary."

"Aye aye, sir!"

He said to Scull, "She's going to fire and board in the smoke!"

Scull could see her decks lined with marines, he saw her officers plain. "Oh, Christ," he muttered again, "here she comes, sir!"

"Hold your fire, Mr. Macgregor!" Barney roared.

"Aye aye, sir," the answer came singing back. Macgregor was up in the hammock nettings. He waved an arm.

"Mr. Jerrell! Mr. Lang! Direct your fire to the decks!"

Scull was swearing steadily. The warship was almost on them again. Towering, looming, she was monstrously close. "Within pistol shot," Scull cried.

Barney judged the distance. A minute more. Just a minute. It passed. He raised his voice to its greatest pitch, so as to be sure it was heard on the enemy quarterdeck. "Helmsman!" The cry rang out. Over the wind, over the water. "Helmsman! Hard aport your helm! Do you want him to run aboard us? Hard aport!"

Barney watched the wheel; he watched the other ship. The wheel was clapped hard to starboard. The helmsman had obeyed the order to its contrary.

Aboard the Britisher, the words, the order was plainly heard. Captain Mason, of his Majesty's ship "General Monk," shouted, "Helm astarboard! And we'll have the Yankee in ten minutes!" Eyes narrowed, he, too, watched. He would have the Yankee in ten minutes; they would board her after the broadside.

Both wheels swung. Too late Captain Mason perceived the trick, too late came his countermanding orders, yelled out frantically as the two ships closed. They were going to foul.

Barney raced fore, down, along Macgregor's loaded starboard guns. "Fire when we foul, Mr. Macgregor!"

Nothing could stop it now; it was much too late. The enemy ship was veering steadily, her great bowsprit, pregnant with headsails, was swinging inevitably as the "Athena" held on her course. The two ships fouled.

The enemy bowsprit tore through the "Athena's" foreshrouds with a fearful ripping and tearing. The "Athena's" foremast shivered. Timbers shuddered and groaned as the enemy prow grazed and then bumped the "Athena's" sturdy oaken side. And Barney yelled:

"Here you are, men! Lash her tight!"

He himself was hanging onto the enemy jibboom, tangled with cut rigging. The crowded forecastle of the "Athena" fell like bees onto their hapless quarry. In sixty seconds the warship was securely and completely lashed to the "Athena." Her heavy guns were useless; in this position she could not use them. But the crash of the "Athena's" guns had already sounded. The musket fire had begun earlier.

They had lashed her there to the sound of Macgregor's first broadside, a broadside which crashed through the English frigate, the heavy shot entering at the starboard bow and making its dreadful whistling way through the larboard quarter. Macgregor had never had such a target before in his life. Hanging there in the hammock nettings, he yelled himself hoarse. A little more than a minute had passed since the first broadside; the guns were ready again.

"Fire," yelled Macgregor.

Orders flew from deck to deck and could be heard aboard each ship. Barney was still fore, because he knew the Britisher would first try boarding, and second he would try to extricate himself from this indefensible position.

"Mr. Macgregor," he roared. "Direct your fire to the rigging!"

Lining the rails here were the marines. The sound of musket fire peppered the air. And Macgregor's next broadside swept through the starboard bow again.

For exactly ten minutes the fighting was concentrated on the forecastles of both vessels, lashed together as they were. Then gradually the English foredecks cleared. The danger of boarding was over. Barney raced back along Macgregor's guns.

"Fire when you will, now, Mr. Macgregor!" There was no need any more for concerted broadsides. Let the gun crews fire as fast as they could.

The carronades were spitting forth death. Barney gained the quarterdeck, he had a word for the helmsman.

"Good man," he shouted, as he took his usual place to watch the progress of the battle. He jumped up on the binnacle head.

"Oh, Christ," muttered Scull.

Barney could see well from here. Musket fire was raining like hail from both ships. The "Athena's" heavier guns had already cut the English shrouds and running rigging so that the English could not handle their ship. And the boarding party was being subjected to such a heavy hail of fire that no human could cross under it. Each time the wild surge from their decks was repulsed, bloodily.

The "Athena's" crew was wild with the lust for battle. Even to Barney's ears the crash of the guns sounded faster than they ever had, though the firing was uneven when individual gun captains and crews fired as they wished.

The "Athena" shook constantly, with the recoils of her heavy guns. The English had been able to fire only five with effect. Three of these had already been put out of action.

A musket ball carried off Barney's cap. A second later, another musket ball passed through the edge of his coat. He looked up to see where those shots came from. "Mr. Lang!" he roared. "Direct your fire to the enemy tops!"

Then he fastened his eyes on the tops to see how well that fire would be directed.

In three minutes he was able to shout, "Well done, Mr. Lang! Good marines we have, Mr. Scull!"

"Sir, it is wonderful," Scull shouted back. He didn't know how it had been possible but they were winning; they had been winning this incredible battle ever since the minute the ships had fouled. Scull looked across at the useless great muzzles that were as harmless as if they had no ammunition.

Barney raised his loaded pistol. He took careful aim. He fired. Then a round shot ploughed into the binnacle head.

From amidships Macgregor saw it. He dropped the axe in his

[251]

hand, and dashed for the quarterdeck. He reached it just as Scull dropped to his knees beside Barney.

Barney lay flat on his stomach, sprawled out. "Sir," cried Macgregor. He didn't even hear the firing of the guns; he reached out to touch Barney's shoulder when suddenly Barney rolled over in a quick movement and sat up.

The relief on Macgregor's face and the look on Scull's face made Barney smile. He got to his feet. "I'm all right," he said. But the blood was trickling down his face. He brushed it with his sleeve. He paid no more attention to them. He dashed for the mizzen shrouds and started up.

Across the restless water, and it was not far, he saw the English decks. They were literally awash with blood. They were a shambles of wounded and dying men, piled about the masts. He could hardly believe his eyes. The damage wrought in so short a time was enormous and terrible. "Have you struck?" he shouted.

There was no answer. Barney saw a wounded officer crawling toward a carronade, and at that moment, exactly twenty-six minutes after battle had been joined, he heard the words of surrender.

"We strike!" And then, "Lower the colors!"

"Hold your fire!" Barney shouted. "Hold your fire!" He clung there in the mizzen shrouds. The crippled cruiser was theirs. He drew a deep breath. Then he slid down onto the deck. Mr. Scull knew what he would say next.

"You may take possession, Mr. Scull."

"Aye aye, sir," breathed Scull. But he didn't move. He looked at the size of the ship of which he was to take possession. He reminded himself it had taken only twenty-six minutes to capture her. Then he realized he hadn't moved and that Barney was looking at him. Scull said, departing from his usual custom, "Allow me to congratulate you, sir!" Then he suddenly smiled widely, just as he turned to go foreward.

42

THE WIND BENT THE TREES ON THE RIVER'S GREEN BANKS. THE SKY was lowering; the blunt northeast wind was the herald of a three-day northeaster which had as yet not unleashed its sheets of rain. The wind moaned and the trees bent, and the river showed little white capped waves like teeth.

With courses furled and the tops and royals reefed, the "Athena" proceeded majestically on her last lap of her voyage. Astern came the crippled English "General Monk," their prize. Her name made Barney think she would probably be rechristened the "General Washington." Barney kept glancing around at her every once in a while.

He stood on the quarterdeck; he hadn't left it since the "General Monk's" flag had been hauled down. There had been too much to do. The "Athena" had suffered eleven of her crew killed and thirty-three wounded. The "General Monk's" jibboom had cut away most of the foreshrouds; there were a couple of shot holes in her sides, and a few sections of counter stove in. But her decks were scrubbed, and as Barney's eyes went over her proudly he could discern no detail which had been left undone, in the time he had had.

Even while he had stood there, for four hours, only part of his mind was concerned with the myriad orders; the larger picture kept intruding—the despatches, safe under his coat, the despatches that meant Washington and his forces would start to move southward within a few days for the coming crucial action which should mean the end of the war and Douglass . . .

He drew a deep breath. He looked over the water to the land beyond. The New Jersey shores stretched, marked with lazy rivers. On the land there, flat, with only gentle rises, were the curving Indian trails he had followed as a boy. On the land were the spreading farms, the furrowed earth terminating abruptly against a belt of pines, or running right down into the bay, or into the waving green of marsh grass and blue seas and white towering dunes that edge the seas. On the land grew so many wild flowers it was impossible to count the varieties. On the cape just passed a colony of eagles flew from the cedar forest. Boats sailed from the Mullica and the Maurice rivers, and came back laden with the finest oysters in the world. He had been born there. He was conscious of the love he bore it, as he sailed past.

He hoped she would learn to love it too. Macgregor's voice broke into his thoughts.

"You know, sir, we fired twenty broadsides in twenty-six minutes."

"I know, Mr. Macgregor. It was fine firing."

"Thank you, sir," Macgregor said. Then he said, looking at the shorn off binnacle head, "You ordered a salute, sir."

"Thirteen guns, Mr. Macgregor."

"Aye aye, sir," said Macgregor. He glanced up at the flag which Barney had ordered left flying for their entrance into the city. "We'll show 'em what a navy can do, sir! Why there must be two hundred shotholes in her mizzen stays'l alone, sir."

Barney smiled. He glanced once more at the "General Monk"; then he left the deck.

He stopped before Douglass' door. He knocked, and it flew open. He gathered her close in his arms.

He knew very well he was dirty, disheveled, bloodstained. "I couldn't wait any longer," he whispered.

"I want to look at you," she answered, leaning back in his arms. She cupped his face in her hands.

"I have a habit of standing on the binnacle head," he said apologetically. He drew her over to the cot and sat her down on it. He put his arms around her and she rested her head on his shoulder, and kept tight hold of one hand. Finally she said:

"I love you, Barney."

He squeezed her hard. They were both silent. After a few minutes he said, "I don't worry about your being happy here, darling. Even if I am a bit like New Jersey."

At the sound of his voice she looked up at his face. He was thinking he couldn't tell her yet what the despatches meant. Not quite yet. He couldn't tell her either that he expected Morris would give him the command of the "General Monk." He wanted to surprise her with that. He said, "I mean I'm a bit raw sometimes. But productive."

Douglass nestled her head closer into his shoulder. She laughed. "Go on, sir."

Barney kissed her. "And while the land does not seem to change, it does, subtly. We have terrible mosquitoes. I'd like to build a house down on the point."

"The war, Barney," she said solemnly.

"Will be over soon. We'll have plenty of time." He drew her closer and kissed her again. "That is like heaven," he whispered. "I

[254]

asked you once if you dropped from heaven. Do you remember?"

"I remember, Barney," she answered.

"And I'll have to leave you now. I must dress. We'll be in port soon. It won't be long, sweetheart." He rose. He went to the door. From the cot she watched him, and she remembered, too, how many times she had heard those words. But this time was different. She said:

"I'll wait, Barney."